The Screaming Staircase

Lockwood & Co.

The Screaming Staircase

JONATHAN STROUD

SCHOLASTIC INC.

ISBN 978-0-545-76587-9

 Published by Scholastic Inc., 557 Broadway, New York, NY 10012, by arrangement with Hyperion Books for Children, an imprint of Disney Book Group, LLC.

12 11 10 9 8 7 6 5 4 3 2 1 14 15 16 17 18 19/0

Printed in the U.S.A. 40

First Scholastic printing, September 2014

For Mum & Dad, with love

Contents

I

The Ghost

Chapter 1

Of the first few hauntings I investigated with Lockwood & Co. I intend to say little, in part to protect the identity of the victims, in part because of the gruesome nature of the incidents, but mainly because, in a variety of ingenious ways, we succeeded in messing them all up. There, I've admitted it! Not a single one of those early cases ended as neatly as we'd have wished. Yes, the Mortlake Horror was driven out, but only as far as Richmond Park, where even now it stalks by night among the silent trees. Yes, both the Gray Specter of Aldgate and the entity known as the Clattering Bones were destroyed, but not before several further (and I now think unnecessary) deaths. And as for the creeping shadow that haunted young Mrs. Andrews, to the imperilment of her sanity and her hemline, wherever she may continue to wander in this world, poor thing, there it follows too. So it was not exactly an unblemished record that we took with us, Lockwood and I, when we walked up the path to 62 Sheen Road on that misty autumn afternoon and briskly rang the bell.

We stood on the doorstep with our backs to the muffled traffic, and Lockwood's gloved right hand clasped upon the bell pull. Deep in the house, the echoes faded. I gazed at the door, at the small sun blisters on the varnish and the scuffs on the letter box, at the four diamond panes of frosted glass that showed nothing beyond except for darkness. The porch had a forlorn and unused air, its corners choked with the same sodden beech leaves that littered the path and lawn.

"Okay," I said. "Remember our new rules. Don't blab about everything you see. Don't speculate openly about who killed who, how, or when. And, above all, don't impersonate the client. Please. It never goes down well."

"That's an awful lot of don'ts, Lucy," Lockwood said.

"I've plenty more."

"You know I've got an excellent ear for accents. I copy people without thinking."

"Fine, copy them quietly *after* the event. *Not* loudly, *not* in front of them, and *particularly* not when they're a six-foot-six Irish dock-worker with a speech impediment, and we're a good half-mile from the public road."

"Yes, he was really quite nimble for his size," Lockwood said. "Still, the chase kept us fit. Sense anything?"

"Not yet. But I'm hardly likely to, out here. You?"

He let go of the bell pull and made some minor adjustment to the collar of his coat. "Oddly enough, I have. There was a death in the yard sometime in the last few hours. Under that laurel halfway up the path."

"I assume you're going to tell me it's only a smallish glow." My head was tilted to one side, my eyes half closed; I was listening to the silence of the house.

"Yes, about mouse-sized," Lockwood admitted. "Suppose it might have been a vole. I expect a cat got it, or something."

"So . . . possibly not part of our case, then, if it was a mouse?"

"Probably not."

Beyond the frosted panes, in the interior of the house, I spied a movement: something shifting in the hall's black depths. "Here we go," I said. "She's coming. Remember what I said."

Lockwood bent his knees and picked up the duffel bag beside his feet. We both moved back a little, preparing pleasant, respectful smiles.

We waited. Nothing happened. The door stayed shut.

There was no one there.

As Lockwood opened his mouth to speak, we heard footsteps behind us on the path.

"I'm so sorry!" The woman emerging from the mists had been walking slowly, but as we turned, she accelerated into a token little trot. "So sorry!" she repeated. "I was delayed. I didn't think you'd be so prompt."

She climbed the steps, a short, well-padded individual with a round face expanding into middle age. Her straight, ash-blond hair was pulled back in a no-nonsense manner by clips above her ears. She wore a long black skirt, a crisp white shirt, and an enormous wool cardigan with sagging pockets at the sides. She carried a thin folder in one hand.

"Mrs. Hope?" I said. "Good evening, madam. My name is Lucy Carlyle, and this is Anthony Lockwood, of Lockwood and Company. We've come about your call."

The woman halted on the topmost step but one, and regarded us with wide, gray eyes in which all the usual emotions figured. Distrust, resentment, uncertainty, and dread: they were all there. They come standard in our profession, so we didn't take it personally.

Her gaze darted back and forth between us, taking in our neat clothes and carefully brushed hair, the polished rapiers glittering at our belts, the heavy bags we carried. It lingered long on our faces. She made no move to go past us to the door of the house. Her free hand was thrust deep into the pocket of her cardigan, forcing the fabric down.

"Just the two of you?" she said at last.

"Just us," I said.

"You're very young."

Lockwood ignited his smile; its warmth lit up the evening. "That's the idea, Mrs. Hope. That's the way it has to be."

"Actually, I'm *not* Mrs. Hope." Her own wan smile, summoned in involuntary response to Lockwood's, flickered across her face and vanished, leaving anxiety behind. "I'm her daughter, Suzie Martin. I'm afraid Mother isn't coming."

"But we arranged to meet her," I said. "She was going to show us around the house."

"I know." The woman looked down at her smart black shoes. "I'm afraid she's no longer willing to set foot here. The circumstances of Father's death were horrible enough, but recently the nightly . . . *disturbances* have been getting too persistent. Last night was especially bad, and Mother decided she'd had enough. She's staying with me now. We'll have to sell, but obviously we can't do that until the house is made safe. . . ." Her eyes narrowed slightly. "Which is why you're here. . . . Excuse me, but shouldn't you have a supervisor? I thought an adult always had to be present in an investigation. Exactly how old *are* you?"

"Old enough and young enough," Lockwood said, smiling. "The perfect age."

"Strictly speaking, madam," I added, "the law states that an adult is only required if the operatives are undergoing training. It's true that some of the bigger agencies *always* use supervisors, but that's their private policy. We're fully qualified and independent, and *we* don't find it necessary."

"In our experience," Lockwood said sweetly, "adults just get in the way. But of course we *do* have our licenses here, if you'd like to see them."

The woman ran a hand across the smooth surface of her neat blond hair. "No, no . . . that won't be necessary. Since Mother clearly wanted you, I'm sure it will be fine. . . ." Her voice was neutral and uncertain. There was a brief silence.

"Thank you, madam." I glanced back toward the quiet, waiting door. "There's just one other thing. Is there someone else at home? When we rang the bell, I thought—"

Her eyes rose rapidly, met mine. "No. That's quite impossible. I have the only key."

"I see. I must've been mistaken."

"Well, I won't delay you," Mrs. Martin said. "Mother's filled out the form you sent her." She held out the manila folder. "She hopes it will be useful."

"I'm sure it will." Lockwood tucked it somewhere inside his coat. "Thank you very much. Well, we'd better get started. Tell your mother we'll be in touch in the morning."

The woman handed him a ring of keys. Somewhere on the road a car horn blared, to be answered by another. There was plenty of time until curfew, but night was falling and people were growing antsy. They wanted to get home. Soon there'd be nothing moving in the London streets but trails of mist and twisting moonbeams. Or nothing, at least, that any adult could clearly *see*.

Suzie Martin was conscious of this too. She raised her shoulders, pulled her cardigan tight. "Well, I'd better be going. I suppose I should wish you luck. . . ." She looked away. "So *very* young! How terrible that the world has come to this."

"Good night, Mrs. Martin," Lockwood said.

Without reply, she pattered down the steps. In a few seconds she had vanished among the mists and laurels in the direction of the road.

"She's not happy," I said. "I think we'll be off the case tomorrow morning."

"Better get it solved tonight, then," Lockwood said. "Ready?"

I patted the hilt of my rapier. "Ready."

He grinned at me, stepped up to the door and, with a magician's flourish, turned the key in the lock.

—

When entering a house occupied by a Visitor, it's always best to get in quick. That's one of the first rules you learn. Never hesitate, never linger on the threshold. Why? Because, for those few seconds, it's not too late. You stand there in the doorway with the fresh air on your back and the darkness up ahead, and you'd be an idiot if you didn't want to turn and run. And as soon as you acknowledge *that*, your willpower starts draining away through your boots, and the terror starts building in your chest, and bang, that's it—you're compromised before you begin. Lockwood and I both knew this, so we didn't hang around. We slipped straight through, put down our bags, and shut the door softly behind us. Then we stood quite still with our backs against it, watching and listening, side by side.

The hall of the house lately occupied by Mr. and Mrs. Hope was long and relatively narrow, though the high ceiling made it seem quite large. The floor was tiled in black and white marble squares, set diagonally, and the walls were palely papered. Halfway along, a steep staircase rose into shadows. The hall kinked around this to the left and continued into a void of black. Doorways opened on either side: gaping and choked in darkness.

All of which could have been nicely illuminated if we'd turned on the lights, of course. And there was a switch on the wall, right there. But we didn't attempt to use it. You see, a second rule you learn is this: electricity interferes. It dulls the senses and makes you weak and stupid. It's much better to watch and listen in the dark. It's good to have that fear.

We stood in silence, doing what we do. I listened; Lockwood

watched. It was cold in the house. The air had that musty, slightly sour smell you get in every unloved place.

I leaned in close to Lockwood. "No heating," I whispered.

"Mm-hm."

"Something else too, you think?"

"Mm-hm."

As my eyes grew used to the dark, I saw more details. Beneath the curl of the banister was a little polished table, on which sat a china bowl of potpourri. There were pictures on the wall, mostly faded posters of old-time musicals, and photographs of rolling hills and gentle seas. All pretty innocuous. In fact, it wasn't at all an ugly hallway; in bright sunlight it might have looked quite pleasant. But not so much now, with the last light from the door panes stretching out like skewed coffins on the floor in front of us; and with our shadows neatly framed inside them; and with the manner of old Mr. Hope's death in this very place hanging heavy on our minds.

I breathed hard to calm myself and shut out morbid thoughts. Then I closed my eyes against the taunting darkness and *listened*.

Listened . . .

Halls, landings, and staircases are the arteries and airways of any building. It's here that everything is channeled. You get echoes of things currently going on in all the connecting rooms. Sometimes you also get *other* noises that, strictly speaking, ought not to be there at all. Echoes of the past, echoes of hidden things . . .

This was one such time.

I opened my eyes, picked up my bag, and walked slowly down the hall toward the stairs. Lockwood was already standing by the little polished table beneath the banister. His face shone dimly in the light from the door. "Heard something?" he said.

"Yep."

"What?"

"A little knocking sound. Comes and goes. It's very faint, and I can't tell where it's coming from. But it'll get stronger—it's scarcely dark yet. What about you?"

He pointed at the bottom of the steps. "You remember what happened to Mr. Hope, of course?"

"Fell down the stairs and broke his neck."

"Exactly. Well, there's a tremendous residual death-glow right here, still lingering three months after he died. I should've brought my sunglasses, it's so bright. So what Mrs. Hope told George on the phone stacks up. Her husband tripped and tumbled down and hit the ground hard." He glanced up the shadowy stairwell. "Long, steep flight . . . Nasty way to go."

I bent low, squinting at the floor in the half-dark. "Yeah, look how the tiles have cracked. He must've fallen with tremendous f—"

Two sharp crashes sounded on the stairs. Air moved violently against my face. Before I could react, something large, soft, and horribly heavy landed precisely where I stood. The impact of it jarred my teeth.

I jumped back, ripping my rapier from my belt. I stood against the wall, weapon raised and shaking, heart clawing at my chest, eyes staring wildly side to side.

Nothing. The stairs were empty. No broken body sprawled lifeless on the floor.

Lockwood leaned casually against the banister. It was too dark to be certain, but I swear he'd raised an eyebrow. He hadn't heard a thing.

"You all right, Lucy?"

I breathed hard. "No. I just got the echo of Mr. Hope's last fall. It was very loud and very real. It was like he'd landed right on top of me. Don't laugh. It's not funny."

"Sorry. Well, *something's* stirring early tonight. It's going to get interesting later. What time is it?"

Having a watch with a luminous dial is my third recommended rule. It's best if it can also withstand sudden drops in temperature and strong ectoplasmic shock. "Not yet five," I said.

"Fine." Lockwood's teeth aren't quite as luminous as my watch, but when he grins, it's close. "Plenty of time for a cup of tea. Then we find ourselves a ghost."

Chapter 2

When you go out hunting wicked spirits, it's the simple things that matter most. The silvered point of your rapier flashing in the dark; the iron filings scattered on the floor; the sealed canisters of best Greek Fire, ready as a last resort . . . But tea bags, brown and fresh and plentiful, and made (for preference) by Pitkin Brothers of Bond Street, are perhaps the simplest and best of all.

Okay, they may not save your life like a sword tip or an iron circle can, and they haven't the protective power of a sudden wall of fire. But they *do* provide something just as vital. They help to keep you sane.

It's never pleasant, sitting in a haunted house, waiting in the dark. The night presses in around you and the silence beats against your ears; and soon, if you're not careful, you start to see or hear things that are the products of your mind. In short, you need distractions. Each of us at Lockwood's has our preference. I do a bit of drawing, George has his comics, Lockwood reads the gossip magazines. But *all* of us like our tea and cookies, and that night in the Hopes' house was no exception.

We found the kitchen at the far end of the hall, just beyond the stairway. It was a nice enough room, neat and white and modern, and noticeably warmer than the hall. It had no supernatural traces of any kind. All was quiet. The knocking sound I'd heard was inaudible here, and there was no repetition of the nasty bumping on the stairs.

I got the kettle going, while Lockwood lit an oil lamp and set it on the table. By its light we took off our rapiers and work belts and laid them out before us. Our belts have seven separate clips and pouches; we went through these in silence, systematically checking the contents while the kettle wheezed and huffed away. We'd already checked everything back in the office, but we were more than happy to do it again. A girl at Rotwell's had died the previous week after forgetting to restock her magnesium flares.

Outside the window, the sun was gone. Faint clouds choked the blue-black sky, and mists had risen to engulf the garden. Beyond black hedges, lights shone in other houses. They were near, but also distant, cut off from us like ships passing across deep water.

We put the belts back on, and checked the Velcro fasteners around the rapiers. I fixed the tea and brought it to the table. Lockwood found the cookies. We sat together while the oil lamp flickered and shadows danced in the corners of the room.

At last Lockwood pulled the collar of his overcoat high around his neck. "Let's see what Mrs. Hope has to say for herself," he said. He stretched out a long, thin hand for the folder lying on the table. Lamplight glimmered darkly in his flop of hair.

As he read, I checked the thermometer clipped to my belt: 59°. Not warm, but roughly what you'd expect from an unheated house this time of year. I took my notebook from another pouch and jotted down the room and temperature. I also recorded details of the aural phenomena I'd experienced in the hall.

Lockwood tossed the folder aside. "Well, that was useful."

"Really?"

"No. I'm being ironic. Or is it sarcastic? I can never remember."

"Irony's cleverer, so you're probably being sarcastic. What's she say?"

"Absolutely nothing of any use. She might as well have written it in Greek for all the good it does us. Here's a summary. The Hopes have lived here for two years. Before that, they were down in Kent somewhere; she gives lots of irrelevant detail about how happy they were. Hardly any curfews, ghost-lamps almost never on, how you could go for a walk late evening and meet only your living neighbors. That sort of thing. Don't believe a word of it myself; Kent had one of the biggest outbreaks of anywhere outside London, according to George."

I sipped my tea. "It's where the Problem *began*, I thought."

"So they say. Anyhow, then they moved up here. All fine, no troubles in the house. No manifestations of any kind. Husband changed his job, started working from home. That's six months ago. Still nothing funny going on. Then he fell downstairs and died."

"Hold it," I said. "How did he fall?"

"Tripped, apparently."

"What I mean is, was he alone?"

"According to Mrs. Hope, he was. She was in bed. Happened during the night. She says her husband was a bit distracted in the weeks before he died. Hadn't been sleeping well. She thinks he got up to get a drink of water."

I grunted noncommittally. "Ri-i-ight . . ."

Lockwood flashed me a glance. "You think she pushed him?"

"Not necessarily. But it would provide a motive for the haunting, wouldn't it? Husbands don't normally haunt wives, except when there's reason. Pity she didn't want to talk with us. I'd have liked to suss her out."

"Well, you can't always tell by looking," Lockwood said. He shrugged his narrow shoulders. "Did I ever tell you about the time I met the notorious Harry Crisp? Sweet-faced man he was, soft-voiced and twinkly-eyed. Good company and very plausible; he actually got me to lend him a ten. Yet it turned out in the end he was the most appalling murderer, who liked nothing better than to—"

I held up a hand. "You *did* tell me that. About a million times."

"Oh. Well, the point is, Mr. Hope could be coming back for a host of other reasons that aren't to do with vengeance. Something left undone, for instance: a will he hasn't told his wife about, or some stash of money hidden under the bed . . ."

"Yeah, maybe. So the disturbances began soon after his death?"

"A week or two later. She was mostly away from the house up until then. Once she'd moved back, she began to be aware of an unwelcome presence." He tapped the folder. "Anyway, she doesn't describe it here. She says she gave a full account to our 'receptionist' over the phone."

I grinned. "Receptionist? George won't like that. Well, I've got his notes with me, if you want to hear them."

"Go on, then." Lockwood sat back expectantly. "What's she been seeing?"

George's notes were in an inside pocket of my jacket. I took them out and unfolded them, smoothing the papers on my knee. I scanned them briefly, cleared my throat. "Are you ready?"

"Yes."

"A 'moving shape.'" With great ceremony, I refolded the papers and put them away.

Lockwood blinked in outrage. "A 'moving shape'? That's it? No further details? Come on, was it big, small, dark, or bright, or what?"

"It was, and I quote, a 'moving shape that appeared in the back bedroom and followed me out across the landing.' Word for word, that's what she told George."

Lockwood dunked a forlorn cookie in his tea. "Hardly the finest description of all time. I mean, you wouldn't want to try to sketch from it, would you?"

"No, but she's an adult: what do you expect? It's never going to be any good. The *sensations* she had are more revealing. She said she felt as if something was looking for her, that it knew she was there but couldn't find her. And the thought of it finding her was more than she could bear."

"Well," Lockwood said, "that's a *little* better. She sensed a *purpose*. Which suggests a Type Two. But whatever the late Mr. Hope's up to, he's not the only one at work in this house tonight. There's *us* as well. So . . . what do you say? Shall we take a look around?"

I drained my mug, set it carefully on the table. "I think that's a very good idea."

For almost an hour we toured the downstairs, briefly turning on our flashlights to check the contents of each room, but otherwise moving in near darkness. We left the oil lantern burning in the kitchen, with candles, matches, and an extra flashlight also on the table. It's a good rule to keep a well-lit place to retreat to if the need arises, and having different forms of light is always advisable, in case the Visitor has the ability to disrupt them.

All was clear in the pantry and dining room at the rear of the house. They had a sad, musty, rather somber air, a sense of lives suspended. Neat piles of newspapers lay curling on the dining room table; in the scullery, a tray of shriveled onions sprouted quietly in the darkness. But Lockwood found no visual traces anywhere, and I heard no noise. The delicate knocking sound I'd detected when we'd first entered seemed to have died away.

As we walked back up the hall, Lockwood gave a little shudder, and I felt the hairs rise on my arms. The air was noticeably colder now. I checked the reading: 48°, this time.

At the front of the building were two squarish rooms, one on either side of the hall. One had a television set, a sofa, two comfy armchairs; here the temperature was warmer, back to the level of the kitchen. We looked and listened anyway, and found nothing. On the opposite side, a formal sitting room contained the usual chairs and cabinets, arranged before large net-swathed windows, and three enormous ferns in terra-cotta pots.

It seemed a little chilly. Fifty-four degrees showed on the luminous dial. Colder than the kitchen. Might mean nothing, might mean a lot. I closed my eyes, composed myself, and prepared to listen.

"Lucy, look!" Lockwood's voice hissed. "There's Mr. Hope!"

My heart jolted. I spun around, rapier half-drawn . . . only to find Lockwood stooped and casual, peering at a photo on a side table. He had his flashlight trained on it: the image hung in a little circle of floating gold. "Mrs. Hope's here as well," he added.

"You idiot!" I hissed. "I might have run you through."

He chuckled. "Oh, don't be so grumpy. Take a look. What do you think?"

It was a gray-haired couple standing in a garden. The woman, Mrs. Hope, was an older, happier version of the daughter we'd met outside: round-faced, neat-clothed, wearing a radiant smile. Her head was level with the chest of the man beside her. He was tall, and balding, with sloped, rounding shoulders, and big, rather cumbersome forearms. He too smiled broadly. They were holding hands.

"Seem cheerful enough there, don't they?" Lockwood said.

I nodded dubiously. "Got to be a *reason* for a Type Two, though. George says Type Two always means someone's done something to somebody."

"Yes, but George has a nasty, gruesome little mind. Which reminds me: we should find the phone and call him. I left a message on the table, but he'll probably be worrying about us, even so. Let's finish off the survey first."

He didn't find any death-glows in the little sitting room and I couldn't hear anything; and that was the ground floor done. Which told us what we'd already guessed. What we were looking for was upstairs.

Sure enough, the moment I set foot on the lowest step, the knocking began again. At first it was no louder than it had been before, a tiny, hollow *tap-tap-tap*ping, like a fingernail on plaster, or a nail being hammered into wood. But with every step I climbed, the echo increased a little, became a little more insistent in my inner ear. I mentioned this to Lockwood, who was treading like a formless shadow at my back.

"Getting nippier, too," he said.

He was right. With every step the temperature was dropping, from 48° to 45° to 43° here, midway up the flight. I paused, zipping up my coat with fumbling fingers, while staring upward into the dark. The stairwell was narrow, and there was no light above me at all. The upper regions of the house were a clot of shadows. I had a strong desire to switch my flashlight on but resisted the impulse, which would only have made me blinder still. With one hand on my rapier hilt, I continued slowly up the stairs, with the knocking growing ever louder and the cold biting at my skin.

Up I went. Louder and louder grew the knocking. Now it was a frantic, scratching, tapping sound. Lower and lower dropped the number on the dial. From 43° to 41° and finally to 39°.

The blackness of the landing was a formless space. On my left, white balusters hung at head height like a row of giant teeth.

I reached the final stair, stepped out onto the landing—

And the knocking noise stopped dead.

I checked the luminous dial again: 39°. Twenty degrees lower than the kitchen. I could sense my breath pluming in the air.

We were very close.

Lockwood brushed past me, flicked his flashlight in a brief reconnaissance. Papered walls, closed doors, dead silence. A piece of embroidery in a heavy frame: faded colors, childish letters, *Home Sweet Home*. Done years ago, when homes *were* sweet and safe, and no one hung iron charms above their children's beds. Before the Problem came.

The landing was L-shaped, comprising a small, square space in which we stood, and a long spur running behind us parallel to the stairs. It had a polished wooden floor. There were five doors leading off: one on our right, one straight ahead, and three at intervals along the spur. All the doors were closed. Lockwood and I stood silently, using our eyes and ears.

"Nothing," I said at last. "As soon as I got to the top, the knocking noises stopped."

Lockwood took a while to speak. "No death-glows," he said. From the heaviness in his voice, I knew that he too felt *malaise*—that strange sluggishness, that dead weight in the muscles that comes when a Visitor is near. He sighed faintly. "Well, ladies first, Lucy. Pick a door."

"Not me. I picked a door in that orphanage case, and you know what happened then."

"That all turned out fine, didn't it?"

"Only because I ducked. All right, let's take this one, but *you're* going in first." I'd chosen the nearest, the one on the right. It turned out to lead to a recently remodeled bathroom. Modern tiling gleamed eagerly as the flashlight swept by. There was a big white bathtub, a sink and toilet, and also a distant smell of jasmine soap. Neither of us found anything noticeable here, though the temperature was the same as on the landing.

Lockwood tried the next door. It opened into a large back bedroom, which had been converted into possibly the messiest study in London. The flashlight beam showed a heavy wooden desk set beneath a curtained window. The desk was almost invisible under stacks of papers, and further teetering piles were placed, higgledy-piggledy, all across the room. A row of dark bookshelves, chaotically filled, ran down three-quarters of the far side wall. There were cupboards, an old leather chair beside the desk, and a faintly masculine smell about the room. I tasted aftershave, whisky, even tobacco.

It was bitterly cold now. The dial at my belt showed 36°.

I stepped carefully around the paper stacks and pulled apart the curtains, disturbing enough dust to set me coughing. Dim white light from the houses across the garden drifted into the room.

Lockwood was looking at an ancient frayed rug on the wooden

floor, nudging it to and fro with the toe of his shoe. "Old pressure marks," he said. "Used to be a bed here before Mr. Hope took over. . . ." He shrugged, surveyed the room. "Maybe he's come back to sort his paperwork."

"This is it," I said. "This is where the Source is. Look at the temperature. And don't you feel heavy, almost numb?"

Lockwood nodded. "Plus, this is where Mrs. Hope saw her legendary 'moving shape.'"

A door slammed, loudly, somewhere below us in the house. Both of us jumped. "I think you're right," Lockwood said. "This *is* the place. We should rig up a circle here."

"Filings or chains?"

"Oh, filings. Filings will be fine."

"Are you sure? It's not even nine o'clock, and its power's already strong."

"Not *that* strong. Besides, whatever Mr. Hope wants, I can't believe he's suddenly turned malevolent. Filings will be more than adequate." He hesitated. "Also . . ."

I looked at him. "Also what?"

"I forgot to bring the chains. Don't stare at me like that. You do weird things with your eyes."

"*You forgot to bring the chains?* Lockwood—"

"George took them out to oil them and I didn't check that he'd put them back. So it's George's fault, really. Listen, it doesn't matter. We don't need them for a job like this, do we? Get the iron set up while I scan the other rooms. Then we focus here."

I had a lot more to say, but now wasn't the time. I took a

deep breath. "Well, don't get into trouble," I said. "Last time you went wandering off during a case, you got yourself locked in the bathroom."

"A ghost shut me in, I keep telling you."

"So you claim, but there was not a shred of evidence that—"

But he was already gone.

It didn't take me long to carry out my task. I hauled several stacks of dusty, yellowed paper to the edges of the room to make space in the center of the floor. Then I pulled the rug aside and scattered the filings in a circle, giving it a fairly small radius, so as not to waste the iron. This would be our primary refuge, where we could retreat if necessary, but we might need other circles too, depending on what we found.

I went out onto the landing. "I'm just going down to get more iron."

Lockwood's voice echoed from a nearby bedroom. "Fine. Can you put the kettle on?"

"Yeah." I crossed to the stairs, glancing at the open bathroom door. When I put my hands on the banister rail, the wood was freezing to the touch. I hesitated at the top, listening hard, then descended toward the grainy illumination of the hall. A few steps down, I thought I heard a rushing noise behind me; but when I turned back, I saw nothing. With my hand on my rapier hilt, I continued to the bottom and walked along the hall to where the kitchen's warm glow shone through a crack in the door. Dim as it was, the lantern light made me screw my eyes up as I went in. I helped myself to a cheeky biscuit, rinsed out the mugs, and put the kettle on again. Then I picked up the two duffel bags and, with some difficulty, pried the hall door open with my foot. I moved back out into the hall, which—thanks to the bright kitchen—seemed even darker than before. There was no sound in the house. I couldn't hear anything of Lockwood; presumably he was still scanning the final bedrooms. I climbed the stairs slowly, from cool, to cold, to colder, holding the heavy bags awkwardly on either side.

I reached the landing and heaved the bags down with a little sigh. When I raised my head to call to Lockwood, I saw a girl standing there.

Chapter 3

I froze; for a tightly packed string of heartbeats, I couldn't stir a muscle. In part, of course, this was due to simple shock, but there was a lot more to it than that. A cold weight pressed like a headstone on my chest; my limbs felt entombed in mud. An icy torpor crept through the roots of my brain. My mind was numbed, the workings of my body dulled; I felt I should never have the strength to move again. A mood stole over me that might have been despair, had I the energy to truly care about it one way or the other. Nothing mattered, least of all me. Silence and stillness and utter paralysis of movement were all I could aspire to, all that I deserved.

In other words, I was experiencing *ghost-lock*, which is the effect Type Twos have when they choose to direct their power on you.

An ordinary person might have stood there helpless and let the Visitor work its will upon her. But I'm an agent, and I'd dealt with this before. So I wrested savage, painful breaths from the frigid air, shook the mist clear of my brain. I forced myself to live. And my hands moved slowly toward the weapons at my belt.

The girl stood halfway across the floor of the study-bedroom, directly ahead of me. I could see her framed by the open door. She was fairly faint, but I saw she stood barefoot on the rolled-up rug—or, more precisely, *in* it, for her ankles were sunk into the fabric as if she were paddling in the sea. She wore a pretty summer-print dress, knee-length, decorated with large, rather garish orange sunflowers. It was not a modern design. The dress and her limbs and her long fair hair all shone with dim, pale other-light, as if lit by something far away. As for her face . . .

Her face was a solid wedge of darkness. No light reached it at all.

It was hard to tell, but I guessed she'd been eighteen or so. Older than me, but not by too many years. I stood there for a time wondering about this, with my eyes locked on the faceless girl, and my hands inching to my belt.

Then I remembered I was not alone in the house.

"Lockwood," I called. "Oh, Lockwood . . ." I said it as lightly as I could. Showing signs of fear is best avoided where Visitors are concerned—fear, anger, and other strong emotions. They feed on it too easily; it makes them faster and more aggressive. No answer came, so I cleared my throat and tried again. "Oh, *Lock*wood . . . !" I was using a merry singsong intonation here, as if I were speaking to a little babe or cuddly pet or something. As I might as well have been, in fact, because he didn't bloody respond.

I turned my head and called a little louder. "Oh, Lockwood, *please* come here. . . ."

His voice sounded muffled, back along the landing. "Hold on, Luce. I've got something. . . ."

"Jolly good! So have I. . . ."

When I looked back, the girl was closer, almost out onto the landing. The face was still in shadow, but the drifts of other-light that spun about her body shone brighter than before. Her bony wrists were tight against her side, the fingers bent like fishhooks. Her bare legs were very thin.

"What do you want?" I said.

I listened. Words brushed soft as spiders' touch against my ear. "*I'm cold.*"

Fragments. You seldom get more than fragments. The little voice was a whisper uttered at great distance, but it was also uncomfortably close at hand. It seemed an awful lot closer to me than Lockwood's reply had been.

"Oh, Lockwood!" I cooed again. "It's *urgent*. . . ."

Can you believe it? I could detect a hint of annoyance in his answer. "Just wait a sec, Lucy. There's something interesting here. I've picked up a death-glow—a really, *really* faint one. Something nasty happened in this front bedroom too! It's so hazy I almost missed it, so it must've been a long while back. But, you know, I think it was traumatic. . . . Which means—it's only a theory, I'm just playing with ideas here—there might possibly have been *two* violent deaths in this house. . . . What do you say to that?"

I chuckled hollowly. "I say that it's a theory I can maybe *help* you with," I sang, "if you'll only come out here."

"The thing is," he went on, "I don't see how the first death's got anything to do with the Hopes. They were only here two years, weren't they? So perhaps the disturbances we're experiencing aren't—"

"—actually caused by the husband?" I cried. "Yes, well done! They're not!"

A brief pause. *Finally* he was paying attention. "What?"

"*I said it's not the husband,* Lockwood! Now, get out here!"

You might notice I'd slightly abandoned my attempts at keeping it lighthearted. That was because the thing in the study had already picked up on my agitation and was now drifting through the door. The toenails on the thin, pale feet were long and curled.

Both my hands were at my belt. One gripped the rapier hilt; the other had closed on a canister of Greek Fire. You shouldn't really use magnesium flares in a domestic environment, of course, but I wasn't taking chances. My fingertips were icy, but sweaty too; they slipped against the metal.

A movement on my left. From the corner of my eye, I saw Lockwood emerge onto the landing. He, too, stopped dead. "Ah," he said.

I nodded grimly. "Yes, and the next time I call you while in an operative situation, do me a favor and get your butt out here double-quick."

"Sorry. But I see you've got it well in hand. Has she spoken?"

"Yes."

"What did she say?"

"She says she's cold."

"Tell her we can fix that for her. No, don't fiddle-faddle with your weapon, that'll only make it worse." The girl had drifted a little closer across the landing; in response, I'd begun to draw my blade.

"Tell her we can fix it," Lockwood said again. "Tell her we can find whatever she's lost."

I did so, in as steady a voice as I could manage. It didn't have much effect. The shape neither shrank nor changed, nor became vaporous, nor departed, nor did any of the other things the *Fittes Manual* claims they'll do when you give them hope of release.

"*I'm cold,*" the little voice said; and then again, much louder, "*Lost and cold.*"

"What was that?" Lockwood had sensed the contact, but he couldn't hear the sound.

"Same words, but I've got to tell you, Lockwood, this time it wasn't much like a girl talking. It sounded really deep and hollow and echoed like a tomb."

"That's never good, is it?"

"No. I think we should take it as a sign." I drew my rapier. Lockwood did likewise. We stood facing the shape in silence. Never attack first. Always wait, draw out its intentions. Watch what it does, where it goes, learn its patterns of behavior. It was so close now that I could make out the texture of the long, fair hair sweeping down around the neck, see individual moles and blemishes on the skin. It always surprised me that the visual echo could be this strong. George called it "the will to exist," the refusal to lose what once had been. Of course, not all of them appear this way. It all depends on their personality in life, and what precisely happened when that life came to an end.

We waited. "Can you see her face?" I asked. Lockwood's Sight is better than mine.

"No. It's veiled. But the rest is *really* bright. I think it's—"

He stopped; I'd lifted up my hand. This time the voice I heard was the barest tremor in the air. *"I'm cold,"* it whispered. *"Lost and cold. Lost and cold . . . and DEAD!"*

The wisps of light that hung about the girl flared bright and desolate, and for an instant the dark veil was lifted from the face. I screamed. The light went out. A shadow swept toward me, bony arms outstretched. Icy air drove into me, forcing me toward the stairs. I stumbled on the lip and toppled backward, over the edge. Dropping my rapier, I threw out a desperate arm, grasped the corner of the wall. I hung above the void, buffeted by the raging wind, fingertips slipping on the smooth, cold wallpaper. The shape drew close. I was about to fall.

Then Lockwood sprang between us, his blade cutting a complex pattern in the air. The shadow reared up, arm raised across its face. Lockwood cut another pattern, hemming it in on several sides with walls of flashing iron. The shape shrank back. It darted away into the study with Lockwood in pursuit.

The landing was empty. The wind had died. I scrabbled at the wall, pulled myself upright at the top of the stairs and sank to my knees. My hair was over my eyes; one foot dangled over the topmost step.

Slowly, grimly, I reached out for my rapier. There was a dull ache in my shoulder where I'd jarred my arm.

Lockwood was back. He bent close to me, his calm eyes scanning the darkness of the landing. "Did she touch you?"

"No. Where did she go?"

"I'll show you." He helped me up. "You're sure you're all right, Lucy?"

"Of course." I brushed my hair away, forcing the rapier viciously back into its belt loop. My shoulder twinged a bit, but it was okay. "So," I said, starting toward the study. "Let's get on with it."

"In a sec." He held out a hand, stalling my movement forward. "You need to relax."

"I'm fine."

"You're angry. There's no need to be. That assault would have caught anyone out. I was surprised too."

"*You* didn't drop your rapier." I pushed his hand away. "Listen, we're wasting time. When she comes back—"

"She wasn't directing it at me. It was all at you, trying to pitch you over the stairs. I guess we know how Mr. Hope came to take his tumble now. My point is, you need to calm down, Lucy. She'll feed off your anger superfast, and grow strong."

"Yeah, I know." I didn't say it gracefully. I closed my eyes, took a deep breath, and then another, concentrating on doing what the *Manual* recommends: mastering myself, loosening the hold of my emotions. After a few moments, I regained control. I withdrew from my anger and let it drop to the floor like a discarded skin.

I listened again. The house was very silent, but it was the silence of a snowfall, heavy and oppressive. I could feel it watching me.

When I opened my eyes, Lockwood was standing with his hands in his overcoat pockets, waiting quietly in the blackness of the landing. His rapier was back at his belt.

"Well?" he said.

"I'm feeling better."

"Anger gone?"

"Not a trace left."

"Okay, because if you don't feel steady, we're heading home right now."

"We're not heading home," I said coolly, "and I'll tell you why. Mrs. Hope's daughter won't let us in here again. She thinks we're too young. If we haven't cracked the case by tomorrow, she'll take us off it and put Fittes or Rotwell's on the job. We need the money, Lockwood. We finish this now."

He didn't move. "Most nights," he said, "I'd agree with you. But the parameters have changed. It's not some poor old boy bothering his widow; it's almost certainly the ghost of a murder victim. And you know what *they're* like. So if your head's not in the right place, Luce . . ."

Calm and steady as I was, I found his condescension slightly irritating. "Yeah," I said, "but it's not really *me* that's the issue, is it?"

Lockwood frowned. "Meaning what?"

"Meaning the iron chains."

He rolled his eyes. "Oh, come on. That's hardly the—"

"Those iron chains are standard equipment for every agent, Lockwood. They're essential for protection when we're up against a strong Type Two. And *you* forgot to put them in!"

"Only because George insisted on oiling them! At *your* suggestion, if I remember."

"Oh, so it's *my* fault now, is it?" I cried. "Most agents would sooner forget their pants than go out without their chains, but you somehow managed it. You were so keen on rushing out here, it's a wonder we brought anything at all. George even advised us not to go. He wanted to do more research on the house. But no. *You* overruled him."

"Yes! Which is what I do, on account of being the leader. It's my responsibility—"

"—to make bad decisions? That's right, I suppose it is."

We stood there, arms folded, glowering at each other across the darkened landing of a haunted house. Then, like the sun coming out, Lockwood's glare softened to a grin.

"So . . ." he said. "How's your anger management going, Luce?"

I snorted. "I admit I'm annoyed, but now I'm annoyed with *you*. That's different."

"I'm not sure it is, but I *do* take your original point about the money." He clapped his gloved hands together briskly. "All right, you win. George wouldn't approve, but I think we can risk it. I've driven her away for the moment, and that gives us breathing room. If we're quick, we can settle this in half an hour."

I stooped and lifted up the duffel bags. "Just lead me to the place."

The place proved to be on the far side of the study: a blank stretch of wall set between two recessed stretches of the chaotic bookshelf. In the harsh light of our flashlights, we saw it was still covered with ancient bedroom wallpaper, drab and faded and peeling near the molding. Puffy, shapeless roses ran floor to ceiling in slanting lines.

In the middle of the space hung a colored map showing the geology of the British Isles. The base of the wall was concealed by thigh-high piles of geology magazines, one or two of which were weighed down by dusty geological hammers. My keen investigative instinct told me that Mr. Hope might possibly have been a geologist by trade.

I inspected the bookshelves on either side, saw how the wall protruded at that point. "Old chimney breast," I said. "So she went in there?"

"She was fading before she reached the wall, but yes—I think so. Would make sense if the Source was hidden in the chimney, wouldn't it?"

I nodded. Yes, it made sense. A natural cavity, big enough for anything at all.

We began shifting the magazines away, carting them in cascading armfuls to the other side of the room. Space was an issue. Lockwood wanted to keep my original circle free and have a good access route to it from the wall where we'd be working, so we dumped most of the magazines by the door and even out onto the landing. Every second armload or so I stopped and listened carefully, but the house remained still.

When we'd cleared a big enough area, I opened the bags and poured out another plastic pot of filings in a curving line across the floor. It formed a rough semicircle that extended outward from the crucial section of the wall. I joined up the two ends with a straight line running along the base of the wall, keeping a yard or so back from it so that the iron wouldn't be messed up by all the falling plaster. Once I'd finished there was enough room inside the lines for us both to stand *and* have our duffel bags too. It would be pretty safe, though not as secure as if we'd used some chains.

I also checked the original circle in the center of the room. A few filings had gotten scattered by our feet as we'd tramped past, but I brushed them back into position.

Lockwood removed the geological map and propped it by the

desk. Then he went down to the kitchen and returned with a couple of lanterns. The time for watching in the dark was past; action was required now, and for that we needed proper light. He set the lanterns on the floor inside our semicircle and switched them on at low intensity, directing the beams toward the empty wall. The light illuminated it like a little stage.

All this took about a quarter of an hour. At last we stood together inside the iron, pocketknives and crowbars ready, looking at the wall. "Want to hear my theory?" Lockwood said.

"Thrill me."

"She was killed in the house decades ago—so long back, she at last grew quiet. Then Mr. Hope set up his study in this room, and that triggered her somehow. It stands to reason, therefore, that something of hers must be concealed here, something she cares about, that makes her linger on. Clothes, maybe, or possessions; or a gift she promised another. Or—"

"Or something else," I said.

"Yes."

We stood and looked at the wall.

Chapter 4

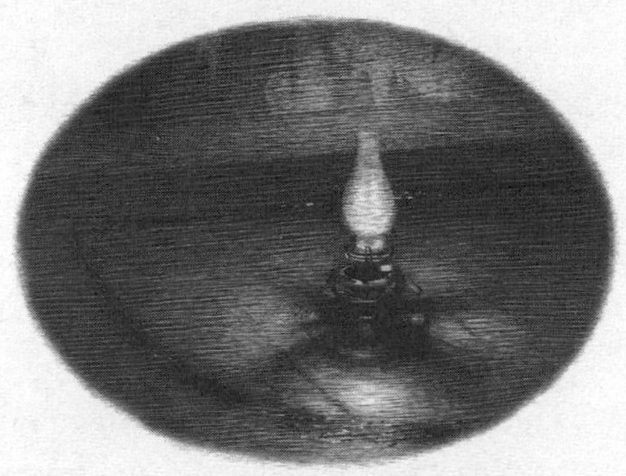

Ever since Marissa Fittes and Tom Rotwell conducted their celebrated investigations, way back in the first years of the Problem, finding the Source of a haunting has been central to every agent's job. Yes, we do other stuff as well: we help create defenses for worried households, and we advise individuals on their personal protection. We can rig up salt traps in gardens, lay iron strips on thresholds, hang wards above cradles, and stock you with any number of lavender sticks, ghost-lights, and other items for day-to-day security. But the essence of our role, the reason for our being, is always the same: to locate the specific place or object connected to a particular member of the restless dead.

No one really knows how these "Sources" function. Some claim the Visitors are actually contained within them, others that they mark points where the boundary between worlds has been worn thin by violence or extreme emotion. Agents don't have time to speculate either way. We're too busy trying to avoid being ghost-touched to worry about philosophy.

As Lockwood said, a Source might be many things. The exact location of a crime, perhaps, or an object intimately connected to a sudden death, or maybe a prized possession of the Visitor when alive. Most often, though (73% of the time, according to research conducted by the Rotwell Institute), it's associated with what the *Fittes Manual* calls "personal organic remains." You can guess what *that* means. The point is, you never know until you look.

Which is what we were doing now.

Five minutes in, we'd almost stripped the central slab of wall. The wallpaper was decades old, its glue dry and turned to dust. We could slip our knives under it and cut away great curls with ease. Some practically disintegrated in our hands; others flopped over our arms like giant folds of skin. The plaster of the wall beneath was pinkish-white and mottled, and speckled with orange-brown fragments of paste. It reminded me of Spam.

Lockwood took one of the lanterns and made a closer inspection, running his hand along the uneven surface. He moved the lantern at different heights and angles, watching the play of shadows on the wall.

"There *was* a cavity here at some point," he said. "A big one. Someone's filled it in. See how the plaster's a different color, Luce?"

"I see. Think we can break into it?"

"Shouldn't be too difficult." He hefted his crowbar. "Everything quiet?"

I glanced over my shoulder. Beyond the little circle of lantern light, the rest of the room was invisible. We were an illuminated island in a sea of blackness. I listened and heard nothing, but there was a steadily mounting pressure in the silence: I could feel it building in my ear. "We're okay for the moment," I said. "But it won't last long."

"Better get on with it, then." His bar swung, crunched into the plaster. A shower of pieces cascaded to the floor.

Twenty minutes later the fronts of our clothes were spotted white, the toecaps of our boots smothered by the heap of fragments ranged beneath the wall. The hole we'd made was half my height and wide as a man. There was rough, dark wood behind it, studded with old nails.

"Some kind of boards," Lockwood said. Sweat gleamed on his forehead; he spoke with forced carelessness. "The front of a box or cupboard or something. Looks like it fills the whole wall space, Lucy."

"Yeah," I said. "Mind the filings." He'd stepped back too far, kicking them out of position. *That* was what we had to focus on. Keep to the rules, keep ourselves safe. If we'd had the chains, it wouldn't have been so difficult; but filings were treacherous, their line easily broken. I crouched down, got the brush, and with small, methodical movements, began to fix the break. Above me, Lockwood took a deep breath. Then came the soft crack of his crowbar biting into wood.

With the line repaired, I scooped away several handfuls of plaster that threatened to spill over the barrier at the front. This done, I remained there, crouching, the fingertips of one hand pressed firmly on the floorboards. I stayed like that a minute, maybe more.

When I got to my feet, Lockwood had done some damage to one of the planks, but he hadn't broken through. I tapped him on the arm.

"What?" He struck the wall again.

"She's back," I said.

The sounds had been so faint that at first, they had merged into the noise we made; and it was only by the vibrations in the floor that I'd noticed them at all. But even as I spoke, they began to rise in volume: three quick impacts—the last a dreadful soft-hard *thud*—then silence, before the sequence started over. It was an endless loop, identical each time: the sound-memory of Mr. Hope falling down the stairs.

I told Lockwood what I heard.

He nodded brusquely. "Okay. Doesn't change anything. Keep watch, and don't let it unsettle you. That's what she's aiming for. She recognizes you're the weak one."

I blinked. "Sorry? What are you saying?"

"Luce, this isn't the time. I just mean emotionally."

"*What?* Like *that's* any better."

He took a deep breath. "All I'm saying is . . . is that your kind of Talent is *much* more sensitive than mine, but, ironically, that very sensitivity leaves you more exposed to supernatural influences, which in cases like this might be a problem. Okay?"

I stared at him. "For a minute there, I thought you'd been listening to George."

"Lucy, I have not been listening to George."

We turned away from each other: Lockwood to the wall, me to face the room.

I drew my rapier, waited. The study was dark and still. *Thud, thud . . . THUD* went the echo in my ears.

A cracking sound told me Lockwood had the crowbar wedged between the boards. He was pushing sideways with all his strength. Wood creaked, black nails shifted.

Very slowly, one of our lanterns began to die. It flickered, faltered, became pale and small, as if something was crushing out its life. Even as it did so, the other lantern flared. The balance of light in the room shifted; our shadows swung oddly across the floor.

A gust of cold air blew through the study. I heard papers moving on the desk.

"You'd think she'd *want* us to do this," Lockwood panted. "You'd think she'd *want* to be found."

Out on the landing, a door banged.

"Doesn't seem so," I said.

Other doors slammed elsewhere in the house, one after the other, seven in a row. I heard the distant sound of breaking glass.

"Boring!" Lockwood snarled. "You've done that! Try something else."

There was a sudden silence.

"How many times," I said, "have I told you not to taunt them? It never ends well."

"Well, she was repeating herself. Get a seal ready. We're almost there."

I bent down, rummaged in my bag. In the pockets we carry a wide range of products designed to neutralize any given Source. All of them are made of those key metals Visitors can't abide: silver and iron. Shapes and decorations vary. There are boxes, tubes, nails and nets, pendants, bands, and chains. Rotwell's and Fittes have theirs specially stamped with their company logos, while Lockwood uses ones that are simple and unadorned. But the crucial thing is to select the right size for your Visitor, the minimum grade necessary to block its passage through.

I chose a chain-net, delicate but potent, made of tightly fused links of silver. It was still carefully folded; when shaken loose it could be draped over objects of considerable size, but for now I could clasp it in my palm. I stood and checked on progress at the wall.

Lockwood had succeeded in forcing out one of the boards a little way. Behind it was a slender wedge of darkness. He heaved and strained, leaning back, grimacing with effort. His boots dug perilously close to our ridge of iron filings.

"It's coming," he said.

"Good." I turned back to face the room.

Where the dead girl stood beside me, just beyond the iron line.

So clear was she, she might have been alive and breathing, gazing out upon a sunlit day. The cold, dim light shone full upon her face. I saw her as she must have been—once, long ago, before it happened. She was prettier than me, round-cheeked, small-nosed, with a full-lipped mouth and large, imploring eyes. She looked like the kind of girl I'd always instinctively disliked—soft and silly, passive when it mattered, and, when it didn't, reliant on her charms to get her way. We stood there, head-to-head, her long hair blond, my dark hair pale with plaster dust; she bare-legged in her little summer dress, me red-nosed and shivering in my skirt, leggings and padded parka. Without the iron line and what it represented, we might have reached out and touched each other's faces. Who knows, perhaps that's what she wanted? Perhaps that severance drove her rage. Her face was blank and without emotion, but the force of her fury broke against me like a wave.

I raised the folded chain-net in a kind of ironic salute. In answer, bitter air whipped out of the darkness, scouring my face, slapping my hair against my cheeks. It struck hard against the iron barrier, making the filings shift.

"I highly recommend finishing this," I said.

Lockwood gave a gasp of effort. There was a crack as wood grains tore.

All across the study came a sudden rustling: magazines flipping open, books moving, dusty papers lifting off their piles like flocks of rising birds. My coat was pressed against me. Wind howled around the margins of the room. The ghost-girl's hair and dress were motionless. She stood staring through me, like *I* was the one made of memory and air.

Beside my boots, the filings began to drift and scatter.

"Hurry it up," I said.

"Got it! Give me the seal."

I turned as quickly as I dared—the key thing now was not to cross the iron line—and offered him the folded net. Just as I did so, Lockwood gave a final heave upon the crowbar and the board gave way. It cracked across its width, near the bottom of our hole, and ruptured forward, carrying with it two others that were nailed to it by connecting spurs of wood. The crowbar slipped from its recess, and suddenly came free. Lockwood lost his balance; he fell sideways and would have tumbled right out of our circle, had I not lunged across to steady him.

We clung together for a moment, teetering above the filings. "Thanks, Luce," Lockwood said. "That was almost bad." He grinned. I nodded in relief.

At which the broken boards fell out toward us, revealing the contents of the wall.

We'd known. Of course we'd known, but it was still a shock. And shocks that make you both jerk backward are never ideal when you're already off balance, when the two of you are already on the brink. So it was that I didn't get much of a look inside the cavity before we toppled over together, arms locked, legs tangled, Lockwood above and me below, beyond the protection of the iron.

But I'd seen enough. Enough to have the image seared upon my mind.

She still had her blond hair; that was the same, though so smirched with soot and dust, so choked up with cobwebs, that it was impossible to tell where it finished or began. The rest was harder to recognize: a thing of bones, bared teeth, and shrunken skin, dark and twisted as burnt wood, and still propped snugly in the bed of bricks where it had rested maybe fifty years. The straps of the pretty summer dress hung loose upon the jutting bones. Orange-yellow sunflowers glinted dimly within a shroud of webs.

I hit the floor. The back of my head struck wood, and the dark was seared by light. Then Lockwood's weight drove down onto me. My breath burst through my mouth.

The brightness faded. My mind cleared, my eyes opened. I was lying on my back, with the silver chain-net still clutched tightly in one hand.

That was the good news. I'd also dropped my rapier again.

Lockwood had already rolled off me and away. I rolled too, knelt back into a crouch, looked frantically for my blade.

What did I see instead? A mess of iron filings, scattered by our fall. Lockwood kneeling, head down, hair flopped forward, struggling to pull his sword clear of his long, heavy overcoat.

And the ghost-girl, floating silently above him.

"Lockwood!" His head jerked up. His coat had gotten twisted tight beneath his knees and was preventing access to his belt. He couldn't free his sword in time.

The girl dropped low, trailing wreaths of other-light. Long, pale hands stretched out toward his face.

I tore a canister from my belt and hurled it without a thought. It passed straight through the stooping shape and struck the wall behind. The glass lid broke; sheets of magnesium fire licked out and sliced across the girl, who vanished in billowing plumes of mist. Lockwood threw himself sideways, iron sparks flickering in his hair.

Greek Fire's good stuff, no question. The mix of iron, magnesium, and salt hits your Visitor three ways at once. Red-hot iron and salt cut through its substance, while the searing light of the ignited magnesium causes it intolerable pain. But (and here's the snag), even though it burns out fast, it has a tendency to set *other* things on fire as well. Which is why the *Fittes Manual* advises against its use indoors, except in controlled conditions.

The present conditions involved a study filled with papers and a very vengeful Specter. Would you call that even the slightest bit "controlled"?

Not really.

Something somewhere wailed with pain and fury. The wind in the study, which had perhaps died back a little, suddenly redoubled. Burning papers, ignited by the first surge from the canister, were plucked aloft, blown directly at my face. I batted them away, watched them whirl off, willed by something unseen. They blew in squalls across the room, landed on books and shelves, on desk and curtains, on curls of wallpaper, on bone-dry files and letters, on dusty cushions on the chair. . . .

Like stars at dusk, hundreds of little fires winked into being, one after the other, high, low, and all around.

Lockwood had risen to his feet, hair and coat both smoking. He flicked his coat aside. A flash of silver: the rapier was in his hand. His eyes were fixed past me on a shadowed corner of the room. Here, in the midst of whirling papers, a shape was starting to reform.

"Lucy!" His voice was hard to make out against the howling wind. "Plan E! We follow Plan E!"

Plan E? What the devil *was* Plan E? Lockwood had so many. And it was hard to think straight with every other stack of magazines going up in flames, and those flames leaping higher, and the way back to the landing suddenly blocked by smoke and flaring light.

"Lockwood!" I cried. "The door—"

"No time! I'll draw her off! You do the Source!"

Oh yes. *That* was Plan E. Luring the Visitor away from where the crucial action was. And already Lockwood was dancing through the smoke, moving with insolent confidence toward the waiting shape. Burning fragments blew about his head; he ignored them, kept his rapier lowered at his side. He seemed unprotected. The girl made a sudden rush; Lockwood leaped back, rapier swinging up at the last minute to parry an outstretched spectral hand. Her long blond hair, blending with the smoke, curled around him from either side; he ducked and feinted, slicing the misty tendrils into nothing. His sword was a blur of movement. Safe behind its flashing steel, he steadily retreated, leading the ghost ever farther from the chimney breast and the broken wall.

In other words, giving me my chance. I plunged forward, fighting against the raging wind. Air slammed into me, screaming with a human voice. Sparks spat against my face; the breath was driven from my lungs. Flames rose up on every side, reaching out as I passed by. The wrath of the air redoubled. I was slowed almost to a standstill, but plowed my way onward, step by step.

Beside the chimney the bookshelves had erupted into walls of flame; trails of racing fire ran like mercury along the floor. Ahead of me the plaster surface swam with orange light. The hole itself was a pool of darkness, the object inside it scarcely visible. Behind the veil of webs, I glimpsed its lipless smile.

It's never good to see such things directly. They distract you from the job. I shook the chain-net loose, held it trailing in my hand.

Nearer, nearer . . . step by step. . . . Now I *was* close. Now I could have looked at her, if I'd chosen to, but I kept my eyes averted from her face. I saw the little spiders clustering on the cobwebs, as they always do. I saw her bony neck, the flowery cotton dress gaping. I also saw a sudden glint of gold—something hanging beneath her throat.

A little golden chain.

I reached the hole, stood with the net held ready, amid the roar of the wind and fire. And, just for a moment, I hesitated, staring at the delicate golden necklace that hung there in the dark. It ended in a pendant of some kind: I could just see it sparkling in the horrid gap between her dress and bony chest. Once, that girl's living hands had put it around her neck, thinking to make herself look lovelier for the day. And still it hung there, decades later, and still it shone, though the flesh beneath was blackened, shrunken and dead.

A rush of pity filled my heart.

"Who *did* this to you?" I said.

"Lucy!" Lockwood's cry rose above the howling wind. I turned my head; saw the ghost-girl come rushing at me through the rising flames. Her face was blank, her eyes bore into mine; her arms were stretched toward me as if in greeting or embrace.

It wasn't the type of embrace *I* fancied. Blindly, I thrust both hands in through the mess of cobwebs, sending the spiders racing. I sought to lower the net—but it had caught on a snag of wood in the mouth of the hole. The girl was almost upon me. I gave a frantic heave; the splinter broke. With a sob, I draped the chain-net over the dry, soft, dusty hair. Iron-and-silver folds dropped down across the head and torso, encasing them as securely as a cage.

At once the girl's momentum stalled; she was frozen in mid-air. A sigh, a moan, a shudder. Her hair fell forward and hid her face. Her other-light grew dim, dim, dimmer. . . . Gone. She winked out of existence as if she had never been.

And, with her, the force that filled the house went too. There was a sudden release of pressure. My ears popped. Wind died. The room was full of burning scraps of paper, drifting slowly to the floor.

Just like that. It's what happens when you successfully neutralize a Source.

I took a deep breath, listened. . . .

Yes. The house was quiet. The girl *had* gone.

Of course, when I say it was quiet, I only mean on a *psychic* level. Fires raged throughout the study. The floor was alight, smoke hid the ceiling. The piles of papers we'd dumped beside the door roared white, and the whole landing was aflame. There was no way out in *that* direction.

On the other side of the room, Lockwood waved urgently, pointing to the window.

I nodded. No time to waste. The house was going up. But first, almost without thinking, I turned back to the hole, reached under the net and (closing my mind to what else I touched there), grasped the little gold necklace—that one uncorrupted reminder of what the living girl had been. When I pulled, the chain came free as easily as if it had been unclasped. I stuffed it all—chain and pendant, webs and dust—into the pocket of my coat. Then, turning, I zigzagged between the fires to the desk below the window.

Lockwood had already vaulted onto it, booting a stack of burning papers to the floor. He tried the window. No go—stiff or locked, it didn't matter which. He kicked it open, splintering the latch. I jumped up beside him. For the first time in hours we breathed in fresh, wet, foggy air.

We knelt there on the windowsill, side by side. Around us, curtains hissed, went up in flames. Out in the garden, our silhouettes crouched in a square of swirling light.

"You all right?" Lockwood said. "Something happen by the hole?"

"No. Nothing. I'm fine." I smiled wanly at him. "Well, another case solved."

"Yes. Won't Mrs. Hope be pleased? True, her house will have burned down, but at least it's ghost-free." He looked at me. "So . . ."

"So . . ." I peered over the sill, hunting vainly for the ground. It was too dark and too distant to be seen.

"It'll be fine," Lockwood said. "I'm almost sure there are some whopping bushes down there."

"Good."

"That and a concrete patio." He patted my arm. "Come on, Lucy. Turn and drop. It's not like we have a choice."

Well, he was right about *that* part. When I glanced back into the room, the flames had spread across the floor. They'd already reached the chimney breast. The hole—and its contents—were being greedily consumed by tongues of fire. I gave a little sigh. "Okay," I said. "If you say so."

Lockwood grinned a sooty grin. "In six months, when have I ever let you down?"

I was just opening my mouth to start the list when the ceiling above the desk gave way. Burning spears of wood and chunks of plaster crashed down behind us. Something struck me on the back. It knocked me out and over the windowsill. Lockwood tried to grab me as I fell. He lost his balance; our hands snapped shut on air. We seemed to hang there for a moment, suspended together between heat and cold, between life and death—then we both toppled forward into the night, and there was nothing but rushing darkness all around.

II

Before

Chapter 5

Some people claim the Problem has always been with us. Ghosts are nothing *new*, they say, and have always behaved the same. There's a story the Roman writer Pliny told, for instance, almost two thousand years ago. It's about a scholar who bought a house in Athens. The house was suspiciously cheap, and he soon discovered it was haunted. On the very first night he was visited by the Specter of a gaunt old man in chains. The Visitor beckoned to him; instead of fleeing, the scholar followed the ghost out into the yard, where he saw it vanish into the earth. The next day the scholar had his servants dig at the spot. Sure enough, they soon uncovered a manacled skeleton. The bones were properly buried, and the haunting ceased. End of story. A classic Type Two ghost, the experts say, with a classic, simple purpose—the desire to right a hidden wrong. Just the same as the ghosts we endure today. So nothing's really changed.

Sorry, but I don't buy it. Okay, it's a decent example of a hidden Source—we've all known plenty of similar cases. But notice two things. First: the scholar in the story doesn't seem at all concerned that he might be ghost-touched, and so swell up, turn blue, and die a painful death. Maybe he was just stupid (not to mention lucky). Or maybe Visitors back in ancient times weren't quite as dangerous as they are now.

And they certainly weren't as common either. That's the second thing. The haunted house in Pliny's story? It was probably the only one in Athens, which is why it was so cheap. Here in modern London there are *dozens* of them, with more springing up all the time, no matter what the agencies do. In those days, ghosts were fairly rare. Now we've got an epidemic. So it seems pretty obvious to me that the Problem's different from what went before. Something strange and new *did* start happening around fifty or sixty years ago, and no one's got a damn clue why.

If you look in old newspapers, like George does all the time, you can find mentions of scattered ghostly sightings cropping up in Kent and Sussex around the middle of the last century. But it was a decade or so later that a bloody series of cases, such as the Highgate Terror and the Mud Lane Phantom, attracted serious attention. In each instance, a sudden outbreak of supernatural phenomena was followed by a number of gruesome deaths. Conventional investigations came to nothing, and one or two policemen also died. At last two young researchers, Tom Rotwell and Marissa Fittes, managed to trace each haunting to its respective Source (in the case of the Terror, a bricked-up skull; in that of the Phantom, a highwayman's body staked out at a crossroads). Their success drew great acclaim;

and for the first time, the existence of Visitors was firmly imprinted on the public mind.

In the years that followed, many other hauntings started to come to light, first in London and the south, then slowly spreading across the country. An atmosphere of widespread panic developed. There were riots and demonstrations; churches and mosques did excellent business as people sought to save their souls. Soon both Fittes and Rotwell launched psychic agencies to cope with the demand, leading the way for a host of lesser rivals. Finally the government itself took action, issuing curfews at nightfall, and rolling out production of ghost-lamps in major cities.

None of this actually *solved* the Problem, of course. The best that could be said was that, as time passed, the country got used to living with the new reality. Adult citizens kept their heads down, made sure their houses were well stocked with iron, and left it to the agencies to contain the supernatural threat. The agencies, in turn, sought the best operatives. And, because extreme psychic sensitivity is almost exclusively found in the very young, this meant that whole generations of children, like me, found themselves becoming part of the front line.

I was born Lucy Joan Carlyle in the fourth official decade of the Problem, when it had already spread across the whole of our islands, and even the smallest towns had their ghost-lamps and all villages had their warning bells. My father was a porter in the railway station of a little town in the north of England, a place of slate roofs and stone walls, set tight among green hills. He was a small, red-faced man, bent-backed, sinewy, and hairy as an ape. His breath smelled of strong brown beer, and his hands were hard and swift in punishing any of his children who disturbed his usual taciturn indifference. If he ever called me by name I don't recall it; he was a distant and arbitrary force. After he fell under a train when I was five years old, my only real emotion was fear that we might not be done with him. In the event, the government's new Untimely Death regulations were followed to the letter. The priests scattered iron on the tracks where the accident occurred; they put silver coins on the corpse's eyes; they hung an iron charm around its neck to break the connection with his ghost. These precautions did the job fine. He never came back. Even if he *had*, my mother said, it wouldn't have caused *us* any problems. He'd only have haunted the local pub.

By day I went to school in a little concrete building set above the river on the outskirts of the town. In the afternoon I played in the water meadows or in the park, but I always kept an ear out for the curfew bells and was back safe in our cottage before the sun had fully gone. Once home, I helped set up the defenses. It was my job to place the lavender candles on the sills and check the hanging charms. My elder sisters lit the lights and poured fresh water in the channel that ran beneath the porch. All would then be ready for when our mother bustled in, just as night was falling.

My mother (think large, pink, and harassed) washed laundry at the town's two small hotels. What active maternal affection she possessed had largely been eroded by work and weariness, and she had little energy to spare for her brood of girls, of whom I was the seventh and the last. By day she was mostly out; after dark, she sat slumped in a haze of lavender smoke, silently watching TV. She seldom paid me any attention whatsoever, and for the most part left me to the care of my elder sisters. My only real point of interest to her lay in how I might eventually pay my way.

Everyone knew, you see, that there was Talent running in my family. My mother had seen ghosts in her youth, while two of my sisters had sufficient Sight to get jobs with the night-watch in the city of Newcastle, thirty miles away. None of them, however, had actually been *agency* material. From the first it was obvious that I was different. I had unusual sensitivity to matters relating to the Problem.

Once, I guess when I was six, I was playing in the water meadows with my favorite sister, Mary, who was the closest to me in age. We lost her ball among the rushes and hunted for it a long time. When finally we found it, wedged deep in the roots and sticky amber mud, the light was almost gone. So we were still trailing back along the path beside the river when the bell sounded across the fields.

Mary and I looked at each other. Since infancy, we had been warned what might happen to us if we stayed out after dark. Mary began to cry.

But I was a plucky little girl, small and dauntless. "Doesn't matter," I said. "It's early yet, so they're still as weak as babes. If there *are* any about around here, which I doubt."

"It's not just that," my sister said. "It's Mam. She'll beat me sore."

"Well, she'll beat me, too."

"I'm older than you. She'll beat me *awful* sore. *You'll* be all right, Lucy."

Privately I doubted this. Our mother washed sheets nine hours a day, mostly by hand, and had forearms as vast as pig's thighs. One smack from her, and your bottom vibrated for a week. We hurried on in gloomy silence.

All around were the reeds and the mud and the deepening grayness of dusk. Up ahead the town lights, twinkling on the spur of the hill, were an admonishment and a beacon to us. Our spirits rose; we could see the grass steps leading up to the road.

"That Mam calling?" I said suddenly.

"What?"

"Is that her calling us?"

Mary listened. "I don't hear anything. Anyway, our house is miles off yet."

Which was true enough. Besides, it didn't seem to me that the faint, thin voice I heard was coming from the town.

I looked off and away across the flats, toward where the river, invisible, flowed brown and deep between the hills. Hard to be sure, but I thought I saw a figure standing far out among the reeds there, a dark notch, crooked as a scarecrow. As I watched it began to move—not very fast, but also not too slow—taking a line that would likely intersect our path ahead of us.

I found I didn't much care to meet that person, whoever it might be. I gave my sister a playful nudge. "Race you home," I said. "Come on! I'm getting cold."

So we ran along the track, and every few yards I jumped up to take a look and saw that unknown someone making the greatest endeavors to reach us, loping and limping through the reed stalks. But the long and short of it was we went faster and got to the steps in safety. And when I looked back down from the railings, the water meadows were a monochrome gray vastness, with nothing in them as far as the river bends, and no voice calling us among the reeds.

Later, once my bottom had stopped tingling, I told my mother about the figure, and she told me about a local woman who had killed herself for love there, back when Mam was a girl. Penny Nolan was her name. She'd waded out into the reeds, lain down in the stream, and drowned herself. As you'd expect, she'd become a Type Two, a needy one, and caused trouble from time to time to people coming back late from the valley. Over the years Agent Jacobs had wasted a lot of iron out there, looking for the Source, but he never found it; so presumably Penny Nolan walks there still. In the end they rerouted the path and let the field lie fallow. It's now a pretty place of wildflowers.

Incidents such as this ensured that before long my Talent was common knowledge in the district. My mother waited impatiently until I was eight years old, then took me up to meet the agent in his office just off the town square. It was excellent timing, as one of his operatives had been killed in action three days before. Everything worked out fine. My mother got my weekly wage, I got my first job, and Agent Jacobs got his new trainee.

My employer was a tall, cadaverous gentleman, who had run his local operation for more than twenty years. Treated by the townsfolk with respect bordering on deference, he was nevertheless isolated from them because of his profession, and so cultivated an aura of occult mystery. He was gray-skinned, hook-nosed, and black-bearded, and wore a slightly old-fashioned jet-black suit in the manner of an undertaker. He smoked cigarettes almost constantly, kept his iron filings loose in his jacket pockets, and seldom changed his clothes. His rapier was yellow with ectoplasm stains.

As dusk fell each evening, he led his five or six child operatives on patrols around the district, responding to alarms or, if everything was quiet, checking the public spaces. The eldest agents, who had passed their Third Grade tests, wore rapiers and workbelts; the youngest, like me, carried only equipment bags. Still, it seemed to me a fine thing to be part of this select and important company, walking tall in our mustard-colored jackets, with the great Mr. Jacobs at our head.

Over the ensuing months I learned how to mix salt and magnesium in correct proportions, and how to scatter iron according to the likely power of the ghost. I became adept at packing bags and checking flashlights, filling lamps, and testing chains. I polished rapiers. I made tea and coffee. And when trucks brought new supplies up from the Sunrise Corporation in London, I sorted through the bombs and canisters and stacked them on our shelves.

Jacobs soon discovered that while I saw Visitors well enough, I *heard* them better than anyone. Before I was nine, I'd traced the whispers at the Red Barn back to the broken post that marked the outlaw's grave. In the vile incident at the Swan Hotel, I'd detected the soft, stealthy footsteps creeping up the passage behind us, and so saved us all from certain ghost-touch. The agent rewarded me with swift advancement. I passed my First and Second Grades in double-quick time, and on my eleventh birthday gained my Third. On that famous day I came home with a rapier of my own, a plastic-laminated official certificate, a personal copy of the *Fittes Manual for Ghost-Hunters*, and (more to the point as far as my mother was concerned) a greatly increased monthly salary. I was now the family's major breadwinner, earning more in my four nights' work per week than my mother did in six long days. She celebrated by buying a new dishwasher and a bigger television.

In truth, however, I didn't spend much time at home. My sisters had all left, except for Mary, who was working at the local supermarket, and I never had much to say to my mother. So I spent my waking hours (which were generally nocturnal) with the other young agents of Jacobs's company. I was close to them. We worked together. We had fun. We saved each other's lives a bit. Their names, if you're interested, were Paul, Norrie, Julie, Steph, and Alfie-Joe. They're all dead now.

I was growing into a tall girl, strong-featured, thicker-set than I'd have liked, with large eyes, heavy eyebrows, an overlong nose, and sulky lips. I wasn't pretty, but as my mother once said, prettiness wasn't my profession. I was quick on my feet, if not especially clever with a rapier, and ambitious to do well. I followed orders effectively and worked smoothly in a team. I had hopes of soon getting my Fourth Grade, and so becoming a section leader, able to lead my own sub-group and make my own decisions. My existence was dangerous but fulfilling, and I'd have been moderately content—if it wasn't for one essential thing.

It was said that as a boy, Agent Jacobs had been trained by the Fittes Agency in London. Once, then, clearly, he'd been hot stuff. Well, he wasn't anymore. Of course, like every adult, his senses had long ago grown dulled; since he couldn't detect ghosts easily, he relied on the rest of us to act as his eyes and ears. This much was fair enough. All supervisors were the same. Their job was to use their experience and quick wits to help guide their agents when a Visitor was sighted, to coordinate the plan of attack and, where necessary, provide back-up in emergencies. In my early years at the agency, Jacobs did this reasonably well. But somewhere down the line, amid all those endless hours of waiting and watching in the darkness, he began to lose his nerve. He hung back at the edge of haunted areas, reluctant to go in. His hands shook, he chain-smoked cigarettes; he shouted orders from afar. He jumped at shadows. One night, when I approached him to report, he mistook me for a Visitor. In his panic he lashed out with his rapier, and took a slice out of my cap. I was saved only by the shaking of his sword arm.

The rest of us knew what he was like, of course, and none of us cared for it. But he was the one who paid our wages, and he was an important man in our little town, so we just got on with it, and trusted our own judgment. And in fact nothing very terrible happened for quite a long time, until the night at the Wythburn Mill.

There was a water mill halfway up the Wythe valley that had a bad reputation. There'd been accidents, a death or two; it had been closed for years. A local logging firm was interested in using it as a regional office, but they wanted it made safe first. They came to Jacobs and asked him to check it out, make sure there was nothing unhealthy there.

We walked up the valley in the early evening and reached it shortly after dusk. It was a warm summer night, and birds were calling in the trees. Stars shone overhead. The mill was a great dark mass, wedged among the rocks and the conifers. The stream idled down below the gravel road.

The main door to the mill had been secured with a padlock. The glass in the door panel was broken; a board had been roughly fixed over the hole. We gathered outside the door and checked our equipment. Agent Jacobs, as was his habit, looked for a seat and found one on a nearby stump. He lit a cigarette. We used our Talents, and made our reports. I was the only one who'd gotten anything.

"I can hear something sobbing," I said. "It's very faint, but quite close by."

"What kind of sobbing?" Jacobs asked. He was watching the bats flit past overhead.

"Like a child's."

Jacobs nodded vaguely; he didn't look at me. "Secure the first room," he said to us, "and check again."

The lock had rusted with the years, and the door was stiff and warped. We pushed it open and shone our flashlights across a large and desolate foyer. It had a low ceiling and plenty of debris on the cracked linoleum tiles. There were desks and easy chairs, old notices on the walls, a smell of rotting furniture. You could hear the sound of the stream running somewhere below the floor.

We went into the foyer, taking with us a drift of cigarette smoke. Agent Jacobs did not come with us. He remained sitting on his tree stump, staring at his knees.

Staying close together, we used our Talents once more. I got the sobbing noise again, louder this time. We turned our flashlights off and hunted about; and it wasn't long before we saw a little glowing shape, crouching far off at the end of a passage that led deeper into the mill. When we switched the flashlights back on, the passageway seemed clear.

I went back out to report our findings. "Paul and Julie say it looks like a little kid. I can't make out the details. It's very faint. And it's not moving."

Agent Jacobs tapped ash into the grass. "It hasn't responded to you in any way? Not tried to approach you?"

"No, sir. The others think it's a weak Type One, perhaps the echo of some child who worked here long ago."

"All right, fine. Pin it back with iron. Then you can search the spot."

"Yes, sir. Only, sir . . ."

"What is it, Lucy?"

"There's . . . something about this one. I don't like it."

The end of the cigarette glowed red in the darkness as Agent Jacobs drew on it briefly. As always these days, his hand shook; his tone was irritable. "Don't like it? It's a child crying. Of course you don't like it. Do you hear something else?"

"No, sir."

"Another voice, maybe? From a second, stronger, Visitor?"

"No . . ." And it was true. I didn't hear anything dangerous. Everything about the visitation was wispy and frail, suggestive of weakness. The sound, the shape . . . they were barely there at all. Just a typical faint Shade. We could snuff it in a trice. All the same, I distrusted it. I disliked the way it cowered, so *very* tight and small.

"What do the others say?" Jacobs asked.

"They think it's easy enough, sir. They're impatient to get on. But it just seems . . . wrong to me."

I could hear him shifting on the stump. Wind moved among the trees. "I can order them to pull back, Lucy. But vague feelings are no good. I need a solid reason."

"No, sir. . . . I guess it's okay. . . ." I sighed, hesitated. "Perhaps you could come in with me?" I asked. "You could give me your opinion."

There was a heavy silence. "Just do your job," Agent Jacobs said.

The others *were* impatient. When I caught sight of them, they were already advancing along the passage, their rapiers up, their salt-bombs ready. Not far away, the glowing form sensed the approaching iron. It quailed and shrank, flickered in and out of vision like a badly tuned TV. It began to drift off toward a corner of the passage.

"It's on the move!" someone said.

"It's fading!"

"Keep it in sight! We don't want to lose it!"

If the apparition's vanishing point was not observed, locating the Source would be that much more laborious. There was a general rush forward. I drew my sword, hastened to catch up with the others. The shade was so faint now it was almost gone. My apprehensions seemed suddenly absurd.

Small as an infant, ever shrinking, the ghost limped forlornly round the corner, out of view. My fellow agents hurried after it; I speeded up too. Even so, I hadn't actually reached the turn when the vicious flare of plasmic light ripped across the wall in front of me. There was a squeal of tortured iron and a solitary burst of magnesium fire. In the brief illumination from the flare I saw a monstrous shadow rising. The light went out.

Then all the screams began.

I twisted my head, looked back down the passage and across the foyer toward the open door. Far off in the distant dusk I saw the cigarette's pinprick point of red.

"Sir! Mr. Jacobs!"

Nothing.

"Sir! We need your help! *Sir!*"

The pinprick flared as the agent took a breath. No answer came. He didn't move. Then wind roared along the corridor and nearly knocked me off my feet. The walls of the mill shook; the open door slammed shut.

I cursed in the darkness. Then I drew a canister from my belt, raised my rapier high, and ran around the corner of the corridor toward the screams.

At the Coroner's Inquest, Agent Jacobs was heavily criticized by relatives of the dead agents and there was talk of him being sent to court, but it never came to anything. He argued that he had acted entirely in accordance with the information I had brought him about the strength of the ghost. He claimed he had not heard my cries for help, nor any other sound from inside the mill, until I'd finally broken through the window on the upper floor and tumbled down the roof to safety. He had not noticed any screaming.

When I gave evidence, I tried to describe the original unease I'd felt, but was forced to admit that I'd detected nothing concrete. The coroner, in his summing up, remarked that it was a pity my report had not been more accurate as to the Visitor's power. If it had, perhaps some lives might have been saved. His verdict was Death by Misadventure, which is usual in such circumstances. The relatives got payouts from the Fittes Fund and little plaques remembering their children in the town square. The mill was demolished and salt strewn over the site.

Jacobs returned to work soon after. It was universally expected that, after a short rest to get over the incident, I would happily rejoin him. This wasn't my opinion. I waited three days to regain my strength. On the fourth morning, early, while my mother and sister slept, I packed my belongings into a small bag, strapped on my rapier, and left the cottage without a backward glance. An hour later I was on the train to London.

Chapter 6

LOCKWOOD & CO.,

the well-known Psychic Investigations agency, requires a new Junior Field Operative. Duties will include on-site analysis of reported hauntings and the containment of same. The successful applicant will be SENSITIVE to supernatural phenomena, well-dressed, preferably female, and not above fifteen years in age. Unsuccessful applicants will include time-wasters, fraudsters, and persons with criminal records.

Apply in writing, together with a photograph, to 35 Portland Row, London W1.

I stood in the street and watched as the taxi drove away. The sound of the engine faded. It was very quiet. Pale sunlight gleamed on the asphalt and on the lines of cars parked nose to tail on either side. Some ways off, a little boy was playing in a dusty patch of sun, moving miniature plastic ghosts and agents across the sidewalk. The agents had tiny swords; the ghosts looked like little floating sheets. Other than the kid, there was no one around.

It was clearly a residential district, this part of London. Its buildings were big-boned Victorian town houses, with pillared porches hung with baskets of lavender, and basement apartments reached by stairs directly from the street. Everything exuded a feeling of shabby gentility—of buildings and people looking back on better days. There was a little grocer's shop at the corner, the cluttered kind that sold everything from oranges to shoe polish, milk to magnesium flares. Outside it rose a battered metal ghost-light, standing eight-feet tall on its scallop-sided stem. The great hinged shutters were closed and blank, the flash bulbs dark, the lenses hidden. Rust bloomed like lichen across the surface of the iron.

First things first. I checked my reflection in the side window of the nearest car, taking off my cap and scuffling my fingers through my hair. Did I look like a good operative? Did I look like someone with the right history and qualifications? Or did I look like a tousled nobody who'd been rejected by six agencies in seven days? It was hard to tell.

I set off up the road.

Number 35 Portland Row was a white-fronted residence of four floors, with faded green shutters and pink flowers in the window boxes. Even more than its neighbors, it had a faint air of dilapidation.

Every surface looked as if it needed a lick of paint, or possibly just a good cleaning. A small wooden sign clamped to the outside of the railing read:

A. J. LOCKWOOD & CO., INVESTIGATORS.
AFTER DARK, RING BELL AND WAIT BEYOND THE IRON LINE.

I paused for a moment, thinking wistfully of the posh town house of Tendy & Sons, of the spacious offices of Atkins and Armstrong; above all, of the glittering glass Rotwell building on Regent Street. . . . But none of those interviews had worked out for me. I didn't have any choice in the matter. Like my appearance, this would simply have to do.

Pushing open a wonky metal gate, I stepped onto a narrow path of broken tiles. On my right, a steep flight of steps led down to a basement yard, a shady space half overhung with ivy and filled with unkempt plants and potted trees. There was a narrow line of iron tiles embedded across the path, and from a post beside this hung a large bell with a dangling wooden clapper. Ahead was a black painted door.

Ignoring the bell, I stepped over the line and knocked sharply on the door. After an interval, a short, fat, tallow-haired youth wearing large, round spectacles looked out.

"Oh, another one," he said. "I thought we'd finished. Or are you Arif's new girl?"

I gazed at him. "Who's Arif?"

"Runs the corner store. He normally sends someone over with

doughnuts about this time. You don't seem to have doughnuts." He looked disappointed.

"No. I have a rapier."

The youth sighed. "So I guess you're another candidate. Name?"

"Lucy Carlyle. Are you Mr. Lockwood?"

"Me? No."

"Well, can I come in?"

"Yeah. The last girl's just gone down. From the look of her, she won't be very long."

Even as he spoke, a scream of the utmost terror rang out from inside the house and echoed off the ivy walls of the yard below. Birds rose from trees up and down the street. I jerked back in shock, hands moving automatically to the hilt of my sword. The scream collapsed into a whimpering gargle and presently died away. I stared wide-eyed at the youth in the doorway, who hadn't stirred.

"Ah, there we are," he said. "Didn't I say? Well, you're next up. Come in."

Neither the boy nor the scream instilled me with much confidence, and I was half inclined to leave. But after two weeks in London, I was almost out of options: mess up here, and I'd soon be signing for the night-watch with all the other no-hope kids. Besides, there was something in the manner of the youth, a subtle impudence in the way he stood, that told me he half-expected me to run. I wasn't having that. So I stepped swiftly past him, and entered a cool, wide hallway.

It had a parquet floor and was lined with bookshelves of dark mahogany. The shelves held a mass of ethnic masks and other artifacts—pots and icons, brightly decorated shells and gourds. A narrow key table stood just inside the door with a lantern on it, its base shaped like a crystal skull. Beyond that sat a vast, chipped plant pot stuffed with umbrellas, walking sticks, and rapiers. I halted beside a rack of coats.

"Hold on a sec," the boy said. He remained waiting by the open door.

He was a little older than me, and not quite my height, though a good deal stockier. He had podgy, rather bland features, nondescript except for a prominently squared jaw. Behind his glasses, his eyes were very blue. His sandy hair, which in texture reminded me of a horse's tail, flopped heavily across his brow. He wore white sneakers, a pair of faded jeans, and a loosely tucked shirt, bulging around the midriff.

"Any minute now," he said.

From deeper inside the house, a murmur of voices rose to a crescendo. A side door burst open: a well-dressed girl emerged at high speed, eyes blazing, face chalk-white, scrunched coat dragging in her hand. She flashed me an expression of fury and contempt, swore roundly at the fat boy, kicked the front door as she passed it, and was gone into the day.

"Hmm. Definite second-interview material, that one," the boy remarked. He closed the door and scratched his pudgy nose. "Okey-doke, if you'd like to follow me . . ."

He led the way into a sunny living room, white-walled and cheery, decorated with further artifacts and totems. Two easy chairs and a sofa surrounded a low-lying coffee table. Also beside it, smiling broadly, was a tall, slim boy dressed in a dark suit. "I win, George," he said. "I *knew* there was one more."

As I crossed to greet him, I used my senses, as I always do. The full range of senses, I mean—outer *and* inner. Just so I didn't miss anything.

The most obvious thing to spot was a rounded, bulky object lying on the table, concealed by a green-and-white-spotted handkerchief. Did it have anything to do with the previous girl's discomfort? I thought it highly likely. There was the subtlest of noises, too—something I could *almost* hear, but it kept its distance from my mind. I suppose if I'd concentrated, I might have pinned it down . . . but that would have meant standing like a plank with my eyes shut and my mouth open, which is never a great way to start an interview. So I just shook the boy's hand.

"Hello," he said. "I'm Anthony Lockwood."

"Lucy Carlyle."

He had very bright, dark eyes and a nice lopsided grin. "Very good to meet you. Tea? Or has George already offered you some?"

The plump boy made a disparaging gesture. "I thought I'd wait until the first test was done," he said. "See if she was still here. I've wasted that many tea bags this morning."

"Why not give her the benefit of the doubt," Anthony Lockwood said, "and go put the kettle on?"

The boy seemed unconvinced. "All right—but I reckon she's a bolter." He spun slowly on his heels and trudged out into the hall.

Anthony Lockwood waved me to a chair. "You'll have to excuse George. We've been interviewing since eight, and he's getting hungry. He was *so* convinced the last girl was the final one."

"Sorry about that," I said. "I'm afraid I haven't brought you any doughnuts either."

He looked sharply at me. "What makes you say that?"

"George told me about your daily deliveries."

"Oh. For a moment there, I thought you were psychic."

"I am."

"I mean, in an unusual way. Never mind." He settled himself on the couch opposite and smoothed out some papers before him. He had a very slender face, with a long nose and a dark mop of unruly hair. I realized almost with shock that he was scarcely older than me. His manner had been so assured, I hadn't noticed his age. I wondered for the first time why there were no supervisors present in the room.

"I see from your letter," the boy said, "that you're from the north of England. From the Cheviot Hills. Wasn't there a famous outbreak in that district a few years back?"

"The Murton Colliery Horror," I said. "Yes. I was five then."

"Fittes agents had to come from London to deal with the Visitors, didn't they?" Lockwood said. "It was in my *Gazetteer of British Hauntings*."

I nodded. "We weren't meant to look, in case they took our soul, and everyone had boarded up their ground-floor windows, but I peeped out anyway. I saw them drifting in the moonlight down the middle of the road. Wee slips of things, like little girls."

He gave me a quizzical look. "Girls? I thought they were the ghosts of miners, who'd died in an accident underground."

"To start with, yes. But they were Changers. Took on many shapes before the end."

Anthony Lockwood nodded. "I see. That rings a bell. . . . Okay, so you obviously knew from early on," he continued, "that you had a Talent. You had the Sight, of course, more than most of the other kids, and the bravery to use it. But according to your letter, that wasn't your real strength. You could listen, too. And you also had the power of Touch."

"Well, Listening's my thing, really," I said. "As a kid in my crib, I used to hear voices whispering in the street—after curfew, when all the living were inside. But I've got good Touch too, though that often merges with what I hear. It's hard to separate them. For me, Touch sometimes triggers echoes of what's happened."

"George can do a bit of that," the boy said. "Not me. I'm tone-deaf when it comes to Visitors. Sight's my thing. Death-glows and trails, and all the ghoulish residues of death. . . ." He grinned. "Cheerful subject, isn't it? Now then, it says here you started out with a local operative up north. . . ." He checked the paper. "Name of Jacobs. Correct?"

I smiled blandly; my stomach clenched with tension. "That's right."

"You worked for him for several years."

"Yes."

"So he trained you, did he? You got your Fourth Grade qualifications with him?"

I shifted slightly in my chair. "That's right. Grades One through Four."

"Okay . . ." Lockwood considered me. "I notice you haven't actually brought your final certificates. Or indeed any letter of referral from Mr. Jacobs. That's a little unusual, isn't it? Official references are normally provided in these situations."

I took a deep breath. "He didn't give me any," I said. "Our arrangement ended . . . abruptly."

Lockwood said nothing. I could see he was waiting for details.

"If you want the full story, I can give it," I said heavily. "It's just . . . it's not something I like dwelling on, that's all."

I waited, heart juddering. This was the moment. All the other interviews had terminated just about *here*.

"Some other time, then," Anthony Lockwood said. When he smiled at me, a warm light seemed to suffuse the room. "You know, I can't think what's keeping George. A trained baboon could have made the tea by now. It's really time for the tests."

"Yes, what tests *are* these?" I said hastily. "If you don't mind my asking."

"Not at all. It's what we use to assess the candidates. Frankly, I don't set much store by people's letters or referrals, Ms. Carlyle. I prefer to see their Talent with my own eyes. . . ." He looked at his watch. "I'll give George another minute. In the meantime, I suppose you want the rundown on us. We're a new agency, been registered three months. I got my full license last year. We're accredited with DEPRAC, but—just to be clear—we're not on their payroll, like Fittes or Rotwell or any of that mob. We're independent, and we like it that way. We take the jobs we want and turn down the rest. All our clients are private customers who have a problem with Visitors, and want it sorted quickly and quietly. We solve their problems. They pay us handsomely. That's about the size of it. Any questions?"

With the issue of my recent past out of the way, I had a clear run now. I wasn't going to mess it up. I sat forward on the sofa, making sure my back was straight, my hands neat in my lap. "Who are your supervisors?" I asked. "Do I get to meet them too?"

A frown flickered across the boy's forehead. "No supervisors here. No adults. It's my company. I'm in charge. George Cubbins is deputy." He looked at me. "Some applicants had a problem with this set-up, so *they* didn't get very far. Does it bother you?"

"Oh no," I said. "No, I like the sound of it fine." There was a brief silence. "So . . . there have always been just two of you? Just you and George?"

"Well, we generally have an assistant. Two's enough to deal with most Visitors, but for tough cases, all three of us go along. Three's the magic number, you know."

I nodded slowly. "I see. What happened to your last assistant?"

"Poor Robin? Oh, he . . . moved on."

"To another job?"

"Perhaps 'passed on' would be more accurate. Or, indeed, 'passed over.' Ah—good! Tea!"

The hall door opened, and the plump boy's posterior backed through it, closely followed by the rest of him. He turned in a stately manner and advanced, carrying a tray with three steaming mugs and a plate of cookies. Whatever he had been doing in the kitchen all this while, he looked more disheveled than before: his shirt was untucked, and his mop of hair now covered his eyes. He placed the tray on the table beside the shrouded object and glanced at me dubiously. "Still here?" he said. "Thought you'd have scarpered by now."

"Haven't done the test yet, George," Lockwood said easily. "You're just in time."

"Good." He took the largest mug and retreated to the sofa.

There was a polite interlude during which mugs were distributed, and milk and sugar offered and declined. "Come on, take a cookie," Lockwood said. He pushed the plate my way. "Please. Or else George'll eat them all."

"Okay."

I took a cookie. Lockwood had a large bite of his and brushed his hands clean. "Right," he said. "Just a few tests, Ms. Carlyle. Nothing to worry about at all. Are you ready?"

"Sure." I could feel George's little eyes fixed upon me, and even Lockwood's casual tones could not disguise a certain eagerness. But they were dealing with someone who'd survived the Wythburn Mill alone. I wasn't going to fret about this.

Lockwood nodded. "We might as well start here, then." He stretched out a languid hand to the spotted handkerchief and, after a ceremonial pause, flicked it away.

Sitting on the table was a stocky cylinder of clear, thick glass, sealed at the top with a red plastic plug. There were small handles near the top to grip it with: it reminded me of the big glass demijohns in which my father used to brew his beer. Instead of stale and brownish liquid, however, it contained a greasy yellow smoke—not quite stationary, very slowly shifting. Sitting in its heart was something large and dark.

"What do you think this is?" Lockwood asked.

I bent forward, scanning the apparatus. On closer inspection, the plug had several safety flanges and double seals. There was a little symbol embossed on the side of the glass: a radiant sun that doubled as an eye.

"It's silver-glass," I said. "Made by the Sunrise Corporation."

Lockwood nodded, gently smiling. I bent closer. With the nail of my middle finger, I tapped the side of the glass; at once the smoke awoke, rippling outward from the point of impact, becoming thicker, more granular as it did so. As it separated, it revealed the object in the jar: a human skull, brown and stained, clamped to the bottom of the glass.

The ripples of smoke contorted, twisted; they took on the horrid semblance of a face, with blankly rolling eyes and gaping mouth. For a moment the features were superimposed upon the skull beneath. I jerked back from the glass. The face devolved into streamlike ribbons of smoke that swirled about the cylinder, and presently became still.

I cleared my throat. "Well, it's a ghost-jar," I said. "The skull's the Source, and that ghost is tied to it. Can't tell what sort. A Phantasm or a Specter, maybe."

So saying, I sat back in a posture of nonchalant unconcern, as if Visitors in jars were something I dealt with every day of the week. In truth, I'd never seen one, and the apparition *had* shocked me. But not unduly so: after the previous girl's scream, I'd expected *something*. Plus, I'd heard of containers like this before.

Lockwood's smile had momentarily frozen, as if uncertain whether to express surprise, pleasure, or disappointment. In the end, pleasure won the day. "Yes, that's right," he said. "Well done." He put the handkerchief back on the cylinder and, with some effort, stowed it out of sight under the table.

The plump boy sipped his tea loudly. "She was shaken," he said. "You could see it."

I ignored the comment. "Where did you get the jar?" I said. "I thought only Rotwell and Fittes had them."

"Time for questions later," Lockwood said. He opened a drawer in the coffee table and pulled out a small red box. "Now, I'd like to test your Talent, if I may. I have some items ready. Please tell me, if you can"—he opened the box and put an object on the table—"what supernatural resonance you detect here."

It was an unassuming cup of old, white porcelain, with a fluted base and a sharp chip in the handle. There was a strange white stain around the inside of the lip, which thickened at the bottom of the cup to become a crusty residue.

I took it in my hand and closed my eyes, turning it this way and that, running my fingers lightly over the surface.

I listened, waiting for echoes. . . . Nothing came to me.

This was no good. I shook my head, cleared my mind of distractions, shut out as best I could the occasional noise of traffic passing on the street, and the less occasional slurps of tea sounding from George's sofa. I tried again.

No. Still nothing.

After a few minutes I gave up. "I'm sorry," I said at last, "I can't detect anything."

Lockwood nodded. "I should hope not. This is the cup George keeps his toothbrush in. Good. On to the next." He picked up the cup and tossed it across to the plump boy, who caught it with a snort of mirth.

I felt myself go cold; I knew my cheeks were scarlet. I took hold of my backpack, and stood abruptly. "I'm not here to be made fun of," I said. "I'll find my own way out."

"Ooh," George said. "Feisty."

I looked at him. His flop of hair, his glossy, shapeless face, his silly little glasses: *everything* about him made me livid. "That's right," I said. "Step over here, and I'll show you *exactly* how feisty I am."

The boy blinked at me. "I might just do that."

"I don't see you moving."

"Well, it's a deep sofa. It's taking me a while to get out of it."

"Hold on, both of you," Anthony Lockwood said. "This is an interview, not a boxing match. George: shut up. Ms. Carlyle: I apologize for upsetting you, but it was a serious test, which you passed with flying colors. You'd be amazed how many of our interviewees this morning have made up some cock-and-bull story about poison, suicide, or murder. It'd be the most haunted cup in London if the mildest of their tales was true. Now then, please sit down. What can you tell me about these?"

From the drawer beneath the table: three new items, laid side by side in front of me. A gentleman's wristwatch, gold-plated around the rim, with an old brown leather band; a piece of lacy red ribbon; and a slim, long-bladed penknife with an ivory inlay handle.

My annoyance at their trick receded. This was a good challenge. With a steely glance at George, I sat and spread the objects out a little, so their hidden textures (if any) didn't overlap. Then I emptied my mind as best I could, and picked them up, one by one.

Time went by; I tested each three times.

I finished. When my eyes refocused, I saw George engrossed in a comic book he had gotten from somewhere, and Lockwood sitting as before, hands clasped, watching me.

I took a long drink of cold tea. "Did any of your other applicants get this right?" I said quietly.

Lockwood smiled. "Did you?"

"The echoes were hard to disengage," I said, "which I suppose is why you threw them at me all together. They're all strong, but distinct in quality. Which do you want first?"

"The knife."

"Okay. The knife has several conflicting echoes: a man's laughter, gunshots, even—possibly—birdsong. If there's a death attached to it—which I suppose there must be, since I can sense all this—it wasn't violent or sad in any way. The feeling I got from it was gentle, almost happy." I looked at him.

Lockwood's face gave nothing away. "How about the ribbon?"

"The traces on the ribbon," I said, "are fainter than the knife's, but much stronger in emotion. I thought I heard weeping, but it's terribly indistinct. What I get so strongly with it is a sense of sadness; when I was holding it, I felt my heart would break."

"And the watch?" His eyes were fixed on me. George still read his comic—*Astounding Arabian Nights*; he idly turned a page.

"The watch . . ." I took a deep breath. "The echoes here aren't as strong as on the ribbon or the knife, which makes me think the owner hasn't died—or not while wearing it, at any rate. But there's death attached to it nonetheless. A lot of death. And . . . it isn't pleasant. I heard voices raised and . . . and screaming, and—" I shuddered as I looked at it glinting gently on the coffee table. Every notch on that gold plate casing, every scuff on that little strip of worn, bent leather filled me with horror. "And it's a vile thing," I said. "I couldn't hold it very long. I don't know what it is or where you got it, but no one should be touching this, not ever. Certainly not for a lousy interview."

I leaned forward, took the final two cookies from the plate, and sat back, crunching. It was one of those moments when a great Don't Care wave hits you, and you float off on it, head back, looking at the sky. I was tired out. It was my seventh interview in as many days. Well, I'd done all I could, and if Lockwood and this stupid George didn't choose to appreciate it—that really didn't bother me anymore.

There was a long silence. Lockwood's hands were clasped between his knees; he was sitting forward like a priest on the toilet, gazing at nothing, a pained, contemplative expression on his face. George's head was still buried in his comic. As far as he was concerned, I might not have been there at all.

"Well," I said finally. "I guess I know where the door is."

"Tell her about the cookie rule," George said.

I looked at him. "What?"

"Tell her, Lockwood. We'll have to get this straight, or there'll be hell to pay."

Lockwood nodded. "The rule here is that each member of the agency only takes one cookie at a time in strict rotation. Keeps it fair, keeps it orderly. Nicking two in times of stress just isn't done."

"One cookie at a time?"

"That's right."

"You mean to say I've got the job?"

"Of course you've got the job," he said.

Chapter 7

Thirty-five Portland Row, the building that would function as both home and headquarters for the operatives of Lockwood & Co., was an unexpected sort of place. Appearing squat and squarish from the street, it was actually positioned at the top of a slight slope, so that its rear elevation jutted out high over a jumble of brick walled gardens. It had four floors, which ranged from tiny (the attic) to sprawling (the basement). Technically, the upper three levels were our living space, while the basement contained the office of the company; in fact, such divisions seemed rather blurred. The living areas, for instance, had all sorts of hidden doors that opened onto weapons racks, or swung out to become dartboards, or spare beds, or giant maps of London festooned with colored pins. Meanwhile, the basement itself doubled as a laundry room, which meant you'd be practicing Wessex half-turns in the rapier room with a row of socks hanging from a clothesline beside your head, or filling canisters from the salt box with the washing machine rumbling loudly in your ear.

I liked it all immediately, though it puzzled me as well. It was a large house, filled with expensive, grown-up things, and yet there were no adults present anywhere. Just Anthony Lockwood and his associate, George. And now me.

On the first afternoon, Lockwood took me on a tour. He showed me the attic first, low-slung beneath steep eaves. It contained two rooms: a minuscule washroom, in which sink, shower, and toilet practically overlapped; and a pretty attic bedroom, just big enough for a single bed, armoire, and dresser. Opposite the bed, an arched gable window looked out over Portland Row as far as the ghost-lamp on the corner.

"This is where I slept when I was little," Lockwood said. "It hasn't been occupied for years; the last assistant, God rest him, chose to live out. You can use it, if you like."

"Thanks," I said. "I'd be pleased to."

"I know the bathroom's small, but at least it's your own. There's a bigger one downstairs, but that'd mean sharing towels with George."

"Oh, I think I'll be fine here."

We left the attic, trooped down the narrow stairs. The landing below was dark and somber, with a circular golden rug in the center of the floor. Bookshelves in a corner were crammed with a random mix of paperbacks: battered copies of the *Fittes Yearbook* and Mottram's *Psychical Theories*, an assortment of cheap novels—mostly pulp thrillers, and detective fiction—and serious works on religion and philosophy. As in the hall and living room below, various ethnic artifacts decorated the wall—including some kind of rattle seemingly made from human bones.

Lockwood caught me staring at it. "That's a Polynesian ghost-chaser," he said. "Nineteenth-century. Supposed to drive away spirits with its raucous sound."

"Does it work?"

"No idea. I've not tried it yet. Might be worth a go." He pointed to a door alongside. "That's the bathroom, if you need it. This one's my room, and that's George's. I'd tread with caution there. I once walked in on him doing yoga in the nude."

With difficulty, I drove the image from my mind. "So this was your house, as a kid?"

"Well, it belonged to my parents then. It's mine now. And yours, of course, for as long as you work here."

"Thanks. Tell me, did your parents—"

"I'll show you the kitchen now," Lockwood said. "I think George is making dinner." He started down the stairs.

"What's through there?" I asked suddenly. There was one door he hadn't mentioned; no different from the others, set close beside his own.

He smiled. "That's private, if you don't mind. Don't worry, it's not very interesting. Come on! There's still lots to see down here."

The ground floor—comprised of sitting room, library, and kitchen—was clearly the heart of the house, and the kitchen was where we would spend the most time. It would be the place we'd assemble for a pre-expedition supper; also where we'd gather for a late breakfast the morning after. Its appearance reflected this fusion of work and leisure. The surfaces had all the usual domestic clutter—cookie tins, fruit bowls, bags of chips—but also sacks of salt and iron, carefully weighed and ready to go. There were rapiers propped behind the garbage bins and plasm-stained work boots soaking in a bucket. Oddest of all was the kitchen table and its great white tablecloth. This cloth was half-covered with a spreading net of scribbled notes and diagrams, and also drawings of several Visitor subtypes—Wraiths, Solitaries, and Shades.

"We call this our thinking cloth," Lockwood said. "It's not widely known, but I located the bones of the Fenchurch Street Ghoul by sketching out the street plan here, over tea and cheese-on-toast at four o'clock in the morning. The cloth lets us jot down memos, theories, follow interesting trains of thought. . . . It's a very useful tool."

"It's also good for exchanging rude messages when a case hasn't gone well and we're not talking to each other," George said. He stood by the cooktop, tending the evening stew.

"Er, does that happen often?" I asked.

"No, no, no," Lockwood said. "Almost never."

George stirred the stew implacably. "You wait and see."

Lockwood clapped his hands together. "Good. Have I shown you the office yet? You'll never guess where the entrance is. Look—it's over here."

It turned out the basement offices of Lockwood & Co. were reached directly from the kitchen. It wasn't exactly a *secret* door—the handle was in plain view—but from the outside it looked like nothing more than an ordinary closet. It had precisely the same wooden veneer and handle shape as all the other kitchen cabinets. When you opened it, however, a little light came on, revealing a set of spiral stairs, curling steeply down.

At the bottom of the stairs lay a string of open, exposed-brick rooms, separated by arches and pillars and stretches of plastered wall. They were lit by a large window looking onto the overgrown yard at the front of the house, and by angled skylights set into the ground along the side. The largest area contained three desks, a filing cabinet, two ratty green armchairs, and a rather wonky bookshelf that Lockwood had assembled to hold his paperwork. A big black ledger sat resplendent on the central desk.

"Our casebook," Lockwood said. "It's got a history of everything we investigate. George compiles it and cross-references everything with the files up there." He gave a little sigh. "He likes that sort of thing. Personally, I take each assignment as it comes."

I glanced at the box files on the shelf. Each one had been neatly labeled by type and subtype: *Type One: Shades*; *Type One: Lurkers*; *Type Two: Poltergeists*; *Type Two: Phantasms*—and all the rest. At the end of the row was a thin file marked *Type Threes*. I stared at this.

"Have you actually encountered a Type Three?" I asked.

Lockwood shrugged. "Hardly. I'm not even sure they exist."

Through an arch off the main office was a side room, completely empty except for a rack of rapiers, a bowl of chalk dust, and two straw-filled Visitor dummies hanging from a ceiling beam by iron chains. One of the dummies wore a bonnet, and the other a top hat. Both were full of holes.

"Meet Joe and Esmeralda," Lockwood said. "They're named after Lady Esmeralda and Floating Joe, two of the famous ghosts from Marissa Fittes' *Memoirs*. Obviously this is the rapier room. We practice here every afternoon. Of course, you'll be proficient with a sword already, if you've passed your Fourth Grade . . ." He glanced at me.

I nodded. "Of course. Yes. Absolutely."

". . . but it doesn't hurt to keep in shape, does it? I look forward to seeing you in action. And over here"—Lockwood led me to a padlocked metal door set in the wall—"is our high-security storeroom. Take a look inside."

This storage area was the only separate portion of the basement—a small, windowless room filled with shelves and boxes. It was here that all the most essential equipment was kept—the range of silver seals, the iron chains, the flares and canisters ordered direct from the Sunrise Corporation. Right now, it was also where the ghost-jar, with its clamped brown skull and ectoplasmic host, was stored, concealed beneath its polka-dotted cloth.

"George gets it out to do experiments sometimes," Lockwood said. "He wants to observe how ghosts respond to different stimuli. Personally, I'd rather he destroyed the thing, but he's gotten attached to it, somehow."

I eyed the cloth doubtfully. Just as during the interview, I thought I could *almost* hear a psychic noise, a delicate hum on the fringes of perception. "So . . . where *did* he get it from?" I asked.

"Oh, he stole it. I expect he'll tell you about it sometime. But actually, it's not the only trophy we've got down here. Come over here and see."

In the back wall of the basement, a modern glass door, fortified with iron ghost-bars, led out onto the garden. Alongside it, four shelves had been riveted to the brickwork: they housed a collection of silver-glass cases, with objects inside each one. Some of these were old, others very modern. I noticed, among them, a set of playing cards; a lock of long, blond hair; a lady's bloodstained glove; three human teeth; a gentleman's folded necktie. The most splendid case of all contained a mummified hand, as black and shriveled as a rotten banana, sitting on a red silk cushion.

"That's a pirate's," Lockwood said. "Seventeen-hundreds, probably. Belonged to a fellow who was strung up and sun-dried on Execution Dock, where the Mouse and Musket Inn stands now. His spirit was a Lurker; he'd given the barmaids a lot of trouble by the time I dug that up. Well, this is all stuff George and I have collected over our careers so far. Some are actual Sources, and very dangerous: they've got to be kept locked up, particularly at night. Others just need to be treated with caution—if you're sensitive—like the three I gave you in the interview."

I'd seen them on the bottom shelf: the knife, the ribbon, the unspeakable watch.

"Yeah . . ." I said. "You never told me what they were."

Lockwood nodded. "I'm sorry that the impressions you got were so grueling, but I didn't expect you to experience them so strongly. Well, the knife belonged to my uncle, who lived out in the country. He took it with him on walks and hunting expeditions. Had it with him when he dropped dead from a heart attack during a shoot. He was a kind man; from what you said, the knife still had something of his personality."

I thought back to the peaceful sensations I'd picked up from the knife. "It did."

"The ribbon came from a grave they opened in Kensal Green

Cemetery, when they were building one of the iron barriers round the perimeter last year. Coffin had a woman in it—and a little child. The ribbon was in the woman's hair."

The memory of my feelings as I'd held the slip of silk returned; my eyes filled with tears. I cleared my throat and made a big business of studying the nearest boxes. It wouldn't do to show weakness to Lockwood. Frailty was what Visitors fed on: frailty and loose emotions. Good agents needed the opposite: firm control and strength of nerve. My old leader, Jacobs, had lost his nerve. And what had happened? I had nearly died.

I spoke in a cool, matter-of-fact voice. "And the watch?"

Lockwood had been observing me closely. "Yes . . . the watch. You were right to sense its sinister residue. It's actually a memento of my first successful case." He paused significantly. "No doubt you've heard of the murderer Harry Crisp?"

My eyes grew round. "Not the coin-in-the-slot killer?"

"Er, no. That was Clive Dilson."

"Oh! You mean the one who kept heads in the fridge?"

"No . . . that was Colin Buchanan-Prescott."

I scratched my chin. "In that case, I've never heard of him."

"Oh." Lockwood seemed slightly deflated. "I'm a little surprised. Do they *have* papers in the north of England? Well, it was thanks to me that Harry Crisp got put away. I was doing a sweep of the neighborhood in Tooting, out hunting Type Twos, you see, and I noticed all the death-glows in his garden. They'd been missed because he'd cunningly scattered iron filings everywhere after the killings, to suppress the ghosts. And it turned out later that, while wearing that watch, it had been his beastly habit to lure—"

"Dinner!" George was standing at the top of the spiral stairs, a ladle in his hand.

"I'll tell you about it another time," Lockwood said. "We'd better go. George gets grouchy if we let the food get cold."

If I knew straight away that I liked the oddities of my new home, I soon formed opinions about my fellow agents, too. And right from the outset these opinions diverged markedly. Lockwood, I already liked. He seemed a world away from the remote and treacherous Agent Jacobs; his zest and personal commitment were clear. Here was someone I felt I could follow, someone perhaps to trust.

But George Cubbins? No. He bothered me. I made heroic efforts not to get annoyed with him that first day, but it wasn't humanly possible.

Take his appearance. There was something about it that acted as a trigger to one's worst instincts. His face was uniquely slappable—a nun would have ached to punch him—while his backside cried out to heaven for a well-placed kick. He slouched, he slumped, he scuffed his way about the house like something soft about to melt. His shirt was always untucked, his sneakers extra-big, the laces trailing. I've seen reanimated corpses with better deportment than George.

And that flop of hair! And those silly glasses! *Everything* about him irritated me. He also had a particular trick of staring at me in a blank, expressionless sort of way that was somehow also rudely contemplative. It was like he was analyzing all my faults and was simply wondering which one I was going to display next. For my part, I did my best to be polite during the first evening meal, and restrained my basic instincts, which were to hit him over the head with a shovel.

Later that night, coming down from my bedroom, I lingered for a moment on the first floor landing. I glanced through the bookshelves, inspected the Polynesian ghost-chaser . . . and suddenly found myself standing outside the *other* bedroom door, the one Lockwood had said was private. It was a very ordinary-looking door. There was a faint pale rectangle marked on the wood grain, just below head height, where a sign or sticker had been removed. Otherwise it was entirely blank. It didn't seem to have a lock.

It would have been easy to peep inside, but clearly that would have been wrong. I was just regarding the door speculatively when George Cubbins emerged from his room, a folded newspaper under his arm. He glanced across. "I know what you're thinking, but that's the forbidden room."

"Oh—the door?" I stepped away from it casually. "Yes. . . . Why does he keep it shut?"

"I don't know."

"Have you ever looked in?"

"No." The spectacles regarded me. "Course not. He asked me not to."

"Of course, of course. Quite right. So . . ." I smiled as amiably as I could. "How long have you lived here?"

"About a year."

"So you obviously know Anthony well?"

The plump boy pushed his glasses briskly up his nose. "What is this? Another interview? It had better be a quickie. I'm on my way to the bathroom here."

"Sorry, yes. I was just wondering about the house and how he came to have it. I mean, it's got all this stuff in it, and yet Lockwood's here on his own. I mean, I don't see how—"

"What you *mean*," George interrupted, "is: where are the parents? Correct?"

I nodded. "Yes."

"He doesn't like to talk about them—as you'll find out, if you last long enough to ask him. I think they were psychic researchers of some kind: you can tell that from all the objects on the walls. They were rich, too: you can tell that from the house. Anyway, they're long gone. I believe Lockwood was in care for years with a relative of some kind. Then he trained as an agent with 'Gravedigger' Sykes, and got the house back somehow." He adjusted his newspaper and marched across the landing. "No doubt you can use your psychic sensitivity to find out more."

But I was frowning after him. "In care? So does that mean his parents—?"

"One way or another, I should think it means they're dead." And with that he closed the bathroom door.

Well, it isn't hard to guess which colleague *I* favored, as I lay awake that night under the attic eaves. On the one hand: Anthony Lockwood—vigorous and energetic, eager to throw himself into each new mystery; a boy who was clearly never happier than when walking into a haunted room, his hand resting lightly on his sword hilt. On the other: George Cubbins, handsome as a freshly opened tub of margarine, as charismatic as a wet tea towel lying scrumpled on the floor. I guessed *he* was never happier than when surrounded by dusty files and piled plates of food and—since he was prickly and seemed to find me irksome—I resolved to keep as far away from him as I could. But it already pleased me to think of walking into darkness with Lockwood at my side.

Chapter 8

Late morning was Lockwood's favorite time for meeting new clients. It gave him a chance to recover from any expeditions of the night before. He always received his guests in the same living room where I'd had my interview, probably because its friendly sofas and displays of oriental ghost-catchers provided an appropriate atmosphere for discussions that bridged the banal and strange.

On my first full day at Portland Row, a single new client came by appointment at eleven o'clock: a gentleman in his early sixties, puffy-faced and plaintive, a few thin strands of hair slicked despondently across his skull. Lockwood sat with him at the coffee table. George was positioned some way off at a sloped writing desk, taking notes from the meeting in the big black casebook. I had no part in the conversation. I sat in a chair at the back of the room, listening to what went on.

The gentleman had a problem with his garage. His granddaughter refused to go in, he said. She claimed she'd seen things; but she was an hysterical girl, and he hardly knew whether to believe her. Still, against his better judgment (here he blew out his cheeks to emphasize his extreme reluctance), he'd come to us for a consultation.

Lockwood was politeness itself. "How old is your granddaughter, Mr. Potter?"

"Six. She's a silly little minx at the best of times."

"And what does she say she's seen?"

"I can't get any sense out of her. A young man, standing at the far end of the garage, beside the tea crates. Says he's very thin."

"I see. And is he always in the same place, or does he move at all?"

"Just stands there, she says. First time out, she reckons she spoke to him, but he never answered her, only stared. I don't know that she isn't making it up. She hears enough about Visitors on the playground."

"Possibly, Mr. Potter, possibly. And you've never noticed anything odd in the garage yourself? It's not unreasonably cold, for example?"

A shake of the head. "It's chilly, but it's a garage, so what do you expect? And, before you ask me: nothing's *happened* there. No one's . . . you know—*died* or anything. It's a new-build, only five years old, and I always keep it safely locked."

"I see. . . ." Lockwood clasped his hands together. "Do you keep pets, Mr. Potter?"

The man blinked; with a stubby finger he encouraged a long

droop of hair back onto his forehead. "I don't see what *that's* got to do with anything."

"I just wondered if you had a dog, perhaps, or cats."

"The wife's got two cats. Milk-white Siamese. Stuck-up bony little things."

"And do they often go into the garage?"

The man considered. "No. They don't like it there. Give it a wide berth. I've always thought it's because they don't like getting their precious little coats dirty, what with all the dust and cobwebs everywhere."

Lockwood looked up. "Ah, you have a problem with garage spiders, Mr. Potter?"

"Well, there's a colony there, or something. They seem to spin new webs fast as I can brush them away. But it's that time of year, isn't it?"

"I couldn't say. Well, I'm happy to look into this. If it's convenient, we'll be along tonight, shortly after curfew. Meanwhile, I'd keep your granddaughter out of that garage, if I were you."

"What's your opinion of the case, Ms. Carlyle?" Lockwood asked, as we sat on the eastbound bus that evening. It was the final service on that route before curfew, the seats empty of adults but crowded with children heading off for night-watch duties in the factories. Some were still half asleep; others stared dully through the windows. Their watch-sticks—six feet long, tipped with iron—bounced and rattled in the racks beside the door.

"Sounds like a weak Type One," I said, "since it's staying put and making no obvious moves toward the girl. But I wouldn't want to take it for granted." My lips tightened as I spoke; I thought of the little shape glowing in the darkness of the haunted mill.

"Quite right," Lockwood said. "Best prepare for the worst. Besides, he says the place is thick with spiders."

"You know about spiders, right, Miss Carlyle?" George was sitting on the seat in front; he glanced casually back toward me.

It's a commonly known fact that while cats can't stand ghosts, spiders *love* them. Or, at least, they love the psychic emanation that some ghosts give off. Strong Sources, remaining active and undisturbed over many years, are often choked by layer upon layer of dusty webs laid there by generations of eager spiders. It's one of the first things agents look out for. Those trails of webbing can lead you directly to the spot. *Everyone* knew that. Mr. Potter's six-year-old granddaughter probably knew that.

"Yes," I said. "I know about spiders."

"Good," George said. "Just checking."

We alighted in an eastern district of the great gray city, not far north of the river. Narrow terraced streets clustered in the shadow of the dockland cranes. With dusk, the local shops were shutting up: psychic healing booths, cheapjack iron dealers, self-proclaimed specialists offering ghost-wards from Korea and Japan. As always in my first few weeks in London, the sheer scale of it all made my head spin. People hurried homeward on every side. At the crossroads, the local ghost-lamp was powering up, the shutters slowly rising.

Lockwood led the way down a side street, rapier glinting beneath a long, heavy overcoat that swung stylishly behind him. George and I trotted alongside.

"As usual, Lockwood," George said, "we're doing this all too fast. You didn't give me enough time to properly research the house and street. I could have found out lots of background if you'd given me an extra day."

"Yes, but research only goes so far," Lockwood said. "There's no substitute for actually *exploring*. Besides, I thought Ms. Carlyle would enjoy the expedition. She might hear something."

"Can be a risky business being a Listener," George remarked. "There was that girl working for Epstein and Hawkes last year. Good ears, incredibly sensitive insight. But she got so freaked out by all the voices she heard, she ended up jumping into the Thames."

I smiled thinly. "Marissa Fittes had my kind of Talent too," I said. "*She* didn't jump anywhere."

Anthony Lockwood laughed. "Well said, Ms. Carlyle! Right, shut up now, George. We're here."

Our client's house was one of four unremarkable semidetached properties set in the middle of an otherwise terraced street. It was of fairly modern construction. The garage was a solid brick affair, with an up-and-over metal door at the front, and a side door that joined up with the kitchen. The garage interior contained three old motorbikes in various stages of repair, this being Mr. Potter's hobby. There was also a long workbench and a wall of tool racks, and toward the rear, a great stack of tea crates, mostly filled with secondhand parts and wheels and dismantled engines.

The first thing we noticed was that though the workbench and tool racks were relatively clean, the storage area was thinly laid with fresh gray webbing. Shimmering threads hung between the crates and slanted down toward the floor; in the light of our flashlights, large-bodied spiders could be seen moving stealthily on unknown errands.

We spent the first few hours carefully taking measurements and making observations. George in particular zealously recorded the minutest drops in temperature, but we all noticed a supernatural *chill* developing as the hour grew late. A sour *miasma* rose up too—a smell of faint decay. Toward midnight, there was a frisson in the air; I felt my neck hairs prickle. A faint apparition appeared in the farthest corner of the garage, close beside the crates. It was very quiet and still; a man-sized nimbus of pale cloud. We watched it quietly, hands ready at our belts, but there was no sense of imminent threat. After lingering for ten minutes, the figure vanished. The air cleared.

"A young man," Lockwood said. "Wearing some kind of leather uniform. Anyone else get that?"

I shook my head. "Sorry, no. My Sight's not as good as yours. But—"

"It's obvious enough what we've got here, Lockwood," George interrupted. "*I* saw the uniform, and it confirms what I guessed before we came inside. This is quite a modern house. Most of the other buildings in the street are older, prewar terraces. Once upon a time there would have been a terraced house here too, right where we're standing. But it's gone. Why? Because it was bombed in one of the air raids in the war. The bomb that destroyed the house probably killed the man we just saw. He's a Blitz ghost, maybe a soldier home on leave, and his remains are in the ground somewhere under our feet." He tucked his pen decisively in his pants pocket, took off his glasses, and wiped them on his shirt.

Lockwood frowned. "You think? Maybe. . . . Though I don't

get any death-glows here." He rubbed his chin thoughtfully. "If so, our client won't be happy. It's going to cost him to knock the garage down."

George shrugged. "Tough. He needs to find the bones. What else can he do?"

"Excuse me," I said, "but I don't agree with you."

They looked across at me. "What?" George said.

"I didn't *see* the Visitor as well as you, of course," I said, "but I perhaps noticed something you missed. I caught a voice just before the apparition faded out. Did you hear it? No? Well, the words were very faint but quite distinct. '*No time. Couldn't check the brakes.*' That was what it said. It repeated it twice."

"Well, what does *that* mean?" George demanded.

"It means that the Source may not be under the floor, and it may be nothing to do with the Blitz. I think it's one of those crates. What are they filled with?"

"Junk," George said.

"Motor parts," Lockwood said.

"Yes, parts of old motorbikes that our client's picked up all over the place. Well, where do they come from? What's their history? I just wonder whether one of them might come from a machine that was once involved in an accident—perhaps a fatal one."

George snorted. "A road accident? You think the Source is a broken *motorbike*?"

"Could the ghost's outfit have been biker's leathers?" I said.

There was a pause. Lockwood nodded slowly. "You know," he said, "they just might have been, at that. . . . Well, we'll have to check. Tomorrow we'll ask the client if we can investigate the crates more closely. Meanwhile—thank you, Ms. Carlyle, for that very interesting insight. Your Talent doesn't disappoint!"

Just for the record, I *was* right. One of the crates contained the smashed remains of a rally motorcycle that provided some *very* curious readings when we assessed it. We subsequently removed it from the garage and had it sent to the Fittes furnaces, and that was the end of that. But on the night in question, when we finally got back to Portland Row, Lockwood's praise still rang loudly in my ears. I was too elated to go straight to sleep. Instead of heading to my attic, I made a sandwich in the kitchen and then wandered to the library, a room I hadn't properly explored before.

It was a dark, oak-paneled room across the hall from the lounge. Heavy curtains shrouded the windows; black shelves crammed with hardback volumes, lined the walls. Above the mantelpiece hung an oil painting of three bright-green pears. Angled standard lamps stood stooped and heronlike; light from one of these illuminated Anthony Lockwood, slumped sideways in a comfy chair. His long, slim legs were draped elegantly over the chair arm; his forelock hung no less decoratively over his brow. He was reading a magazine.

I hesitated at the door.

"Oh, Ms. Carlyle." He jumped up, gave me a grin of welcome. "Please—come in. Sit wherever you like, except possibly that brown chair in the corner. That's George's, and I'm afraid he's been known to lounge there in his underwear. I hope that's a habit he'll snap out of, now you're here. Don't worry, he won't come now; he's already gone to bed."

I sat in a leather chair opposite his. It was soft and comfy, and only slightly marred by a shriveled apple core laid neatly on one arm. Lockwood, who had come over to switch on a light behind my head, plucked it deftly away without comment and put it in a wastebasket. He flung himself back into his seat, where he set the magazine in his lap and folded his hands on top of it.

We smiled across at each other. All of a sudden I remembered we were strangers. Now that all the interviews, tours, and investigations were over for the moment, I found I didn't have a clue what to say.

"I saw George going upstairs," I said finally. "He seemed a little . . . crotchety."

Lockwood made an easy gesture. "Oh, he's fine. He has these moods sometimes."

There was a silence. I became aware of a steady ticking noise coming from an ornate mantel clock above the fireplace.

Anthony Lockwood cleared his throat. "So, Ms. Carlyle—"

"Call me Lucy," I said. "It's shorter, and easier, and a bit more friendly. Since we're going to be working together, I mean. And living in the same house."

"Of course. Quite right. . . ." He looked down at his magazine, then up at me again. "So, *Lucy* . . ." (We both laughed awkwardly.) "Do you like the house?"

"Very much. My room's lovely."

"And the bathroom . . . it's not too small?"

"No. It's perfect. Very homey."

"Homey? Good. I'm glad."

"About *your* name," I said suddenly. "I notice George calls you 'Lockwood.'"

"I answer to that, most of the time."

"Anyone ever call you 'Anthony'?"

"My mother did. And my father."

A pause. "So what about 'Tony'?" I said. "Ever been called that?"

"Tony? Look, Ms. Car—sorry—*Lucy*. You can call me whatever you like. As long as it's Lockwood or Anthony. Not Tony, please, or Ant. And if you ever call me Big A, I'm afraid I'll have no option but to throw you out into the street."

Another silence. "Er, has someone actually *called* you Big A?" I asked.

"My first assistant. She didn't last long." He smiled at me. I smiled back, listened to the ticking of the clock. It seemed noticeably louder. I began to wish I'd gone up to my room.

"What's that you're reading?" I asked.

He held it up. The cover showed a blond woman with teeth as bright as ghost-lamps getting out of a black car. She wore a big spray of lavender on the lapel of her dress, and the windows of the car were fortified with iron grilles. "*London Society*," he said. "It's a dreary rag. But you get to see what's going on in town."

"And what is going on?"

"Parties, mainly." He tossed the magazine across. It consisted of endless photographs of fashionably dressed men and women preening in crowded rooms. "You'd think the Problem would make people consider their immortal souls," Lockwood said. "But, for the rich, it's had the opposite effect. They go out, dress up, spend all night dancing in a sealed hotel somewhere, thrilling with horror at the thought of Visitors lurking outside. . . . That party there was thrown last week by DEPRAC, the Department of Psychic Research and Control. The heads of all the most important agencies were there."

"Oh." I scanned the photos. "Were you invited? Can I see your picture?"

He shrugged. "No. So no."

I flipped through the pages a little longer; they made a rhythmic flapping sound.

"When you said in your advertisement that Lockwood's was a *well-known* agency," I remarked, "that was a bit of a lie, wasn't it?"

The pages flapped, the clock ticked. "I'd call it a mild exaggeration," Lockwood said. "Lots of people do it. Like *you*, for example, when you said you had the full Agency qualifications up to the Fourth Grade. I rang up DEPRAC's North of England branch straight after your interview. They said you'd only completed Grades One to Three."

He didn't seem angry, just sat there looking at me with his big dark eyes. All of a sudden, my mouth was dry, my heart thumping in my chest. "I—I'm . . . sorry," I said. "It's just that. . . ." I cleared my throat. "I mean, the point is I'm *good* enough to have that qualification. It's just that my traineeship with Jacobs ended very badly, and I never took the test. And when I came here . . . well, I *really* needed the job. I'm sorry, Lockwood. Would it help if I told you about Jacobs—how it happened?"

But Anthony Lockwood had held up a hand. "No," he said. "No. It doesn't matter. Whatever happened then is in the past. What counts now is the future. And I already *know* you're good enough for that. For my part, I can assure you that one day this *will* be one of the three most successful agencies in London. Believe me, I *know* it will. And you can be part of that, Lucy. I think you're good, and I'm glad you're here."

You can bet my face was flushed right then—it was a special triple-combo of embarrassment at being found out, pleasure at his flattery, and excitement at his spoken dreams. "I'm not sure George agrees with you," I said.

"Oh, he thinks you're special too. He was amazed by what you did in the interview."

I thought back to George's vocal range of snorts and yawns, to his spikiness that evening. "Is that how he usually shows approval?"

"You'll get used to him. George dislikes hypocrites—you know, people who say nice things to your face and criticize you behind your back. He takes pride in being the reverse. Besides, he's an excellent agent. He had a job at Fittes once," Lockwood added. "They value courtesy, secrecy, and discretion there. Know how long he lasted?"

"I should think about twenty minutes."

"Six months. *That's* how good he is."

"If they put up with his personality for that long, he must be superb."

Lockwood gave me a radiant smile. "My view is: with you and George on my team, nothing can stand in our way."

For a moment, as he said this, it all made perfect sense. I soon learned that when he smiled like that, it was hard not to agree with him.

"Thank you," I said. "I hope so too."

Lockwood laughed. "There's no 'hope' about it. With our combined talents, what can possibly go wrong?"

III

The Necklace

Chapter 9

It's amazing how quickly a fire can spread through an average suburban house. Even before Lockwood and I toppled from the window, perhaps while we were still grappling with the ghost-girl, a neighbor must have sounded the alarm. The emergency services responded quickly too; they arrived in minutes. But by the time special night crews in their chain-mail tunics came charging into the garden, escorted by a troop of Rotwell agents, the upper floor of Mrs. Hope's house was thoroughly ablaze.

White flames poured from the first floor windows like upturned waterfalls. Roof tiles cracked and shimmered in the heat, their edges glowing in the night like rows of dragon scales. Thin fiery pennants twirled and twisted from the chimney tops, sending sparks raining down on nearby trees and buildings. Below, the mists churned orange; agents, medics, and firefighters ran frantically through a cloudscape of light and shadow.

At the center of it all, Lockwood and I sat hunched at the base of the bushes that had saved our lives. We answered the medics' questions; we let them do their thing. Around us, hoses gushed and timbers snapped; supervisors shouted orders at grim-faced kids in jackets scattering salt across the grass. Everything seemed unreal—muffled and far away. Even the fact that we'd survived was hard to comprehend.

It was fortunate for us that neither Mr. nor Mrs. Hope had ever been keen gardeners. They'd let the bushes behind the house grow large and sprawling, thick and tall and spongy-boughed. And so it was that when we'd fallen down and struck them—smashing through the upper branches, ripping through the lower ones, coming to an abrupt and painful halt almost at the ground—our clothes had torn and our skin had been pierced, but we *hadn't* done the obvious thing, which was break our necks and die.

A gout of fire erupted from the chimney stack and fountained out across the roof. I sat there, staring into space, while someone wound a bandage around my arm. I thought of the girl behind the wall. There'd be little left of her by now.

So much chaos . . . and all because of me. We needn't have confronted her ghost at all. We could have left her—no, we *should* have left her when we discovered how dangerous she was. Lockwood had wanted to pull back, but I'd persuaded him to stay and get it done. And because of that decision . . . it had come to *this*.

"Lucy!" It was Lockwood's voice. "Wake up! They want to take you to the hospital. They're going to patch you up."

The side of my mouth was puffy. It was difficult to talk. "What . . . what about you?"

"I've got to speak with someone. I'll follow in a bit."

My vision was woozy; my left eye had completely closed. I thought I saw a man in a dark suit standing just behind the crowd of medics, but it was hard to be sure. Someone helped me to stand; I found myself being led away.

"Lockwood. This is all my fault—"

"Rubbish. It's my responsibility. Don't worry about it. I'll see you soon."

"Lockwood—"

But he was already lost among the mist and flames.

The hospital doctors did their job. They patched me up okay. By morning my cuts were cleaned and covered; my rapier arm was in a sling. Overall I was stiff and sore and out of joint; still, nothing was broken and I only limped a little. I knew I'd gotten off lightly. There was talk of keeping me in for observation, but I'd had enough by then. The doctors protested a bit, but I was an agent, and that gave me leverage. Just after dawn, they let me go.

When I got back to Portland Row, the ghost-lamp had recently gone off; I could hear the hum of its electronics inside the stem. At Lockwood's, the office lights were on in the basement, but the upper stories of the house were dark and quiet. I couldn't be bothered to look for my keys. I leaned against the doorway and rang the bell.

Running footsteps sounded. The door opened with violent haste. George stood there, cheeks red, eyes staring. His hair was even more disheveled than usual. He wore the same clothes as the day before.

When he saw my scratched and swollen face, he made a small noise between his teeth. He didn't say anything. He stood aside, let me walk in, and quietly closed the door.

The hall was dark. I reached over to the crystal skull on the key table and switched the lantern on. It threw a frail halo around us, the skull grinning at its center. I stared dully at the ethnic knick-knacks on the bookshelf opposite: the pots and masks, the hollow gourds that, according to Lockwood, certain tribesmen wore instead of pants.

Lockwood . . .

"Where is he?" I said.

George had stayed by the door. His glasses shone with lantern light, and I couldn't see his eyes. Something pulsed halfway up his neck. "Where is he?" I said again.

His voice was so tightly wound I could scarcely hear it. "Scotland Yard."

"With the police? I thought he was at the hospital."

"He was. DEPRAC has got him now."

"Why?"

"Ooh, I don't know. Possibly because you burned down someone's house, Lucy? Who can tell?"

"I have to go and see him."

"You won't get in. I asked to as well. He told me to wait here."

I looked at George, then at the door, then down at my boots, still dusted with soot and plaster. "You spoke to him?"

"He called me from the hospital. Inspector Barnes was waiting to take him away."

"Is he okay?"

"I don't know. I think so, but . . ." He changed tack abruptly. "*You* look terrible. What about your arm? Is it broken?"

"No. Minor sprain. It'll be okay in a few days. You just said 'but.' But what? What did he tell you?"

"Nothing much. Except—"

Something in the way he said it . . . My heart beat fast; I leaned back against the wall. "Except what?"

"He'd been ghost-touched."

"George—!"

"Would you mind not leaning there? You're making black marks on the wallpaper."

"Stuff the wallpaper, George! He wasn't ghost-touched! I'd have seen!"

Still he hadn't moved; still he spoke in a quiet monotone. "Would you? He said it happened while you were dealing with the Source. When he was fighting off the Visitor, she got him with a curl of plasm. Touched him on the hand. They gave him a shot of adrenaline in the ambulance and stopped the rot. He *says* he's fine."

My head was awhirl. *Could* it have happened? Everything had moved so quickly in the study, and the period in the garden was a blur. "Was it bad?" I said. "How far had it gone?"

"By the time they treated it?" He shrugged. "You tell me."

"Well, how do *I* know?" I snapped. "I wasn't there."

George gave a roar of fury that made me jump. "Well, you *should* have been!" He slammed his palm against the wall so hard, an ornamental gourd fell off the bookcase and rolled upon the floor. "Just like you *should* have stopped him getting touched in the first place! Yes, I think it *was* bad! His hand had started swelling. He told me his fingers were bulging out like five blue hot dogs by the end, but they still had to manhandle him into the ambulance. Why? Because he wanted to go find *you*. See if you were okay! He couldn't be talked down, even though the ghost-touch was on him and he'd have died within the hour if someone with some common sense hadn't jabbed a needle in his bum. He couldn't be talked down! Like he wasn't prepared to wait for me to get back last night! Like he wasn't prepared to let me do some proper research, so I could find out *exactly* what you were getting into. No! As always he was in far too much of a hurry. And if he'd only waited"—he kicked out viciously at the fallen gourd, sending it spinning away to crack in half against the skirting—"none of this stupid mess would have happened!"

Let's see. In the previous twelve hours, I'd almost been murdered by a vicious ghost. I'd fallen from an upstairs window into a small tree. I'd sprained my arm. I'd had a spotty bloke with tweezers pulling twigs and thorns out of sensitive portions of my anatomy half the night. I'd also set fire to a small suburban house. Oh, and Lockwood had been ghost-touched and, whatever state he'd been left in, was now being grilled by the police. What I badly needed was a bath, some food, a lot of rest—and getting to see Lockwood again.

Instead I got George having a hissy fit.

That didn't make my day.

"Shut up, George," I said wearily. "This isn't the time."

He wheeled around on me. "No? Well, when *is* going to be the time? When you and Lockwood are both dead, maybe? When I open the door one night and see the two of you hovering beyond the iron line, plasm trailing, worms poking from your eyes? Yeah, fine. Let's have our little catch-up then!"

I snorted. "Charming. I wouldn't come back like that. I'd have a nicer guise."

George gave a hoot of rage. "Really? How do you *know* what kind of Visitor you'd make, Lucy? You know nothing about them. You don't read anything I give you. You never make notes on what you see. All you and Lockwood care about is going out and snuffing Sources, as quickly as you can!"

I stepped forward, close to him. Probably if my arm had been less sore, I'd have prodded him in his puffed-up chest. "Because that's what makes our *money*, George," I said. "Faffing about with old papers like you do gets us nothing."

His eyes flashed behind the stupid round glasses. "Oh? Nothing?"

"That's right. If you were less obsessed with it, we'd have done twice as many cases in the last few months. Take yesterday. We waited all afternoon for you. You could have gotten back any time, come along with us. But no. You were too busy in the library. We left you a polite note on the thinking cloth. Didn't go out till almost five."

He spoke quietly now. "You *should* have waited."

"So what that we didn't? What difference would it have made?"

"What difference? Come on! I'll show you what difference!" He drew back and, turning, led me up the hall and into the kitchen. Ignoring my gasps of disgust at the piled dishes festooning the surfaces, he threw open the basement door and clattered away down the iron steps. "Come on!" he shouted up. "*If* you can be bothered!"

The curse I gave would probably have curdled the milk if it

hadn't been sitting out on the table for thirty-six hours already. I was *really* angry now. I too banged down the spiral stairs. In the office, the light was on over George's desk; scattered papers, dirty cups, apple cores, chip bags, and half-gnawed sandwiches marked the scene of his recent vigil. The ghost-jar was sitting there too, uncovered, the skull faintly visible in the yellowish murk. For some reason the disembodied head was floating upside down.

George plucked several of the papers from the desk. I didn't wait for him to start, but launched right in.

"You know what *your* problem is?" I said. "You're jealous."

George stared. "Of what?"

"Of me."

He gave a harsh guffaw. Over in the corner, the head in the ghost-jar aped his outrage. It made a face of theatrical dismay. "Oh sure!" George said. "You're fantastic. You've just burned down our client's house. You're our best assistant yet."

"Too right, I am. The last one's dead."

He hesitated. "That's not the point."

"It's exactly the point. Remind me how Robin died again."

"Met a Raw-bones. Panicked and ran off a roof."

"Right, whereas I've survived, and have done so out on the front line. Which is where *you* seldom go, George. And it's starting to get to you, isn't it? You're feeling a bit left out. Well, tough. And don't try to make me feel guilty for going out and *doing* things. This job's not all about dusty books. It's about efficient action."

"Okay." He pushed his glasses up his pudgy nose. "Okay. Maybe you're right. I'll have to think about what you said. While I'm doing that, perhaps you can take a little peek at this dusty old research I did yesterday, while you were back here efficiently forgetting to pack your iron chains. This first bit of paper is from the Housing Registry. It's for Sixty-two Sheen Road, where you've just been. Gives a rundown of all the owners of the house for the last one hundred years. Look, there's Mr. and Mrs. Hope at the end, but you knew about them. What you didn't know about was *this* one: a Miss Annabel E. Ward, who bought it fifty years ago. Remember that name for a minute. Now, the reason I was so long yesterday was that I was down at the National Archives, cross-referencing all these names against stories from the newspapers. Why? Because I don't like surprises, and funnily enough I *did* find a surprise. You see, I was just wondering if any of these owners had come to public attention for any reason. And—guess what?—one of them had."

With ink stained fingers, he pushed another sheet of paper forward on the desk, a smudged photocopy of a small newspaper article. It was from the *Richmond Examiner*, dated forty-nine years before.

Missing Girl: POLICE APPEAL FOR HELP

Police investigating the disappearance of popular young socialite, Miss Annabel Ward, yesterday appealed for fresh information from the public.

Miss Ward, 20, of Sheen Road, Richmond, has not been seen since late on the night of Saturday 21st June, when she dined with a group of friends at the Gallops nightclub on Chelsea Bridge Road. She left shortly before midnight, and failed to keep an appointment the following day. Detectives have since questioned her circle of associates, but have yet to make

a breakthrough with the case. Anyone with any information is urged to call the number below.

Searches for the missing girl, an aspiring actress and a familiar figure on the society circuit, have been carried out in and around her home and surrounding areas over the last few days. Police divers are searching ponds and rivers. Meanwhile Miss Ward's father, Mr. Julian Ward, has issued a statement, offering a substantial reward for any—

"Having trouble reading it?" George said. "No wonder—it must have, ooh, at least two paragraphs. Let me help you figure it out. They don't mention her exact address, but I think it's pretty obvious this Annabel Ward must be the same one from the Housing Registry. The dates fit too. So she'd lived at Sixty-two Sheen Road, the house where you and Lockwood were busy investigating an apparition. Coincidence?, Maybe, but finding this made me sit up and take notice. So I hurried home to tell you—only when I got there, surprise, surprise, off you'd gone already. Even then, I wasn't worried. I thought you were well equipped. It was only later I saw you'd left the chains behind."

Silence. The ghost in the jar had now devolved into a grainy, luminous mass of plasm, swirling slowly like green water at the bottom of a well.

"So what about it?" George said. "Any of this fit with your experiences last night?"

It was like a hole had opened in me somewhere, and all my anger had drained through it. I just felt very weary now. "Got a picture of her?" I said.

Of course he did. He stretched out among the papers. "That's all I have so far."

From another edition of the *Examiner.* A girl in a long fur coat, caught in flashbulbs as she stepped outdoors. Slim glimpse of leg, bright teeth, primped hair up in a beehive look. She was probably coming out of one of those society clubs or bars the papers loved so much. If she'd been alive now, she'd have been a glassy-eyed half-page feature in one of Lockwood's magazines, and I'd have hated her.

As it was, I only saw that other face—eyeless, shrunken, and cupped in cobwebs, propped behind the bricks. It made me very sad.

"Yes," I said. "It's her."

"Grand," George said. He didn't say anything else.

"It says they searched her house," I murmured. "They can't have looked very hard."

We stood by the table staring at the photo and forgotten newspaper, fifty years old.

"Whoever hid her did the job well," George said at last. "And this was before the Problem was widely accepted, don't forget. They wouldn't have sent any psychics in."

"But why wouldn't the ghost make trouble from the start? Why the long time gap?"

"Could be as simple as too much iron in the house. An iron bed frame in that room might have been enough. If the Hopes did a clear-out, changed the furniture, that would have freed the Source again."

"They *did* make a change," I said. "He turned it into a study."

"Anyway, it doesn't matter now." He took his glasses off and rubbed them on his untucked shirt.

"I'm sorry, George. You were right. We should have waited."

"Well, I should have gone out to join you. It's so hard to get a night cab. . . ."

"There was no call for me to get so mad. I'm just worried. I hope he's all right."

"He'll be okay. Look, I shouldn't have lost my temper, or kicked that fertility gourd. I broke it, didn't I?"

"Oh, he'll never notice. Just put it back on the shelf."

"Yeah." Back went the glasses. He looked at me. "I'm sorry about your arm."

We would probably have kept on being sorry about stuff indefinitely, but right then I was distracted by the face in the jar, which had stealthily re-emerged and was now pulling expressions of extravagant disgust. "That thing can't hear us, can it?"

"Not through silver-glass. Let's go back up. I'll make you something to eat."

I headed for the spiral stairs. "You'll have to wash up first. That'll take some time."

I was right. So much time, in fact, that I'd bathed and changed, and come stiffly downstairs again before George had gotten the eggs and bacon on the plate. I was just parking my sprained elbow on the table and reaching gingerly for the salt when the doorbell rang again.

George and I looked at each other. We both went to the door.

Lockwood stood there.

His coat was torn and burned, his shirt ripped at the collar. His face was scratched; he had the bright, staring eyes and hollow cheekbones of an invalid risen from his bed. Far from being swollen, as I'd feared, he seemed thinner than ever. When he stepped slowly into the hall's light, I saw his left hand was bandaged in thin white gauze.

"Hi, George," he said, and his voice shook. "Hi, Lucy . . ." He wobbled, seemed about to fall. We rushed forward to support him between us, and Lockwood acknowledged us with a smile. "Glad to be home," he said, and then, "Hey, what happened to my gourd?"

Chapter 10

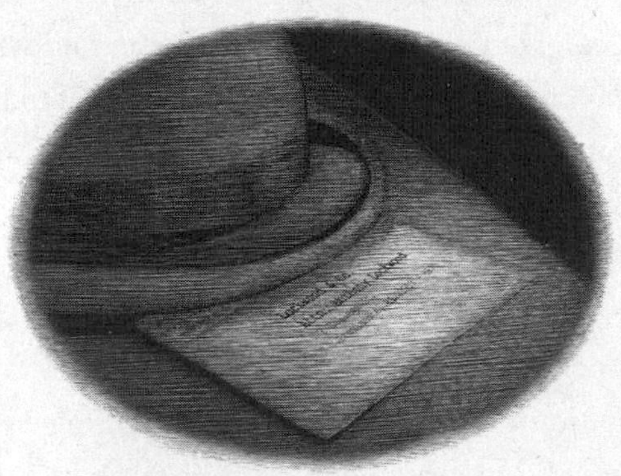

Whether the chill of the ghost-touch still ran in his veins, or whether his other injuries—together with his long interrogations at Scotland Yard—had simply exhausted him, Lockwood was in a mopey state all day. He slept (as I did) for much of the morning; at lunch he ate little, scarcely picking at George's fresh-made pot pie and peas. He moved slowly; he hardly spoke, which for Lockwood was unusual. After lunch he went into the living room and sat with his wounded arm swathed in hot water bottles, staring dully out of the window.

George and I stayed near him in companionable silence throughout the afternoon. I read a cheap detective novel. George conducted experiments on the trapped ghost in its jar, using a small electrical circuit to apply shocks to the glass. Whether out of protest or for some other reason, the ghost did not respond.

Toward four o'clock, when the light was already failing, Lockwood startled us both by suddenly asking for our casebook. It was the first time he'd said anything in hours.

"What've we got coming up, George?" he said when the black ledger had been fetched. "What cases have we got outstanding?"

George turned the pages to the latest entries. "Not a *great* deal," he said. "Got a report of a 'terrifying black shape' seen in a parking lot, early evening. Could be anything from a Dark Specter to a Gray Haze. We were going to visit there tonight, but I've called them to postpone. . . . We've also got a 'sinister rapping sound' heard in a house in Neasden. . . . Possibly a Stone Knocker, even a weak Poltergeist; but again there's not enough info yet to be sure. Then there's a 'dark, still shadow' seen at the bottom of a Finchley garden—probably a Lurker or a Shade. . . . Oh, and an urgent request from Mrs. Eileen Smithers of Chorley. Every night, when alone in the small hours, she hears—"

"Hold it," Lockwood said. "Eileen Smithers? Didn't we work for her before?"

"We did. That time it was a 'ghastly disembodied howling' resounding around her kitchen. We thought it might be a Screaming Spirit. In fact it was her neighbor's cat, Bumbles, trapped inside the wall cavity."

Lockwood made a face. "Oh lord, I remember. And this time?"

"An 'eerie, childlike wailing' heard in her attic. Starts around midnight, when—"

"It'll be the bloody cat again." Lockwood removed his left hand from beneath the water bottles and flexed the fingers carefully. The skin was slightly blue. "All in all, it's not the most thrilling program in the history of psychic detection, is it? Lurkers, Shades, and Bumbles the ginger tomcat. . . . What happened to the *good* cases, like the Mortlake Horror and the Dulwich Wraith?"

"If by 'good' you mean a powerful, challenging ghost," I said, "last night's was pretty fine. Trouble was—we weren't expecting it."

"As the police at Scotland Yard repeatedly pointed out to me," Lockwood growled. "No, by 'good,' I mean cases that might make us some money. None of this stuff's exactly big time." He subsided back into his chair.

It was rare for Lockwood to mention money; it wasn't his usual motivation. There was an uncomfortable silence. "Funnily enough, George has found out a bit about our ghost-girl," I said brightly. "Tell him about it, George."

George had been dying to get it off his chest all day. He whipped the article out of his pocket and read it through. Lockwood—who seldom had much interest in the identity of Visitors, even when they *hadn't* injured him—listened indifferently.

"Annabel Ward?" he said at last. "So that was her name? I wonder how she died. . . ."

"And who it was who killed her," I added.

Lockwood shrugged. "Fifty years is a long time. We'll never know. I'm more concerned about *now*. Her ghost has created a real mess for us. The police aren't at all happy about the fire."

"So what *did* happen with them last night?" George said.

"Not much. They took my statement. I argued our case pretty well—*dangerous Visitor, our lives at risk, had to act on the spur of the moment,* all the obvious stuff. But they didn't seem convinced." He broke off, stared out of the window again.

"And now?" I said.

He shook his head. "We'll have to see what happens."

As to *that,* we found out sooner than expected. Not twenty minutes later a brusque hammering sounded on the front door. George went to answer it. He returned with a blue-fringed visiting card and an expression of grim dismay.

"Mr. Montagu Barnes of DEPRAC," he said bleakly. "Are you at home?"

Lockwood groaned. "I'll have to be. He knows I'm in no state to go out today. All right. Show him in."

The Department of Psychic Research and Control, or DEPRAC, is one of the most powerful organizations in the country. It's sort of part of the government, and sort of part of the police, but is actually run by lots of old operatives who've grown too slow and decrepit even to be supervisors anymore. One of their main jobs is to keep tabs on the agencies and make sure we all follow the rules.

Inspector Barnes liked the rules more than most. He was famously officious and had a deep dislike of anything that didn't follow DEPRAC guidelines to the letter. Lockwood and George had crossed paths with him on several occasions, mostly before I'd joined the company. This was the first time I'd seen him up close, so I studied him with interest as he entered the living room.

He was a small man, wearing a dark, rather crumpled suit. His shoes were brown and scuffed, his pants just too long for him. He was dressed in a long brown raincoat that extended to his knees, and he had a brown suede bowler on his head. His hair was lank and thin, except under his nose, where sat a resplendent mustache, as coarse and tufty as a brand-new scrubbing brush. His age was uncertain; perhaps he was a lived-in fifty. To me he seemed inexpressibly old, one short step from becoming a Visitor himself. He had a melancholy, drawn expression, as if all light and joy had been surgically removed from his person under local anesthesia, leaving his skin loose and saggy beneath the eyes. These eyes, however, were shrewd and keen.

Lockwood rose stiffly, gave him a cordial-enough greeting, and ushered him to a seat. George removed the ghost-jar to the sideboard and concealed it under the polka-dotted veil. I went to make some tea.

When I got back, Barnes was sitting in the middle of the sofa, still wearing his coat and hat, his hands flat on wide-spaced knees. It was a posture that managed to be both domineering and awkward at the same time. He was staring at the collection of artifacts on the wall.

"Most people," he was saying, in a somewhat nasal voice, "make do with landscape paintings or rows of ducks. This stuff can't be hygienic. What's *that* moth-eaten thing?"

"Tibetan spirit-pole," Lockwood said. "At least a hundred years old. My guess is that the lamas somehow directed roaming ghosts into those hollow metal globes hanging between the flags. Clever of you to pick it out, Mr. Barnes; it's one of the best pieces in my collection."

The inspector snorted into his mustache. "Looks more like foreign mumbo-jumbo, if you ask me. . . ." He pulled his gaze around to meet with ours. "Well," he said, "I'm pleased to see you're both in such good shape. Surprised, too. When I saw you in the garden last night, I thought you'd be in the hospital for a week." There was just enough ambiguity in his tone to make me wonder if he'd perhaps *hoped* for this outcome, as well.

Lockwood made a regretful gesture. "I'm sorry that I wasn't able to stay and help out," he said. "I wanted to, but the doctors were insistent."

"Oh, you couldn't have done anything," Barnes said. "You'd just have been in the way. It was a heroic effort by the firefighters and agents who fought the blaze. They managed to save the bulk of the house. But the upper floor is a complete write-off, thanks to you."

Lockwood nodded stiffly. "I've made my statement to your colleagues at the Yard."

"I know. And *I've* spoken with Mrs. Hope, whose house you destroyed."

"Ah. And how's she doing?"

"She's distraught, Mr. Lockwood, as you might imagine. I couldn't get much sense from her. But she and her daughter are also very angry, and they're demanding compensation. This my tea? Lovely." He took a cup.

Lockwood's face, already pale, grew paler. "I quite understand that they're upset," he said, "but, speaking as professionals, accidents like this happen in our work. Lucy and I dealt with a dangerous Type Two, which had killed before and was threatening our lives. Yes, the collateral damage was unfortunate, but I trust DEPRAC will support us in meeting any costs that—"

"DEPRAC won't help you with a penny of it," Barnes said, sipping his tea. "That's why I'm here. I've already checked with my superiors, and they take the view that you disregarded several basic safety procedures in your investigations at Sheen Road. Most crucially, you chose to engage with the Visitor without your iron chains: the fire was a direct result of that decision." The inspector wiped his mustache dry with the side of a finger. "As far as compensation goes, you're on your own."

"But this is ridiculous," Lockwood said. "Surely we can—"

"There's no 'we' about it!" Barnes seemed suddenly irate. He got to his feet, brandishing the cup. "If you and Ms. Carlyle had done the *sensible* thing—if you'd left the house when you'd first encountered the Visitor, if you'd returned with better equipment or"—he glared around at us—"with better agents, that house would still be standing! It's your fault, and I'm afraid that I can't help you. Which brings me to the real point." He took a packet from his coat. "I have an envelope here from the Hope family solicitors. They're demanding immediate settlement for the damage caused by the fire. The sum is £60,000. You've four weeks to pay up, or they'll launch court proceedings against you." He pursed his lips. "I hope you're as well-off as you seem to be, Mr. Lockwood, because I can assure you that if you fail to meet this obligation, DEPRAC will have to wind your agency up, shut Lockwood and Co. down."

Nobody moved. Lockwood and I sat as if we'd both been ghost-locked. Slowly, George took his glasses off and wiped them on his sweater.

Now that he'd given us that fatal news, Inspector Barnes seemed restless and ill at ease. He stalked around the room, glaring at the artifacts, sipping his tea.

"Put the letter on the sideboard, please," Lockwood said. "I'll look at it later."

"No use feeling miffed, Mr. Lockwood," Barnes said. "This is what happens when an agency isn't properly run. No supervisors! Agencies with adults ensure everything's done with maximum care for property and minimum loss of life. But you—" He waved a hand disgustedly. "You're nothing but three kids, playing at grown-up games. Everything in this house is testament to that, even this rubbish on the wall." He peered at a small label. "'An Indonesian ghost-catcher?' Fiddle-faddle! Belongs in a museum!"

"That collection was my mother's," Lockwood said quietly.

The inspector didn't hear; he tossed the envelope on the sideboard and, in the same moment, noticed the object concealed beneath the spotted handkerchief. Frowning, he flicked the cloth aside, revealing the jar of yellow smog. His frown deepened. He bent close, peered into its depths. "And this? What's this monstrosity? Some other appalling specimen that should have been incinerated long ago. . . ." He tapped dismissively on the glass.

"Er, I wouldn't do that," Lockwood said.

"Why not?"

There was a rush of yellow plasm; the ghost's face congealed into existence directly opposite Barnes's own. Its eyes bulged out as if on stalks; its mouth yawned wide, revealing an Alpine range of jagged teeth. It was doing something improbable with its tongue.

It was hard to guess exactly how much of the apparition the

inspector saw. Certainly he sensed *something.* Emitting a whoop like a howler monkey, he sprang back in terror. His hand jerked high; hot, strong tea rained down over his face and shirt front. The cup clattered to the floor.

"George," Lockwood said mildly. "I *told* you to keep that jar downstairs."

"I know. I'm so forgetful."

Barnes was blinking, gasping, wiping at his face. "You irresponsible idiots! That hellish thing—what is it?"

"Not sure," George said. "Possibly a Specter of some kind. Sorry about that, Mr. Barnes, but really you shouldn't have looked so close. It's easily startled by grotesque shapes."

The inspector had snatched up a napkin from the tea tray and was dabbing at his shirt; now he scowled around at us all. "This is *exactly* what I'm talking about," he said. "Jars like that shouldn't be kept in private homes. They need to be at secure locations, under the control of responsible institutions—or, better still, destroyed. What if that ghost got free? What if some kid came in and found it? *I* could barely see the outline, and it frightened me half to death; and you go leaving it casually on a sideboard." He shook his head, sourly. "Like I say, you're just playing games. Well, I've said what I came for. Read those documents, Mr. Lockwood, and think about what you want to do. Remember—four weeks is all you've got. Four weeks and £60,000. No, don't bother seeing me out; I can manage, assuming some ghoul doesn't devour me in the hall."

He slapped his hat on his head and stomped from the room. We waited until we heard the front door slam.

"Rather a tiresome meeting in so many ways," Lockwood said, "but it perked up a little toward the end."

"Didn't it?" George chuckled. "That was priceless. Did you see the look on his face!"

I grinned. "I've never seen anyone move so fast."

"He was absolutely petrified, wasn't he?"

"Yeah. That was great."

"*Really* funny."

"Yes."

Our laughter drained away. There was a long silence. We all stared out at nothing.

"*Can* you pay the Hopes off?" I said.

Lockwood took a deep breath; the effort seemed to pain him—he rubbed irritably at the side of his ribs. "In a word: no. I've got this house, but not much in the bank. Nothing like enough to fix the Hopes' place, anyway. The only way I could raise the cash is to put 35 Portland Row up for sale, and that's effectively the end of the agency, as Barnes well knows. . . ." For an instant, he seemed to shrink back into his chair; then a switch was flicked, and energy returned. He flashed us both a bruised, resplendent smile. "But it's not going to come to that, is it? We've got four weeks! That's *plenty* of time to earn some real money! What we need is a *really* high-profile case that gives us a bit of significant publicity, gets the ball rolling." He pointed at the casebook on the table. "No more of these measly Shades and Lurkers—we want something that'll truly make our name. Well . . . we'll get on to it tomorrow. . . . No thanks, George, I don't want supper. I'm a little tired. If it's all the same to you, I'm off to bed."

He said good night and left. George and I sat there, saying nothing.

"I didn't tell him, but we're off one of those cases already," George said at last. "They called today and canceled. Heard about the fire, you see."

"The cat lady?"

"I'm afraid not. One of the interesting ones."

"Four weeks isn't *really* long enough to get that money, is it?" I said.

"No." He was cross-legged on the sofa, chin resting gloomily on his hands.

"It's *so* unfair," I said. "We risked our lives!"

"Yeah."

"We faced down a formidable ghost! We made London a safer place!"

"Yeah."

"We should be getting *praised* for this!"

George stretched, prepared to rise. "Nice thought, but it's not the way things work. You hungry?"

"Not really. Just exhausted. I think I'm going to bed too." I watched him gather up the tea things, and retrieve the inspector's fallen cup from under the settee. "At least Annabel Ward's dealt with," I said. "That's a little consolation."

He grunted. "Yeah. You did *that* bit right, at least."

Chapter 11

I awoke sometime in the middle of the night, with the room in darkness and all my body aching. I lay on my back—the least uncomfortable position—turned slightly toward the window. One arm was bent and resting on my pillow, the other stretched out on the bedspread. My eyes were open, my mind alert. It almost seemed as if I hadn't been asleep at all, but I must have been, for all around me was the heavy, velvet silence of the dead hours.

My cuts felt raw, my bruises tender; a whole day after the fall, my muscles were in the process of stiffening nicely. I knew I should probably get up and take some aspirin, but the bottle was in the kitchen far below. It was too much effort to go and fetch it. I didn't want to move. I was stiff, the bed was warm, and the air was much too cold.

I lay quiet, staring at the sloping attic ceiling. After a short time, a pale white glow showed beyond the window, dim at first, then flaring. That was from the ghost-lamp, regular as a lighthouse beam, shining way off on the corner of the street. Every three and a half minutes, it pierced the night with its harsh white radiance for exactly thirty seconds before switching off again. Officially this was designed to keep the roads safe, discourage Visitors from lingering. In reality—since few ghosts wandered the open roads—it was about reassurance, to make people think the authorities were doing something.

It worked in its way, I guess. It gave a little comfort. But when it shut off, it made the night seem blacker still.

While the light was on, I could see the details of my little room: the ceiling beams, the dark strips of the iron ghost-bars around the window, the flimsy little armoire that was so shallow, all my hangers had to go in at an angle. There was scarcely any room in it—usually I ended up chucking my clothes in a heap on the chair beside the door. I could see that heap out of the corner of my eye. It had risen mighty high. I'd have to sort it out tomorrow.

Tomorrow . . . Lockwood's brave face notwithstanding, it didn't look as if there were many tomorrows left to us. Four weeks . . . Four weeks to find an impossible amount of money. And it had been *my* insistence that had kept us in the house after the ghost-girl's first attack. It had been me who drove us on to face her again, when it would have been so easy just to pack our things and leave.

My fault. I'd made the wrong decision, like at the Wythburn Mill. That time I'd not obeyed my instincts. *This* time I'd followed my instincts, and they'd been wrong. One way or another, when it came to a crisis, the end result was the same. I messed up, and disaster followed.

Out in the street, the ghost-lamp switched off; the room was dark once more. Still I hadn't moved. I was hoping I could con my mind into going back to sleep. But who was I kidding? I was too sore, too awake, too guilty—and also much too cold. I needed another blanket from the linen closet in the bathroom below.

Too cold . . .

My heart gave a little tremor as I lay there in my bed.

It really *was* too cold.

And not the ordinary damp middle-of-November kind, either. It was the sort of cold that causes your breath to plume above you as you sleep. It was the sort that causes little crystal webs of ice to grow on the inside of your windowpanes. It was a spreading, numbing, lung-scouring chill, and it was very well known to me.

I opened my eyes *wide*.

Darkness. I saw the faintest outline of the gable window and, through it, the orange-tinted London night. I listened—heard only the blood pounding in my ears. My heart beat against my chest so hard, I guessed the quilt above it was jumping in response. All my muscles tensed; I'd become superaware, feeling every inch of contact on my skin—the brush of my cotton nightie, the warm, smooth pliancy of the sheet, the press of the bandages on my wounds. My hand that lay on the pillow twitched involuntarily; sweat broke out on my palm.

I'd seen nothing, heard nothing, but I *knew*.

I was not alone in the room.

A small part of my mind screamed at me to move. Throw off the heavy bedspread, get to my feet. What I'd do *then*, I didn't know—but anything was better than just lying there helpless, clenching my panic tight between my teeth.

Just get up. Throw open the door. Run downstairs. . . . *Do* something!

I lay quite still.

A trickle of cold memory told me that making for the door might not be wise. Because I'd seen . . . What *had* I seen?

I waited. Waited for the light.

Sometimes three minutes takes a long, long time.

Down by the corner store, in the ghost-lamp's hidden circuitry, the electronic switch clicked on. Behind the great round lenses, magnesium bulbs ignited, bathing the street in cool white light. High up at my attic window, the glow returned.

My eyes flicked in the direction of the door.

Yes. There. The chair and heap of clothes. They formed: a black and shapeless blot—but it was *higher* than usual, far higher than it should have been. If I'd taken all the clothes I owned in the world and piled them there with my skirts and sweaters at the bottom and my socks teetering at the top, they wouldn't have been anywhere as tall, or thin, as the shape that stood just visible in the dark place by the door.

It didn't move. It didn't have to. I stared at it for thirty seconds, lying frozen in the bed. And I *did* feel frozen, too. The ghost-lock had stolen up on me so subtly, so stealthily, that I'd been entirely unaware of it till now.

The light from the street went out.

I bit my lip, ignited my concentration, drove the feeling of helplessness from my mind. I wrenched my muscles into action, threw my bedclothes off me. I hurled myself sideways, rolled off, landed on the floor.

I lay quite still.

All my muscles throbbed with pain; the violent action hadn't done my stitches any good. But I'd put the bed between me and the door, and the thing that stood beside it, which *was* good. It was all that counted now.

I was pressed low against the carpet, head resting on my hands. Ice-cold air bit the exposed skin of my feet and legs. The carpet was covered with a faint luminosity, a thin white, swirling haze: ghost-fog, an occasional side-product of a manifestation.

I closed my eyes, tried to calm down, open my ears, and *listen*.

But what's easy when you're fully clothed and equipped, and have a gleaming rapier at your side, isn't so simple when you're in your pink-and-yellow nightie, sprawling on the floor. What's fine when entering a haunted house on agency business doesn't work so well when you're in your very own bedroom, and have just seen something dead standing a few feet away. So I picked up no supernatural sound at all. What I got were life's essentials—my beating heart, the pumping of my lungs.

How the hell did it get in? There was iron on the window. How could it get so high?

Calm down! *Think*. Did I have any weapons in my room, anything I could use?

No. My workbelt was on the kitchen table, two full floors below. Two floors! It might as well have been in China. As might my rapier, lost back at Sheen Road, burned and melted in the fire. All our spares were in the basement, and that was *three* floors down! I was completely defenseless. There was probably plenty of equipment scattered nearer in the house, but that was useless too, because the thing was hovering by the door.

Or was it? Air shifted. My skin crawled.

Lying on my stomach as I was, I couldn't raise my head too far, not without supporting myself on my hands. All I could see was the nearest bed leg, gray and granular, strands of white-green ghost-fog, and the wall. My back was to the open room. Something could be drifting up behind me that very moment, and I wouldn't know anything about it.

Dark or not, I *had* to look right now. I steeled myself, prepared to rise.

The light in the street came on again. I straightened my arms, craned my head up, peeped back over the edge of the mattress . . .

And felt my heart nearly stop in fear. The shape was no longer by the door. No. It had moved up, slowly, silently, and was now hovering *above the bed*. It hung there in a stooped, investigative posture, plasm trailing on the mattress, its long dark fingers blindly probing the warm patch on the sheet where I'd just been lying.

If it had stretched those fingers to the side, it would have touched me.

I ducked back down.

In many ways the spare bed that I slept in was a dismal affair. Probably it was the very one Lockwood had snoozed in all those years ago as a little kid. Its joints were rickety, its mattress a wilderness of humps and springs. But one good thing about it: it lacked those built-in drawers you get with modern beds. So there was plenty of room beneath for crumpled hankies, books, and dust, even for my little box of stuff from home.

And plenty of room, right then, for a swiftly moving girl.

I don't know whether I crawled or rolled; I don't know what I crushed or broke. I think I hit my head, and I must've torn the bandages off my forearms, because I found them later all bloodied on the carpet. One second, maybe two: that was all it took for me to shoot beneath the bed and out the other side.

As I emerged I was engulfed by something cold.

It was big and soft, and flopped on me from above. For a split second I thrashed about in utter terror—then I realized it was just my bedspread, slumping off the bed. I hurled it away, struggled to my feet. Behind, on the bed, came a flare of angry other-light. The patch of darkness sprang into focus: a pale, thin shape drifted after me with outstretched arms.

I leaped to the door, tore it open with a crash, and launched myself desperately down the stairs.

Onto the first floor landing, colliding with the banisters, threads of cold air clutching at my neck. "Lockwood!" I shouted. "George!"

Lockwood's door was on the left. A little crack of light appeared beneath it. I scrabbled at the handle, staring over my shoulder at the pale glow extending swiftly down the stairs. The handle moved uselessly up and down; the door was locked, it wouldn't open. I raised a desperate fist to hammer on the wood. Around the angle of the stairs came fingers, a shining, outstretched hand. . . .

The door swung open; soft yellow lamplight almost blinded me.

Lockwood stood there, dressed in striped pajamas and his long, dark bathrobe.

"Lucy?"

I pitched past him into the room. "A ghost! My room! It's coming!"

His hair was a little rumpled, his bruised face tired and drawn, but he was otherwise as self-possessed as ever. He didn't ask questions but stepped backward, keeping his face toward the black opening of the door. There was a dresser beside him. Without looking, he opened the uppermost drawer with his good hand, reached purposefully inside. I felt a warm surge of relief. Thank goodness! It would be a salt-bomb, or a canister of iron filings maybe. Who cared? *Anything* would do.

He brought out a crumpled mess of wood and string and bits of metal. The metal pieces were shaped like animals and birds. Lockwood took hold of a wooden pole and began untangling the strings.

I stared at it. "That's all you've got?"

"My rapier's downstairs."

"What the hell is it?"

"Toy mobile. Had it when I was a kid. You hold it here, and the animals hang from this rotating wheel. Makes a jolly sound. My favorite was the smiley giraffe."

I looked toward the open door. "Well, that's very nice, but—"

"They're made of iron, Lucy. So what happened? Your knees are bleeding."

"An apparition. Dark aura at first, but other-light's kicking in now. Secondary effects of ghost-lock, and chill. It just followed me down the stairs."

Lockwood seemed satisfied with the mobile. When he held it up and flexed his wrist, the little circle of dangling animals turned freely. "Turn off the bedside lamp, will you?"

I did so. We were plunged into darkness. No spectral glow showed on the landing.

"Take it from me, it's out there," I said.

"Okay. We're making for the door. As you pass my bed, pick up a boot."

We stole toward the door, with the mobile held in front of us, and peered cautiously out. There was no sign of the apparition on the landing or the stairs.

"Got the boot?"

"Yes."

"Chuck it at George's door."

With as much strength as I could muster, I hurled it across the landing. It struck the door opposite with a dramatic thump. We waited, watching darkness.

"It followed me down the stairs," I said.

"I know. You said. Hurry it up, George. . . ."

"You'd have thought he'd be awake already, the noise I made."

"Well, he's a heavy sleeper. In more ways than one. Ah, here he is."

At last George had stumbled from his room, blinking and peering like a myopic vole. He wore an enormous pair of saggy blue pajamas that were at least three sizes too big for him, and were decorated with garish and ill-conceived spaceships and planes.

"George," Lockwood called, "Lucy says she's seen a Visitor, here in the house."

"I *have* seen it," I said tersely.

"Got any iron handy?" Lockwood said. "We need to check this out."

George rubbed his eyes; he fumbled at his belt-cord in a vain effort to keep his pants from sagging dangerously low. "Not sure. Maybe. Hold on."

He turned and trudged inside. There was a pause, followed by various rummaging sounds. A few moments later George returned, wearing a gaucho-style shoulder belt bristling with magnesium flares, salt-bombs, and canisters of iron. An empty silver-glass box hung beneath it on a string. He carried a coil of chain, and a long, ornate-handled rapier, and had a flashlight poking nonchalantly from the waistband of his pajamas. His feet were encased in enormous boots. Lockwood and I gazed at him.

"What?" George said. "Few little bits and pieces I keep by my bedside. Always good to be prepared. You can borrow a salt-bomb if you want to, Lockwood."

Lockwood hefted his tinkling mobile resignedly. "No, no, I'll be all right with this."

"If you're sure. So where's this apparition, then?"

With a few terse words I filled them in. Lockwood gave the order. We began to climb the stairs.

To my surprise, the way was clear. Every few steps we stopped to look and listen, but with no result. The sense of fearsome cold had gone; the ghost-fog too had faded; and I heard nothing with my inner ear. Lockwood and George drew a blank as well. The only obvious peril was provided by George's pajama bottoms, which, with the weight of his equipment, were in perpetual danger of falling down.

We rounded the corner at last. George plucked the flashlight from his pajamas and flashed it around my room. Everything was dark and quiet. My rumpled bedspread lay where I'd cast it, beside my disarranged bed. The clothes from my chair, which I must have knocked over in my flight, lay scattered on the floor.

"Nothing here," George said. "Are you sure about this, Lucy?"

"Of *course* I am," I snapped. I crossed swiftly to the window, looked down onto the distant street. "Though I admit, I can't feel it now."

Lockwood was kneeling, squinting under the bed. "From what you say, it must've been a weak one—slow-moving, only faintly aware of its surroundings—otherwise it would have caught you, surely. Maybe it's used up its energy, gone back into its Source."

"Which would be *what*, precisely?" George said. "Where's this new Source that's just mysteriously sprung from nowhere in Lucy's room? The house is well defended. Nothing can get in." He peered into my armoire, rapier at the ready. "Well, there's nothing in here but some charming tops and skirts and. . . . Ooh, Lucy—I've never seen you wearing *that*."

I slammed the door closed, narrowly missing his pudgy hand. "I *tell* you I saw a ghost, George. You think I'm going blind?"

"No, I just think you're deluded."

"Now, *look* . . ."

"This makes no sense at all," Lockwood interrupted, "unless Lucy's brought one of our psychic artifacts up here. You haven't, have you, Luce? You haven't brought that pirate's hand up for a closer inspection, for instance, and forgot to put it back in its case?"

I gave a little cry of anger. "Don't be stupid. Of *course* I haven't.

I wouldn't *dream* of taking anything that wasn't properly . . . that wasn't properly secured. . . . Oh."

"Well, George is always moving that jar of his about—" Lockwood noticed my expression. "Lucy?"

"Oh. Oh no."

"What is it? *Have* you taken something?"

I gazed at him. "Yes," I said in a very small voice. "Yes, I think I have."

George and Lockwood both turned to me, their backs to the armoire and the mess of scattered clothes. As they began to speak, pale radiance flared across the wall. A figure rose from the floor behind them. I saw thin, thin arms and legs, a dress with orange sunflowers, long blond tresses dissolving into whirling snakes of mist, a contorted face of cold, hard rage. . . . I gave a cry. Both boys wheeled around, just as sharp-nailed fingers reached out for their necks. George swung his sword, embedded it in the corner of my armoire. Lockwood thrust frantically with the mobile. There was an impact pulse as the iron struck; the ghost-girl vanished. A wave of cold air blasted across the room, pressing my nightie tight against my legs.

The attic room was dark once more.

Somebody coughed. George tugged at the rapier hilt, trying to get it free.

"Lucy . . ." Lockwood's voice was dangerously quiet. "Didn't that look like—"

"Yes. It was. I'm so, so sorry."

George gave a heave; the blade came free. He stepped awkwardly to the side and, as he did so, there was a sharp crack beneath his boot. He frowned, bent down, picked up something from among the scattered clothes beside the chair. "Ow!" he said. "It's freezing!"

Lockwood took the flashlight and trained the light upon the object dangling from George's fingers. A pendant, slightly squashed, glinting as it spun on a delicate golden chain.

Lockwood and George stared at it. They stared at me. George unhooked the silver-glass box from his belt and stowed the necklace inside. He shut it with a crisp and final click.

Slowly Lockwood raised the flashlight until I was transfixed by a silent, accusatory beam of light.

"Er, yes," I said. "The girl's necklace. . . . Um, you know I was *going* to mention that to you." Standing there in my rumpled nightie, in my bandaged, disheveled state, I did my best to smile at them as prettily as I could.

Chapter 12

The following day dawned bright and clear. Pale November sunshine flowed through the kitchen window and extended cheerily over the usual breakfast clutter. Cornflakes boxes glowed, bowls and glasses sparkled; every scattered crumb and blob of jam was picked out perfectly in the morning light. The air was warm, and heavy with the scent of good strong tea, of toast, fried eggs, and bacon.

I wasn't enjoying myself at all.

"*Why*, Lucy?" Lockwood demanded. "I just don't understand! You *know* an agent has to report any artifact she finds. Particularly one so intimately connected with a Visitor. They *must* be properly contained."

"I know that."

"They've *got* to be put in iron or silver-glass until they can be studied or destroyed."

"I know."

"But you just shoved it into your pocket and didn't tell me or George!"

"Yes. I said I'm sorry! I've never done that sort of thing before."

"So why did you do it *now*?"

I took a deep breath. My head was lowered; for some minutes, while my reprimand proceeded, I'd been grimly doodling on the thinking cloth. It was a picture of a girl, a thin girl wearing an old-style summer dress. Her hair whipped around her head, and her eyes were vast and blank. I pressed the pen down hard, probably scoring the table below.

"I don't know," I muttered. "It all happened so fast. Maybe it was because of the fire—maybe I just wanted to save something of her, so she wouldn't be completely lost. . . ." I sketched a big black sunflower in the middle of the dress. "In all honesty, I hardly remember taking it at all. And afterward . . . well, I just forgot."

"Better not mention this to Barnes," George remarked. "He'd be livid if he knew you'd absentmindedly carried a dangerous Visitor around London without proper precautions. It would give him yet another reason to close this agency down."

Out of the corner of my eye, I watched him complacently spread another dollop of lemon curd on his toasted bun. Oh, he was in fine fettle that morning, George, chipper as a ferret. I reckoned he was enjoying my discomfort big-time.

"You forgot?" Lockwood said. "That's it? That's your excuse?"

Defiance flared; I raised my head, brushed my hair back. "Yeah," I said, "and if you want to know *why*: for starters, I was probably preoccupied with being in the hospital, and after that, too busy worrying about *you*. But actually, if you think about it, I didn't have any reason to believe it was dangerous. Did I? Because we'd just sealed the Source."

"No!" Lockwood jabbed a finger of his good hand on the tablecloth. "That's just it! We *thought* we had, but we hadn't! We *hadn't* sealed the Source, Lucy, because obviously the Source is *there*."

He indicated the small silver-glass box, which sat quietly between the butter and the teapot. It glittered in the sunshine; inside, the golden necklace could just be seen.

"But how *can* it be the Source?" I cried. "It should've been her bones."

He shook his head pityingly. "It only *seemed* that way, because her ghost vanished the moment you covered her body with the silver net. But obviously you'd covered the necklace too, in the self-same action, which was more than enough to seal it up. Then, when you stole the necklace—"

I glared at him. "I didn't steal it."

"—you put it straight into your coat pocket, which was stuffed full of iron filings and packets of salt, and other agency bits and pieces that were more than enough to keep the Visitor constrained for the remainder of the night. The following day, though, you slung your coat down on your chair, and the necklace fell out. Then it lay hidden in the pile of clothes until darkness, when the ghost was able to return."

"The only puzzler is why it wasn't as fast or powerful as the previous night," George said. "From what you say, it was almost sluggish when you first escaped from the room."

"Most likely some of the iron and salt fell out of your coat with the necklace," Lockwood said. "They'd have been enough to keep the ghost weak, and prevent it from sustaining its presence very long. That's probably why it couldn't follow you downstairs, and wasn't able to rematerialize swiftly when we came back up."

"Luckily for us," George said. He shivered, took a consoling bite of toasted bun.

I held up my hands to silence them. "Yes, yes. I understand all that. But that's not what I'm saying. What I mean is, the Source is whatever the Visitor is most attached to, isn't it? It's what it holds most dear. So surely it really *ought* to have been her bones." I reached out, picked up the glass case by its cord, and turned it in my fingers, so that the pendant and spool of chain inside slid softly to and fro. "But instead, it turns out to be this. This necklace is more significant to the spirit of Annabel Ward than her own bodily remains. . . . Isn't that a little odd?"

"No different from that motorbike rider we had one time," George pointed out.

"True, but—"

"I hope you're not trying to change the subject, Lucy," Lockwood said in a cold voice. "I'm in the middle of telling you off, here."

I set the case down. "I know."

"I'm not finished, either. Not by a long shot. I've a whole heap more to say." There was a protracted pause. Lockwood gazed sternly at me, then out of the window. Finally he gave an exasperated cry. "Unfortunately, I've lost my train of thought. The point is: *Don't do it again*. I'm disappointed in you. When you joined the company I told you I wasn't bothered if you kept stuff hidden about your past.

That's still true. But keeping secrets about things that happen *now* is different. We're a team and we've got to work that way."

I nodded. I stared at the tablecloth. My face felt cold and hot at the same time.

"You can forget wondering about this necklace, too," Lockwood said. "I'm taking it to the Fittes furnaces in Clerkenwell today to get it incinerated. Good-bye, Source. Good-bye, Annabel Ward. Good riddance to the whole affair." He scowled petulantly into his mug. "And now my tea's gone cold."

The events of the night certainly hadn't helped matters, but Lockwood's mood was poor for other reasons too. His ghost-touched hand was troubling him. Barnes's bad tidings weighed heavily on his mind. Worst of all, the public fallout from our Sheen Road disaster had begun. To his horror, the fire had made the *Times* that morning. In the *Problem Pages*, where prominent hauntings were covered daily, an article entitled "Independent Agencies: More Control Needed?" described how an investigation carried out by Lockwood & Co., ("an independent outfit, run by juveniles"), had resulted in a dangerous, destructive blaze. It was clearly implied that Lockwood had lost control. At the end of the piece, a spokeswoman for the giant Fittes Agency was quoted. She recommended "adult supervision" for nearly all psychic investigations.

The repercussions of this article had been quick and definite. At 8:05 a.m. there'd been a phone call to the office, canceling one of our ongoing cases. A second call followed at 9:00 a.m. We fully expected several more.

The chances of raising £60,000 within a month seemed remote to say the least.

Our meal tailed off into frosty silence. Lockwood sat across the table from me, nursing his cold tea, flexing his injured fingers. Life was returning to them, but they still had a bluish look. George shuffled about the kitchen, gathering plates and bunging them into the sink.

I turned the glass case over and over in my hand.

Lockwood's anger was justified, and that made me miserable. The strange thing was—though I knew I'd been in the wrong, both in taking the necklace and forgetting all about it—I couldn't wholly regret what I'd done. That night in Sheen Road I'd heard the voice of a murdered girl. I'd seen her too—both as she'd once been, and as the wretched, shriveled object she'd become. And, despite the fear and fury of the haunting, despite the terrible malignancy of the vengeful ghost, I couldn't quite throw those memories aside.

With the body turned to ashes, this necklace was all that remained: of Annabel Ward, of her life and death, of her whole unknown story.

And we were going to toss that in the fires too.

It didn't seem right to me.

I lifted the case closer to my eyes, staring through the glass. "Lockwood," I said, "can I get the necklace out?"

He sighed. "I suppose. It's daytime. It's safe enough for now."

It was certainly true that Annabel Ward's ghost was not going to spring forth from the pendant during the day. But it *was* linked to her, whether she was somehow contained within it or simply using it as a conduit from the other side. So I couldn't help feeling a frisson of anxiety as I flicked aside the slender iron bolt and eased the silver-glass open.

There it was: looking scarcely more sinister than the jam spoons and butter knives that littered the sunlit table. A delicate piece of jewelry on a delicate golden chain. I took it out of the case, flinching a little at its chill touch on my skin, and studied it properly for the first time.

The chain was formed of twisted loops of gold, mostly clean and bright, except in a couple of spots where something black had clogged between the links. The pendant itself was roughly oval, about the dimensions of a walnut. Thanks to George's galumphing boot, it had a slightly squashed look. At one time the exterior must have been lovely. It had been lined with dozens of flakes of mother-of pearl, pinkish-white and glittering, and neatly embedded in a mesh of gold. But many of the pieces had fallen out and, as with the chain, the surface was tarnished in places with ominous black flecks. Worst of all (and again thanks probably to George), the entire oval had been ruptured down one side. I could see a clear split along a seam.

More interesting than all that, however, was a slightly raised heart-shaped symbol halfway down the pendant at the front. Here, a faint and spidery pattern marked the gold.

"Oh!" I said. "There's an inscription on it."

I held it up so it caught the light, and ran my finger over the letters. As I did so, I caught a sudden sound of voices—a man and woman talking, then the woman's laughter, high and shrill.

I blinked; the sensation faded. I gazed at the object in my hand. My curiosity had infected the others. Despite himself, Lockwood had gotten up and moved around the table. George had stopped doing the dishes and, flourishing a dish towel, was peering over my shoulder from the other side.

Four words. We gazed at them in silence for a time.

Tormentum meum
laetitia mea

It didn't make much sense to me.

"'*Tormentum*' . . ." George said at last. "That sounds cheerful."

"Latin," Lockwood said. "Haven't we got a Latin dictionary somewhere?"

"It's from the man who gave her the necklace," I said. "The one she loved. . . ." The echo of the two voices still resounded in my mind."

"How d'you know it's a bloke?" George put in. "It could have been a female friend. Could have been her mum."

"No way," I said. "Look at the symbol. Besides, you wear these things so you can have your loved one's message next to your heart."

"Like you know anything about that," George said.

"Like *you* do either."

"Let's have a look at it," Lockwood said. He perched on the chair next to mine and took the necklace from my hand. He held it close, brow furrowing.

"Latin phrases, a loved one's gift, a long-lost girl . . ." George flipped his damp dish towel over his shoulder and headed for the sink. "Bit of an exotic mystery. . . ."

"*Isn't* it?" Lockwood said. "*Isn't it, though*?" We looked at him.

His eyes were shining; he'd sat up suddenly. The gloom that had enveloped him all morning had suddenly dispersed, like white clouds on the wind. "George," he went on, "do you remember that famous case that Tendy's had, a year or two back? The one with the two entangled skeletons?"

"The Wailing Tree affair? Of course. They got an award for it."

"Yes, and masses of publicity. And the reason for that was they figured out who the Visitors were, didn't they? They found a diamond tie pin on one of the skeletons and traced it back to the jeweler who made it, and that told them that the owner—"

"—was young Lord Ardley," I said, "who'd gone missing back in the nineteenth century. Everyone thought he'd run off overseas. But there he was, buried in the family garden, where his younger brother must've put him, in order to inherit the estate." There was a pause; I looked at them. "Why so surprised? I read issues of *True Hauntings* too."

"Fair enough," Lockwood said. "And you're spot on. The point is, it was a great story, and by solving that old mystery Tendy's did very well. They became a more prominent agency off the back of it; they're fourth-biggest in London now. So I'm just wondering . . ." He trailed off, gazing at the locket in his hand.

"Whether Annabel Ward might do the same for us?" George said. "Lockwood, you know how many Visitors there are in London? Across the country? It's a plague. People don't care about the stories behind them. They just want them gone."

"You say that, but good cases make big headlines," Lockwood said. "And this one *could* be good. Think about it. A glamorous girl, brutally slain and lost for decades, two tragic lovers, a small but enterprising agency that uncovers the truth behind the killing. . . ." He grinned at us. "Yes . . . if we play it right, we might make a splash with this. We could turn our fortunes around after all. But we'll need to get moving. George—that Latin dictionary is on the second floor landing, I think. Mind bringing it down? Thanks! And Lucy," he continued, as George padded away, "maybe there's something *you* can help with too."

I gazed at him. His transformation from the grumpy, woebegone figure of a few minutes previously was utterly complete. His movements were quick and light, his injuries forgotten; his dark eyes sparkled as he looked into mine. In that instant it was as if nothing in the world fascinated him as much as me.

"Tell me something," he said. "I almost don't want to ask this, given our experiences these last two days, but when you held the locket just now, I don't suppose you . . . felt anything, did you?"

I nodded slowly. "If you mean a psychic residue, yes, I did. Voices, laughter . . . Not much. I wasn't trying."

"And, do you think," Lockwood said, smiling, "if you *did* try . . . ?"

"You want me to see what sensations I can get?"

"Yes! Isn't it a great idea? You might pick up something vital; a clue that we can use."

I looked away, embarrassed by the intensity of his gaze. "Sure, maybe . . . I don't know."

"If anyone can do it, *you* can, Luce. You're brilliant at this. Give it a go."

Moments before, he'd been promising to incinerate the locket. Now, it was the key to all our troubles. Moments before, he'd been giving me a rollocking; now, I was the apple of his eye. This was the way it was with Lockwood. His shifts were sometimes so sudden that they took your breath away, but his energy and enthusiasm were always impossible to resist. I could hear George thumping eagerly around upstairs; and I, too, felt a sudden unbidden thrill—excitement at the prospect of uncovering the ghost-girl's story, hope at the thought of maybe helping save the agency somehow.

Despite myself, of course, I also couldn't help being flattered by Lockwood's words of praise.

I sighed heavily. "I could *try*," I said, "but I can't promise anything. You know that with Touch it's normally just emotions and sounds you get, not concrete facts. So if—"

"Great! Well done." He pushed the pendant toward me along the table. "Can I help in any way? Would you like me to make you a cup of tea?"

"No. Just shut up and let me concentrate."

I didn't pick it up at first. This wasn't, after all, something to do lightly. I'd already had ample evidence of the ghost-girl's wrath and hatred. I knew her fate had not been a pleasant one. So I took my time. I sat looking at the pendant and the coil of chain, and tried to rid my mind of thoughts as best I could. I set aside all the rushing, garbled feelings of the day-to-day.

At last I took it in my hand. The cool of the metal sank through me.

I waited for any echoes that might come.

And very soon, they *did* come, same as before. First, a man and woman talking, the woman's high-pitched laughter, the man's voice joining her as one. Then a sensation of fierce joy, of passion shared;

I felt the elation of the girl, her feverish delight. A great bulb of happiness spread out to fill my world. . . . The laughter changed, became hysterical in tone. The man's voice grew harsher, the sound twisted. I felt a cold, sharp jolt of fear. . . . And then at once the joy was back, and all was well, well, well. . . . Until the next reversal, until contentment curdled, and the voices rose once more in anger, and I was sick with jealousy and rage. . . . And so it went on, back and forth, back and forth, the mood swings flashing past, like I was on that merry-go-round in Hexham as a kid, the one time my mother let me go, and I was full of joy and terror mixed together, and I knew I couldn't get off no matter how I tried. And all at once came sudden silence, and a cold voice talking in my ear, and a final blaze of fury that ascended to a desperate shriek of pain—a shriek I realized was my own.

I opened my eyes. Lockwood was supporting me in the chair. The door burst open; George pelted into the room.

"What the hell's going on?" he cried. "Can't I leave you two alone for a minute?"

"Lucy," Lockwood said. His face was white. "I'm so sorry. I should never have asked you to do that. What happened? Are you okay?"

"I don't know. . . ." I pushed him away and, in the same motion, dropped the pendant on the kitchen table. It rocked there briefly, glittering. "I shouldn't have done that," I said. "It's too strong. It's completely bound up with her spirit and her memories. I felt I *was* her for a moment, and that wasn't nice at all. Her anger is terrible."

I sat quiet for a moment in the sunny kitchen, letting the

sensations peel away from me like fading fragments of a dream. The others waited.

"There's one thing I *can* tell you," I went on at last. "Maybe it's what you were after, Lockwood, and maybe it isn't, but it's something I *do* now know for certain. It came through in the emotions loud and clear." I took a deep breath, looked up at them.

"Yes?" Lockwood said.

"The man who gave her this necklace? He's the one who killed her, too."

Chapter 13

Early that afternoon we took the short walk to Baker Street Underground station. It was good to be outdoors again, and in pleasant sunlight, too. Each of us felt the change; our mood had lifted. We put on casual clothes. Lockwood wore a long brown leather coat that emphasized his slimness and easy stride. George wore a hideous puffy jacket with a high elastic waistband that emphasized his bottom. I had on my usual gear: coat, roll-neck sweater, short dark skirt, and leggings. All of us wore our rapiers (in my case a spare one from the hall). These—and the cuts and bruises on our faces—were the marks of our profession and our status; people moved aside for us as we went by.

The Jubilee Line train was crowded and heavy with the sweet protective smell of lavender. Men wore sprigs of it in their buttonholes; women had them in their hats. All across the carriage, silver brooches and tie pins winked and glittered beneath the neon lights.

We stood silent and serious as the train rattled through the tunnels on the five-minute journey to Green Park. No one spoke. The eyes of the crowd followed us as we alighted and set off along the platform.

During the trip George had been flicking through the Latin dictionary. As we went up the escalator, he took his pencil out of his mouth and made a last notation on a scrap of paper.

"Okay," he said. "I've done the best I can. It's '*Tormentum meum, laetitia mea*,' right? Well, *tormentum* means 'torment' or 'torture.' *Laetitia* equals 'joy' or 'bliss.' *Meum* and *mea* are both 'my.' So I translate the inscription in our locket as 'My torment, my bliss.'" He snapped the dictionary shut. "Not the healthiest of love messages, is it?"

"Fits exactly with what I sensed," I said shortly. "It *wasn't* a healthy relationship. It veered between extremes. Half the time it was sort of happy; half the time eaten up by jealousy and hate. And *that's* what triumphed in the end."

"Don't think about it anymore, Lucy," Lockwood said. "You've done your part. Now George and I will do ours. How long do you think it'll take us at the Archives, George?"

"Not long," George said. "We'll go back to the local newspapers, starting at the date where I left off. If there's any more about Annabel Ward—whether they ever arrested anyone, for instance—we should find it straight away. Then we can check the gossip magazines, too—it said she was a society girl."

We left the station and started up Piccadilly. Afternoon light lanced steeply between tall buildings; we walked from bright sun to blue shadow and back again. It being late autumn, preparations for evening were already underway. A salt-spreader pushed his cart along the roadside, scattering fresh grains left and right like snow. Outside the big hotels, attendants filled trash cans with bunches of dried lavender ready for burning; others polished the ghost-lamps hanging above the doors.

I let my bruised muscles stretch out as I walked; it was nice to feel my strength returning. Lockwood was limping slightly, but otherwise full of zest. He'd removed the bandages from his ghost-touched arm to let the sunshine bathe his skin. "If we can solve this old case," he said, "if we can uncover the murderer and get justice for the girl, it'll be *brilliant* publicity. It'll totally offset the fact we burned that woman's house down."

"And help us save Lockwood & Co in the bargain," I said.

"That's the hope. . . ." He steered past a man offering tourist maps of the "safe zones" of the city and ignored the entreaties of an iron-seller. "But only if we get good cases, and get them soon."

"You realize DEPRAC will be working on this also," George pointed out. "It's never their priority, but they *do* investigate old murders, if they happened within living memory."

"All the more reason to act fast," Lockwood said. "Okay, let's cross here."

We ducked out across the street, stepping over the open drain, or 'runnel,' of running water that separated the sidewalk from the asphalt. The wandering dead were known to dislike moving water; consequently narrow runnels crisscrossed many of the great shopping streets in the West End, allowing people to walk in safety well into the evening. Earlier governments had hoped to extend this system across the city, but it had proved prohibitively expensive. Aside from ghost-lamps, the suburbs fended for themselves.

Up a side road, under a great stone arch out onto the sweeping curve of Regent Street. Not far ahead, a stand had been set up on the sidewalk. Flags fluttered above a cheery blood-red canopy. On each flag reared a gold heraldic lion, and an ornate letter 'R.'

"Ooh, look," George said. "Hot chestnuts! Who wants some?"

A group of boys and girls in dark-red jackets were arranged around the stand, giving out free sprigs of lavender, salt-bombs, and sweets to passers-by. Roasting chestnuts popped and crackled on an open grill; an acned youth with a giant scoop stood by to tip them into paper cones. The agents' hair was carefully brushed, their swords polished, their faces scrubbed and smiling; all seemed to have been pressed out of the same anemic mold. They were representatives of Rotwell's, the second-oldest psychic investigation agency in London and, thanks to its publicity campaigns, the most popular by a wide margin. Behind the stand, set back a little from the street, the central Rotwell office rose—a vast, smooth-fronted edifice of glass and marble. Snarling lions, holding rapiers in their forepaws, had been inscribed into the glass of its sliding double doors. I knew the interior of that office; I'd failed an interview there.

A smiling boy, no more than ten years old, held out a little cone of chestnuts as we approached. "Gift courtesy of Rotwell's," he said. "Go safe tonight."

"We're not having any," Lockwood growled. "George, I want you just to walk on by."

"But I'm hungry."

"Tough. You're *not* walking down the street with one of those cones in your hand. It would be a crime to advertise a competitor."

He ignored the boy and stalked on past. George hesitated, then took the cone and popped it in his pocket. "There," he said. "Nicely out of sight. *I* say it's a crime to refuse free food."

We pushed on through the pressing crowd and came out the other side. A few minutes later we had reached a quiet, leafy square a block behind Regent Street. It was dominated by an ugly, brick-fronted building of colossal size. An iron plaque on the door read: NATIONAL NEWSPAPER ARCHIVES.

George's spectacles gleamed. This was his territory; he had the nearest I'd seen to a smile on his chestnut-stained face. "Here we go. Keep your voices down. The librarians are picky here." He ushered us over the iron-line and through the revolving doors.

I'd never been a big one for reading as a kid. My family rarely had a book in the house, and I'd been apprenticed out to Jacobs almost before starting school. Of course, I had needed to read in order to complete my studies—you can't get any of your certificates without a simple written exam—and I'd memorized the *Fittes Manual for Ghost-Hunters* by the time I was twelve. But after that? To be honest, I was too busy working to spend much time with books. True, Jacobs had occasionally sent me to the local library to look up historical details on hangings (the region around Gibbet Hill, half a mile from our little town, being a notorious spot for Visitors), so I wasn't entirely unused to buildings full of printed paper. But the National Newspaper Archives was on a bigger scale than anything I'd seen before.

The complex had six enormous floors, piled about a central concrete atrium. When you stood at the bottom, among palms and other indoor trees, the ascending levels of shelves and racks and reading tables seemed to reach the sky. A large iron sculpture hung from the domed roof high above, part-decoration, part-defense. On every level, hunched figures flipped through yellowed newspapers and magazines. Some, perhaps, researched the Problem, looking for clues to the plague that beset us. Others were agents: I saw blue Tamworth jackets dotted about, the lilac tones of Grimble, and here and there the somber dark-gray hues of Fittes. Not for the first time, I wondered why Lockwood hadn't chosen to clothe us in a coordinated uniform of our own.

Like me, Lockwood seemed somewhat overawed, but George bustled us along in a confident manner. Within a few minutes he had taken us by elevator to the fourth floor, sat us down at an empty desk and, after disappearing for a moment, plunked down the first great gray files before us.

"Here're the local papers from the Richmond district, forty-nine years ago," he said. "Annabel Ward disappeared in late June. The article I found came out a week or so later. Lockwood, why don't you start with the July editions? They're the most likely to be helpful. Lucy, you check the autumn file. I'll go get some issues of *London Society*."

Lockwood and I took off our coats and immersed ourselves obediently in the thrill-a-minute pages of the *Richmond Examiner.* I soon found it contained more local parties, lost cats, and best-kept garden competitions than I could have believed existed in the universe. There was quite a bit about the Problem too, the nature of which was beginning to be discussed. I found early calls for ghost-lights to be erected (they eventually were) and for graveyards to be bulldozed and salt-sown (they weren't: it was far too expensive and controversial; instead they were simply ringed with iron). But I discovered nothing more about the hunt for the missing girl.

Lockwood and George—who was flipping through the glossy black-and-white photos of the society magazine—were having a similar lack of luck. Lockwood grew restless; he looked sighingly at his watch.

Shadows fell over my page. Looking up, I discovered three people standing by the table, watching us with ill-concealed amusement. Two were teenagers, a boy and a girl; the other was a very young man. All three wore the soft gray jackets and crisp black pants of the oldest, most prestigious company of ghost-hunters in London, the Old Gray Lady of the Strand—the celebrated Fittes Agency. Their rapiers had complex, Italian-style hilts, much more old-fashioned and expensive than ours. They carried neat gray briefcases, emblazoned (like their jackets) with the Fittes symbol, the rearing silver unicorn.

Lockwood and George got to their feet. The young man smiled at them.

"Hello, Tony," he said. "This *is* novel. Haven't seen you here before."

Tony. No one, in the six long months I'd known him, had so much as dared to call him Anthony. For a split second I assumed there was great friendship between this Fittes supervisor and Lockwood; then I realized it was the other thing.

Lockwood was smiling too, but not in a way I'd ever seen before. It was somehow wolflike. Deep creases hid his eyes. "Quill Kipps," he said. "How's life treating you?"

"Busy. Very busy. What about you, Tony? You look rough, if you don't mind my saying."

"Oh, it's nothing serious. Just a few knocks. Can't complain."

"Yes, I imagine you haven't got time for that," the young man said, "what with all the other people complaining about *you*. . . ." He was very slightly built, almost birdlike in his delicacy of form. He probably weighed less than I did. He had a small, rather upturned nose, a narrow, freckled face, and auburn hair cropped severely short. He had four or five medals pinned to the breast of his jacket, and in the pommel of his rapier was a glittering green stone. Not that he could *use* the sword much these days. I guessed he was about twenty, so his days of active service were behind him. His Talent had mostly shriveled up and gone. Like my old leader, Jacobs, and all the other useless supervisors choking the industry, all he could do now was boss the kids around.

Lockwood didn't seem overly perturbed by the jibe. "Well, you know," he said, "these things happen. So . . . what are you researching?"

"Cluster of ghosts in a road tunnel near Moorgate. Trying to figure out what they are." He eyed our open files. "I see you're looking into something too."

"Yes."

"*Richmond Examiner* . . . Oh, *I* see. The notorious Sheen Road case. Of course, here at Fittes, we tend to do our research *before* we take on a Visitor. We're not completely stupid, you know."

The boy at his side, a tall and gangling youth, with a large, big-boned head and a thatch of mousy hair, laughed dutifully. The girl didn't respond. Humor—even the snide and easy sort that she was meant to side with—didn't seem to be her thing. Her chin was small and slightly pointy. Her blond hair had been cut short at the back, but she had a sharp flick angled across her forehead; its tip almost reached her eye. I thought her striking, in a hard and plastic sort of way. She gazed at me. "Who's this?"

"New assistant," Lockwood said. "Well, newish."

I held out a hand to the girl. "Lucy Carlyle. And you are?"

The girl gave a little laugh and looked away up the aisle as if there was a chip bag or something lying there that she found more interesting than me.

"You ought to watch out, being with Tony, sweetheart," Quill Kipps said. "His last assistant came to a nasty end."

I smiled blandly. "Don't worry about me. I'm fine."

"Yeah, but bad things happen to people he's close to. It's always been that way. Since he was *ever* so young."

He tried to make it sound casual, but his tone betrayed him. There was a catch in his voice that I didn't understand. I glanced across at Lockwood. The way he stood was different. His studious unconcern had stiffened, become something harder and less pliable. I knew he was about to say something, but before he could speak, George stirred.

"I've been hearing things about *you* too, Quill," he said. "That young lad you sent into the Southwark catacombs alone, while you 'waited for reinforcements' at the door. What became of that kid, Quill? Or haven't they found him yet?"

Kipps frowned. "Who told you that? That wasn't the way it happened—"

"And that client who got ghost-touched because your agents left an arm bone in his trash can."

The man flushed. "That was a mistake! They threw away the wrong bag—"

"Plus, you have the highest mortality rate of any Fittes team leader, so I'm told."

"Well—"

"It's not a *great* record, is it?" There was a silence.

"Oh, and your fly's undone," George said.

Kipps looked down and discovered the unhappy truth of the statement. His face went bright red. His fingers strayed to his sword hilt; he took a half step forward. George didn't move but unblinkingly pointed to a QUIET sign hanging on the wall.

Quill Kipps took a deep breath. He smoothed his hair back, smiled. "Pity I can't close that fat mouth of yours here, Cubbins," he said. "But there'll come a time when I will."

"Okay," George said. "Meanwhile, why not pick a fight with someone your own size? I suggest a gerbil or a mole."

Kipps made a small sound with his lips. He moved; the blade was in his hand—

A blur of movement at my side; a tang of steel on steel. Lockwood scarcely seemed to have changed position, but the line of his rapier now stretched out diagonally across the table, intersecting Kipps's blade, pressing it firmly down.

"If you're going to mess about with swords, Quill," Lockwood said, "you'd better be able to use them."

Kipps said nothing. A vein pulsed halfway up his neck; under the smart material of his soft gray sleeve, his arm exerted pressure. I could see that he was trying to shift his rapier, first one way, then the other, but Lockwood, without appearing to expend any effort whatsoever, forestalled him. The blades remained still, their owners almost motionless; George and I, and the two Fittes agents, were likewise frozen, as if by some magical extension. All around us, the library's quiet hum went on.

"You can't keep this up forever," Kipps said.

"True." Lockwood's arm twisted; he flicked his wrist. Quill Kipps's rapier was snatched from his hand. It flew straight up and embedded itself, point-first, in the ceiling.

"Nice," I said.

Smiling, Lockwood returned his sword to his belt and sat back down, leaving Kipps breathing loudly through his nose. After a moment he gave a little jump, hoping to reach the hilt of his hanging sword, but missed by several inches. He jumped again.

"Little bit higher, Quill," George said encouragingly. "You almost got it then."

At length Kipps had to scramble onto the table in order to wrestle his rapier free. His agents watched in silence, the boy smirking, the blond girl as stony-faced as ever.

"You'll pay for that, Lockwood," Kipps said, when he'd returned to the ground. "I swear I'll make you pay. Everyone knows DEPRAC's going to close you down, but that won't be enough for me. I'll find a way of making you *really* suffer, you and these idiot friends of yours. Bill, Kate, come on."

He spun around. His lackeys did too. Like a small, poorly trained dance ensemble, they flounced away in unison toward the elevator.

"Even when I worked with him, Kipps had a terribly short fuse," George observed. "He's got to learn to lighten up a bit. Wouldn't you say so, Lockwood?"

But Lockwood was already buried in the files again, his lips a thin hard line. "Come on," he said. "We've got a job to do here. We mustn't waste more time."

In fact, it was only another minute or so before the breakthrough came, and it was Lockwood himself who made it. With a low, long whistle of triumph, he pointed to the newspaper before him. There she was. Annabel Ward. A different photograph, same familiar splash of blond hair, curves, and gleaming teeth. This time she was wearing some kind of ball gown; this time she'd made the front cover of the *Richmond Examiner*, forty-nine years ago.

Annie Ward: EX-BOYFRIEND QUESTIONED

The case of Miss Annabel "Annie" Ward, the local woman missing for almost two weeks, took a new turn last night when police arrested one of her former boyfriends. Mr. Hugo Blake, 22, a well-known gambler and society figure, is currently being held at Bow Street Police Station. He has not yet been formally charged.

According to police sources, Mr. Blake was one of Miss Ward's dining companions at the Gallops nightclub on Saturday 21st June, the night she disappeared. He is said to have left the club soon after Miss Ward and, under repeated questioning, has admitted driving her home. Sources say that the pair had been close some months previously, but that their relationship had cooled. Blake's association with Miss Ward caused much comment in fashionable circles. Under his influence, she had largely abandoned a promising acting career, though she had recently made attempts to find new roles in—

"Hugo Blake," I said softly. "Her former boyfriend. I bet he gave her the necklace."

George nodded. "And he took her home that night. . . . Well, I think we know what he did there."

"Keep looking," Lockwood said. "They arrested him, but was he charged? For all we know, he may have gone to prison, even though they didn't locate the body."

It didn't take long to find the answer. A small piece dated a few days later tersely recorded that Hugo Blake had been released without charge. Scotland Yard sources were quoted saying the Annabel Ward inquiry had "run up against a brick wall."

"A brick wall is right!" I gasped. "Those idiots! She was right there, all along!"

"They didn't have enough evidence to nail Blake at the time," Lockwood said, scanning the page. "He was the only real suspect in the case, but they couldn't back it up. He claimed he'd escorted her home and left her there, but hadn't gone inside. No one could prove otherwise, and since they didn't have the body, or anything else to go on, they couldn't press charges. . . . So they let him walk. This is perfect. Looks like Blake's our man."

George sat back in his chair. "How old was Blake then?"

"Twenty-two," I said. "Poor Annie Ward was only twenty."

"Well, that was forty-nine years ago. Long time, but he'd only be seventy-one now. He's probably still alive."

"I bet he is," I said savagely. "I bet he's been living it up ever since. He got away with murder."

"Until now," Lockwood said. He grinned at us. "This is just what we need—as long as we treat it right. So here's the plan. We contact

DEPRAC. If Blake's still living, he'll be arrested. Meanwhile, we go to the papers, tell them the story. Killer caught after fifty years! *That* should make some waves."

"That's fine," George said slowly, "but I'm not sure we should go public yet. There's a lot more research we could do, checking into Annie Ward's past." He patted the pile of *London Society* magazines beside him. "She's bound to be here somewhere. And, if we're lucky, we can probably find juicy stuff on Blake, too, which might—"

"You carry on." Lockwood scraped his chair back, got to his feet. "Let me know what you find. Meantime, I'm going to talk to some people. We lost three clients this morning. For the sake of the agency, we can't afford to hang around."

"Well . . ." George adjusted his glasses doubtfully. "Don't be too hasty, that's all."

Lockwood gave us both a gleaming smile. "Oh, I'll be careful. You know me."

Chapter 14

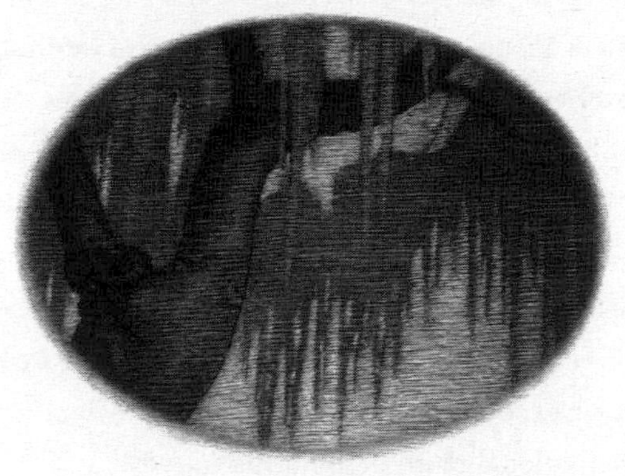

DISCOVERED AFTER 50 YEARS!

MURDER VICTIM'S BODY FOUND

TRIUMPH OF DETECTION BY LOCKWOOD AGENCY

In one of the most incredible examples of "cold case" detections of recent years, the body of Annabel "Annie" Ward, who vanished almost half a century ago, has been discovered in a house in southwest London. Operatives working for the Lockwood & Co. agency battled half the night with the terrifying spirit of the victim, before locating and making safe the remains.

"We barely escaped with our lives," says young agency head, Anthony Lockwood. "But destroying the ghost wasn't enough for us. We wanted justice for the unknown girl."

The team subsequently employed sophisticated research techniques to establish the identity of Miss Ward. DEPRAC has since agreed to open a murder investigation.

"There's no case too old or too difficult for us," says Mr. Lockwood. "In fact, the tricky ones suit us best, because of our high professionalism and distinctly personal approach. We want to dispose of Visitors, of course, but we're also interested in the human stories behind the hauntings. Poor Annie Ward died long ago, but her killer can still be brought to account. Lucy Carlisle, one of our top agents, communicated psychically with the Visitor during the operation and, despite a raging inferno started by the vengeful spirit, gained vital evidence that we think will lead us to the culprit's door. That's all I can say for now, but we expect to have more news soon, when we'll reveal the full sensational truth behind this tragedy."

"What a great article," Lockwood said, for the twentieth time that day. "Couldn't have been better."

"They spelled my name wrong," I pointed out.

"They didn't mention me at all," George said.

"Well, in all the essentials, I mean." Lockwood grinned around at us. "Page six of the *Times*. Best bit of publicity we've ever had. This is the turning point. Things are finally looking up." He shivered and moved his boots from one foul smelling portion of compost to another.

It was almost 8:00 p.m., the day after our trip to the Archives. We were standing in a mucky gooseberry patch in a dark and chilly garden, waiting for a ghost. It wasn't the most glamorous assignment known to man.

"Temperature?" Lockwood asked.

"Still dropping." George was checking his thermometer. It

glowed faintly amid the tangles of the gooseberries. Up in the house, the lights were masked by drab curtains. A dog barked a good way off. Twenty feet away from us, the thin black branches of a willow tree hung like frozen shafts of rain.

"Miasma's intensifying," I said. My limbs were heavy, my brain tugged by alien emotions of futility and despair. The taste of decay was bitter in my mouth. I took another mint to freshen things.

"Good," Lockwood said. "Shouldn't be too long."

"Telling DEPRAC about Annie Ward," George said suddenly, "is all well and good. But I *still* don't think you should have gotten the press involved so early. The police investigation's hardly started, has it? We don't know where it's going."

"Oh, yes we do. Barnes wasn't very pleased that we'd beaten them to the girl's identity, but he *was* very interested in the connection to this Hugo Blake. He looked him up in their records. Turns out that he's something of a successful businessman, but has been in prison several times for fraud, and once for serious assault. He's a nasty piece of work. And we were right: he's still alive and well, and living here in London."

"So they're bringing him in?" I said.

"They were going to do it today. Probably arrested him already."

"Ghost fog coming," George said. Faint tendrils had risen from the earth, coldly luminous, thin as spaghetti, winding between the willow and the wall.

"What do you hear, Lucy?" Lockwood asked.

"Still the same. Wind in the leaves. And a rasping squeak, squeak, squeak."

"Rope, you think?"

"Might be."

"George—see anything?"

"Not yet. What about you? Death glow still off-ground?"

"Well, it wouldn't have moved, would it? Yeah, still up there among the branches."

"Can I have a mint, Lucy?" George said. "Forgot mine."

"Sure."

I handed the packet around. Conversation lapsed. We watched the willow tree.

Despite Lockwood's high hopes for his article, we had not yet felt any benefits from its publicity, and this evening's vigil represented the last case remaining on our books. Our clients, a young married couple, had regularly experienced feelings of unease and terror near the bottom of their urban garden. On recent nights their children (ages four and six) had reported looking from the house and seeing "a dark, still shadow" standing among the trailing branches of the tree. The parents, who were with the children on each occasion, had seen nothing.

Lockwood and I had carried out an initial survey of the area that morning. The willow was very old, with high, thick branches. We'd both noticed faint background phenomena in the vicinity, mainly miasma and creeping fear. Meanwhile, George, who had been at the Archives all day, had investigated the history of the house. He had discovered one significant incident. In May, 1926, the owner, a Mr. Henry Kitchener, had hung himself somewhere on the premises. The exact location was not specified.

We had reason to suspect the tree.

"I still don't know why you mentioned me but not the necklace,"

I said. "You make it sound like Annie Ward told me personally who killed her, which we all know is rubbish. Ghosts don't communicate clearly enough. Psychic connection is a fragmentary thing."

Lockwood chuckled. "I know, but it doesn't hurt to emphasize what a star you are. We want other clients to come running, eager for your services. And I deliberately didn't mention the necklace, partly because I'm holding that back for future articles, and partly because I haven't told Barnes about it either."

"You didn't tell Barnes?" George said incredulously. "Even about the inscription?"

"Not yet. He's still livid with us, and since taking dangerous artifacts as Lucy did is kind of an offense, I thought it was safer to keep quiet about it now. Besides, why bother? The necklace doesn't really *add* anything. Even without it, Blake's clearly guilty. That reminds me, did you find anything else about the Ward case, George?"

"Yeah. Some pictures. They're interesting. I'll show you when we get back."

Time passed. The chill increased. The desolate emotions of the restless suicide seeped out from the willow, spreading between the shrubs and flower beds, the plastic bikes and children's toys scattered about the garden. The willow twigs began to rustle gently, though there wasn't any wind.

"Wonder why he did it," Lockwood murmured.

"Who?" George said. "Hugo Blake?"

"No, I was thinking about *this* case. Why the man hung himself."

I stirred. "He lost someone dear to him."

"Really? Why do you say that, Luce? Wasn't in the report, was it, George?"

My mind had been empty; I'd been listening to the squeaking in the tree. "I don't know. I'm probably wrong."

"Hold it." Lockwood's voice was sharp. "I've got a shape. . . . Yes! You both see that?"

"No. Where?"

"He's right there! Can't you see him? He's standing under the tree, looking up."

I'd felt the thing's arrival—the invisible disturbance wave, rippling outward, had made the blood pulse in my ears. But my Sight's not as good as Lockwood's, and the tree was still a web of shadows.

"He's got the rope in his hand," Lockwood muttered. "He must have stood there such a long time, willing himself to do it. . . ."

Sometimes the trick, like with stars, is to look slightly away. When I moved my eyes toward the garden wall, shadows under the tree contracted into sudden focus: I saw a pale outline, slim and motionless, the willow branches superimposed on it like bars.

"I see it." Yes, he was looking up, the head tilted, as if his neck was already broken.

"Don't look at his face," George said.

"Okay, I'm going in close," Lockwood said. "Let's all keep calm. Aaah! Something's got me!"

Twin squeals of iron: George and I had drawn our rapiers. I flicked my flashlight beam at Lockwood, who was frozen beside me, staring.

I flicked it off again.

"Nothing's got you," I said. "Your coattail's caught on a gooseberry bush."

"Oh, fine. Thanks."

A snort from George. "That coat! It's too long! It almost killed you the other night as well."

Small sounds followed as Lockwood pried his coat clear of the gooseberries. Below the willow tree, the shape had still not moved.

"Keep me covered," Lockwood said.

He drew his rapier and stole past, moving toward the tree. Ghost-fog clung about his calves and churned in milky eddies as he took each cautious stride. George and I kept pace behind him, salt-bombs ready in our hands.

We drew near the willow's outer fronds.

"Okay . . ." Lockwood breathed. "I'm close, but it hasn't reacted. It's just a Shade."

I could see it better now: the rudimentary outlines of a man in shirtsleeves, high-waisted pants, suspenders . . . A pale face tilted upward. I kept my eyes averted from that face, but I felt the echoes of an ancient grief, a loved one lost, despair beyond enduring. . . . I sensed a man's deep-throated groan.

All at once the shape moved; I saw a flash of rope, a coil flung high into the branches—

At which a small, pale missile shot past and burst upon the tree. A shower of salt cascaded out, cut through the shape. It writhed and vanished. Salt grains ignited with green fire. They pattered down like emerald snow.

I turned to George. "What did you do that for?"

"Keep your hair on. It moved. Lockwood was right there. I'm not taking chances."

"He wasn't attacking," I said. "He was too busy thinking about his wife."

"His wife? How do you *know* that? Did you hear him speak?" George said.

"No . . ."

"So how—"

"It doesn't matter." Lockwood pushed the willow twigs aside. Around his boots, green sparks winked and faded into nothing. "He's gone. Let's lace the ground with iron, and get back in the warm."

Some cases are like that—quick and easy, over in a trice. For what it's worth, the following day, an ancient ring of rope, deeply embedded in a high branch, was discovered directly above the place where the apparition had been. The rope was fused to the wood and could not be removed, so the whole branch was sawn off and burned in a salt-fire. Three days later, the owners had the tree cut down.

Arriving back at Portland Row after our vigil in the garden, we were surprised to find a police car parked outside our house, with the lights on and the engine running. A DEPRAC officer got out as we approached: a big fellow, shaven-headed, all muscle and no neck. He wore the usual night-blue uniform.

He regarded us unsmilingly. "Lockwood and Co.? At bloody last. You're to come to Scotland Yard."

Lockwood frowned. "Now? It's late. We've just been on a case."

"That's nothing to me. Barnes wants you. He *wanted* you two hours ago."

"Could it wait until tomorrow?"

The policeman's hand, pink and massive as a ham joint, alighted slowly on the iron truncheon at his belt. "No."

Lockwood's eyes flashed. "Eloquently put," he said. "All right, Sergeant. Let's go."

Scotland Yard, the headquarters of London's conventional police force, and also of the DEPRAC units that served the city in the grim night hours, was a wedge shaped block of steel and glass halfway up Victoria Street in the middle of the city. Close by stood the Gravediggers' Guild and the Union of Undertakers; also the Fairfax Iron Company; United Salts; and above all, the vast Sunrise Corporation, which manufactured equipment for most agencies in the country. On the opposite side of the road lay the offices for most of the major religions. Each one of these powerful organizations was at the heart of the ongoing war against the Problem.

Outside the Yard, lavender fires smoldered in metal tubs, and runnels of fresh water gushed across the pavement. Two red-nosed night-watch kids stood near the doors, guarding against supernatural threat. They drew back their sticks and stood at attention as the officer led us past and up some stairs to DEPRAC's center of operations.

As always after dark, the room was a hive of activity. On the back wall a giant street map of London was dotted with dozens of tiny lights, some green, some yellow, each marking the night's emergencies. Men and women in sober uniforms bustled back and forth below it, carrying sheaves of paper, talking loudly on telephones, giving orders to team leaders from the Rotwell and Fittes agencies, which often helped DEPRAC in its work. A young agent ran past us, carrying a bundle of rapiers in his arms; beyond, two policemen stood drinking coffee, their body-armor steaming from ectoplasm burns.

The officer showed us into a waiting room and left us. It was quieter here. Above our heads, iron mobiles moved in the breeze from hidden fans. Air conditioning thrummed.

"What do you think he wants?" I asked. "Something more about the fire?"

Lockwood shrugged. "I *hope* it's news about Blake. Maybe they've got him. Maybe he's confessed."

"Speaking of which . . ." George foraged in his bag. "While we're waiting, you might take a look at these clippings from the Archives. I've found out more about Annie Ward. Seems that, fifty years ago, she was part of a glitzy set—mostly rich kids, but not all—who hung out in the swankiest bars in London. A year before she died, *London Society* did a photo piece on them. Check it out. She's not the only name you'll recognize."

The pictures, photocopied from the originals, were in black and white. They were mostly of balls and parties, but of casinos and card games, too. Young, glamorous people clustered in every shot. Apart from the dress styles (and the lack of color) they were little different from those in the modern magazines that Lockwood read, and just about as dull—but on the third or fourth sheet, I was suddenly brought up short. There were two photos on this page. The first was a studio shot of a sleek young man, smiling at the camera. He wore a black top hat, a black bow tie, a jet-black jacket. There was probably a frilly shirt as well, but that was mercifully hidden behind the cane in his hand. He had white gloves, too. His hair was long, dark, and luxuriant; his face handsome in a fleshy way. The smile was confident and ingratiating. It said it *knew* how much you'd like him, if you'd only take the chance.

Underneath, a caption: *Mr. Hugo Blake: Today's Man About Town.*

"There he is," Lockwood breathed.

I stared at the glossy, self-satisfied face. As I did so, *another* face—laced with dust and cobwebs—came into my mind.

"And he's in this one too," George said.

Directly below it, another picture. This was a group photo, taken from some high vantage point. Young men and women standing by a fountain. It must have been some tedious summer gala, because all the men were in white tie and tails, while the girls wore full ball dresses. There were straps and sequins and ruched shoulders, and I don't know what else. Dresses aren't my thing. It was a black-and-white shot, but those dresses had beautiful colors, you could just tell. The girls were arranged mostly at the front, with the men crowding in behind. They were all grinning up at the camera like they owned the world, which some of them maybe did. And right in the center was Annie Ward. She was so radiant, it was like the other-light was already on her. The women standing next to her wore resigned smiles, as if they knew they were being put in the shade.

"Here's Blake," George said, pointing to a tall figure grinning in the row behind. "Right at her shoulder. It's like he's stalking her, even here."

"And look. . . ." With a jolt I noticed a tiny oval smudge just visible beneath the girl's white throat. I felt my own throat tightening. "She's got the necklace on."

"Oh, you've *all* come, have you?" Inspector Barnes stood in the doorway, glaring down at us. He looked weary; even his mustache had a slightly mournful droop. He carried a file of reports in one hand and a styrofoam cup of coffee in the other. "What joy. Going to make me spill my drink again?"

Lockwood stood. "We've come at your request, Mr. Barnes," he said coolly. "How can we be of service to you?"

"Well, not all of you *can*." He looked particularly at George. "You got rid of that ghost-jar yet, Cubbins?"

"Certainly have, Mr. Barnes," said George.

"Mm. Well, as it happens I don't need you tonight—nor you either, Lockwood. It's Miss Carlyle I want to speak to." The hangdog eyes appraised me; I felt the keenness of his stare. "Please come with me now, miss. You others wait here."

A pang of fright speared through my chest; I looked anxiously at Lockwood, who'd stepped forward, frowning. "Nothing doing, Inspector," he said. "She's my employee. I insist on being present whatever you're—"

"*If* you want to be charged with obstructing an investigation," Barnes growled, "keep right on talking. I've had enough of you this week. Well? Anything more to say?"

Lockwood fell silent. I smiled as best I could at him. "It's fine," I said. "I'll be okay."

"Of course she will." Barnes pulled the door aside and ushered me past. "Don't fret. We won't be long."

He led me out and across the operations room to a smooth steel door on the far side. Here he keyed in a number on a pad; the door slid open, revealing a quiet corridor lit by neon strip-lights.

"Your friend Lockwood *tells* me," Barnes said, as we set off down the corridor, "that you achieved a psychic connection with the ghost of Annie Ward. Is that true?"

"Yes, sir. I heard her voice."

"He also *says* you gained an important insight about her death—that she was killed by a man she'd once loved."

"Yes, sir." Well, that was true too—up to a point. I'd had that insight when I touched the necklace. I hadn't learned it from the ghost-girl herself.

Barnes looked at me sidelong. "When she spoke to you, did she give you his name?"

"No, sir. It was just . . . random fragments. You know what Visitors are like."

He grunted. "They say Marissa Fittes held whole conversations with Type Three ghosts back in the old days, and so learned many things. But that's a rare power, and those are rare ghosts. The rest of us have to make do with whatever pathetic scraps we can get. Okay . . . this is the High Security Zone. We're almost there."

We had taken a concrete staircase to a lower level. The doors around us were heavier now, and made of banded iron. Several of them had black-rimmed warning signs fixed against the wall: yellow triangles showing a single grinning skull, red triangles showing two. The air had grown cool; I guessed we were now underground.

"Now, listen," Barnes said. "Thanks to your discoveries, I've reopened the Annabel Ward case." He glared at me askance. "Don't think we weren't close to figuring out her identity too. You may have gotten there quicker, but that's because you're three kids messing about, who have nothing better to do. Be that as it may, I've looked into the connection with this Hugo Blake and I think he's guilty. I arrested him today."

My heart leaped. "Good!"

"However . . ." Barnes had stopped outside a plain iron door. "Fifty years later, Blake still denies it all. He says he dropped the girl off at the house and never went inside."

"He's lying," I said.

"I'm sure he is, but I'd like more evidence. And that's where you come in. All right, in you go, please."

Before I could speak he had ushered me past the door and into a small, dark room, empty except for two steel and leather chairs and a little table. The chairs faced the opposite wall, which consisted of a single pane of fogged gray glass. There was a switch built into the table, and also a black telephone receiver.

"Sit down, Miss Carlyle." Barnes picked up the receiver and spoke into it. "Okay? Is he there? That's fine."

I stared at him. "What are you talking about? Please tell me what's going on."

"Psychic links like you had with the dead girl," Barnes said, "are very subjective things. Hard to put into words. You remember some things and forget others. Basically, they mess with your mind. So it's possible that the ghost *did* communicate more about her killing than you recall. The face of her murderer, for instance."

I shook my head, suddenly understanding. "You mean Blake? No. I just saw a photo of him now. It didn't mean a thing to me."

"It may be different in the flesh," Barnes said. "We'll see, shall we?"

Panic filled me. "Mr. Barnes, I really don't want to do this. I've told you everything."

"Just take a look. He won't be able to see you. It's one-way glass. He won't even know you're there."

"No, please, Mr. Barnes . . ."

The inspector ignored me. He pressed the switch on the table. In front of us, bright light split the center of the pane of glass. The brightness widened. Internal shutters drew aside like curtains to reveal a spotlit room.

A man sat on a metal chair in the center of that room, facing toward us. If you disregarded the one-way glass, he was about six to nine feet away.

He was an elderly gentleman in a smart, sharp suit, black with a thin pink pinstripe. His shoes were brightly polished, his tie bright pink; a hot-pink handkerchief erupted from his breast pocket like a flame. Hugo Blake clearly retained the dandyish taste that he'd displayed in that black-and-white photo, fifty years before. The hair was slate-gray, but still long and still luxuriant; it brushed against his shoulders with soft, indulgent curls.

So much, then, was still the same—but not the face.

The smooth, complacent looks of youth had been replaced by a ravaged expanse, gaunt and gray and lined. Bones jutted like plowshares beneath the skin. The nose had a net of thick blue veins that had begun to spread across the cheeks and chin. The lips were shrunken—tight and thin and hard. And the eyes—

The eyes were the worst. Sunk deep in hollow sockets, they were bright and cold, and full of anger and intelligence. They moved ceaselessly, staring all about him, scanning the surface of the blank glass wall. The man's fury was apparent. His hands dug like claws into his knees. He was speaking, but I couldn't hear the words.

"Blake's rich," Barnes chuckled, "and used to getting his own way. He's not at all happy to be here. But that's not your problem. Take a good look, Miss Carlyle. Let your mind empty; think back to what you got from the girl. Does this trigger anything?"

I took a deep breath, squashed my anxiety down. After all, it *was* going to be okay. He couldn't actually see me. I'd do what Barnes wanted, then be gone.

I focused my attention on the face—

And as I did so, the old man's eyes locked suddenly into mine. They became quite still. It was as if he saw straight through the barrier and knew that I was there.

He smiled at me. It was a smile full of teeth.

I jolted right back in my seat. "No!" I said. "That's enough! I don't get anything. It's triggered nothing. Please. Please stop now! That's enough."

Barnes hesitated, then pressed the button. The shutters drew together, unhurriedly blocking out the spotlit, smiling man.

Chapter 15

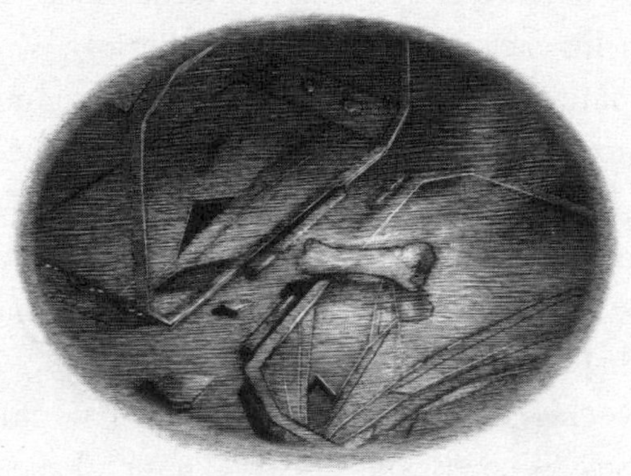

"Lucy," Lockwood said. "Stop. You need to talk to me."

"No. No, I really don't."

"Stop going so fast. I understand why you're angry, but you've got to realize—I didn't know Barnes was going to ask you to do that."

"No? Maybe you should have guessed. Thanks to your stupid article this morning, the whole *world* knows about my psychic link to Annie Ward. I'm suddenly considered central to the case!"

"Lucy, please—" Lockwood grabbed my sleeve, forced me to stop in the middle of the street. We were in Mayfair somewhere, about halfway home. The mansions were quiet, mostly hidden behind high walls and the swirling mist. It had just turned midnight. Not even the ghosts were around.

"Don't touch me," I said. I shook myself clear. "Because of your article, I came face-to-face with a murderer tonight, and funnily enough, I didn't enjoy the experience. You didn't see his *eyes*, Lockwood. But *I* saw them—and it felt like he saw *me*."

"He can't have." George's face was turned away from us; with his hand on his rapier hilt he watched the fog. We'd only seen one Visitor during our walk—in Green Park, a figure drifting far off along a tree-lined avenue—but it always paid to be careful. You could never tell what was around the next corner in London. "He can't have seen you," George repeated. "You were behind the glass. Obviously he knew *someone* was there, and he just wanted to freak them out. That's all there is to it."

"You're wrong," I said quietly. "Blake *knew* it was me. He'd have seen that article like everybody else. He knows all about Lockwood and Company, and how Lucy 'Carlisle' has gained vital evidence against him. He can easily find where we live, too. If he walks free, there's nothing to stop him from coming after us!"

Lockwood shook his head. "Lucy, Blake is *not* going to come after us."

"Or if he does," George said, "it'll be very, very slowly, hobbling on a stick. He's over seventy years old."

"What I *mean* is, he's not walking free at all," Lockwood went on. "He's going to be charged, found guilty, and go to prison, which serves him right. Meanwhile, so what that he's got strange eyes? George's are pretty odd too, and we don't hold it against him."

"Thanks for that," George said. "I thought they were my best feature."

"They are—that's the tragedy of it. Listen, Lucy. I can see why you're mad. I'm furious too. Barnes had no right to put you through that against your will. It's typical DEPRAC behavior—they think they rule the show. But they don't—or at least, they don't rule *us*." Lockwood raised his arms and gestured at the swirling fog, the silent road. "Look around you now. It's past midnight. We're alone in an empty city. Everyone else is asleep, with their doors locked and their charms hanging at the windows. Everyone's afraid—except for you, me, and George. We go wherever we choose, and we're not beholden to Barnes or DEPRAC or anybody. We're completely free."

I drew my coat around me. What he said made sense, as usual. It *was* good to be out in the night again, with my sword and my colleagues at my side. The distress of my brief encounter at Scotland Yard was slowly fading. I felt a little better. "I suppose you're right. . . ." I said. "You really think Blake's staying in custody?"

"Of course he is."

"By the way, Lucy," George said, "here's something that might cheer you up. We saw Quill Kipps while we were waiting for you. He's part of a Fittes group working for DEPRAC tonight. Has to do it regularly—it's part of the deal between the organizations. Well, let's just say he's been patrolling the sewers this evening. His team's clearly had a close encounter with *something* nasty down there, and I don't mean a Visitor. Yeuch, you should have seen them. Soaked."

I couldn't help but laugh. "At least Kipps still *has* a job. Our casebook's empty now."

"Better to be poor than sticky," George said.

Lockwood squeezed my arm. "Come on," he said. "Don't worry about tomorrow. Something will turn up. Let's get home. I fancy a peanut-butter sandwich."

I nodded. "Cocoa and chips for me."

The mist grew thicker as we went; it coiled about the iron

railings, and wound around the ghost-lamps, muffling and twisting their intermittent beams. Our boots rang on the empty sidewalks, echoing strangely on the other side of the road, so that it sometimes seemed as if another trio walked invisibly alongside us.

In Portland Row there had been a malfunction with the ghost-lamp; blue sparks flickered at the base of the headpiece and, instead of their usual fierce brightness, the lenses glowed a frail, resentful red. Most of our neighbors' windows were dark, and all were shut and curtained. The mist clung close about us as we drew level with our door.

Lockwood was in the lead; he reached out his hand to open the gate and suddenly stopped dead. George and I both bumped into him.

"George," Lockwood said quietly. "You had Annie Ward's necklace last. What did you do with it?"

"I put it on the shelves with all the other trophies. Why?"

"Its silver-glass case was sealed? It wasn't loose or anything?"

"Of course not. What—"

"I just saw a light in our office window."

He pointed down over the railing. The basement yard was a pool of blackness, diagonally sliced by the faint orange glow from the street-lamp outside Number 37. Half in and half out of that glow sat the window in question. By day it gave a glimpse of my work chair, and the vase of flowers on the center of my desk. Right now it was entirely flat, as if a black rectangle had been painted on the brickwork.

"I don't see anything," George breathed.

"It was just for a second," Lockwood said. "I thought it might be a trace of other-light, but maybe— No, there it is again!"

This time we'd *all* seen the shimmer, faint and fleeting, glinting off the interior of the glass. Shock held us in its grip; none of us moved.

"That was a flashlight," George said softly.

I nodded; my skin crawled. "Someone's in our house."

"Someone," Lockwood said, "who's not afraid of being out at night. Which means that they're armed. They'll have rapiers or flares, at the very least. All right, let's think. How did they get in?"

I squinted up the path. "Front door looks okay."

"You want me to check out the back?" George said. "They may have busted in through the garden door."

"But if they haven't, you'll be stuck outside. . . . No, we need to work together on this. We'll go in the front as usual—only *quietly*. Come on."

Lockwood flitted up the path, moving soundlessly on the tiles. At the porch he halted, pointing in silence to a little patch of splintered wood halfway up the door jamb. When he pushed the door, it swung slowly open.

"They jimmied the lock," George hissed.

"If this was their way in," Lockwood said, "we can trap them down below." He beckoned us close, whispered in our ears. "Okay. We check the ground floor, then go down the spiral stairs. I don't want to hear a sound."

"What about the upper floors?"

"Can't risk it. The landing squeaks. Besides, it's clearly the office that they're raiding. So: rapiers ready? We find them, corner them, ask them to disarm."

"And if they don't?" I said.

Lockwood's teeth glinted briefly. "We use what force we need."

—

The hallway was black; no sound came from deeper in the building. We halted a moment, with the door pulled closed behind us, letting our eyes adjust. The crystal skull lantern grinned from its side table; our coat rack was a dark mass on the wall. Lockwood pointed with his rapier at the display shelves opposite. At first sight they were the same as ever; then I saw that some of the masks and gourds were slightly out of position, as if someone had sorted through them with a hasty hand. Far ahead of us, I made out the dull white glow of the thinking-cloth beyond the kitchen door. I listened again, heard nothing. I realized I was automatically using *all* my senses, both outer and inner, as if we were away on business, doing the agent thing.

But this was *our* house, *our* home, and we had an intruder here.

Lockwood motioned with the blade to left and right. George flitted into the living room; I stepped like a shadow into the library. I could sense right away it was empty: there was no trace of a lingering presence. But it hadn't escaped our guest's attention. Below the shelves, books and papers lay strewn upon the floor.

Back in the hall, Lockwood waited by the stairs. George's report was similar to mine. "Someone's working the place over," he breathed. "Hunting for something."

Lockwood only nodded. We stole forward to the kitchen.

Whether or not our enemy had rifled through our possessions here was hard to say, since the room was its usual mess. The table was strewn with the remnants of the meal we'd eaten before going out on the garden job, and the work surfaces were clogged with clutter. I noticed the pots of iron filings nestling by the cereal, and a little pile of salt-bombs stacked where George had been preparing them. None of that was useful to us now: we went in search of human prey.

Lockwood advanced to the little basement door. It was very slightly open. With the tip of his blade he caught the handle, pulled it softly outward. Darkness, silence, the top of the spiral stairs. . . . Warm air rose from below, heavy with its smells of paper, ink, and magnesium. The lights were out, and we didn't try to switch them on. From somewhere came a little scuffling noise, like rats nosing through tight spaces in the dark.

We looked at one another, clenched our sword hilts tight. Lockwood set foot upon the topmost step. He descended, moving swiftly. George and I followed, boots barely making contact with the iron. In moments we were at the bottom.

The exposed-brick room we stood in was an empty portion of the cellar, occupied only by filing cabinets and sacks of iron. Without the lights, it was entirely black, except for a faintly greenish glow shining from the archway on the right. From the opposite arch came the ratlike scuffling. A teasing hint of flashlight darted momentarily and was gone.

Drifting softly as Visitors ourselves, we double-checked the right-hand arch and found a scene of chaos. Files upended, cupboards opened, a sea of papers on the office floor. On George's desk the ghost-jar had been uncovered. The skull was silhouetted in its luminous green plasm. Above it, the disembodied face spun dismally around and around.

The rapier room was empty, our storeroom door still locked. All that remained was the rear of the basement—where the trophy shelves were. We flitted closer. Ahead of us it seemed that someone grew impatient in their search. The rustling noises sounded rather louder than before.

We reached the final arch, and looked in.

The trophy room was not entirely dark. It rarely is, by night, thanks to the glow of the cases on the shelves beside the door. Some of Lockwood's prizes—the bones and bloodstained playing cards, for instance—are entirely harmless. You could give them to a toddler to play with, because they have no supernatural power. But others are active Sources still, with spectral force that manifests during the hours of darkness. Soft lights glint beneath the glass—pale blues and yellows, lilacs, greens, maroons—shifting, ever-changing, always looking for escape. It's a beautiful sight—but also eerie, and best not studied for too long.

Someone *was* studying them now.

A shape stood beside the shelves, a hulking figure dressed in black. It was a man, broad in the shoulder and half a head taller than Lockwood; he wore a coat, with the hood drawn up to hide the face. A rapier hung at his belt. He was turned away from us, examining one of the smaller cases in a black-gloved hand. He had his flashlight trained on it closely; spears of light reflected off its facets and extended over the ceiling.

Whatever he sought, he didn't find. He tossed the case contemptuously on the floor.

"Can I offer you some tea while you ransack our place?" Lockwood said politely.

The figure wheeled around. Lockwood shone his flashlight full into the intruder's face.

Despite myself, I let out a gasp. The hood hung forward, curving like a raptor's beak. Beneath this cowl, the face was covered by a white cloth mask. The eye sockets were black slashed holes. Another slash, jagged and off-center, formed the mouth. Nothing of the man beneath it could be seen.

The intruder was clearly blinded by the flashlight. He raised an arm against the beam.

"That's right. Put up your hands," Lockwood said.

The arm shot down. It reached for the rapier.

"It's three against one," Lockwood pointed out.

A swish of metal: the sword was drawn.

"Be like that, then." Lockwood raised his blade, stepped slowly forward.

Plan C seemed the obvious maneuver in the circumstances. We normally use it on powerful Type Twos, of course, but it works for mortal enemies as well. I went to the left, George to the right. Lockwood held the center. Our blades were up and ready. We moved steadily inward, hemming the intruder in.

Or so we thought. The white-masked figure seemed unconcerned. He raised his left hand to the shelves and grasped a case that glowed with a dim blue light. Turning, he threw it with appalling force, so that it struck the floor at George's feet. Hinges cracked, the case broke open; a fragment of finger bone fell out. At once the light escaped, bled outward like a little cloud. A faint blue apparition rose from the floorboards. It took the shape of a hopping, deformed creature dressed in rags. It rolled its head, threw back its arms and, with a sinuous sidelong plunge, sprang straight at George.

I saw no more, for the intruder had seized two other cases and thrown them at Lockwood and at me. Lockwood's bounced, but didn't open. Mine shattered completely, emitting a woman's hair fastener, six streams of yellow plasm, and a violent psychic wail. The streams rolled and tumbled on the floor, then rose like striking cobras and swung in my direction. With frantic hacks and swipes, I sliced them to ribbons. Some instantly dissipated and were gone; others fused and returned to the attack.

A clash of blades. Lockwood had leaped past and closed in on the enemy. Their rapiers met, and met again. Beyond, George parried the Specter's flailing blows. He drove it back, wove iron patterns in the air.

The Visitor I faced was weak and tentative. It was time to snuff it out. I scrabbled in my belt, located a bag of filings. Ripping it clear, I tossed it down. A burst of sparkling light. The thrashing plasm shrank and dwindled, became a smoking puddle on the floor.

Beside me iron smote on iron; Lockwood and the intruder moved back and forth in the center of the room, exchanging rapid strikes. The man in the mask was fast, his attacks accurate and heavy, but Lockwood remained at ease. He moved in a swaying dance step, a sashaying, drifty sort of motion. His boots hardly touched the ground. His rapier arm gave delicate twitches, the blade tip changing position like some nimble dragonfly.

George grew impatient with his contest; dropping back a little, he took a salt-bomb from his belt and blew his shambling Specter into twinkling motes of sapphire light. The noise distracted Lockwood, who glanced aside. At once the masked enemy swung his rapier at Lockwood's face. It would have been an awful injury—if it had struck. Lockwood leaned away; the edge swished past his cheek. With his enemy unbalanced, Lockwood stepped to the side, jabbed his sword forward. The figure gave a cry, clutched at his midriff. With desperate strikes, he drove Lockwood back and, plunging past him, ran across the room. George reached out to stop him. A gloved fist swung, caught George across the cheek, sent him crashing with a moan against the wall.

The intruder raced across the room toward the spiral stairs, with Lockwood in pursuit. I jumped over the fading ribbons of yellow plasm and closed in, swiping blindly with my rapier. The man fled past the stairs and through the arch into the front office. For a moment his silhouette was illuminated by the faint light seeping through its window, and I understood what he was going to do.

"Lockwood!" I cried. "Quick! He'll—"

Lockwood already knew the danger; even as he ran, he reached to his belt, plucked out a canister of Fire.

The intruder put on a spurt, drew near my desk. He leaped upon it and, as he did so, threw his arms across his face. He collided with the window in a crouched position, smashing through the pane in a whirl of spinning shards.

Lockwood cursed; from the far end of the office, he hurled the flare. It passed straight through the broken window and out into the yard. We heard the canister crack upon the stones. A silver-white explosion lit up the night, sending the remaining fragments of window glass hurtling back into the room. They spilled across the desk, clattering against the ghost-jar, so the head inside it winced and goggled. Shards like spilled ice fanned out across the floor.

Lockwood sprang onto the table, sword in hand; I came to a halt behind him. We went no farther. We knew we were too late. Out in the yard, little white fires flickered in the broken flowerpots, and danced and dwindled like Christmas lights across the hanging ivy. Smoke rose toward the street; somewhere up above us, a variety of car alarms beeped and yammered. But it had all been for nothing. The intruder was gone. At the top of the steps, the front gate swung gently, gently. It came slowly to a halt.

Lockwood jumped back to the floor. Behind us, a shape emerged: George, shuffling painfully, clutching the side of his jaw. He was bleeding from a cut to his lower lip. I gave him a wan smile of sympathy; Lockwood patted his arm.

"That was exciting," George said thickly. "We should have guests over more often."

All at once I felt lightheaded. My legs gave way; I supported myself upon the desk. For the first time since the fight began, I remembered the aches and strains left over from the Sheen Road fall. Lockwood must have experienced a similar come-down. It took him two or three tries to fix his rapier back into his belt.

"George," he said. "The Annabel Ward necklace. You said you put it with the trophies. Mind going to see if it's still there?"

George dabbed at his lip with his shirtsleeve. "Don't need to. I already thought of that. Just had a look. It's gone."

"You're sure you put it on the shelves?"

"This very morning. It's definitely not there."

There was a silence. "You think that's what he came for?" I asked.

Lockwood sighed. "It's possible. Anyway, he's clearly got it now."

"No," I said. "He hasn't." At which I pulled my collar aside, to reveal the silver-glass case with the pendant in it, hanging safely on its cord around my neck.

Chapter 16

I should point out, I guess, that I'm not in the habit of secreting haunted objects on my person. I certainly don't have any other sinister artifacts stuffed down my socks, as George suggested. The necklace was a weird one-off for me.

I'd seen it the previous afternoon, as we got ready for the assignment by the willow tree. George had put it on the trophy shelf along with all the other curios. It just lay there in its little protective case, sparkling dully behind the glass. And instead of leaving it, as any ordinary person would have, I'd picked the case up, hung it around my neck, and simply walked away.

Explaining *why* I'd done this wasn't exactly easy, especially considering the state we were all in after the fight. So it wasn't until after a very late breakfast the following day that I tried to give my reasons.

"I just wanted to keep the necklace close at hand," I said. "Not shoved in with all the other trophies. I think it's because of what happened when I touched it, when I got that psychic connection with Annie Ward. The sensations I experienced then were *her* sensations. I felt what *she* felt, I got a glimpse of *being* her. So—"

"That's the danger of your Talent," Lockwood said abruptly. He was pale and serious that morning; he regarded me with narrowed eyes. "You're almost too sensitive. You get too close to them."

"No, don't get me wrong," I said. "I'm not close to Annie Ward at all. I don't think she was a particularly nice person when alive, and she's certainly a cruel and dangerous ghost. But, because of my Touch, I *do* understand something of what she went through. I understand her pain. And that means I want justice for her now. I don't want her forgotten. You saw her lying in that chimney, Lockwood! You know what Blake did. So, when I saw the necklace dumped there with all the other trophies, it just . . . it just seemed wrong to me. Until that man's been punished, and justice is properly done, I don't think we should . . . discard her." I gave them a rueful smile. "Don't tell me . . . that's basically a bit crazy, isn't it?"

"Yep," George said.

"You need to be careful, Lucy," Lockwood said, and his voice was flat and cold. "Wicked ghosts aren't things to trifle with. You're keeping secrets again, and any agent who does that is endangering the rest of us. I'm not having anyone on my team who can't be trusted. You understand what I'm saying?"

I did understand. I looked away.

"However . . ." he went on, in a slightly lighter tone, "by chance it's all worked out quite well. This necklace would probably have been stolen, if it wasn't for you."

He had it in his hand as he spoke, the gold surface of the pendant glinting in the sun. We stood in the basement, beside the open garden door. Cool air drifted in, diluting the taint of decay left by the freed Visitors in the night. The floor was littered with broken glass and plasm stains. George had been working at the trophy shelves, sorting through the cases. He wore an apron with slightly lacy edges, and he had his sleeves rolled up. "Nothing else has been nicked," he said, "which, if that guy was a normal thief working for the black market, *is* a little strange. There are some first rate pieces here. The pirate hand, for instance, or this lovely fibula . . ."

Lockwood shook his head. "No. It's the necklace he wanted. It's too much of a coincidence otherwise. *Someone* needs it badly."

"Well, we know who that someone is," I said. "Hugo Blake."

George paused. "Only one problem. He's currently locked up."

"He's in custody," Lockwood agreed, "but that doesn't mean much. He's a wealthy man. He might easily have arranged the raid. But I must admit, I don't quite understand why the necklace is so important to him. That Latin inscription doesn't prove him guilty, does it?" He hesitated. "Unless . . ."

"Unless," I said, "the necklace contains *another* clue or secret that Blake doesn't want found out."

"Exactly. Let's look at it in daylight."

We stepped outside into the little garden. Lockwood held the necklace up for us to inspect. It seemed exactly as before: an oval pendant, gold with pearly flakes, rather squashed and split along one side.

I gazed at it. Split along the side . . .

"We're idiots," I gasped. "It's staring at us in the face."

Lockwood glanced at me. "Meaning . . ."

"Meaning it's *supposed* to have a split! It's a *locket*. It opens! We can open it."

I took the pendant from him and pressed the corners of my thumbnails into the narrow crack. I pried gently. Despite its distorted shape, there was an immediate, satisfying click; the pendant split in two, neatly swiveling on its hinge. I pulled the halves apart, held it open on my palm.

I don't quite know what I expected, but I expected *something*. A twist of hair, maybe? A photograph? People keep things in lockets. That's what they're for.

As one, we stared at the locket's open halves.

There wasn't any hair. Or a photograph, a keepsake, or a tiny folded letter. But that didn't mean the locket was empty. No. There *was* something there.

It was another inscription, neatly scored into the smooth gold of the interior:

A ‡ W
H.II.2.115

"Here it is," Lockwood said. "The hidden clue. *This* is what he wanted to hide."

"The AW's obviously Annabel Ward," I said.

"And the H is for Hugo," George breathed. "As in Hugo Blake . . ."

Lockwood frowned. "That's good as far as it goes. But there

must be more. What about these numbers? This is some kind of code. . . ."

"We'd better give this to DEPRAC," I said suddenly. "We can't hold on to it. This is serious evidence, which the police will need to see. And Blake knows it's here."

"You're probably right," Lockwood said. "Not that I *really* want to come clean with Barnes. I'd rather we figured this out ourselves. Still . . ." The phone rang shrilly in the office. "Maybe we haven't got much choice. Answer that, would you, George?"

George departed and was gone for a long time. When he returned, Lockwood had returned the locket to its case and I'd started sweeping up the debris on the floor.

"Don't tell me," Lockwood said. "Barnes again?"

George's features were slightly flushed. "Actually, no. A new client."

"I assume some old lady with a ghost-cat up a tree?"

"Nope, and you might want to leave that, Lucy, and start tidying upstairs. That was Mr. John Fairfax, Chairman of Fairfax Iron, and he's coming over now."

It was generally accepted that the Problem afflicting the British Isles was a bad thing for the economy. The dead returning to haunt the living, apparitions after dark—these things had consequences. Morale and productivity were low. No one wanted late-shifts. In winter, businesses closed mid-afternoon. But some companies *did* flourish, because they fulfilled a vital need. One of these was Fairfax Iron.

Already a leading manufacturer of iron products when the crisis began, Fairfax Iron immediately set about supplying seals, filings, and chains to the Fittes and Rotwell agencies. As the Problem worsened, and the government began to mass-produce ghost-lamps, it was Fairfax Iron that provided the vast quantities of metal required. This alone secured the company's fortune. But, of course, there was more. Those ugly iron gnomes that people dotted around their gardens? Those dorky Protecto® necklaces? Those little plastic bracelets with the smiley iron faces they put on babies' wrists before they left the hospital? Fairfax products, every one.

The company's owner, John William Fairfax, was, as a result, one of the richest men in the country, up there with the silver barons, with the heirs of Marissa Fittes and Tom Rotwell, and with that bloke who owns the great lavender farms on the Lincolnshire Wolds. Fairfax lived somewhere in London, and when he snapped his fingers, the ministers of whichever government was currently in office scampered hot-foot to his house.

Now he was coming here in person.

You can be sure we tidied that living room double-quick.

A few minutes later, the purr of a large vehicle sounded in the street. I peeped out, to see a shiny Rolls-Royce idling to a halt. It seemed to fill the street. It had polished silver-coated grilles on the windows, and threads of silver tracery running down the sides. On the hood, a small silver figurehead glinted in the winter sun.

The chauffeur emerged; smoothing down his crisp gray uniform, he marched around the car to open a rear door. I ducked back inside, where Lockwood was frantically plumping cushions, and George brushed cake crumbs beneath the sofa. "He's *here*," I hissed.

Lockwood took a deep breath. "Okay. Let's try to make a good impression."

We stood up when Mr. John Fairfax entered the room, not that it made much difference. He was a very tall, thin man. He towered over me, towered over Lockwood. George, trailing in his wake, was entirely in his shadow. Even at seventy or eighty, or whatever age he'd reached, he was built on an impressive scale, like something you'd expect to launch down a slip at Southampton docks. Yet his limbs were thin and wasted. The sleeves of his long silk jacket hung loose; his legs, despite the walking stick that supported him, trembled as he walked. My immediate impression was of a peculiar mix of strength and weakness. In a room of a hundred people, he would have been impossible to ignore.

"Good morning, sir," Lockwood was saying. "This is Lucy Carlyle, my associate."

"Delighted." The voice was deep, the outstretched hand vast and all-encompassing. A great square head, bald and liver-spotted, bent in my direction from on high. The nose was hooked, the black eyes bright and shining; the lines on the brow were heavy. When he smiled (it was scarcely a smile at all, rather an acknowledgment of my existence) I saw the teeth were capped in silver. It was a face used to exerting authority and command.

"Pleased to meet you," I said.

We sat. Our guest engulfed his chair. His walking stick was mahogany, with an iron handle shaped like a dog's head: a mastiff or bulldog, maybe. He rested it against one great bent knee and spread his fingers on the seat arms.

"It's an honor to have you here, sir," Lockwood said. "Would you like some tea?"

Mr. Fairfax inclined his head, gave a rumble of assent. "Pitkins' Breakfast, if you have it. Tell your boy to bring the sugar, too."

"My boy? Er, yes. Off you go, George. Teas all round, please."

George, who had neglected to remove his apron, rotated a leg, and exited the room, expressionless.

"Now, Mr. Lockwood," John Fairfax said, "I'm a busy man, and as you'll be wondering why I've called upon you unannounced on a Friday morning, we'll dispense with the small talk and get down to business. There is a haunting that is proving most troublesome to me. If you can help me with it, I shall make it worth your while."

Lockwood nodded gravely. "Certainly, sir. We'd be glad to."

Our visitor cast his gaze around the room. "A nice house you have. Excellent collection of New Guinean ghost-wards, I see. . . . Business going well?"

"Tolerably, sir."

"You lie like a politician, Mr. Lockwood," the old man said. "Smooth and effortless. My mother, God rest her soul and may she never walk at night, told me to speak plainly and honestly to all men. I have followed her advice all my life. So, come—" He slapped his knee with his great flat palm. "We shall get on much better if we are open with each other! Your business is *not* going well. I read the papers! I know you are in financial difficulty . . . in particular following a certain incident with a house you managed to burn down." He chuckled, a dry reverberation. "You have a heavy fine to pay."

A muscle twitched in Lockwood's cheek; otherwise he gave no

sign of irritation. "That's correct, sir, though I am in the process of raising the money. We have plenty of other excellent cases, which give us a healthy income."

Fairfax made a dismissive gesture. "Fibbing again, Mr. Lockwood! I should tell you I have contacts in DEPRAC, and I have read your recent files. I know the extent and quality of those 'excellent' cases. Gray Hazes! Cold Maidens! Gibbering Mists! The weakest and most humdrum Type Ones imaginable! I'm surprised you earn enough to pay Miss Carlyle here."

Which was a good point, come to think of it. I *hadn't* been paid for a month.

Lockwood's eyes glinted. "That being so, sir, might I ask why you have come to us today? There are many other agencies in London."

"Indeed there are." Fairfax raised his tufted eyebrows and fixed us both with his black and beady stare. "But it so happens that your recent publicity surrounding that case drew my favorable attention. I was impressed by the way in which you not only found the body of—" He hesitated. "What was the name of the girl?"

"Annie Ward, sir."

"Of Annie Ward, but discovered her identity, too. I like your panache, I like your attention to detail. I also like your youth and independence of mind!" The old man leaned forward on his stick. There was something new in his face; not warmth, exactly, more a fierce enthusiasm. "I began as an outsider too, Mr. Lockwood. I struggled hard to make my way when I was a lad. I fought against big companies, knew lean times. . . . I understand the passion that drives you on, each day! Besides, I've no interest in giving yet more money to Fittes or Rotwell. They're rich enough already. No, I propose to give you an opportunity you've never dreamed of, to see if you can bring your powers to bear on a different, more dangerous puzzle. . . . Ah, your fellow's back again."

George had returned, carrying the tray, on which he'd assembled a tea service I'd never before set eyes on. It was all fine bone china and little pink flowers, the kind of dainty cups that are so delicate and brittle, you expect them to shatter when you put them to your lips. This classy effect was slightly undermined by a teetering pile of fat jelly doughnuts on a plate beside them.

"Thanks, George," Lockwood said. "Put them down here."

George set the tray on the table, poured out the tea, and offered the doughnuts around. Since no one took one, he pried the biggest of all from the bottom of the stack, fingering most of the others in the process, plonked it on a plate, and sat next to me with a lingering sigh of gratification. "Shove over," he said. "So, have I missed anything?"

The old man's eyes widened. "Mr. Lockwood, this is an important consultation! Surely your office help should wait outside."

"Er, he's not actually an office boy, sir. This is George Cubbins. He works with me."

Mr. Fairfax appraised George, who was busily licking jelly off his fingers. "I see. . . . Well, in that case, I shall delay no longer." He put a hand inside his jacket and rummaged awkwardly within. "Take a look at this." He threw a crumpled photograph on the table.

A house. More than a mere house, in fact: it was a country mansion, set on extensive grounds. The photo had been taken from some distance across a stretch of attractively mown lawn. Willow trees and flowerbeds were featured on the margins, and there was also the suggestion of a lake, but the house beyond dominated all—a tall, dark slab of several floors. You could see columns and sweeping entrance stairs, and a profusion of thin, irregularly positioned windows, but the precise age and nature of the building was hard to make out. The photo seemed to have been taken either very early or very late. The sun was somewhere behind the building, and the long black shadows of its many ancient chimneys stretched out like grasping fingers across the lawns.

"Combe Carey Hall," Fairfax said, rolling the syllables off his tongue. "In Berkshire, just to the west of London. Have you heard of it?"

We shook our heads. None of us had.

"No, it is not well known, and yet possibly it is the most haunted private house in England. I believe it may well be the most deadly. To my certain knowledge, four previous owners of the estate have died there as a result of its apparitions. As for the numbers of servants, guests, or other folk who have been frightened to death, or ghost-touched, or otherwise drawn to their doom across the house and grounds . . ." He gave a small, dry chuckle. "Well, the list is extensive. In fact, the place was boarded up thirty years ago after some gruesome scandal of that kind, and not reopened until recently, when it came into my possession."

"You live there, sir?" I asked.

The domed head tilted, the dark eyes flashed at me. "It is not my *only* property, if that is what you mean. I visit it from time to time. The place is very old. In origin, it was a priory, founded by a breakaway group of monks from one of the local abbeys. The stones at the heart of the West Wing go back to that period. Subsequently a series of local lords owned it, rebuilding and adapting the ruins, before it was converted into its current form around the turn of the eighteenth century. Architecturally it is a peculiar mishmash of a place—passages leading nowhere or doubling back upon themselves, odd changes of level. . . . But more to the point, it has always had a sinister reputation. Stories of Visitors here go back centuries. In short, it is one of those sites where hauntings were *already* in evidence, well before the start of the Problem. It's said that—"

"Is that someone looking out?" George said suddenly. He had been studying the photograph closely while the old man talked, staring at it quizzically through his thick, round glasses. Now he picked it up and, with a chubby finger, indicated a point on the main wall of the house. Lockwood and I bent close, frowning. High above and to the left of the entrance portico, a dark triangular notch indicated the presence of a narrow window. There was a slight gray smudge inside the notch, almost too faint to be seen.

"Ah, you've noticed that, have you?" Fairfax said. "Yes, it *does* look like a figure, doesn't it? Standing just inside. The curious thing is that this photograph was taken a couple of months *before* I inherited the estate. The house was shut and locked. There was no one living there."

He took a sip of tea, his black eyes twinkling. Again, I thought I detected amusement in his manner, as if he took a certain pleasure in that smudge and its implications.

"What time was the picture taken?" I asked.

"Approaching dusk. The sun's setting, as you can see."

Throughout all this, Lockwood's face had been glowing with scarcely suppressed excitement. He sat hunched forward, bony elbows balanced on his knees, his hands pressed together, every sinew tense with interest. "You were about to tell us something of the phenomena, sir," he said. "About how they manifest, I mean."

Mr. Fairfax placed his cup down on the table, and sat back with a sigh. One great hand grasped his iron-headed walking stick; the other gestured as he spoke. "I am an old man. I cannot see apparitions myself, and as a general rule, I don't sense 'em, either. But the malignant aura of this house is evident even to me. I feel it the moment I walk in the door; I taste it in my mouth. Ah, it is a sickly atmosphere, Mr. Lockwood, which works to sap the soul. As for specifics—" He leaned a little on the stick, adjusted his position slightly as if his bones hurt him. "Well, there are many stories. The caretaker, Bert Starkins, is the one to ask about it; he seems to know them all. But certainly the two best-known tales in the neighborhood—the key hauntings, if you will—concern the Red Room and the Screaming Staircase."

There was a profound silence, abruptly broken by an enormously loud rumble from George's stomach. Plaster didn't actually fall from the ceiling, but it was close.

"Sorry," he said cheerfully. "Famished. I think I'll have another doughnut, if you don't mind. Any takers?" No one paid him any heed. He reached out for the plate.

"The Red Room?" I said.

"The Screaming Staircase?" Lockwood edged forward eagerly in his chair. "Please, Mr. Fairfax, tell us more."

"I'm delighted to see that you display such interest," the old man said. "I can see that my high opinion of you was correct. Well, the Red Room is a bed chamber on the first floor of the West Wing of the house. At least, it *was* used as a bedroom once. No longer. It is completely empty now. It is one of those places where the supernatural presence is so potent that it spells disaster to all who visit it. No one can spend the night there and live—or that's the story."

"Have you been in there, sir?" Lockwood asked.

"I *have* peered in. By day, of course."

"And the atmosphere—"

"Thick, Mr. Lockwood. Thick with evil." The old head drew back; Fairfax looked down his great hooked nose at us. "And I have good reason to believe in the power of this room, as I shall tell you presently. Then there is the Screaming Staircase. To me, this is a more mysterious tale. The stairs wind from the Long Gallery on the ground floor, up to the landing. They are made of stone and are very ancient. I myself have never experienced any ill sensation on these stairs, and I do not know of anyone who has. But it's said that long ago they witnessed some great horror, and that the souls of those involved are trapped within. At certain times, perhaps when the power of these Visitors is at its height, perhaps when they sense the presence of a new victim, you can hear their frenzied howling. It emanates from the stairs themselves."

Lockwood spoke softly. "The actual staircase screams?"

"Apparently. I have never heard it."

"About the Red Room—" George was finishing his doughnut; he paused and swallowed. "You say it's on the first floor? Would that be the same level as the window in this picture?"

"Yes . . . I suppose it would be about there. Do you mind not spraying sugar on the photograph? I don't have another copy."

"Sorry."

"This is fascinating," Lockwood said. "From what you're saying, there is more than one Visitor in the house. More than one Source. A cluster of ghosts, in other words. You believe that to be true?"

"Certainly," Fairfax said. "I can feel them."

"Yes, but how did it begin? There must have been some key event, some central trauma that started it all. . . . It begs the question—which Visitor was first?" Lockwood tapped his fingertips together. "Is the house empty now?"

"The West Wing is certainly unoccupied, for that is where the danger is concentrated. My man, Starkins, has been caretaker for many years. He lives in an adjacent building."

"And where do *you* stay, sir, when you visit the property?

"I have a suite in the East Wing, which is relatively modern. It has its own entrance and is separated from the main section of the house by iron doors on every floor. I installed them myself, along with the best defenses money can buy, and my sleep has not been disturbed." The old man regarded us all fixedly, each in turn. "I am by no means a coward, but I would not for any consideration spend the night alone in the old wing of Combe Carey Hall. However"—he fingered the iron bulldog lovingly—"that is precisely what I am asking *you* to do."

My heart jumped. I made some small adjustment to my skirt but was otherwise quite still. Lockwood's eyes were shining. George's were as ever, expressionless; slowly he took off his glasses and rubbed the lenses on the front of his sweater. We waited.

"You would not be the first to make this attempt," Fairfax went on. "The same questions Mr. Lockwood has just articulated were on the mind of the previous owner too. Thirty years ago he decided to investigate, and he hired a small team from the Fittes Agency—a youth, a girl, and their adult supervisor—to conduct initial explorations. They agreed to spend the night in the house, focusing their attention on the so-called Red Room. Well, they followed standard procedures. The main door to the house was left unlocked, so they had a clear avenue of escape. They rigged up an internal telephone in the Red Room itself; this was connected to the phone in Bert Starkins's lodge, so that help—if necessary—might be summoned. They were all highly experienced operatives. The owner left them there at dusk. Some hours later, when he went to bed, Starkins noticed their flashlight beams moving steadily in the windows of the upper floors. Around midnight the caretaker's phone began to ring. He picked it up: it was the supervisor. He said that there had been some odd phenomena, and that he wished to check the connection was working properly. Otherwise all was well. He was quite calm. He hung up, and Starkins went to bed. The phone did not ring again that night. In the morning, when Starkins and the owner met on the front steps, the Fittes group had not emerged. At seven-thirty they entered the Hall. The place was quiet; no one answered their calls. They knew where they had to go, of course; when they opened the door of the Red Room, they found the body of the supervisor lying facedown beside the telephone. He was ghost-touched and quite dead. The girl was on the far side of the room, crouched beside a window. I say crouched: she was so tightly curled up they could not unbend her to see her face or check her pulse. Not that there was much point in that. She was stone dead too, of course. I am sorry to say they never discovered what happened to the boy."

"You mean they couldn't tell how he died?" George asked.

"I mean they never found him."

"Excuse me, sir," Lockwood said, "but when the man used the telephone at midnight, did he say what kind of phenomena they'd been experiencing?"

"No. He did not." Mr. Fairfax took a pocket watch from his jacket and consulted it briefly. "Time is passing. I need to be in Pimlico in fifteen minutes! Very well, to the point. As I say, your agency has caught my eye; I am surprised and intrigued by your capabilities. So: here is my proposition for you. I am prepared to pay your costs in the Sheen Road case. That will settle the damages caused by the fire, and keep DEPRAC quiet in the bargain. To earn your £60,000, all you need to do is commit yourself to the investigation. In fact, I shall wire the sum to your account the moment you arrive at the Hall. Additionally, if you succeed in uncovering its mysteries and locate the Source within it, I shall pay you a further handsome fee. What is your standard charge?"

Lockwood named a figure.

"I shall pay twice that. Combe Carey, I can assure you, is not to be taken lightly." Mr. Fairfax grasped the bulldog's head and shuffled forward, preparing to rise. "Another thing: when I require something, I act quickly. I would want you there in two days."

"Two days?" George said. "But we'd need time to—"

"Let me tell you at once," Fairfax said, "that my proposal is not up for negotiation. You are not in a position to impose terms. Oh, and I have another stipulation. No flares or explosive devices may be brought into the Hall, which contains a great deal of ancient and valuable furniture. It is not that I don't trust you, but, forgive me"—the silver-capped teeth glittered—"I do not want my property burned down." Squeaks of protest from the chair; he stood, towering over us on his brittle limbs like some kind of giant insect. "Very well. I don't expect a decision from you now, of course. Let me know by the end of the day. You'll find my secretary's number on this card."

I sat back in the sofa, blowing out my cheeks. Too right he wouldn't get an immediate decision. Fittes agents were the best, we all knew that. And three of them had died in Combe Carey Hall! To follow them in, without time for proper preparation, would be bordering on madness. The Red Room? The Screaming Staircase? Yes, the money Fairfax was offering might save the company, but what good was that if we lost our lives? There was no doubt about it: we needed to debate this *very* carefully.

"Thank you very much, sir," Lockwood was saying, "but I can give you our answer now. We'll definitely take the case." He stood up and held out his hand. "We'll make arrangements to be down at the Hall as soon as possible. Shall we say Sunday afternoon?"

IV

The Hall

Chapter 17

It's fair to say we'd had our differences, George and I, during the months I'd been at Lockwood's. We'd bickered about the big things (such as the times one of us had gotten a face full of salt or been nearly scalped by the other's wildly swinging blade), and we'd bickered about the small (the laundry rotation, the tidiness of the kitchen, George's habit of leaving the ghost-jar in unexpected places, like behind the bathroom door). We fought about almost everything. What we almost never did was argue on the same side.

That lunchtime, after Fairfax left, was one of those rare occasions.

No sooner had the Rolls-Royce purred away than we both rounded on Lockwood for not consulting us in his decision. I reminded him of the deadly reputation of the Hall. George argued we'd need at least a fortnight, and preferably a month, to properly research its history. Anything less was probable suicide.

Lockwood heard us out in cheerful silence. "Are you done?" he said. "Good. Three things. First: this is probably our only chance to save the company before we go bust. We can pay off the Hopes in one fell swoop and get DEPRAC off our back. It's an extraordinary opportunity, and we simply can't turn it down. Second: I'm in charge here, and whatever I say goes. Thirdly: isn't this the most enticing job any of us have ever had? The Screaming Staircase? The Red Room? Come on! At *last* we've got a mission worthy of our talents! Do you want to spend the rest of your lives snuffing drab Shades in the suburbs? This is the real thing at last! It would be a crime to turn it down."

His reasoning, particularly the second point, did not completely convince us. George rubbed his glasses on his sweater in a passion. "The true crimes," he said, "are Fairfax's outrageous preconditions. No magnesium flares, Lockwood! That's completely mad!"

Lockwood stretched back on the sofa. "It's certainly an interesting requirement."

"*Interesting?*" I cried. "It's outrageous!"

"The man's a fool," George said. "If this place is half as dangerous as he tells us it is, it would be insane to go in without every single weapon available!"

I nodded. "No one takes on a Type Two without canisters of Greek Fire!"

"Right! And this is a *cluster* of Type Twos we're talking about—"

"With a proven death count to its name—"

"Plus, we're not getting anything *like* enough time to do some—"

"—research in the historical records," Lockwood said. "Yes, yes, I *know*, as you both keep bellowing it in my ear every thirty seconds. Will you two fishwives shut up and listen? As eccentric as he seems to be, Fairfax is our client, and we have to go along with his wishes. We'll have our swords, won't we? And plenty of defensive chains. So we're not exactly going in unarmed." He flinched. "Lucy, you're doing that starey thing with your eyes again."

"Yes, I am. Because I don't think you're taking this seriously."

"Wrong. I'm taking it very seriously indeed. We go to Combe Carey Hall, we put our lives at risk, make no mistake about that." He smiled. "But isn't that what we do?"

"Only when properly equipped," George growled. "And another thing. What Fairfax said about choosing us doesn't make sense. There are fifteen agencies in London bigger and more successful than Lockwood & Co. Yet you don't seem surprised that he came knocking on *our* door."

Lockwood shook his head. "On the contrary, I think it's remarkable that he did so. It's almost the most fascinating thing about the case. Which is why we should take full advantage and see what happens. Now, if that's all—"

"It isn't," I said. "Not quite. What about Hugo Blake and the locket? Maybe it slipped your mind, but we got burglarized twelve hours ago. What are we doing about that?"

"I haven't forgotten Blake," Lockwood said. "But Fairfax and his offer have to be our priorities now. He's given us forty-eight hours to prepare, and we've got to make that count. Blake's in jail. There's no need to take the locket over to Barnes right now. Besides, I wouldn't mind trying to crack that code before we do. It would be something else to tell the papers about—hopefully along with details of our triumph at Combe Carey Hall." He held up a hand as I tried to interrupt him. "No, Lucy, we won't be burgled again—they'll know we're forewarned now. And your friend Annie Ward has been waiting fifty years for justice, so a couple more days won't make any difference. Okay, it's time to get to work. George, I've a few things for you to look into."

"Obviously," George growled. "The Hall."

"Yes, and some other stuff, as well. Get yourself ready, and try to cheer up. It's research time—you should be hopping with delight. Lucy, *your* job today is to help me fix the house and sort through the equipment. Everyone happy? Good."

Happy or not, there was no arguing with Lockwood when he was in that mood, and George and I knew better than to try. Soon afterward, George set off for the Archives, while I joined Lockwood in the basement. And so two days of frantic activity began.

That first afternoon, Lockwood supervised the repair and strengthening of our home defenses. New locks were placed on the front door, and firm iron bars—suitable for keeping out the living as well as the dead—placed on the basement window. While the workmen labored, he sat at the telephone, making calls. He rang Mullet & Sons, the rapier dealer, to order brand-new blades; he spoke with Satchell's of Jermyn Street, the main supplier of agency goods in London, requesting fresh stocks of iron and salt to compensate for leaving behind our flares.

Meanwhile I spent my time laying out our weapons and defenses on the basement floor. I polished the chains and swords; I refilled the pots of filings. I reassessed our collection of silver seals, selecting all the strongest boxes, bands, and chain-nets, and setting the smaller stuff to one side. Finally, regretfully, I removed our flares from our workbelts and put them back in the storeroom. The head in the ghost-jar watched the whole process with great interest, mouthing at me urgently through the murky glass, until I grew annoyed and covered it with the cloth.

Throughout our preparations, Lockwood seemed distracted by the scale of the coming adventure. He was vigorous—I'd never seen him more buoyant, bounding around the house, taking the stairs three steps at a time—but also oddly preoccupied. He seldom spoke, and he occasionally broke away from what he was doing to stare off into space, like he was following some complicated pattern in his head, trying to see its end.

George remained at the Archives all day; he still hadn't returned when I went to bed, and had already left again by the time I got up next morning. To my surprise, I discovered Lockwood preparing to go out too. He stood beside the mirror in the hall, carefully adjusting an enormous flat cloth cap on his head. He wore a cheap suit and had a battered briefcase at his side. When I spoke to him, he replied in a broad country accent quite different from his usual tones.

"How's this sound?" he asked. "Suitably rural?"

"I suppose so, yes. I can barely understand you. What are you doing?"

"I'm going to Combe Carey. I want to check a few things. I'll be back quite late."

"You want me to come too?"

"Sorry. There's important work that needs doing here, Lucy, and I need you to hold the fort. There'll be the Satchell's and Mullet deliveries later. When they arrive, could you get out the new rapiers and check them over? Give old Mr. Mullet a call if there are any problems. Don't worry about the Satchell's stuff; I'll open it when I'm home. Then can you double-check the equipment bags and start getting the food supplies ready? Also"—he felt in his jacket pocket and produced the little silver-glass case—"I want you to have the ghost-girl's necklace. We'll deal with it in a couple of days, but in the meantime, look after it carefully for me. Keep it on you, as before." He picked up the briefcase, set off down the hall. "Oh, and Luce, apart from the deliveries, don't let anyone in. Our masked friend might try a subtler approach next time."

Late afternoon came: the winter sun shone low over the rooftops, a faint and lilac disc. Thirty-five Portland Row was cold and empty, full of gray planes of a dozen shades and shadows. I was alone in the house. Neither George nor Lockwood had returned. I'd received the deliveries, rearranged our equipment bags, assembled our food and drink, and ironed my clothes ready for the morning start the next day. I'd practiced rapier play on Esmeralda in the basement. Now I paced the house in the steepening dusk, wrestling with my frustrations.

It wasn't the Fairfax case that truly bothered me, though its dangers clustered like phantoms at the corner of my mind. I could see that Lockwood was right—we simply couldn't afford to pass up such a generous, extraordinary offer if we wanted the company to survive. And as numerous as the questions surrounding the case were—the exact nature of the Red Room and the Screaming Staircase, for a start—I had enough confidence in George's powers of research to know we'd not be going in *entirely* blind.

But while this deservedly took our attention, it also annoyed me that I was being a bit left out. George was doing his thing with books and papers. Lockwood was (presumably) gathering fresh information about the Hall. And me? I was stuck at home, making cheese sandwiches and stacking weapons. No doubt it was vital work, but it didn't exactly thrill me. I wanted to make a better contribution.

What *really* bothered me, however, was the way we were neglecting our *other* case. I didn't agree with Lockwood that we could let the locket wait for another couple of days. What with the burglary and the strange inscription, it seemed to me it was vital that we keep things moving, and this belief was confirmed by a shocking phone call during the afternoon. It was Inspector Barnes, reporting that Hugo Blake was about to be released.

"Not enough evidence," Barnes snapped. "That's the long and short of it. He hasn't confessed, and we haven't proved he went inside that house. Now his lawyers are getting busy, and that means we're running out of time. Unless we stumble on something else, Miss Carlyle, or unless the man himself comes clean—I'm afraid he'll walk out of here tomorrow."

"What?" I cried. "But you can't let him go! He's obviously guilty!"

"Yes, but we can't *prove* it, can we?" I could almost see Barnes's mustache rippling as he spoke. "It's not enough that he took her home. We haven't got the final piece of proof that connects him to the crime. If you idiots hadn't burned the place, we might perhaps have found something there. As it is, I'm sorry, but he's likely to get away scot-free." Giving a final snort, the inspector hung up, leaving me to my indignation.

We haven't got the final piece of proof . . . But maybe, of course, we *had*.

I took the little case from around my neck and held it so that it caught the dying light. Behind the glass, the locket's sliver of gold hung, distorted, like an eel in shallow water. *Tormentum meum, laetitia mea* . . . I could just about read the words. And inside: what was it? A‡W; H.II.2.115 . . . Somehow, those letters and numbers concealed the final clue. That's what Blake was after. That's why he was so desperate to get it back. Perhaps, when we gave the piece to Barnes, he'd figure out the problem.

Or perhaps he wouldn't. Perhaps the murderer *would* continue to get away with it, as he had for fifty years.

Cold, hard anger rose within me. If we didn't crack the code, it would be the last chance gone. Blake would never admit what had happened, and there was no one else who knew.

No one else, except . . .

I stared down at the glass case in my hand.

The idea that had suddenly occurred to me was so forbidden that for a little while I could only stand there, listening to the uneasy pounding of my heart. It would certainly put my life at risk, though I thought I could easily get around that; worse, it would risk the wrath of Lockwood, who had already warned me against doing anything dangerous without permission. If I had any sense at all I should wait for his return, but I knew quite well he'd forbid me to carry out the experiment I planned. And then I really *would* have spent a useless day, while the vile Blake waited expectantly for his release.

I wandered through the house, following an aimless course, turning my plan over in my mind. The light faded; I found myself in the kitchen. Slowly I took the iron steps to the basement below. On the back wall, the artifact shelves were a grid of black. Tonight the pirate hand glowed faintly lilac, while the other trophies remained dark.

It was worth the risk. If I succeeded, we could bypass the locket's weird number code altogether. I could get the final confirmation of Blake's guilt. If I failed, what did it matter? Lockwood need never know.

The iron chains were laid out on the floor, oiled and tested, ready to be packed. I took one of the longest and thickest, a stout two-incher, and hauled it into the practice room, where the ragged straw-filled forms of Joe and Esmeralda hung in melancholy silence. I laid it out to form a loop of double thickness, about four feet in diameter, with the ends folded over each other. Just to be sure they couldn't be forced open, I clipped the two end links together with a bicycle lock. This was a heavy-duty defense, guaranteed against Type Twos. It was probably made by Fairfax Iron. Ordinarily the agents would stand inside, safe against any roaming ghosts.

Today, I'd change the rules.

There were no windows in the practice room, so it was already very dark. My watch told me it was only five p.m., which is ordinarily too soon for full manifestations. But I didn't have the option of waiting. Lockwood and George might be at back any time. Besides, when a ghost is eager, who knows how early it might come?

I stepped over the chains into the circle and took the silver-glass case from my pocket. Kneeling on the floor, I pushed open the bolt, flipped the lid, and let the locket drop out into my palm. It was painfully cold, like something taken from the freezer. I placed it carefully on the floor. Then I stood up and stepped back across the iron.

Easy enough, so far. I didn't expect results straight away, so I went to the office area to get a couple of things. I was only out for two minutes, but when I got back, the air in the practice room had chilled. Joe and Esmeralda were swinging gently from their chains.

"Annie Ward?" I said.

Nothing—no response, but I felt a tightness against my temples, a faint force gathering in the room. I stood a little distance from the chains, with a bag of salt in my pocket and a paper in my hand.

"Annie Ward?" I said again. "I know it's you."

A shimmer of silver light inside the circle of iron chain. A faint outline of a girl in two dimensions, folding, bending; now here, now gone.

"Who killed you, Annie?" I said.

The outline warped and flickered as before. I listened, heard no voice. The tightness in my head was painful now.

"Was it Hugo Blake?"

No change—at least not *visually*. For a fleeting second I thought I picked up the slightest murmur, as if someone was talking quietly in a distant room. I strained hard, listened; my forehead throbbing with the effort. . . . No. Gone. If it had ever been there.

Well, it was too much to hope I'd pick up anything. If interrogating the dead was as simple as that, all the great Talents would have mastered the art. As it was, only Marissa Fittes had ever done it, in her legendary conversations with Type Threes. No, who was I kidding? In a moment I'd get the salt grains out, get this mess cleared up.

Still, I had one last thing to try.

I already had George's photocopy in my hand, held hidden behind my back. Now I brought it around, unfolded it, and stepped close to the chains. I flipped the paper so that the photographs of Blake faced the circle. There he was twice over—in that main mug shot, grinning away in black tie, hat, and gloves, and ditto in the group picture beside the fountain, standing close by Annie Ward.

"Here," I said. "Was it him? Was it H—"

A piercing psychic scream, a howl of grief and fury, knocked me off my feet. Air blasted out across the room, forcing the iron chains outward into a perfect circle, blowing brick dust from the basement walls. The straw dummies swung up so far, they struck the ceiling; I skidded on my back almost to the door, crying out as I did so, for the pressure in my head was so great, I thought my skull would split. I looked up, saw the ghost careering back and forth inside the chains, colliding with the boundary, spurts of plasm fizzing off whenever it touched the rim. Its shape was grotesquely distorted, the head long, misshapen, the body spindly, cracked like a broken bone. All semblance of a girl had gone. And still the psychic wail rolled out, so that I was stunned and deafened.

I'd dropped the paper when I fell, but the salt-bomb was still in my pocket. I scrambled into a sitting position and lobbed it hard into the circle.

Plastic burst, salt scattered; the thrashing, mewling thing vanished. Instantly, the noise in my head snapped off.

I sat sprawling on the floor, mouth open, eyes blinking, hair in my eyes. Opposite me, the two straw dummies swung madly back and forth; they swiftly slowed, hung still.

"Ow," I said. "That *hurt*."

"I should just about think it did."

Lockwood and George stood in the archway, faces blank with astonishment, staring down at me.

"Wait!" I said. "Stop talking, George! Wait! I'll show you!"

Two minutes had passed, and I hadn't got a word in edgewise. Okay, I'd been busy: my first job, once my head had stopped ringing, had been to retrieve the locket from the circle—which was easier said than done, since it was covered in frozen salt flakes that almost blistered my skin. Then I had to get it back in the case—again not easy, when you've got George Cubbins shouting in your ear. But I needed to speak, and do it fast. Lockwood hadn't said a thing to me. There were spots of color on his cheeks, and his mouth was tight and hard.

"Look," I said, picking up the paper from the floor. "I did what we should have done originally. I showed Annie Ward these pictures. What are they of? Hugo Blake. What did she do? She went ballistic. I've never heard such a scream."

"You deliberately let her free?" Lockwood said. "That was a stupid thing to do."

When I looked at his face, my heart quailed. "Not free," I said desperately. "Just . . . freer. And it got results, which nothing else has done so far."

George snorted. "What results? Did she actually speak with you? No. Did she sign a legal document that would stand up in court? No."

"The reaction was clear, George. Cause and effect. You can't deny the connection."

Lockwood nodded. "Even so, you shouldn't have done it. Give me the paper."

I handed it over wordlessly, my eyes prickling. I was done for now. I'd made the wrong decision yet again, and I knew Lockwood would not forgive me. I could see it in his face. This was the end of my stint at the company. All at once I understood the preciousness of what I'd thrown away.

Lockwood stepped aside, his boots crunching across the salt, to stand and study the paper beneath the light. No such luck with George; he came in close, his eyes bulging so much behind his spectacles, they almost pressed against the glass.

"I can't *believe* you did that, Lucy. You're crazy! *Purposefully* freeing a ghost!"

"It was an experiment," I said. "Why are you complaining? You're always messing about with that stupid jar of yours."

"There's no comparison. I keep that ghost *in* the jar. Anyway, it's scientific research. I do it under carefully controlled conditions."

"Carefully controlled? I found it in the bathtub the other day!"

"That's right. I was testing the ghost's reaction to heat."

"And to bubble bath? There were bubbles all over the jar. You put some nice soapy fragrance in that water, and . . ." I stared at him. "Do you get in the tub with it, George?"

His face flushed. "No, I do not. Not as a rule. I—I was saving time. I was just getting in myself when it occurred to me I could do a useful experiment about the resistance of ectoplasm to warmth. I wanted to see if it would contract. . . ." He waved his hands wildly in the air. "Wait! Why am I explaining myself to *you*? You just unleashed a ghost in our house!"

"Lucy . . ." Lockwood said.

"I didn't unleash it!" I cried. "Take a look at all the salt. I was in total control."

"Yeah," George said, "which is why we found you spread-eagled on the floor. If you kept the ghost constrained it was more by dumb luck than skill. That bloody thing nearly had our heads off the other night, and now—"

"Oh, quit complaining. *You* got naked with a ghost."

"*Lucy!*" We broke off. Lockwood was still in exactly the same pose he'd been when we started bickering, under the ceiling light, holding the paper before him. His face was pale and his voice was strange. "You showed the Visitor this paper?"

"Well, yes. I—"

"How did you hold it? Like that? Or like that?" He adjusted his hand grip rapidly.

"Er, the last one, I suppose."

"It definitely saw the whole paper?"

"Well, yes, but only for a second. Then it went crazy, as you saw."

"Yeah," George said grimly. "We saw. Lockwood, you've been pretty quiet so far. Can you tell Lucy that she is *never* to do anything like this again? This is twice now we've been put at risk. We need to say—"

"We need to say, well done," Lockwood interrupted. "Lucy, you're a genius. I think you've made a key connection. This is a crucial clue."

I was almost as surprised as George, whose lower jaw now resembled a gently moving swing. "Oh. Thanks . . ." I said. "You think . . . you think this will help the case?"

"Very much so."

"So shall we take it to the police? Shall we show the locket to Barnes?"

"Not yet. George is right: the ghost's reaction can't strictly count as evidence. But don't worry—thanks to you, I'm confident we can bring the Annie Ward story to a satisfactory conclusion very soon."

"I hope so. . . ." Baffled as I was, I was also mightily relieved. "But there's something you should know. Hugo Blake's going to be released." I told them about the call.

Lockwood smiled; he seemed suddenly relaxed, cheerful even. "I shouldn't worry," he said. "We've made the house secure. They won't burgle us again. All the same, I don't think we should leave the locket here when we go down to Combe Carey. Bring it with you, Lucy—keep it around your neck. I promise we'll deal with the matter soon. But first"—he grinned—"there's the Fairfax job. George has got some news on that."

"Yeah," George said. "I uncovered a bit about the haunting."

I stared at him. "And is it as bad as Fairfax said?"

"Nope." George took off his glasses and wearily rubbed his eyes. "From what I've seen, it's almost certainly a whole lot worse."

Chapter 18

To get from the London offices of Lockwood & Co. to the village of Combe Carey is a fairly simple business. All it takes is a quick taxi up the street to Marylebone Station, a leisurely wait at platform six, and finally a gentle forty-minute train ride—through rolling, gray-brown suburbs, then the wintry Berkshire fields—before you arrive below the mossy flanks of St. Wilfred's Church in old Combe Carey station. An hour and a half journey, tops. Easy, quick, straightforward, and as pleasant as a trip can be.

Yeah, right. That's the theory. But it isn't so much fun when you're helping to carry six super-massive duffel bags weighed down with metal, plus a rapier bag with four old ones stuffed inside as spares, *and* you have a brand-new rapier at your belt getting in your way. It also doesn't help if your leader and his deputy both conveniently mislay their wallets, so it's *you* who has to fork out for the train tickets, *and* pay supplements for the heavy luggage. Or that you spend so much time haggling, you end up missing the first train. Yes, all that *really* improves your mood.

Then there's the small matter of heading toward one of the most haunted houses in England, and hoping you aren't going to die.

This last factor wasn't improved en route by George's giving us a full briefing on the things he'd discovered over the previous two days. He had a binder filled with neatly written notes and, as the train pootled cheerily past the spires and ghost-lamps of villages hidden in the wooded folds of gentle hills, he regaled us with nasty details from them.

"Basically, it seems what Fairfax told us was right," he said. "The Hall's had a bad rep for centuries. You remember it started off as a priory? I found a medieval document about that. It was built by an outfit known as the Heretic Monks of St. John. Apparently they 'turned awaye from the laweful worshippe of God to the adoration of darke things,' whatever *that* means. Before long a group of barons got wind of this and burned the place down. They took over the priory's land and divided it among themselves."

"Possibly a setup?" I said. "They framed the monks in order to take the land?"

George nodded. "Maybe. Since then it's been owned by a succession of rich families—the Careys, the Fitz-Percys, the Throckmortons—all of whom benefited from the wealth of the estate. But the Hall itself is nothing but trouble. I couldn't find too many details, but one owner abandoned it in the fifteenth century because of a 'malign presence.' It's almost burned down two or three times, and—get this—in 1666, an outbreak of plague killed off its inhabitants. Seems a guest turned up at the door and found everyone inside lying dead, except for one little baby, left crying in a cradle in a bedroom."

Lockwood whistled. "Grisly. That could be your cluster of Visitors, right there."

"Did they save the baby?" I said.

George consulted his notes. "Yeah. He was adopted by a cousin and became a school teacher. Which is a tough break, but he was lucky to get out. Anyway, the bad vibes in that house continue right up until this century. There've been a succession of accidents, and the last owner before Fairfax—a distant relative—shot himself."

"No shortage of potential Visitors for us, then," Lockwood mused. "Any mention of this Screaming Staircase, or the dreaded Red Room?"

"One fragment, from Corbett's *Berkshire Legends*." George turned a page. "It claims two children from Combe Carey were found unconscious at the bottom of the 'old steps' in the Hall. One died right away, but the other recovered sufficiently to report being beset by a 'foul and devilish ululation, a cruel and unholy outcry.'" He snapped the folder shut. "Then she died too."

"What's a ululation?" I said.

"That would be the screaming." Lockwood stared out at the passing landscape. "Stories, stories . . . What we badly need are *facts*."

George adjusted his glasses in a complacent manner. "Aha. Maybe I can help you there, too." From inside the folder he brought out two pieces of paper, which he unfolded and set on the little table beneath the window of our compartment. The first was a hand-drawn floor plan of a large building, showing two extensive levels, each with walls, windows, and stairs carefully rendered in ink. Here and there were annotations, written in blue: *Main Lobby, Library, Duke's Chamber, Long Gallery*. . . . At the top, in George's neat little handwriting, was written *West Wing: Combe Carey Hall.*

"This is superb work, George," Lockwood said. "Where did you find it?"

George scratched his pudgy nose. "The Royal Architectural Society on Pall Mall. They've got all sorts of plans and surveys there. This one was done in the nineteenth century. Look at the great staircase: it's an absolute monster. Must dominate the hall. The other plan"—he swapped the papers over—"is much older; might even be medieval. It's a very rough sketch, but it shows the place when it was still basically the ruins of the priory. It's much smaller, and there are lots of rooms that must have been knocked down when they rebuilt it as a house, because they're not on the later map. But look, you can see that the massive staircase is already there, and also the areas that became the lobby and Long Gallery. The Long Gallery was the monks' refectory, where they ate. Some upstairs rooms correspond to the nineteenth-century plan too. So between them," George said, "these plans tell us where the oldest regions of the West Wing are."

"And that," Lockwood said, "is where the ultimate Source is most likely to be. Excellent. We'll start our searches in those areas tonight. What about the other material I asked you for, George? Can I have a look?"

George produced a slim green file. "There you go. Everything I could find on Mr. John William Fairfax. As he said, he inherited the place six or seven years ago. Didn't seem put off by its reputation. Anyway, you've lots of articles on him there—interviews, profiles, that sort of thing."

Lockwood settled back with the file. "Let's see. . . . Hmm, seems that Fairfax is a firm advocate of fox hunting. Likes hunting and fishing . . . Supports a *lot* of charities. Ooh, and he was a keen amateur actor in his youth. . . . Look at this review: 'Will Fairfax gives an intense performance as Othello . . .' The mind boggles. But it makes sense, in a way. He's a bit theatrical even now."

"That's not really relevant, is it?" I said. I was still studying the floor plans, tracing the curve of the staircase, pondering the location of the infamous Red Room.

"Oh, it's good to have the full background to a job. . . ." Lockwood became engrossed. Conversation faltered; the train rushed on. Once or twice I touched the front of my coat, feeling a small hard outline hanging beneath: the case containing the ghost-girl's locket. I'd kept it on me, safe, just as Lockwood had instructed. I hoped he was right, that we'd soon bring her story to a conclusion. Assuming, of course, that we survived the night in Combe Carey Hall.

Outside the village station, a car was waiting for us. A tousle-haired youth lounged against the hood, reading an old issue of *True Hauntings*. As we staggered out under our burden, like three trainee Sherpas back from Everest, he lowered the magazine and regarded us with callous amusement mixed with pity. He touched his forelock in a slightly ironic gesture.

"Mr. Lockwood, is it? Got your message. I'll take you to the Hall."

Our bags were stuffed into the back, and with some difficulty George and I squeezed in alongside. Lockwood bounded into the front beside the driver. The taxi veered out into the road, sending ducks squalling across the village pond and me sprawling headlong onto George's lap. Grimly, I levered myself upright. The lad whistled through his teeth as we drove between stark gray elms.

"No extra ironwork on the car, I see," Lockwood said, by way of conversation.

"No need, around here," the boy replied.

"Safe district, is it? No Visitors around?"

"Nope. They're all up at the house." The boy turned sharply to avoid a pothole, so that I was flung bodily across George's lap again.

George looked down at me. "Want a hand? You can stay there if it's easier."

"No. No, thank you. I can manage."

"You mean Combe Carey Hall?" Lockwood was saying. "Good. That's where we'll be staying tonight."

"In the new wing? Or with old Bert Starkins the caretaker?"

"In the main house."

There was a pause, during which the youth took his hands off the wheel to cross himself, touch a small religious icon on the dashboard, and spit ritually out of the window. He looked in the rearview mirror in a ruminative manner. "I like that red duffel bag," he said. "I could use one for my football gear. Mind if I nip up to the Hall tomorrow and ask for it? Mr. Fairfax wouldn't be wanting it, would he? Nor old Starkins."

"Sorry," Lockwood said. "*We'll* still have need of it tomorrow."

The youth nodded. "I'll drop by anyhow," he said. "No harm in seeing."

We drove uphill, through straggling woods, amid a tangled grid of cold, dark fields lined with winter greens. "You ever been inside the Hall?" Lockwood said.

"What? You think I'm crazy?"

"You must know something about it, though. About its haunting."

The youth turned abruptly up a narrow side lane, a miracle of last minute steering, so that everything in the back of the car shifted violently to the left, and my head was brutally sandwiched between the window glass and some soft portion of George's face. For a few seconds I heard nothing except his breathing in my ear; by the time he pried himself loose, with much gratuitous fumbling, we had passed through a tumbledown gateway and were racing up a long, straight drive.

". . . murdered, hidden, and never found," the boy was saying. "*That's* how it all began, I reckon. Everyone around here knows it. One death leads to another, and so it becomes a chain of deaths that'll keep on growing as long as the house shall last. Whole place should be burned down and salt sown on the ashes, that's what my mum says. Not that we can get the owner to see that kind of sense. He's so set on his little experiments. So: here we are. That'll be ten pounds fifty, plus two for the extra bags."

"Interesting," Lockwood said. "Particularly the first part. Thanks."

We had come to a halt at the end of the gravel drive. Through my window I saw rolling parkland spotted with oaks and beeches, and part of the lake I'd noticed in Fairfax's photograph. It all had a wild, unkempt look. The grass was high, and the lakeshore overgrown with matted sedge. On the other side, past George, I could just make out the pale trunk of a tree, two vast urns on plinths and, behind it all, the blank gray stone of a house.

Lockwood was busy talking with the driver. I got out and helped George with the bags. Combe Carey Hall rose vast and tall above me. The air was dank and chill.

Far above, long brick chimneys sprouted like horns against the clouds. This left-hand portion of the house, which I assumed to be the older, western, wing, was mostly of ancient stone, switching to brickwork near the roof and on the margins. It had a great number of windows, of many sizes and at a variety of levels, each one blankly reflecting the gray November sky. Cracked columns supported an ugly concrete portico above the double entrance doors, which were reached by a splaying flight of stairs. A monumental ash tree, of considerable age and size, stood by the far end of the wing. Its bone-white branches pressed against the bricks like the legs of giant spiders.

To the right of the entrance stairs, the smaller, eastern, wing was also brickwork, but of clearly modern construction. By a curious accident of architecture, the wings were set at a slight angle to each other, so the effect was of the entire house subtly reaching out to encircle me. It was an ugly, oppressive mongrel of a building, and I'd have disliked it intensely even if I hadn't known its reputation.

"Lovely!" Lockwood said cheerily. "Here's our hotel for the night." He had been talking animatedly with the driver for a surprisingly long time. As I watched, he handed over a wad of notes—considerably more than £12.50—and a sealed brown envelope. "You'll deliver it, won't you?" he said. "It's important."

The youth nodded. In a shower of gravel, the taxi roared away, leaving behind a smell of fear and gasoline, and the sight of an elderly man descending the steps of the house.

"What was all *that* about?" I demanded.

"Little package I needed posting," Lockwood said. "I'll tell you later."

"Hush," George whispered. "This must be 'old Bert Starkins.' He *is* old, isn't he?"

The caretaker was certainly very ancient, a tight and desiccated thing from which all softness and moisture had long since been extracted. Where Mr. Fairfax had been bullishly vigorous despite his age and infirmity, this man was more like the ash tree by the house: gnarled and twisted, but holding tenaciously to life. He had a shock of gray-white hair, and a narrow face that disintegrated, as he drew near, into a web of lines, a limestone surface with bumps and fissures. His clothes carried an air of somber correctness: he was dressed in an old-fashioned tail coat of dark black velvet, from the sleeves of which gray, liver-spotted fingers protruded. His striped pants were incredibly thin, his shoes as long and pointed as his nose.

He came to a halt and surveyed us dismally. "Welcome to Combe Carey. Mr. Fairfax is expecting you but is presently indisposed. He will be ready to receive you shortly. In the meantime, he's asked that I show you around the grounds, introduce you to the Hall." His voice was broken, querulous, like the rustling of willow fronds.

"Thank you," Lockwood said. "Are you Mr. Starkins?"

"I am, and I've been caretaker here for fifty-three years, man and boy, so I know a thing or two about the place and I don't care who knows it."

"I—I'm sure you do. That's excellent. Where shall we put our bags?"

"Leave them here. Who's going to take them? Not the Inhabitants of the Hall, I'm sure; *they* don't stir before sundown. Come then, I'll show you the gardens."

Lockwood held up a hand. "Excuse me, but it's been a long journey. Do you have . . . any *facilities* nearby?"

The net of wrinkles grew deeper, shadows enveloped the old man's eyes. "When we get to the house, boy. I can't escort you now. Mr. Fairfax wants to show you the interior himself."

"It's a bit urgent."

"Cross your legs and wait."

"Well, you could give me directions."

"No! Impossible."

"I'll just nip behind one of those urns, then. No one will know."

Starkins scowled. "Up the steps, across the lobby, little room to the left of the stairs."

"Thanks *so* much. Won't be a moment." Lockwood hurried away.

"If he can't hold it in now," the old man said, "how will he cope tonight, when the light begins to drain away from the Long Gallery?"

"Er, I don't know," I said. Lockwood's behavior had slightly perplexed me, too.

"Well, we don't have to wait for him," Starkins went on. He pointed up at the western wing. "This stonework marks the oldest portion of Combe Carey. It's the shell of the original priory—you can see one of the chapel windows there—built by the notorious Monks of St. John. Ah, they were a wicked order! It's said they turned away from God to the worship of—"

"—darke things," I murmured.

Starkins looked at me askance. "Who's doing this tour, me or you? But you're right. Such depraved sacrifices and rituals . . . Ooh, it's terrible to think of it. Well, the rumors spread, and finally the priory was sacked by the barons. Seven of the wickedest monks were thrown down a well. The rest were burned inside the building. Yes, they all died screaming inside those walls! By the way, I've prepared your beds in the guest rooms on the first floor. There're *en suite* bathrooms, too. You've all the modern conveniences."

"Thanks," I said.

"Is the well still open?" George asked.

"No. You could still see a disused well out here in the courtyard when I was a lad, but they sealed it up with an iron plug, years ago, and buried it in sand."

George and I scanned the silent building for a time. I was trying to work out which, in Mr. Fairfax's photograph, had been the window with the apparent spectral figure standing at it. It was very hard to tell. There were several potential candidates, seemingly up on the first or second or third floor.

"Are the monks the ultimate Source of the haunting, do you think?" I asked. "Sounds like they must be."

"It's not my place to speculate," Bert Starkins said. "Might be the monks; then again, it might be Mad Sir Rufus Carey, who built the first Hall from the ruins of the priory in 1328. . . . Ah, here's your weak-bladdered friend back. About time too."

Lockwood was pattering toward us, a spring in his step. "Sorry about that," he said. "Have I missed anything?"

"We were just hearing about Mad Sir Rufus," I said.

Starkins nodded. "Yes. He was known hereabouts as the Red Duke, on account of his flaming hair and addiction to spilled blood. It's said he brought his enemies to a torture chamber deep inside the house, where—" He hesitated. "No, I can't say more, not with a young girl present."

"Oh, go on," George said. "Lucy's terribly jaded. Look at her. She's seen it all."

"I *have* seen a lot," I said sweetly.

The old man grunted. "Let's just say they provided his nightly . . . entertainments. When he'd finished off each one, he set their skulls on the steps of the central staircase with candles burning behind the eye sockets." Starkins's aged, rheumy eyes rolled in horror at the thought. "So it went for years, until the stormy night one of the victims broke free and cut Sir Rufus's throat with a rusted manacle. From that day to this, whenever the Red Duke's ghost stalks the corridors, you can hear the souls of his victims howling. They say it's like the very staircase screams."

Lockwood, George, and I glanced at each other. "So that's the origin of the Screaming Staircase?" Lockwood asked.

Starkins shrugged. "Maybe."

"Have *you* ever heard it?" I said.

"Not a chance! Wouldn't catch *me* going into the Hall by night."

"Well, what about anyone you know? Have they heard it? Any of your friends?"

"Friends?" The caretaker's forehead creased in puzzlement at the concept. "It's not my place to have *friends*. I'm a servant of the Hall. Well, let's continue the tour."

Old Mr. Starkins took us on a rambling circuit of the house, pointing out external features, and giving us a canned speech. It soon became apparent that, in his opinion at least, every stone and tree had some horrid association. Sir Rufus and the monks had set the tone. Almost all the subsequent owners of the Hall had been mad, or bad, or a messy combination of both. As they hacked and strangled their way down the years, countless killings had taken place. Theoretically, any one of them might have contributed to the terrible atmosphere of the Hall, but the sheer volume of anecdotes was both numbing and hard to believe. I could see Lockwood struggling to keep an incredulous smile off his face, while George dawdled behind, yawning and rolling his eyes. For my part, I soon gave up trying to remember all the stories and spent my time studying the house. I noticed that, the main entrance aside, there were no obvious exits from the ground floor, except in the modern East Wing, which Mr. Fairfax used. His Rolls was parked outside this side door; the chauffeur, stripped to his shirtsleeves despite the bitter air, stood polishing the hood.

In the grounds beyond the East Wing stretched the boating lake, drab and kidney shaped. Nearby were rose gardens, and a tall, round tower with ruined battlements.

Bert Starkins pointed. "I draw your attention to Sir Lionel's Folly."

"An unusual tower," Lockwood ventured.

"Wait for it," George whispered.

The old man nodded. "Yes, it was from the top of that tower that Lady Caroline Throckmorton threw herself in 1863. Lovely summer evening it was. She stood astride the crenellations, skirts flapping, silhouetted against a bloodred sky, while the servants tried to coax her back in with tea and seed cake. No good, of course. They said she stepped off as casually as if she was alighting from a bus."

"At least it was a serene end," I said.

"You think so? She screamed and flapped her arms all the way down."

There was a short silence. Wind ruffled the cold waters of the lake. George cleared his throat. "Well . . . it's a nice rose garden."

"Yes. . . . Built where she landed."

"A pleasant lake—"

"Where old Sir John Carey perished. Took off for a swim one night. They say he swam to the middle, then dropped like a stone, weighed down by guilty memories."

Lockwood pointed hastily to a little cottage surrounded by shrubs and hedges. "What about that house—"

"Never found his corpse, they didn't."

"Really? Shame. Now, that cottage—"

"It's down there still, cradled among the mud and stones and old drowned leaves. . . . I'm sorry, what did you say?"

"That little house. What's the appalling story about that?"

The ancient man sucked his gums meditatively. "Ain't none."

"There's nothing?"

"No."

"You're sure? No suicide pacts or crimes of passion? Must at least be a quick stabbing or something, surely."

The caretaker appraised Lockwood in a thoughtful manner. "Perhaps, sir, you'd be making one of your clever college jokes about me?"

"I wouldn't dream of it," Lockwood said. "And actually, I've never been to college."

"Perhaps you don't believe the tales I've told," the old man said. Like cart wheels slipping in thick mud, his rheumy eyes swiveled around to George and me. "Perhaps none of you do."

"No, no. We do," I said. "We believe every word. Don't we, George?"

"Almost all of them."

Bert Starkins scowled. "You'll discover very shortly whether or not what I say is true. In any case, there's no ghost in that cottage, because that's where *I* live. I keep it clean of Visitors." Even from a distance the iron defenses dangling from the tiled roof were clear. The old man said no more. He stalked onward, rounded the final corner, and led us back to the front of the house, where we discovered our duffel bags had been moved to the top of the entrance steps, and a tall, emaciated figure stood at the open doors, waving his iron-handled walking stick in greeting.

Chapter 19

"Welcome, Mr. Lockwood, welcome!" John William Fairfax ushered us over the threshold, shaking Lockwood's hand, nodding curtly to George and me. He seemed even taller and thinner and more mantislike than I remembered; the cloth of his dark-gray suit hung off his wasted limbs in empty folds. "Right on time, exactly as you promised. And you will find that I have kept *my* promise too. I wired the money to your bank account ten minutes ago, Mr. Lockwood, so your company's future is assured. Congratulations! If you will accompany me now to my apartments in the East Wing, you may telephone your bank manager, as we discussed. Mr. Cubbins, Miss Carlyle—yonder in the Long Gallery you will find refreshments laid out by the fire. No, don't bother with your bags! Starkins will see to them."

He continued talking loudly as he walked away, his stick tapping on the flagstone floor. Lockwood went with him; George lingered a moment, stomping his boots clean on the entrance mat. Me, I lingered too, but not to clean my boots. For the first time since I was a tiny kid and Jacobs had forced me inside a haunted farmhouse with a stick, I disobeyed the first, most crucial rule.

I hung back at the doorway, hesitant and afraid.

The lobby of the Hall was a great square chamber with a vaulted wooden ceiling and plainly whitewashed walls. George's floor plans had told us it was a relic of the original priory, and in its scale and simplicity it was still very much like a church. Up on the ceiling, where ancient crossbeams met, small carved figures gazed inscrutably down, winged and robed, their faces worn away by the years. The walls were hung with oil paintings, mostly portraits of lords and ladies from long ago.

On either side of the lobby, recessed arches led to other rooms. Directly opposite me, however, a much larger arch rose almost as high as the ceiling, and beyond that arch—

Beyond that arch was a staircase. The steps were broad and made of stone. Time and the feet of centuries had worn them thin at the center, smoothed them sheer as marble. On either side, stone balustrades swept up toward a quarter landing, beneath a circular glass window. Through this the final rays of sunlight gleamed, splashing the stairs with red.

I looked at that staircase, and I couldn't move. I looked at it and *listened.*

Beside me, George stomped his great fat feet. Old Starkins hefted the first duffel bag, wheezing and gasping as he thumped it down into the lobby. Footmen walked by, carrying trays of cups, cakes, and clinking cutlery. I heard Lockwood laugh as he passed into another room.

There was plenty of noise around, in other words. But when I listened, it was something else I heard. A silence. The deeper silence of the house. I sensed it all around me, sentient and aware. That silence stretched away from me, along the corridors and levels, up that great stone flight of stairs, through open doors and under lonely windows, on and on, to an ever more frightening distance. There wasn't any end to it. The house was just the gate. The silence continued forever. And it was waiting for us—I could feel it waiting. I had the impression of something towering over me, massive and clifflike, ready to crash down on my head.

George finished stomping his boots; he set off in pursuit of the footmen and their cakes. Starkins wrestled with the luggage. The others were gone.

I looked over my shoulder at the gravel driveway and the park beyond. Light drained across the winter countryside. Out in the fields, furrows filled with shadow; soon they'd brim over and flood the land with spreading dark, and the silence in the house would stir. . . .

Panic gripped my chest. I didn't *have* to go in. There was still time to turn back.

"Nervous, are we?" Bert Starkins remarked, shouldering his way past me with a duffel bag in his arms. "Don't blame you if you are. That poor little Fittes girl, thirty years back: she was fearful too. Tell you what, I wouldn't blame you if you ran for it." He regarded me with dour commiseration.

His voice cut through my self-absorption. The moment passed; my paralysis was gone. I shook my head dumbly. With slow, mechanical steps I stepped over the threshold, crossed the chilly hallway, and entered the Long Gallery.

This was a darkly beautiful room, lit along its enormous length by a line of mullioned windows. It was clearly the same age as the lobby: the same whitewashed stone, oak ceiling, carved figures in the shadows, rows of darkened paintings. Halfway along, a fire leaped and spat in a vast brick fireplace; at the far end, a faded tapestry filled the wall. It showed a scene of obscure mythological interest, involving six cherubs, three plump semi-naked women, and a disreputable-looking bear. Beside the fireplace was a table, and the footmen setting out high tea.

George had already helped himself to a cake, and he was surveying the tapestry with interest. "Nice tarts," he said. "You should try a custard one."

"Not now. I need to talk with Lockwood."

"Good timing. Here he is."

Lockwood and Fairfax had entered the room from the lobby. Lockwood moved over to intercept us. His face was calm, but there was a bright gleam in his eye.

"Have you felt the *atmosphere* in this place?" I began. "We—"

"You'll never guess what," he said over me. "They've been through our bags."

George and I stared. "*What*?"

"While we were walking around with Starkins. Fairfax got his men to check them over. They wanted to make sure we hadn't brought any canisters of Greek Fire."

George whistled. "They can't do that!"

"I know! When we'd given them our word."

Over at the tea table, Fairfax belabored the footmen for some error. He waved an arm, stamped his stick upon the floor. "How do you *know* he did it?" I said softly.

"Oh, he told me straight out, after I called the bank. Bold as brass he was. Said he'd do the same to anyone. Have to protect the fabric of the ancient building, and its *highly* expensive furniture—blah, blah, blah. But the *real* message he was giving me was: it's his house, his rules. We play it his way, or not at all."

"It's been like that from the start," George said. "This whole thing is screwy. Nothing makes sense. He doesn't allow us to take flares. He gives us no time for research. Then he throws us into what he claims is one of the most haunted sites in Britain, and—"

"It's not just a *claim*," I said. "Can't you feel it? All around us?" I stared at them.

Lockwood nodded curtly. "Yes. I feel it."

"Well then, do you really think we should—?"

"Mr. Lockwood!" Fairfax's deep voice rolled out across the gallery. "Your tea awaits! Come to the table, and let me advise you about the evening."

The meal was good, the tea was Pitkins' best, and the warmth of the crackling fire drove back the deathly silence for a while. Fairfax sat alongside us while we ate, watching us with his black and hooded eyes, and talking generalities about the Hall. He discussed its many treasures—the late medieval ceilings, the collections of Sèvres porcelain and Queen Anne furniture, the unique Renaissance oils hanging in the lobby and stairs. He told us of the extensive wine cellars, running beneath our feet; of the herb gardens, which he hoped in due time to restore; of the ruined priory cloisters drowned beneath the lake. He did not mention anything of any relevance to our assignment until the tea was done. Then he dismissed the footmen and got down to business.

"Time presses," he said, "and Starkins and I are keen to leave before the light fails. No doubt you have your own preparations to make before you can begin your work, so I shall be brief. As I told you the other day, this wing is the afflicted region of the house. Perhaps you have sensed as much already."

He waited. Lockwood, who was chasing a raisin around his plate with a long thin finger, smiled urbanely. "It promises to be a very intriguing night, sir," he said.

Fairfax chuckled. "That's the spirit. Very well, here are the ground rules. As dusk falls, I shall shut you in, but be aware that those main doors will remain unlocked all night, should you need to leave the building. In addition, on each level you will find an iron door leading to my apartments in the East Wing. These will be locked, but in case of emergency, rap on them loudly and I will come to your aid. Electrical equipment does not work well in this wing, owing to psychic influences, but we will rig up a telephone in the lobby that will connect you to Starkins's cottage. All internal doors will, with one exception, be unlocked so you can roam where you please. As for that exception"—he tapped his jacket pocket—"I have the key here, and will give it to you presently. Any questions so far?"

"It would be useful if you could indicate the areas of most activity, sir," Lockwood said quietly. "If you have the time."

"Yes. Yes, of course. *Starkins!*" The old man raised his voice in a roar; from the lobby the even older man came scuttling, wringing his bony hands. "Get Boris and Karl to set up the phone," Fairfax said. "I'm taking Mr. Lockwood on a tour. He's a good servant, Starkins," he confided, once the caretaker had bobbed and shuffled away, "only hellish timorous. Wouldn't catch *him* going upstairs this late, even with the sun still in the sky. Well, I suppose caution's kept him alive this long. Let's get on."

We left the table and followed Fairfax out across the room. He indicated a door on the far side of the fireplace. "Through there you'll find the garden rooms, reception areas, conservatory, and kitchens. They're old, but not as ancient as this gallery here, which is part of the original priory. It used to lead to other buildings, but they were pulled down long ago." He pointed to the tapestry at the end. "That's where the house ends now."

He led us back through the lobby and over to an archway beyond. Here was a square, carpeted room made dark by rows of towering bookshelves; on the far side was a studded metal door. Uncomfortable looking modern chairs of iron and leather stood among reading tables. One wall was almost covered by a large collection of framed photographs, some in color, most in black and white. The largest of all, right in the center, showed a serious young man, in doublet, ruff, and tights, scrutinizing a moldy-looking skull.

Lockwood regarded it with interest. "Excuse me, sir, but isn't that you?"

Fairfax nodded. "Yes, that's me. I played Hamlet in my youth. Indeed, I played most Shakespearean roles, but the Dane was perhaps my favorite. Ah, 'To be or not to be,' the hero caught suspended between life and death. . . . If I must say so myself, I was rather good. So then: this is the library, where I spend most time during my visits. My predecessor's taste in books was poor, so I have replaced his with my own collection and refurbished it a little. It is just a step through the door there to the safety of my chambers, and the iron furniture—made by my own company, of course—keeps the ghosts away."

"A very pleasant room, if I may say so," Lockwood commented.

"You won't spend much time here during your search." Fairfax returned us to the lobby, where Starkins was setting a black, old-fashioned telephone on a side table, beside an ornate vase. "The Source, whatever it is, is doubtless in the oldest portion of the house. The lobby, the Long Gallery or, most probably, upstairs. Hey, careful there!" Two footmen were unraveling a coil of telephone wire around the table. "That's Han Dynasty! Do you know the *value* of that vase?"

He continued to rebuke them, but I had tuned him out. I walked across the lobby, listening with my inner ear, hearing only my heart beating in the waiting silence. Ahead of me the great stairs rose, curving to the quarter landing and onward into darkness. Strange creatures, with lots of scales and horns, were carved into the sides of the balustrade every other step. Each supported a small plinth between its claws.

"Hear anything?" George murmured. He'd drifted alongside me.

"No. The reverse. It's like it's cloaked, or something."

"I see you've found the legendary Screaming Staircase!" Fairfax was back with us once more. "See those plinths beside the carven dragons? Those are where the Red Duke set the skulls of his victims—or so the story goes. Perhaps, after tonight, you will be able to confirm the story of the stairs. I hope, for your sake, you do not hear it scream."

He led the way up the flight, stick tapping on the stone. We followed in a silent, ragged procession, each ignoring the others, letting our senses take the lead. I let my fingers run across the hand-rails, opening my mind to psychic traces, listening all the time.

We crossed below the window, four slow figures stained with the sun's last rays, climbed another flight, and arrived at a landing. A deep burgundy carpet and flocked red wallpaper absorbed all sounds. There was a strange sweet smell up here, like tropical flowers, heavy with the taint of decay. A long, wide corridor that I remembered from George's plans ran east-west, following the line of the house. Numerous rooms opened on both sides; through half-open doors I glimpsed dark-toned furniture, paintings, heavy golden mirrors. . . . Fairfax ignored them all. He led the way west along the corridor until it ended in a door.

Fairfax halted; whether it was the effort of the stairs, or the suddenly stifling quality of the air, he was out of breath.

"Beyond this barrier," he said finally, "is the place I told you of. The Red Room."

It was a sturdy wooden door, closed and locked, and no different from the others we'd passed—except for the mark upon it. Someone, at some time, had slashed a great, rough X upon its central panel. One stroke was short, the other long; both were made with violence, scoured deep into the wood.

Fairfax adjusted the position of his stick upon the floor. "Now, Mr. Lockwood, pay close attention. Because of its particular danger, this room is always kept locked. However, I have the key here, and I hereby transfer it to your possession."

He made a great show of it, patting and rummaging. Finally the key appeared: a small gold thing on a loop of dark-red ribbon. Lockwood took it coolly.

"It is my belief," Fairfax said, "that the Source is in that room. Whether you decide to pursue it is a matter for yourselves. You do not *have* to enter. I leave it up to you. I think you can already sense, however, that I am right. . . ."

He may have said more, but I was too busy trying to block out the faint, insistent whispering sounds that had suddenly broken through the silence. They were somewhere very close, and I did not like the voices. I noticed that Lockwood had gone ashen, and even George looked green and queasy; he'd drawn his collar high about his neck as if he felt the cold.

Down in the lobby, the telephone had been rigged up beside the vase, its cable running across the stones to a socket somewhere in the library. The footmen had gone. Old Bert Starkins jittered by the doors, silhouetted in the half-dark, desperate to follow them.

"Ten minutes, sir!" he cried.

Fairfax regarded us. "Mr. Lockwood?"

Lockwood nodded. "That's fine. Ten minutes is all we need."

We worked in silence, beneath the high thin windows of the Long Gallery, emptying out the bags, collecting the equipment, tightening straps, and adjusting gear. Each of us had our usual tools—plus a few extra, to make up for our lack of flares.

At my belt I carried my rapier, a flashlight and extra batteries, three candles with a lighter and a box of matches, five small silver seals (each of a different shape), three sachets of iron filings, three salt-bombs, two flasks of lavender water, my thermometer, my notebook and pen. Next, on a separate strap, looped like a sash across my shoulder, I had two lines of plastic canisters, arranged in pairs. Each pair contained half a pound of iron filings and half a pound of salt. Next, also over my shoulder: I had a loop of slender iron chain, six feet long when fully unfurled, and tightly wound with Bubble-Wrap to prevent excessive noise. Last, in an outer pocket of my coat, I kept: a pack of emergency provisions—energy drink, sandwiches, and chocolate. Our thermos flasks of good hot tea, and the larger chains and seals were carried in a separate bag.

In addition to my normal clothes I wore thermal gloves, a thermal vest and leggings, and thick socks under my boots. It wasn't cold enough yet for my hat, so I stuffed this in the pocket of my parka. And I still had the necklace in its silver-glass case, hidden around my neck.

The others were outfitted more or less the same, though Lockwood also had his dark glasses clipped to the breast pocket of his coat. The equipment weighed us down and was more cumbersome than usual, but we each carried enough iron to be individually self-reliant. If we were separated, and the need came, we could set up our own circles of defense. The duffel bags still contained double sets of two-inch iron chains—which even the strongest Visitor would find pretty hard to move—but we weren't wholly dependent on those now.

We finished. The light outside the windows was almost gone. Over in the fireplace, the orange flames danced low. Darkness crept along the ceiling of the Long Gallery and weltered in the crooks and angles of the great stone staircase. But so what if it did? Yes, the day was dead and the night had come, and the Visitors of the Hall were stirring, but Lockwood & Co. were ready. We worked together, and we wouldn't be afraid.

"Well, that's it," Fairfax said. He stood beside Starkins at the door. "I shall re-enter here at nine tomorrow morning to receive your report. Are there any final questions?"

He gazed around at us; we stood there waiting, Lockwood smiling softly in that way he had, hand resting on his rapier, seemingly as relaxed as if he was lining up for a cab. Beside him, George—as awkwardly impassive as ever, blinking through his thick, round specs, his pants hitched high against the weight of salt and iron. And me . . . How did *I* look, I wonder, in those final moments? I hope I carried myself well. Hope I didn't let the fear show.

"Any questions?" Fairfax repeated.

Each of us stood there quietly, waiting for him to shut his trap and go.

"Until the morning, then!" Fairfax raised his hand in ponderous farewell. "Good luck to you all!" He nodded crisply to Bert Starkins, and turned to descend the steps. Starkins reached out to close the doors. Twin squeals of hinges; the doors swung in. For a moment the caretaker's body was framed between them, silhouetted against the twilight like a gaunt and twisted gallows-tree. . . . Then the doors slammed shut. The reverberation of their closing rang sharply around the lobby and away along the galleries. I could hear the echoes drifting on and on into the dusty reaches of the house.

"Wouldn't it be good if he'd forgotten his stick," George said, "and he had to scurry back in again to pick it up? That would absolutely *ruin* the effect, wouldn't it?

Neither of us answered. The echoes had faded, and now the eager silence of the house rose to enfold us like the waters of a well.

Chapter 20

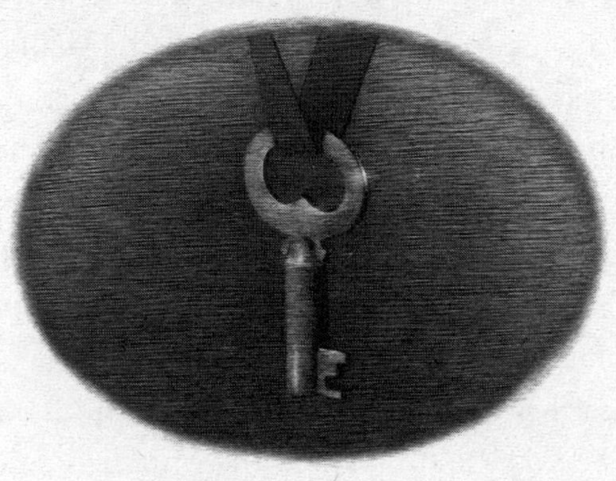

"First things first," Lockwood said. "Wait here."

He walked away across the lobby, boots tapping on the flagstones, under the gaze of the old lords and ladies of Combe Carey, to a small door beside the staircase. He opened the door and disappeared within. The door shut. There was a pause. George and I looked at each other. An oddly ceramic sound followed, then silence; then a toilet flushing. Lockwood emerged, wiping a hand on his coat. He strolled back to us unhurriedly. "That's better," he said. He was carrying a glistening wet packet under his arm.

"What's this?" George asked.

Lockwood flourished the packet. "Seven of the strongest magnesium flares Satchell's could provide," he said. "Strap them in your belts as usual and off we go." He broke the tape seal round the bag and unfolded the wet plastic. When he tipped it, two bright silver canisters fell out onto his palm.

"Lockwood . . ." George began, "how did—"

"You had the flares under your clothes!" I cried. "You hid them when we arrived! While we were waiting outside with Starkins!"

He smiled; his teeth glinted dimly in the half-light. "That's right. They were strapped to the lining of my coat. As soon as we got here I nipped to the loo and hid them in the toilet tank. Here you go, Lucy. Hold out your hands."

I took comforting possession of the cylinders and fixed them to my belt in their proper place. Lockwood tipped out two more and handed them to George.

"I guessed that Fairfax would frisk us or check our equipment eventually," he said, "and I wanted them stashed away and out of sight before that happened. I must admit, though, I didn't think he'd have the nerve to rifle through our bags while we weren't looking. But there you go, that's a measure of the man he is."

"Why, what kind of a man *is* he?" George said, staring at his canisters.

"A dreadful one. Isn't it obvious? And here are two for me. . . ."

I shook my head, marveling. "If Fairfax *knew* you'd done this . . ."

"Ah, but he doesn't." Lockwood wore his wolflike smile. "And I'm not going to lose any sleep over deceiving him. He's laid out the rules so far. This is where we start to adjust them in our favor."

"I'm not arguing, Lockwood," George said. "This is great work. But you know that if we set fire to so much as the leg of a Queen Anne chair, we won't be getting the rest of our money. In fact, Fairfax will probably sue us, like the Hopes did, so we'll be right back where we started."

"Oh, he'd sue us, all right," Lockwood agreed. "But who cares? This Greek Fire just might save our lives. Remember what happened to the last group of agents who spent the night here? No one's finding *us* stone dead on the floor. Which brings me to my last little purchase yesterday. . . ."

He tapped the upturned packet. Out rolled a seventh cylinder, slightly larger than the rest. Like the others, it had the Sunrise Corporation's rising sun logo stamped on its side, but the paper wrapper was dark red instead of white. It had a long fuse at one end.

"New type of flare," Lockwood said, attaching it next to the other canisters on his belt. "The guy at Satchell's said Fittes and Rotwell agents have begun using them on cluster cases—Blitz victims, plague sites, and so on. It sends out a broad blast wave of silver, iron, and magnesium. We'll have to be *far* away when it goes up, because it's industrial strength, apparently. I hope so; it cost enough. Now—where can I hide this trash?" He crumpled the wet packet, and stuffed it inside the opening of Fairfax's Han vase. "Good," he said briskly. "Let's get to work."

We chose the library as our base of operations. It was close both to the main exit and the door connecting to the safer wing, and its profusion of iron chairs would likely dampen Visitor activity. We dragged our bags inside and set up an electric lantern on one table. Lockwood turned it down low.

"Well, we've had a quick look around already," he said. "Any thoughts?"

"The whole place is heaving with them," I said.

George nodded. "Particularly—"

"The corridor near the Red Room?"

"Yeah."

"Did you hear anything, Lucy?"

"In that corridor? A lot of whispering. It was too quiet to make out any of the words, but the voices were . . . wicked, I think. Everywhere else, just silence. But it's a silence that I *know* is going to break as the night goes on." I gave an apologetic smile. "Sorry, that doesn't make much sense, does it?"

Lockwood nodded. "Actually, it does. It's just the same with me. I can sense death-glows *everywhere*, but I can't quite see them yet. What about you, George?"

"I'm not as tuned in as you two," he said, "but one thing I *have* noticed." He unclipped his thermometer and held the reading toward us. "When we were in the library, with Fairfax, the temperature was sixty degrees. It's down to fifty now. That's dropping fast."

"It'll go a lot lower yet," Lockwood said. "All right, we'll be systematic. We'll map temperatures and record sensations. Ground floor first, including the staircase—then the cellars. Then we'll take a break. After that: the other floors. The night's long, and it's a big house. We stick together at all times. No one wanders off alone. For *any* reason. If you need to take a leak, we all go. Simple as that."

"No more tea for me, then," I said.

I was right. The place *was* heaving with them. And it wasn't long before the ghosts began to show themselves.

Thanks to the iron furniture, the library—where we started—had relatively few paranormal traces. But even here, with the lantern briefly switched off and us standing in darkness, we started to notice little flecks and threads of light darting across our vision. They were too faint and fleeting to build into a true manifestation, but they were plasmic traces all the same. Following the traditional Fittes technique, George took temperature readings in all four corners and in the center of the room. He noted them carefully on his floor plan. I stood guard with the rapier while he did so; Lockwood and I then used our Talents to check sensations. We didn't pick up much. The silence blanketed my ears. Lockwood reported some faint illuminations that he guessed were ancient death-glows. He seemed more interested in the cheesy theatrical photos on the wall.

In the lobby, George's readings gave an average of fifty degrees. The flecks of plasm were noticeably stronger now, shooting around us like fireflies in the dark. Here too came the first glimpse of green-white ghost-fog, a haze so subtle that trying to focus on it hurt your eyes. It clung close to the floor and built slowly in the margins of the room.

And now the other phenomena began to gather pace. When I concentrated, I began to hear a low-lying crackling sound, like radio static, at the far edge of perception. It died and swelled repeatedly, forever threatening to cohere into meaningful noise, but never quite doing so. For some reason its obscurity disturbed me. I did my best to shut it out.

Meanwhile Lockwood had detected three death-glows in the lobby, each one disconcertingly bright.

"Recent, you think?" I said.

He took off his sunglasses and clipped them to his coat. "Or a record of an old but horribly traumatic event. Impossible to say."

The great staircase itself provided surprisingly low-key readings. Its temperature (George made measurements on several steps, then took the average) was no different from the lobby. I detected no variation in the underlying sounds there, and certainly no screaming. When (rather tentatively) I touched its stonework and sought psychic impressions, I got nothing except a sensation of strong unease, which—speaking frankly—I was already feeling anyway.

In the Long Gallery, the far wall was lost in shadows and the air was chill. The roaring fire in the grate had shrunk down to a single palsied flame; it shook and quivered, but never quite went out. George consulted the thermometer again. "Forty-six degrees," he said, "and falling."

"I'm starting to detect malaise," I said. "Anyone else pick that up?"

They nodded. Yes, it was starting. That old familiar drooping of the spirits, that leaden weight pressing cruelly on your heart, so that all you wanted to do was curl up in a ball and close your eyes. . . .

We drew close, hands on rapiers, and walked together down the room.

The feelings of despair grew stronger as we proceeded, past the tea table and the fireplace, toward the faded tapestry at the far end of the gallery. The temperature dropped fast. Ghost-fog drifted at our ankles and lapped against the sofas. And now, when we looked back, the first true apparitions came into view, dim figures standing in the center of the lobby.

By the peculiar rule of weak Type Ones, they were clearest when viewed out of the corner of your eye, granular notches of gray and black that flickered briefly and melted into nothing. Two were child-size, one was adult: aside from that you couldn't tell anything about them.

Ignoring them as best we could, we took turns standing guard while we did our readings at the farthest wall. It was noticeably colder here. Lockwood raised a corner of the tapestry and looked beneath it.

"I wondered about that too," George said. "Anything?"

Lockwood let the tapestry drop. "Just stone. This *is* a cold spot, though."

"Yeah. Forty-two degrees, going on forty-one. Okay, we're done here. Let's keep going."

By the time we'd finished with the ground floor and arrived back at the staircase, we'd been exposed to a whole range of sinister mists, sounds, and odors, not all of them courtesy of George. Nowhere else had proved to be quite as chilly as the Long Gallery, or so baleful in atmosphere, but supernatural phenomena extended throughout the wing. The malignant static noise had grown louder. Several other death-glows had been mapped. Apparitions were frequent. They never came close to us, but always materialized at the far ends of corridors, in places we'd just been, or were just about to go to. Their details could not be picked out, though some were clearly children. The impression they gave was typical of your standard Type Ones: unresponsive, unaggressive, just a little sad.

"They're the small stuff," George said as, with the frail orb of Lockwood's candle out in front, we descended the narrow cellar stairs. "Shades, Lurkers, Hazes . . . They're just the outlying manifestations that have gathered around the original, deeper haunting. Nothing we've seen so far is the Source itself, or even close to it, except maybe the cold spot by the tapestry. And you know what room *that's* directly under, don't you?"

I didn't answer. None of us had mentioned the Red Room for over an hour, even though it was clear to all of us where our investigation was likely to lead.

It was pitch black in the cellar, and there was a nasty draft. The candle blew out almost immediately, and we had to resort to flashlights. The beams picked out a spreading complex of vaulted passageways, gray stones, ancient pillars, and an uneven flagstone floor across which the ghost-fog curled. Some of the alcoves were filled with broken casks and empty racks once used for storing wine; the rest contained firewood, lumber, spider webs, and rats. As we scuffed our way ever farther in, the cobwebs grew thicker and the ghost-fog brighter. The temperature kept going down.

The last room ended in a blank stone wall.

"Same pattern as above," George said, scribbling on his map while I held the flashlight. Lockwood stood beside us with the rapier. "We're directly below the far end of the Long Gallery, and again we've hit a cold spot. It's forty-one degrees here too: that's the coldest reading in the cellars. Look at the webs up there. . . . There's something about this wall that—Ow!"

Lockwood had shoved us aside. He sliced frantically downward with his rapier. The tip struck the stonework of the end wall; yellow sparks ignited in the dark.

He gave a curse. "Missed!" he snarled. "It's gone."

I had my sword out; George, overbalanced by his backpack and chains, had capsized on the flagstones. Both of us stared wildly all around. My flashlight beam spun in crazy circles. It was like we were surrounded by a thin gray hoop of rushing stone.

"What was it?" I said. "Lockwood—?"

He brushed his hair out of his eyes, breathing hard. "Didn't you see?"

"No."

"It was there. Standing right beside you. God, it was quick."

"*Lockwood. . . .*"

"A man—swimming out of the dark beside the wall. Just a face and hand. It was like he was reaching out to grab you, Lucy. It was a monk, I think. The top of his head was bald. His hair was cut in one of those tonsil things."

"Tonsure," George said, from the floor.

"*Tonsil, tonsure*—whatever. I didn't like his face."

We returned upstairs. A few coils of ghost-fog had penetrated a little distance into the library, but the lantern still gleamed strongly, and the apparitions had been kept at bay. Lockwood turned the light up a little. We took off our loops of iron chains to give our backs a rest, laid our flasks and rations out on Fairfax's reading desks, and sat together in silence. It was a little after ten p.m.

For some while I'd been conscious of a cold weight pressing on my chest, and I took the opportunity to pull the silver-glass case out from beneath my coat. A faint blue gleam shone from within: the first time I'd seen the ghost-girl's locket give a spectral glow. Clearly her spirit was still active. Perhaps she was responding to the strength of Visitor activity all around; perhaps there was some other reason for the light. When it came to Visitors, it was all guesswork. Even after fifty years, there was so much we didn't know.

George had his floor plans spread out on his ample knee; with his pencil, he tapped an irritating rhythm on his teeth as he considered our annotations. Lockwood finished his cookies; flashlight in hand, he got up to inspect the bookshelves. Out in the lobby a solitary ghost stood shrouded in the darkness, flickered suddenly, and was gone.

"Got it," George said.

I tucked the glass case out of sight. "Got what?"

"The Source. I know where it is."

"I think we can all guess that," I said. "The Red Room." It was time *someone* brought it up. After we'd rested, we were due to go upstairs.

"Possibly," George said. "And possibly not." He had his glasses off, so he could rub his tired eyes. Now he put them back on. It's a curious thing with George. With his glasses off, his eyes looked small and weak—blinky and a bit baffled, like an unintelligent sheep that's taken a wrong turn. But when he put them on again, they went all sharp and steely, more like the eyes of an eagle that eats dumb sheep for breakfast. They did that now. "Something's just occurred to me," he said. "It's been staring us in the face in these old floor plans all this time. But our readings confirm it, I think. Look here—"

He positioned the two plans together on the table.

"Here's the old sketch of the priory ruins," he said, "done in medieval times. Here's the refectory, which becomes the Long Gallery. Upstairs, these rooms here are the monks' dormitories. Many of them are gone, but this one still exists—it's now known as the Red Room."

"Lockwood," I said, suddenly, "are you listening to this?"

"Mm. Yes . . ." Lockwood was standing by Fairfax's wall of photographs. He'd gotten a large book from the shelves and was flipping through it idly.

"The medieval sketch," George went on, "shows passages beyond the Red Room, and beyond the Long Gallery, too, which have since been knocked down. They led to a series of rooms on both levels—more dormitories, perhaps, or stores, or chapels for praying in. There was probably an extension on the cellar level, too—I don't know, that's not shown on the plans. But when you look at the nineteenth-century floor plan, those extra areas are gone. It shows the wing as it ends today—with that big stone wall, where the cold spots are."

"It's a very sturdy wall, isn't it?" I said.

"It's a very *thick* wall," George said. "And that's the point. It's *much* thicker than the wall shown on the original plan. It extends out across where those earlier passages were."

A tremor of excitement, like a little electric surge, ran through my chest and prickled the muscles of my arms. "You think . . ."

His glasses glinted. "Yeah. I think we're talking secret rooms."

"So . . . when the rest was destroyed, they might have sealed up some of the connecting passages? I guess it's possible. What do you say, Lockwood?"

No answer. When I looked back, Lockwood had taken several other volumes from the shelves and was deeply engrossed in them. He had his back to us, his thermos balanced on the stack of books. As I watched, he took a leisurely sip of tea.

"Lockwood! What the hell are you doing?"

He turned; his eyes had that same detached look I'd noticed

before during the past few days. It was like he was seeing something far away. "Sorry, Lucy. Did you speak?"

"It was more of a yell. What are you doing? George is on to something here."

"Is he? Excellent . . . I was just looking through Fairfax's scrapbooks. He's kept a record of all the plays he acted in when he was young: programs, tickets, reviews . . . that sort of thing. It's fascinating. He was quite the actor, once upon a time."

I stared at him. "Who cares? Why is that relevant? What's it got to do with us finding the Source?"

"Nothing . . . I'm just trying to put my finger on something. It's close, but it keeps slipping out of reach . . ." A switch flicked in him, his face cleared. "And you're right, it's not the priority quite yet." He bounded over, sat down next to us, gave George a friendly slap on the back. "You were saying, George? Secret rooms in the far wall?"

"Rooms or passages, yes." George adjusted his spectacles; he spoke quickly. "You remember Fairfax's story about the doomed Fittes expedition thirty years ago? That settles it for me. Two agents were found dead in the Red Room. The third one—the boy—vanished. Far as we know, ghosts don't eat their victims. So where is he?" He prodded the floor plan with a stubby finger. "Here. Somewhere in that unusually thick end wall. He found the entrance and went inside. A Visitor—perhaps *the* Visitor at the heart of all this—got him. He never returned. He's in there still, and I'll bet you three of Arif's best chocolate doughnuts *that's* where the Source is too."

We sat looking at the plan in our little pool of lantern light, the sea of ghost-fog lapping at its fringes. Lockwood had his head bowed, hands pressed tight together. He was deep in thought.

"Okay," he said at last, "I've something important to say."

"It's not about Fairfax's scrapbooks again, is it?" I said.

"No. Listen. George, as usual, has gotten it right. The Combe Carey Source is probably hidden in that wall. To find it we'd have to find the entrance, and that's almost certainly in the Red Room. Now, some of the stories about the Hall might be bunk—I don't think there's anything in that Screaming Staircase yarn, for instance—but the Red Room is clearly different. We all felt the atmosphere outside that door. It would be no small thing to go inside." He looked up, surveyed us each in turn. "But we don't have to. Fairfax said so himself. We don't *have* to go into that room. Just by turning up here this evening, we've earned the money to pay off the damages caused by the Sheen Road fire. Fairfax has already paid—I checked with the bank when we arrived. Sure, we can get more if we track down the Source, but that's not essential. The company will survive without it."

"Will it, though?" George said. "Exactly how many more cases are you expecting to get, Lockwood? Apart from Fairfax's surprise offer, our reputation's up in flames."

Lockwood didn't try to deny it. "Like I keep saying," he said quietly, "we need a big success to turn it all around. Solving the Annie Ward murder would do it, of course, and we're close there, thanks to Lucy. But . . . it's not guaranteed." He sighed. "I can't quite make the final jump. As for finding the Source here—well, that's certainly another option. But it's a risky one. Whatever's hidden in this place is frighteningly strong." He sat back and smiled—and this time it wasn't the full megawatt version, the one you obeyed despite yourself: just a warm, companionable grin. "You know me," he said. "I think we'd be a match for it. But I'm not going to impose that belief on you. If you want to steer clear, that's fine. I leave it up to you."

George and I looked at each other. I waited for him to speak; he waited for me. And in my head, the crackling ghostly static died away, as if the thing that controlled the house awaited my decision too.

Before that evening? I might have held back. I'd chosen wrongly too many times in crisis situations to fully trust my instincts now. But since stepping through the door, and particularly since we'd begun our explorations, my confidence had slowly risen. We'd worked well together, so much better than ever before. We'd been careful, rigorous, even competent. . . . It showed me what Lockwood & Co. might one day become. This wasn't something I wanted to give up lightly. I took a deep breath.

"I vote we take a quick look," I said, "*providing* we keep an avenue of retreat open behind us. If things go bad, we leave and get out of the building as quickly as possible."

Lockwood nodded. "Fair enough. And George?"

George puffed out his ample cheeks. "Amazingly, Lucy's talked some sense for once. I feel exactly the same way. Provided"—he patted the cylinders at his belt—"we're allowed to use all our weapons if we have to."

"That's settled, then," Lockwood said quietly. "Gather the bags, and let's go."

Now that we'd made the decision, we didn't hang around—but we weren't reckless, either. We made cautious progress up the stairs, always watching and listening a few steps ahead. As before, the phantoms kept their distance, but the ghost-fog billowed around our knees. Lockwood saw death-glows on the landing and beyond the bedroom doors. For my part, the towering silence was back: it pressed tightly against my temples. The air felt thick and syrupy. The cloying sickly-sweet smell followed us from the landing.

Outside the defaced door the whispering had died away. When I looked back along the passage I could sense the apparitions clustering beyond the fringes of the flashlight beam.

"It's like they're waiting," I muttered. "It's like they're waiting for us to go in."

"Who's got the mints?" George said. "I just *know* we're going to need the mints in there."

Lockwood took the key from his pocket and put it in the lock. "Turns easily," he said. There was a single, solid click. "Okay, that's done. Here we go. Like Lucy said, we take a quick look, and that's all."

George nodded. I did my best to smile.

"Don't worry," Lockwood said. "It'll be fine."

Then he took hold of the handle and pushed, and the horror of the night began.

Chapter 21

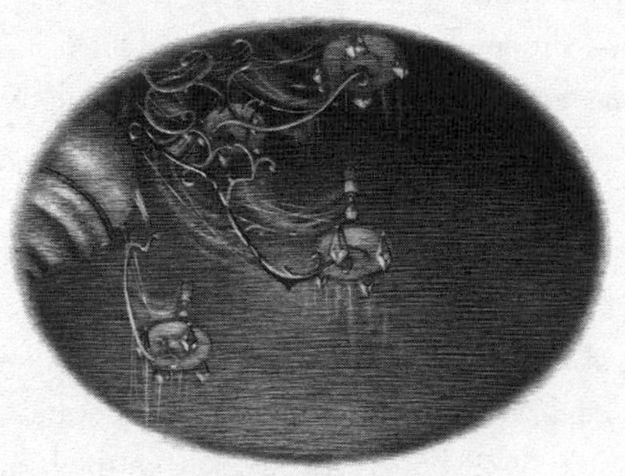

The hinges didn't squeak eerily or anything. To be honest, they didn't need to.

As the door swung open, there was a sigh of dry, cool air, a smell of dust and absence. It was the same sensation you get in any unused room. Lockwood shone his flashlight into the darkness; its soft round glow picked out bare floorboards, running left to right. They were gray and dark and stained. In places, ragged strips of some old rug were visible, fused to the boards by centuries of grime.

He moved the beam upward until it hit the opposite wall. A glimpse of high white wainscotting, then dark-green wallpaper, almost black with dirt and age. In places it had been ripped away, revealing the bricks beneath. Still the beam rose: we saw a strip of heavy molding, then a ceiling of ornate plasterwork, covered with swirls and spirals. The light reached a single chandelier hanging from the center of the ceiling. Fronds of soft gray webbing dangled from its scrolls and chains, swaying in currents stirred by the opening of the door.

Spiders. . . . A sure sign.

Lockwood dropped the flashlight low. Down at our feet, the corridor carpet ended precisely at the line of the door. A thick strip of iron had been embedded here. Beyond were dust and floorboards and the utter desolation of the Red Room.

"Anyone sense anything?" Lockwood said. His voice sounded strange and hollow.

Neither of us did. Lockwood stepped over the iron band, and George and I followed him, bringing the heavy duffel bags. Cool air swirled around us. Our boots tapped softly on the boards.

I'd expected to be hit by strong phenomena right off, the moment we went in. But all was very quiet, though the pressure in my skull was worse than ever. The ghost-fog had not manifested in the room, and I couldn't hear the static or the whispering right now. We put our bags down, and with our flashlights surveyed our surroundings.

It was a large, rectangular space, taking up the full depth of the wing. The wall opposite marked the end of the house and corresponded to the tapestried wall in the Long Gallery directly below. This wall had no doors or windows, but in places the paper had been stripped away to reveal bricks or stones beneath.

The wall on the right had no windows; that on the left had originally had three, but two had been bricked up. The last one had a shutter, folded back against the sides of its recess.

Other than the chandelier, there was no furniture at all.

"Not very 'red,' is it?" George said. That had been my thought too.

"First things first," Lockwood said briskly. "Lucy, help me make a circle. George, secure our retreat, please."

Holding our flashlights in our teeth, Lockwood and I opened the duffel bags and pulled out the heavy duty two-inch chains. We laid them on the floor and began to shape them into the necessary circle—our defense against whatever waited in the room.

George, meanwhile, bent to his backpack. He unzipped a side pocket and felt inside. "I've a Visitor-proof DFD somewhere in here," he said. "Hold on a sec. . . ."

"DFD?" I said.

"Door-Fixing Device. Just a bit of the latest tech. Got it from Satchell's. Pricey, yes, but worth it. Ah, here we go." He produced a rough hewn triangle of wood.

I stared at it. "Isn't that just a wedge?"

"No. A DFD, my friend. A DFD. It's got an iron core."

"It looks like you found it in a Dumpster. How much did you pay for it?"

"I can't remember." George kicked it firmly into position, so the door was held ajar. "Call it what you like. It'll stop the door from closing, and that might keep us alive."

He was right to that extent. In the case of the Shadwell Poltergeist the year before, two Grimble agents had been separated from their colleagues when the bathroom door blew shut on them. The door had then stuck fast; no one could get through, and the two agents had been battered to death by whirling ceramics. When the visitation had ended, the door had opened freely.

"Scatter salt across the doorway, too," Lockwood said. "Just to be sure." We'd finished the chain circle now and were hauling the bags inside. "Right, we retreat in here if anyone gives the word. Temperature?"

"Forty-three degrees," George said.

"So far, so good. At the moment this seems the quietest place in the house. Let's make the most of it. We'll hunt for hidden doors. It's the end wall, isn't it, George?"

"Yes. We're looking for any signs of a concealed entrance. Buttons, switches, that sort of thing. Try knocking for hollow areas too."

"Okay. Lucy and I will do the first search. George, stay here and watch our backs."

Lockwood and I went to opposite ends of the wall, our boots echoing in emptiness, flashlight beams focused small to minimize the disruption to our inner senses. I chose the lefthand corner, not far from the single unblocked window. Through the dirty glass I could just make out lights from a distant village, and a couple of winter stars.

I turned off the flashlight and ran my hands along the wall. It seemed smooth enough, the paper level and unbroken. I shuffled sideways, feeling high and low. Every now and then I stopped and listened, but all remained still.

"Anyone smell that?" Lockwood said suddenly. His profile hung at the edge of his flashlight beam. He was frowning, wrinkling his nose.

"Smell what?"

"Something sweet but sour. . . . I can't think what it is. It's familiar, but strange."

"Sounds a lot like Lucy," George remarked. He was behind us, in the center of the room.

The minutes passed. Lockwood's hand met mine in the darkness; we'd reached the middle of the wall. After a moment we each started going back the way we'd come, this time rapping the surface with our knuckles.

"A few wisps of plasm building," George called.

"You want us to stop?"

"Keep going for now."

At last, near the end of the wall, at the corner by the window, I detected a slight variation in the quality of sound. The ring of my knock seemed higher and more resonant, as if echoing from a space within.

"I may have something here," I said. "There's a place that sounds hollow. If you—"

"What was *that*?" George said. We'd all heard it: somewhere in the dark, a soft, decisive *tap*. Lockwood and I turned around.

"Come back to the circle," George said. "And keep your flashlights off. We'll use mine." His beam cut slowly, carefully past us as we hurried back to join him, strafing the ceiling, walls, and floor. All seemed exactly as before.

Or did it? Discreetly, insidiously, something in the atmosphere had changed.

We stood back to back in the center of the circle, shoulders pressing tight together.

"I'm going to turn the flashlight off," George said.

He did so. We gazed out into the blackness of the empty room.

"Lucy," Lockwood's voice said, "what do you hear?"

"The whispering's kicked off," I said. All at once it was very loud. "It's like before. A host of wicked voices."

"Can you tell where?"

"Not yet. Seems all around."

"Okay. George: what do you see?"

"Wisps and whirls of light. Bright, but brief. No one location."

There was a pause. "And you, Lockwood?" I said.

He spoke heavily. "I can see the death-glows now."

"More than one?"

"Lucy, there are *dozens*. I don't know how I didn't see them before. The whole room's a death chamber. . . ." He took a breath. "Everyone, draw your rapiers now."

Three sets of shoulders bumped and shifted. There was the collective rasp of iron.

"It sensed that," George said. "The wisps went into a frenzy. They've calmed again."

"Lucy?"

"The whispering got louder, angrier, then it died back. What do we do?"

"That smell!" Lockwood said. "It's there again. So strong! Surely you can—" He gave a little cry of frustration. "Don't *either* of you smell it?"

"No," I said. "Lockwood—concentrate. What do we do? Do we leave?"

"I think we've got to. Something big's coming. Ahh . . . these glows are bright!" I could hear him fumbling with his sunglasses, hurrying to put them on.

"But didn't Lucy say she'd found a door?" George said. "Shouldn't we—?"

"Not a door," I said. "I got a hollow thump, like the wall was thin, somehow."

"It doesn't matter either way," Lockwood said. "We're leaving the room now."

A *tap* sounded in the darkness, soft but heavy, the same as the first. Another followed. And then another.

"That's between us and the door," George said.

"No, it isn't."

"Quiet," Lockwood said. "Just listen."

Tap, tap, tap . . . Slow and regular: I timed five fast heartbeats between each sound. It wasn't easy to tell where the noise was coming from, or what it might be, but it seemed familiar. I'd heard the like before. For some reason the bathroom back in Portland Row came to mind—the lower one, where I sometimes took a shower, and where George's discarded underwear lay in wait for unwary feet. At first I thought it might be the shared sense of danger and foreboding that made me make the connection, then I realized it was something else. The shower head in that bathroom was faulty. It dripped.

Tap, tap, tap . . .

"Turn the light on, Lockwood," I whispered. "Direct it in front of you."

He obeyed without question. Perhaps he'd realized too.

The beam fell on the floorboards like a delicate ring of gold. Something black and irregular lay in its center. It looked rather like a large misshapen spider with innumerable legs. *Tap.* A new leg grew, splayed out to the side. *Tap.* Another leg: longer, thinner, stretched far across the wood. . . . With each tap there came a flash of movement in the middle of the shape. The black thing glistened. There was a hint of red.

Lockwood raised the flashlight slowly, in time to catch the next drip as it fell, midair. He lifted the flashlight to the plaster ceiling, where a wider, darker stain was spreading along the spiral molding. At its center, stuff as thick and dark as molasses sagged, grew heavy, broke loose in drops—to splash down upon the floor below.

"Now I know what the smell was," Lockwood muttered.

"Blood. . . ." I said.

"Well, technically, of course, it's plasm," George said. "The Visitor's just chosen a highly unusual, non-anatomical guise, which—"

"I don't care about *technically*, George!" I cried. "It *looks* like blood, it *smells* like it. It'll do as blood for me."

Even as we watched, the weight of substance pooling in the ceiling became too great to be released by a single steady outflow. Drips broke loose in a second place, slightly closer to us, and the rate of fall was faster. I flicked on my flashlight too, saw the floor stain spattering out. Broken fingers of blood reached in the direction of our chains.

"Don't let it near you," George said. "It'll ghost-touch just like any other kind of plasm."

"We're going," Lockwood said crisply. "Gather the bags. No, forget the chains; we're carrying spares. Ready? Quick, then. Follow me."

We stepped over the barrier of iron and looped out across the room, keeping far away from the spreading mass. Malevolence radiated off it in waves. The room was icy cold.

"Good-bye and good riddance to you," George said, as we approached the door.

But when we got there, it was closed.

For a moment none of us moved. I felt a coil of panic slide slick and tight around my belly. Lockwood stepped forward. He covered the ground in three quick strides, and tried the handle. He rattled at it urgently. "Shut," he said. "I can't open it."

"What the hell happened to the wedge?"

George's voice was faint. "The DFD."

I gave a wild curse. "I don't care what it was called, George! It didn't work! *You* didn't secure it properly."

"I secured it fine."

"No, you just nudged it in with your BFF! That's Big Fat Foot, by the way."

"Shut *up*, Lucy!"

"Will you *both* shut up," Lockwood snarled, "and help me with this door?"

We grasped the handle together and tugged as hard as we could. The door didn't budge.

"Where's the key?" I said. "Lockwood—*the key*. What did you do with it?"

He hesitated. "I left it in the door."

"Oh, that's great," I said. "Between you and George, we might as well have put up a sign for the Visitor saying *Be Our Guest*."

"I tell you I secured it *fine*," George shouted. "And I put the salt down too." He kicked out viciously at the grains beneath our boots. "See? It shouldn't have been able to go *near* the door."

"Calm down," Lockwood said. He had shone the flashlight back to the ceiling, where a new spur of blood had begun to well downward ominously close to where we stood. "It's responding to our panic. Let's get back to the circle."

We managed this okay, though we had to loop noticeably farther out across the room than before. Several of the drips had now intensified into unbroken streams, like taps left gently running. The noise they made was no longer a series of sharp clicks, but a continual liquid thrum. There was a considerable puddle of blood spreading on the floor.

"We're going to get surrounded," I said. "How much plasm has it *got* in there?"

"This is *huge*," George muttered. "It's not an ordinary Type Two. A Poltergeist would have the advanced telekinetic powers—shutting the door, keeping it closed, turning the key—but that doesn't fit with the manifestation. The blood makes it a Changer, surely. But Changers don't turn keys. . . ."

"I've been stupid," Lockwood said. "*Really* stupid. I underestimated everything. . . . Lucy, we're going to have to find the secret exit. You've got to show us where you felt the difference in the wall."

An arm of blood extended swiftly from the central pool upon the floor. Its tip drew close to the iron chains and retreated, fizzing, spitting. The air was thick with the smell of blood; it was difficult to breathe.

"Or we stay here. . . ." I said. "At least it can't get in."

George gave a yell; I felt him jump to the side. He stumbled over the duffel bags and nearly fell beyond the iron.

Lockwood cursed. "What the hell are you—?" He shone the

flashlight. George crouched on the bags, clutching at his jacket. A ribbon of smoke curled from his shoulder.

"Up above," he said hoarsely. "*Quick*."

The beam snapped upward. There—the chandelier, choked with dust and webs. A single rivulet of red had trickled from the ceiling, down the central column, and out along a curving crystal arm. At its lowest point, a new pendant of blood was slowly building.

"It—it can't do that," I stammered. "We're inside the iron."

"Move out of the way!" Lockwood pushed me back just as the drop fell, spattering on the floor in the center of the circle. We were all standing almost atop the iron chains. "We've made it too big," he said. "The power of the iron doesn't extend into the very center. It's weak there, and this Visitor's strong enough to overcome it."

"Adjust the chains inward—" George began.

"If we make the circle smaller," Lockwood said, "we'll be squeezed in a tiny space. It's scarcely midnight; we've seven hours till dawn and this thing's just gotten started. No, we've got to break out—and that means Lucy's corner. Come on."

Keeping our flashlights pointed up above us, we stepped out of the circle on the opposite side to the spreading pools and began to move around toward the left corner of the end wall. But no sooner did we do so than thick dark trails extended on the ceiling, flowing fast in our direction. The panic in my belly twisted tighter; I fought down the urge to scream.

"Wait," I said. "It's sensing where we are. If we *all* go there, it'll quickly hem us in."

Lockwood nodded. "You're right. Well done. Come on, George. We'll try to distract it. Lucy: get over there and keep on looking."

"Okay . . ." I hurried on. "But why me?"

"You're a girl," Lockwood called. "Aren't you supposed to be more sensitive?"

"To emotions, yes. To nuances of human behavior. Not necessarily to secret passages in a wall."

"Oh, it's much the same thing. Besides, flailing about with rapiers is basically all George and I are good at." He danced off across the room, swirling his flashlight, waving his sword high toward the ceiling. George did likewise, making for another corner.

Whether the Visitor was suitably distracted, I didn't have time to see. I put my rapier away, set my flashlight to its weakest setting, held it tight between my teeth so I could see roughly where I was. To my left was the window recess. Beyond the glass was the fresh cool air of nighttime, and a thirty-foot bone-snapping drop down to the gravel driveway. Who knows, perhaps we'd have to jump for it, before we were done. Perhaps that would be the better way to die.

Sweat poured down my face, despite the cold. My hands shook as I set them to the wall. As before, I ran my hands all over it, keeping to the area where I'd gotten the hollow sound.

No luck. Nothing but smoothness.

I reached the corner, felt up and down along the join. On sudden impulse I tried the adjoining wall. Maybe a switch or door was there. I stood on tiptoe, stretched as high as I could. I bent down low. I pressed and pushed. I shoved. I did all this until I reached the window recess. Still I had no luck.

Looking back, I discovered our tactics had worked up to a point. George and Lockwood were banging about in the far regions of the room, channeling their panic into whoops and whistles, and rude insults shouted at the Visitor. In response, the central ceiling pool had thrown out new branches: long angry streams of blood diverged around the chandelier, came lancing out toward them.

But I hadn't been forgotten either. To my shock, a stream of blood now stretched almost to my feet along the floor. Up above, an arm of the central stain extended perilously close, and from this a dark, thin stream was falling. Black spatters laced the boards beside my boots. One fell against my heel. There was a hiss; a thin white coil of smoke curled upward as I jumped away, up onto the deep sill below the window.

This was no good. Now I risked being completely trapped. I turned, crouched, prepared to leap down—and as I did so my fingers touched the wooden shutter that was folded back against the sides of the recess. I looked at it. And in that desperate moment, inspiration came.

I shone my flashlight full upon the shutter. It was a single solid panel, as high as the recess and almost as wide. At the back, near the window, great black hinges fused it to the stone. If you pulled it, it would swing out to cover the glass.

And—possibly—reveal something else.

I grasped the wood, tried to pull it to me. I wanted to see beneath it—just in case. Somewhere, something gave. I felt the shutter move. I flashed a quick look with my flashlight—and saw a crack had opened, a gap just wide enough to get my fingers in. Perhaps there was nothing but stone beneath; perhaps it really *was* a shutter. Or perhaps . . .

"George! Lockwood!" I shouted out to them over my shoulder, past a column of gushing blood. "I may have found it! Quick—I need your help!"

Without waiting, I pulled at the wood. I heaved, I tugged. It didn't shift at all.

Something shoved me to the side. It was Lockwood, throwing himself into the recess. The blood was nearing the edges of the room. He'd had to flatten against the wall as he ran toward the ledge. George careered after him, holding his rapier at an angle above his head. Falling blood splashed against the sword-tip, fizzing and sparking as it touched the iron. He jumped up next to us. No one spoke. George handed me the rapier. He and Lockwood grappled the wood, braced themselves, and pulled.

I turned and held the blade above us all as an ineffective shield.

The bloodstain on the ceiling now spread almost wall to wall; in our corner, a single triangle of clean space remained. Elsewhere torrents of blood fell in curtains, roaring, driving, gusting like rain waves in a thunderstorm. The floor was awash. It pooled between the floorboards and lashed up against the wainscotting. The chandelier dripped with it: the crystals shone red. Now I knew why the chamber was without furniture of any kind, why it had been deserted for so many years. Now I knew why it had the name it did.

George gasped, Lockwood gave a cry. They fell back, knocked against me, dragging the shutter open. Behind it, matted cords of cobwebs trailed like corpse hair. My flashlight showed darkness too—a narrow arch inside the wall.

Blood spattered on the corner of the shutter and on the tilted blade above my head. I felt it fizz against my gloves and arms.

"In! In!" I gestured to the others; they tumbled through. I followed, moving backward, stepping from sill to ancient stone. Blood poured down the inside of the shutter; it ran down the sides of the recess, flooding toward my feet.

On the inside of the shutter door we saw an ancient rope, fixed there by an iron ring. George and Lockwood seized it, heaved. The door swung slowly inward. Blood cascaded through the closing crack, splashed thickly on George's arm. He cursed, fell back; I lost my balance too. Lockwood gave a final tug. The door closed shut—and we were left in darkness, listening to the crashing and drumming of the blood as the unnamed Thing wrought its fury on the far side of the wall.

Chapter 22

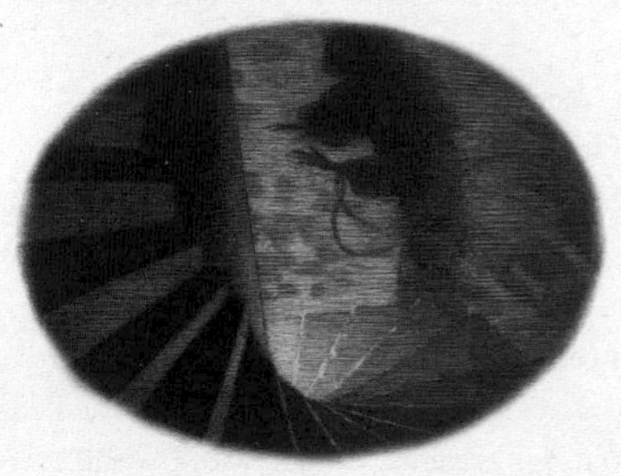

All at once, like a switch had been flicked or a plug pulled, the terrible noise cut out. We were alone.

The sudden silence made me flinch. I sat against rough stone, head raised, mouth open, panting for breath. My own blood hammered in my ears. My chest rose and fell in jerks; each movement gave me pain. Though it was utterly black, I knew the others were sprawled beside me in the tightness of the passage. Their wheezes mirrored mine.

We'd collapsed in a single heap, one on top of the other. The air was cold and sour, but at least the overpowering smell of blood was gone.

"George," I croaked, "are you okay?"

"No. Someone's buttocks are flattening my foot."

I shifted my position irritably. "I meant the *plasm*—where you got hit."

"Oh. Yes. Thank you. It didn't touch my hand, though I think this jacket's *ruined.*"

"That's good. It's an awful jacket. Who's got a flashlight? I just dropped mine."

"Me too," Lockwood said.

"Here." George clicked his on.

Flashlights never show you to your best advantage. In the sudden harshness, George and I crouched close together, eyes bulging, hair matted with sweat and fear. George's arm was stained a livid white and green where the plasm had struck him. Smoke rose from it, and also from the rapier across my knees. When I looked down I saw that my boots and leggings were spattered with the substance too.

Lockwood, miraculously, appeared to have escaped the worst of the assault. His coat was lightly stained, and the tip of his forelock had been burned white by a drop of plasm. But where George's face shone bright red, his had just gone paler; where George and I gasped and groaned and flopped about, he lay calm and rigid, waiting for his breathing to grow quiet. He had taken off his sunglasses, and his dark eyes glittered. His jaw was set. I could see at once that he had drawn his emotions deep inside himself, made them hard and steely. There was something in his face I hadn't seen before.

"Well," he said. "It's over for the moment."

George angled the flashlight toward the inside of the secret opening. Seconds before, thick fingers of blood had been pouring down it. Now the wood was dry, dusty, and unstained. There was no visual sign that anything had happened. If we'd gone back into the empty room, no doubt that would have been dry and clean as well.

Not that we *were* going back there anytime soon.

Lockwood sat up awkwardly, adjusting his Bubble-Wrapped loops of chain. "We're in good shape," he said. "We've lost the heavy duty chains and the stuff in the bags, but we've got our rapiers, iron, and silver seals. And we've found what we wanted now."

I stared at the clean, calm surface of the door. "Why couldn't it come after us? Ghosts can pass through walls."

Lockwood shrugged. "In some cases a Visitor is tied so completely to the room where it met its death that it no longer has any conception of there being any adjacent space at all. So . . . when we left its hunting ground, it was as if we ceased to exist, as if we ceased to be. . . ."

I looked at him. "You haven't really got a clue, have you?"

"No."

"Here's a possibility," George said. He gestured with the flashlight. "See that ring we pulled to close the door? It's made of iron. And look, there's a lattice of iron strips all across the wood. And down the stone here, too. . . . They look old to me. Someone attached them sometime long ago as a way of hemming in that particular Visitor. It keeps the passage safe."

He circled the flashlight around us in an arc, allowing us to consider the space in which we were confined. It was a very narrow corridor, walled and floored with old, thin bricks. It ran a short distance, then hit the corner of the western wall—the one that showed up as suspiciously thick on George's plans. Here, the bricks were replaced by solid stone and the passage turned to the right. The bend was almost entirely choked with swathes of webbing that hung like fat gray curtains from the roof of the passage to the floor.

"Don't like all those spiders," I said.

"This side passage is mainly clear of them," Lockwood said, "because of all the iron. But once we turn the corner, we're back in the original priory building, and we'll be getting near the Source. That means more spiders and stronger visitations. From now on we use all available weapons as soon as anything shows up."

We struggled to our feet. I gave George back his rapier, and drew my own. I found my flashlight where I'd dropped it on the bricks, but the bulb had broken. Lockwood's was gone, and George's seemed dimmer than before.

"Save it," Lockwood said. He brought out candles and distributed them between us; when lit, their flames were mustard-yellow, tall, and strong. "They'll be a good indicator of psychic build-up, too," he said. "Keep your eye on them."

"Shame we can't use caged cats, like Tom Rotwell did," George remarked. "They're the most sensitive indicator of all, apparently—*if* you can stand the yowling."

"I can't believe the Source isn't in the Red Room," I said. "That Visitor was *so* strong."

"And *so* weird," George added. "Mix of Poltergeist and Changer. That's new."

"No, it was just a Changer." Lockwood held his candle out, surveying the way to the corner. "It didn't have telekinetic properties at all."

"You forget it closed and locked the door," I said.

"Did it?" Lockwood said. "I don't think so."

I frowned at his retreating back; he was already on the move. "Wait," I said. "You think another ghost—" The answer came to me. "You mean someone *living* did it? Deliberately locked us in? But that means—"

George gave a long, low whistle. "Fairfax or Starkins. . . ."

"But they wouldn't come in here," I protested. "Not after dark."

"*Starkins* wouldn't," Lockwood said. "Come on, we've work to do."

But I still stared at him. "*Fairfax*? But why? Lockwood—"

He held up his hand to hush me; he was at the corner now, ducking low to avoid the hanging webs. When he raised his candle to the webbing, dozens of shiny black bodies scurried to the margins, fleeing the sphere of light. "It's instantly colder here," he said, "once you step off the bricks. And there's miasma, too, and immediate malaise. . . . George, do a temp check there, then cross over to the stones."

George pushed past me and began the readings. I followed reluctantly.

"I know you don't like Fairfax," I said, "but if you're saying he's insane—"

"Oh, he's certainly not insane," Lockwood said. "Temp difference, George?"

"Drops from forty-eight to forty-one in the space of a stride."

Lockwood nodded. "It's all in the stones. And it'll only get colder when we go down *there*."

He indicated the arch beside him: as black and gaping as an open mouth. Our candlelight didn't penetrate too far. George briefly switched on his flashlight to reveal the beginnings of another passage, taller and broader than the one we'd come from. It stretched away inside the wall.

Lockwood had been right about the temperature drop. For the first time, I really felt the cold. I pulled my hat out, put it on; zipped my coat up tight. The others were doing likewise. I glared at Lockwood as I did so, irritated by his refusal to talk about Fairfax and the Red Room door. *Yet again* he was keeping quiet, not sharing what he knew. He'd been like this for days, ever since Fairfax first came calling. Maybe even before that—since the burglary, even since we found the necklace. . . .

I put my hands to my throat, checked the hidden cord around my neck. Beneath my coat the silver-glass pressed cold and hard against my chest. I wondered if it glowed, whether the ghost was emitting any light. Well, she was secure enough. It wasn't Annie Ward we had to worry about now.

Lockwood put on his gloves; George crammed his head inside his foul green bobble-hat. We started up the passage, Lockwood taking the lead. He held his candle high. Drifts of cobweb danced above its meager flame.

A few steps in, George called us to a halt. He pointed to the right-hand wall, at a rough arch of brickwork embedded in the stone. "There's the original way through from the Red Room," he said. "Blocked up when they rebuilt the house. We're in one of the priory passageways now."

"Fine," Lockwood said. "Let's look at the map. Then we can see where—"

His head snapped around. The wick of his candle had quivered;

its light shrank dim and pale. All of us had felt the change—the shift that comes when a Visitor walks near.

We waited, rapiers at the ready, hands hovering at our belts.

One moment there was nothing, and the next . . . a boy stood ahead of us in the dark. He shone with a frail glow. It wasn't easy to tell how far away he was, or whether he floated or touched the stones. His other-light lit nothing but himself. When I listened, I thought I heard faint weeping, but the apparition's face was blank and clear. It looked toward us with that open, empty expression so many of them have.

"Check out the *clothes*," Lockwood whispered.

The boy had been quite young, probably not as old as me. He was fair-haired and stocky, tending to the stout, with a soft and rounded face. If George had been scrubbed up and forcibly inserted into something smart and ironed, he might almost have been his cousin. He wore dark pants and a long gray jacket, which seemed slightly too big for him. Something about the cut of the jacket and the pants (I'm no good with fashion) told me this was an apparition decades old. But there was no mistaking the essential uniform, or the Italianate hilt of the rapier at his side.

"Oh, lord," I said, "it's the Fittes kid. The one who died in here."

The weeping grew louder. The apparition flickered; it slowly turned away from us and drifted off along the passage.

All sight and sound winked out. Nothing but darkness, silence, a sweet-sour smell fading in my nose. The candlewicks flared up bright as day. We remembered to breathe again.

"I could *really* do with a mint now," George said.

"Did he speak to you, Lucy?" Lockwood asked.

"No. But he was trying to tell us something."

"That's the trouble with ghosts. They never spell it out. Well, it was presumably a warning, but we've got to keep on going. There's nothing else we can do."

We continued along the passage, more slowly than before. Not a yard farther on, roughly where we'd seen the apparition, we came to a flight of stairs.

It was a spiral staircase, tight and narrow and heading steeply downward. The passage led directly to it, and the entrance was fringed with smaller blocks of stone.

"Thirty-nine degrees," George said matter-of-factly. The light of his thermometer shone against his glasses and made his frosted breath plume green.

"Seems we're going down," Lockwood said. "Was this on the medieval floor plan, George?"

"I don't know. . . . Actually—yes, I think so. A connecting stair from dormitories to refectory. Want me to check?"

"No. No, let's get it done."

We set off down the steps. Lockwood went first, then me, with George bringing up the rear. It was not a comfortable place. There was a strong feeling of being somewhere very old and very far from natural light. Despite the cold, the air was close, and the walls pressed tight on either side. We had to bend our necks to avoid the layers of cobwebs on the ceiling. The smoke from our candles made my eyes water, and their guttering wicks cast disconcerting shadows on the smoothly curving stones.

"Don't trip on a piece of the Fittes kid, Lockwood," George said. "He's down here somewhere."

I scowled back at him. “Ugh, George. Why would you even *say* that?”

“I guess because I’m nervous.”

I sighed. “Yeah . . . fair enough. So am I.”

We all felt the strain now; our senses were on red alert, waiting for the slightest trigger. Outwardly it all seemed quiet—no sounds, no death-glows, no floating wisps of plasm. But this meant nothing. The Red Room had started the exact same way.

The staircase opened out briefly into a tiny squared chamber, with blocked arches on either side, before continuing its way down. Lockwood paused. “We’re at ground level here,” he said. “Must be right behind that tapestry. You remember—the one with the picture of that suspicious-looking bear.”

“I remember,” I said. “This is where that cold spot was.”

“Yes, we’re down to thirty-eight degrees,” George said. “That’s the coldest reading in the house.” His voice was tight. “We’re getting close.”

“We’d better go slow now.” Lockwood handed out some spearmint gum. Chewing mechanically, we started down the steps again, spiraling toward the cellar level. A thought occurred to me.

“This staircase,” I said in a casual voice. “It’s not . . . it wouldn’t be *the* staircase, would it?”

Behind me, George chuckled. “No. Don’t worry. That was the other one.”

“You’re sure? Did the legends definitely say it was the main staircase of the hall?”

“Yes.” We descended steadily, step by careful step, going around and around and down. Lockwood’s candle dimmed and flickered, then grew strong again. "Well," George continued, "they didn't *expressly* say it, as it happens. They just mentioned some 'old steps.' But everyone's always assumed it was the main one, what with those carved dragons, and skull niches, and all the rest of it."

"Right. . . . So they just *assumed*. . . . But naturally, it would *have* to have been that main staircase, wouldn't it, if it had been anywhere."

"Yep. That's right."

"Though we didn't get any psychic readings at all there, did we?"

"No. And we're not getting any *here*, either." George spoke with unusual firmness. "It's just a legend."

It certainly seemed so. I didn't doubt it for a minute. And so it was only for my private reassurance that I took off a glove and tucked it in my pocket. It was only out of merest curiosity that I let my fingertips trail against the stonework as we spiraled slowly down.

To my relief, all I could feel was the chill in the wall. It was a deep, dry, lifeless cold that had sunk into the stones over a great many years. It stippled my skin, and made an electric charge run up the hairs on the back of my neck. An unpleasant feeling—but that was all it was. Just cold.

I was about to take my fingers away when I heard the sounds.

They were faint at first, but swiftly drawing nearer. Boots stamping. Boots, and the clink of metal. The stairwell echoed with it, and with the voices of many men. There were the rustle of their tunics, the scrape of swords. Suddenly they were all around us, keeping pace with our descent. I smelled burning tar and smoke and sweat, and an overwhelming stink of fear. Someone cried out in a language I didn't understand. It was a simple cry of desperation, a plea for help. Chainmail clinked, a blow fell; I heard a moan of pain.

Onward, downward went the boots, and with every step we took, the dreadful atmosphere of terror grew stronger and more palpable. Now there was not one pleading voice, but several—and as I listened, their cries began to rise in volume and become more desperate and shrill. Louder, ever louder . . . soon they swallowed up the other sounds, the tramping boots and rattling mail, until it seemed there was just a single swelling outcry deep down in the earth, an hysterical screech of fear. . . .

I snatched my hand away.

Gone. I took a gulp of smoky air, and anxiously scanned the wall. Thank goodness. Just for a moment my shadow had seemed a little different. Taller, thinner, sharper, and more hunched. . . . No, it was still the same. And the sound was gone.

I fumbled my glove back onto my numbed fingers. Gone . . .

Except that it wasn't. I could still hear it. Faint and far away, the echo of the scream went on.

"Erm, guys . . ." I said.

Lockwood stopped dead in front of me. He gave a cry. "Of *course*! I've been an idiot!"

George and I stood and stared. "What?" George said. "What is it?"

"It's been right in front of us all this time!"

"What has?"

"The answer to it all. Ah, I'm *such* a fool!"

Frowning, I held my gloved palm against my head. I was listening, listening hard. "Lockwood, wait," I said. "Can't you hear—"

"I've had enough of this," George said. "Lockwood, you've

been acting odd for days. Tell us what's going on. Clearly it's about Fairfax, and since it's *his* job that's put us in such danger, I think you owe us an explanation."

Lockwood nodded. "Yes, I do. But first we've got to find the Source. Then—"

"No," George said. "Not good enough. Tell us now."

The scream was swelling, faint but growing in force. Candles flickered. Shadows distorted on the walls. "Lockwood," I pleaded, "*listen*."

"We've got to stay alert, George," Lockwood said. "There's no time to explain."

"Speak quickly, then, and use short words."

"*No! Both of you—shut up!*" They looked at me. My fingers scraped at my temples; my teeth were clenched. The dreadful sound had just erupted at full volume from the walls. "Can't you hear it?" I whispered. "It's the *screaming*."

Lockwood frowned. "What? No . . . I don't think so."

"Take it from me! *This* is the Staircase! We need to get off it *now*."

There was a moment's hesitation, but Lockwood was too good a leader to ignore so strong a warning. He grasped my hand. "All right, we'll get you down to the bottom. Maybe the noise will stop there. Maybe it's only you, Lucy, who can—" He broke off. His fingers clenched mine; I felt him stagger on the steps. There'd been another swell in the sound; for the first time it broke through some physical barrier, became audible to ears less sensitive than mine.

I looked back. George had frozen too, his eyes stretched wide.

He said something, but I couldn't hear him. The scream was just too loud.

"Down!" Lockwood shouted; at least, I could see him mouthing the word. "*Down!*" He was reeling, but he still held my hand tightly. He pulled; behind me George came tumbling, fists jammed against his ears. We threw ourselves downward through the spiraling light and dark, with the candle flames leaping crazily and our shadows veering up the walls.

All around us rose the scream, issuing directly from the steps and stones. Its volume was appalling—as painful as repeated blows—but it was the psychic distress it carried that made it so unbearable, that made your gorge rise and your head split and the world spin before your eyes. It was the sound of the terror of death, drawn out indefinitely, extending on forever. It spiraled around us, clawing at our minds.

Down, down, and around and around—and all at once, the shadows rushing with us were not our own but darker shapes with sharp, cowled heads, and thin, thin arms stretched high along the walls. Down and down—falling, jumping, tearing through the clinging cobwebs. Around and around—and on the walls, the hooded figures rose and fell, keeping pace on either side. Shadow fingers swooped and plunged; the stairs went on forever; and still the screams tore into our skulls like stakes of red-hot iron, so that all I wanted was for the terrible noise to cease.

At which we fell out at the bottom of the steps into a small, square room.

We collapsed on the floor. Our candles fell from our fingers, went skidding along the stones. Our heads spun; we could not get up, thanks to the noise and the sickening giddiness of the descent. The screaming had not stopped. And now the racing shadows spilled out from the stairs along the margins of the room, their silhouettes swooping faintly across the walls as they danced and capered in a hellish frenzy. Shadowy ropes swayed broken on their wrists.

"The monks," I gasped. "It's the monks! The ones they killed here."

Seven monks, the story said. Seven monks, for crimes of blasphemy, had been thrown into a well.

I raised my head, looked across the tilting floor. There, lit by horizontal candlelight: a broad, round, stone-lined hole of fathomless blackness, set into the center of the floor. And close beside it—

Between us and the well a small and shrunken figure lay: a huddled heap of bones and rag, its outlines softened by successive layers of cobwebs. The neck was twisted at an odd, unnatural angle. One hollow jacketed arm reached out toward the hole as if it wished to drag itself forward and slip down into the dark.

The Fittes boy had almost made it to the foot of the stairs, then, before the screaming killed him. I guessed he'd tripped and tumbled in his frantic flight, and finished up breaking his neck. At least it had been a quick end for him.

The sound was driving me mad. I pulled myself to my feet. It was hard to do it; it was hard to move or think. At my side, Lockwood and George did likewise. Blood was trickling from Lockwood's ear.

Like a drunken man, he grappled us by the collars, pulled us in close. "Find the Source!" he shouted. "It *must* be here. Somewhere in this room!"

He shoved us away. George stumbled; and, as he did so, drew close to one of the silhouettes on the wall. At once a translucent hand stretched out of the stonework beside him, long-fingered and bony, with white hairs on the arm and a frayed rope-end dangling from the wrist. It reached for George. Lockwood was faster; he wrenched a salt-bomb from his belt and threw it at the stones. Grains ignited, burning green. The arm drew back. On the wall the shadow flexed and undulated furiously like a snake.

Out across the room we went, Lockwood, George, and I, stumbling, flailing, searching to and fro. It wasn't any good. The room went nowhere. It had no exits, no shelves; there was nothing in it but the walls and the stones and the deep, dark, waiting well.

A flash of whiteness, an explosion of salt and iron. George had flung a canister of Greek Fire at shadows in the far corner of the room. Mortar fell from the stones; the chamber shook. For a moment the nearest silhouettes flickered, then their dance went on.

Desperation took us. We were all at it now, mounting a last attack. Iron filings, salt-bombs, flares—we threw them at the walls, trying to obliterate the ghostly shadows, trying to silence the dreadful sound. Stones cracked, smoke licked outward, curtains of cobwebs went up in flames. Burning particles of salt and iron skimmed and spattered across the room in a dozen colors. And still the shapes of the murdered monks kept dancing, still their screams went on.

No good. A great heaviness suddenly engulfed me. We'd never find the Source, and now our belts and shoulder straps were empty, our ammunition used up, our energies spent. I slowed, came to a dragging standstill. Elsewhere, George had drawn his rapier and was striking blindly all around him, scarcely conscious of whether he made contact with the wall or not. Lockwood stood close beside the well itself, brow furrowed, looking about wildly, evidently still hunting for a solution.

Poor Lockwood. There *was* no solution. Our Talents were useless, our weapons gone. My arms dropped; my head hung low. We'd *never* find the Source. We'd never find it, and the noise would never, ever stop.

Unless . . .

I looked dully at the well.

How stupid I'd been. There *was* a way to make the screaming stop. To go at once from noise to silence, from pain to peace and quiet. And it would be so, *so* easy to achieve.

Over by the steps George had dropped his rapier. He'd flopped down on his knees and was cowering low, arms cradling his head. On the wall behind, the exultant shadows danced in triumph.

I shuffled forward. Ahead of me: the brick-lined lip, the shaft of soft gray stones leading into peaceful darkness. . . .

Yes. It was easy, it was obvious. I'd known it all along. After all, *this* was what the house had promised, when I stood hesitating in the lobby all those hours ago. This was where I'd known it would lead me—step by easy step, past all those flittering Type Ones and the ghost-fog and the evil whispers, past the bloody room and, finally, spiraling down the stairs. This was where it was always going to end. In this place. The place where the silence was, at the heart of the Hall and its haunting, where the silence went on forever. It was very simple now. Just a couple more strides and the screaming would stop. I'd be part of that silence too.

I took the first step swiftly; as I began the second, a sudden pain flared at my chest: a sharp, cold spasm. I hesitated, clawing at the cord around my neck. It had come from the locket. . . . A burst of energy; I'd felt it even through the silver-glass. That Annie Ward—troublesome to the end! Well, no matter. She could be lost along with me.

The well shaft waited. It promised me so much. I would hesitate no longer. With nothing but relief, I took the last steps forward and walked out over the edge—

And hung there, leaning out above an abyss of black.

Something had grasped me, something held me tight. Something hauled me back onto the safety of the stones.

Lockwood: his face haggard, hair disheveled, his overcoat torn and stained. Blood ran down the collar of his shirt. He gripped me tighter around the waist and pulled me to him.

"No," he said into my ear. "No, Lucy. That's *not* the way it's going to be."

With that he let me go, ducked his head, shuffled off his loop of chains, and dropped it to the floor. "Matches!" he shouted. "Give me your matches. And your chains, too!" He fumbled at his belt. "I want the extra iron, and any silver seals you've got. Come on, *do* it! We're being dumb," he cried. "The *well*'s the Source, of course it is. *That's* where the Visitors are."

The force of his will broke through the ghost-lock, broke through the sapping power of the relentless scream. I threw off my chains, unclipped the seals. I opened a belt pouch, took out the box of Sunrise matches, while Lockwood ripped a final canister free of his belt. The big one. The one with the dark red wrapper. The industrial strength flare with the long, long safety fuse, to give you time enough to get far away.

Lockwood brought out his pocketknife and sliced the fuse away, so that only a tiny nub remained.

"Take it!" he shouted. "Light the end!"

He was already away from me, dragging our chains toward the well, fighting against the suffocating sound. Around the walls the seven shapes paused in their swooping; they too seemed suddenly alert. Spectral arms pushed through the stone, reached out toward us; alongside them the first cowled heads broke clear.

I struck a match, put it to the oiled fuse. A spark flared, a tiny filament of light.

At the well's lip, Lockwood kicked the chains and seals into the hole. He stumbled back, took the canister from me, shouted in my ears.

"Run, Lucy! Get to the stairs!"

But I couldn't move. I still felt the deathly pull toward the well. My body felt immersed in tar; I didn't even have the strength to turn.

The Visitors were free of the walls now; they drifted inward from all sides. Two of the nearest were almost at George, still hunched upon the floor. The rest converged on us, bone-white faces insubstantial beneath their rotting hoods. Sockets gaped, sharp teeth glittered. And still the screaming rose.

Lockwood took the cylinder, stumbled to the edge. The nub of fuse had almost burned away.

He dropped it in. The fuse glow lit the well stones for an instant and was gone.

Lockwood turned. I saw for an instant his slim, pale face, his dark eyes meeting mine.

Hooded shadows swooped in on us.

Then the screaming stopped; the shadows froze; and a millisecond later, the world exploded in a soundless burst of light.

Chapter 23

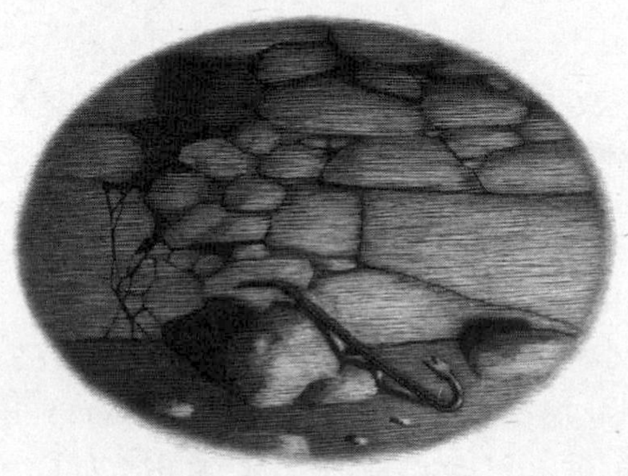

I woke suddenly, in a state of pain. My eyes snapped open, and for a long-held moment my sisters were there, and Lockwood, and Annabel Ward in her pretty summer dress with its orange flowers. They were all smiling at me; I saw them distinctly, their shapes gently overlapping. They probably floated in some kind of cloud.

I didn't buy any of it; besides, I had a pounding headache, too. So I stared at them grimly until they broke apart and faded, and I was left in a different, darker place.

Dark, but not pitch-black. It shone with a silver glow.

Quiet, but not entirely silent. I heard a ringing in my ears.

It was a high-pitched, tinny sort of ring, like a mosquito's whining buzz, and when I heard it I instantly felt a kind of joy. Because it meant my ears were sore, and that in turn meant I wasn't dead. I wasn't in that silent place at the bottom of the well.

Additionally there was a strong smell of smoke and gunpowder, and a chemical taste on my tongue. The side of my face was pressed against hard stone.

When I moved, I hurt. It was like the fall from Mr. Hope's study window all over again; every muscle ached. I could feel a light coating of something dusty falling off my hair and skin as I rolled over and pushed myself upright.

I was sitting in a far corner of that terrible underground chamber, where the force of the blast had blown me. My forehead was sticky with blood. I was covered—like everything else in the room—with a whitish layer of the ash and iron fragments that were still settling from the air. I coughed, spat the stuff out of my mouth. The cough made my head hurt even more.

A column of pale white smoke rose slowly from the well shaft in the center of the room. It was lit by an angry silver radiance in the depths beneath, an eerie glow that pulsed and flared. The whole room shone with magnesium light. Somewhere, faint reverberations still sounded; I could feel the impacts in the stone.

At the well rim, several bricks had disappeared, and a curling crack now ran outward from the edge across the floor. A portion of the floor had tilted upward. Where the crack met the wall, a number of stones had been dislodged; one or two had fallen, and others protruded at queasy angles. Smaller fragments of rock littered the chamber. Some rested on the bodies lying there.

Three bodies, covered with white dust. Three bodies, scattered by the explosion from the well. None of them was moving.

Which was reasonable enough in the case of the poor Fittes boy. He'd had a lot of practice at that.

But Lockwood and George . . .

I got to my feet slowly, carefully, supporting myself against the wall. Dizzy as I felt, it was a whole lot better than when the screaming had filled my head. There was a kind of hole in my mind from the psychic attack; I felt scoured out and hollow, as if I were a convalescent, newly risen from my bed.

George was closest. He lay on his back with his arms and legs spread wide. He looked like a kid caught making an angel in the snow, except his glasses had been blown off and one of his hands was bleeding. He breathed heavily; his belly rose and fell.

I knelt close. "George?"

A groan, a cough. "It's too late. Leave me. . . . Let me sleep. . . ."

I shook him firmly, slapped the side of his face. "George, you've got to wake up! George, *please*. Are you okay?"

An eye opened. "Ow. That cheek was the one part of me that *wasn't* sore."

"Here, look—your glasses." I scooped them out of the ash, put them on his chest. One of the lenses had cracked. "Get up now."

"Lockwood?"

"I don't know."

I found him on the opposite side of the room, lying on his side with his coat blown outward like a single broken wing. He was very still. With its coating of ash, his face looked like that of an alabaster statue, smooth and white and cold. A piece of masonry had struck him, and there was blood in his hair. I knelt by him, brushed the ash from his forehead.

His eyes opened. He looked at me with a clear, unclouded gaze.

I cleared my throat. "Hi, Lockwood. . . ."

Awareness returned. I saw bafflement first, then gradual recognition.

"Oh . . . Lucy." He blinked, coughed, tried to sit up. "Lucy. For a moment I thought you were . . . It doesn't matter. How *are* you, Lucy? You're okay?"

I stood abruptly. "Yes, I'm fine."

George was watching me through cracked spectacles. "I saw that."

"What?" I said. "Saw what? Nothing happened."

"Precisely. Where was *his* slap in the chops? Where was *his* firm shaking? There're double standards at work here."

"Don't worry," I said. "I'll be sure to slap him next time."

George grunted. "Great. . . . Though that means you'll probably *kick* me awake."

"I'll certainly bear that in mind."

The silver smoke continued to gout up from the hole, and by its light we got organized again. We'd escaped the force of the explosion relatively unharmed, though both Lockwood and George had been hit by pieces of debris, and all of us were shaky from what had gone before. We had our rapiers, but all our iron and salt was gone. George had his loop of iron chain; Lockwood and I had thrown ours down the well.

The first thing we did was share the remnants of our sandwiches and energy drinks. George and I sat on a lump of masonry to eat our portions, huddling together to keep warm. Lockwood stood a little way off, staring stony-faced into the smoke.

"We should have attacked the well from the start," George said.

"I reckon we would have, if it hadn't been for that hellish noise addling our brains. It *had* to be the Source, really. That's where the monks' bones are; that was where they died."

I nodded without speaking. Yes, that was where they died—after being roped together and taken down the stairs. They'd known what was coming, all right. The terror of their final journey still infused the stones. . . .

"I reckon I see how it fits together now," George went on. "The monks' spirits are so old, and their death so terrible, that their influence has pervaded the whole house. It underlies all the other Visitors. It's because of what happened in this room that so many later inhabitants of the Hall went mad and did appalling things."

"All those murderous dukes and suicidal ladies that Starkins loved so much," I said. I swallowed my last bite of sandwich. "You think it's over now?"

"Hope so." George considered the broiling smoke. "That flare must've scattered a *lot* of iron, silver, and magnesium down there. With luck it'll be nicely mingled with the bones, and that'll keep things quiet till we can get the well sealed up. The stairs will be safe. And probably the Red Room."

"You believe the blood in there was linked to the monks?" I asked.

"I believe it *was* them, manifested differently. They were Changers: they took different forms in each location. Gushing blood in the Red Room, screaming shadows on the staircase; down here they even became bodily apparitions, though it wasn't their favorite guise. I say 'their.' Really, their ghosts more or less acted as one. That's why it was such a powerful haunting. Fusing like that's not unheard of. Wasn't there that famous case at Castle Sherbourne?"

"Maybe. What do you think, Lockwood?" I said. "You're very quiet."

He didn't answer at first, just watched the smoke. His body was a thin, dark silhouette, his coat hanging limp and torn like the plumage of a storm-blown bird. "What do *I* think?" he said softly. "I think that's twice now we've nearly died." He turned to look at us, his face bloodied, hair disheveled; as he moved, ash fell from him in a little cloud. "I think that we're very lucky to be alive. I think that I've been far too slow on the uptake and have severely underestimated our enemy. It's been an unforgivable lapse in a leader, and I'm sorry for it. However"—his voice grew harsh; he spoke between clenched teeth—"all that ends now."

George and I stared at him. "Er, that's good," I said. "So perhaps you could tell us exactly what's going o—"

"I need a lever!" Lockwood cried, so suddenly that both George and I flinched back. He burst into life, strode across the room, ragged coat flapping behind him. "A stick, a crowbar, something! Come on! Hurry! There's no time to waste!"

"I've got a bar," I said, scrabbling at my belt. "But—"

"That'll do. Hand it over." He snatched the crowbar from me, sprang across the room to the damaged wall, and plunged it in between two stones. "Don't just sit around," he growled. "What, are you having a picnic? We're going to break out here."

"Hold on, Lockwood," George began, as he and I struggled to our feet. "We're deep underground. How can you know that's a possible way through?"

"Look at the smoke!" Lockwood wrenched at the crowbar,

levered a loose stone clear, and jumped aside as it cracked on the flags between his feet. "If the smoke's escaping, so can we!"

And it was true, though neither George nor I had noticed before, that the smoke from the well wasn't pooling in the room; instead it flowed across the ceiling in a soft gray current, and was being sucked out between the stones of the damaged wall.

"There's a pressure difference," Lockwood shouted. "It's being drawn out into a bigger space. That'll be the cellar. The cellar must be through that wall. The explosion's done half our job already. We just need to make a bigger hole. Come on!"

His energy stirred us into action. Shaking off our stiffness and fatigue, George and I set to with knife and crowbar, shifting the loosest blocks, prying at the others. Alongside us, Lockwood worked at speed, heaving on the crowbar and, where necessary, wrenching at the stones with his bare hands. His eyes glittered; his mouth was a taut, white line.

"We've been dealing with two separate problems tonight," he said, hacking at the mortar. "They *seem* connected, but really they're quite different. The first, the haunting of Combe Carey Hall, is over. With the monks gone, the other apparitions can be steadily mopped up. The danger's finished here. The second issue"—he tossed his bar aside and helped George pull a medium-sized stone free of the wall—"concerns our friend Mr. John William Fairfax, and *that* story is not yet done."

The stone fell, broke into segments. I pushed the debris clear. Lockwood and George returned to attacking the weakest area half-way up the wall.

"So," I said, "Fairfax. What about him?"

"It's been obvious from the first that something's seriously wrong with all this," Lockwood said. "His invitation to come here was more than a trifle odd. True, the terms were amazingly generous, but that just made it odder still. Why did he choose to come to *us*, when he could have had Fittes or Rotwell, or any of a dozen other agencies? Our record recently has been . . . patchy, but he claimed to have been impressed by it."

"He said he'd been an outsider too," I said, tugging on a lump of rock. "He said he liked our passion and—watch your feet! Oh, sorry, George—our independence of mind."

Lockwood's lip curled. "Yes, that's what he *said*, didn't he? A rather thin claim, particularly when you read about his youth and discover he inherited all his wealth from his father. But aside from choosing us, there were three other questions that bothered me. One: why now? He'd owned the Hall for years, so why was he suddenly so desperate to resolve its haunting? Two: why the blazing hurry? He gave us a ridiculous two days to prepare! And three: why on earth were we forbidden to bring flares?"

"Yeah, I couldn't get over that last one," George said. "Nobody in their right mind would take on an A-grade Visitor without sufficient flares."

"We would," Lockwood said. "And Fairfax knew it. He knew we were desperate for the cash. And he was just as desperate for us to come, so much so that he offered to pay off our £60,000 debt if we simply turned up at the door. To me that was either insanely generous, or linked to an ulterior motive, and I wanted to find out which. So my first act, the next day, was to pay a quick visit to the village of Combe Carey."

"We've broken through!" George said. He'd wrestled another stone free: a small gap now showed in the center of the fractured wall. Beyond was darkness and empty space.

Lockwood nodded. "Good. Let's rest for a minute. What's the time, Lucy?"

"Three a.m."

"The night's passing. We've got to be away from here by dawn. Okay, so I went to the village. I pretended to be a traveling salesman, going from door to door."

"Selling what?" George demanded.

"Your comic collecton, George. Oh, don't worry, I didn't get rid of any. I made the price too high. But it gave me an excuse to talk to the locals."

"And how did you get on?" I said.

Lockwood made a rueful face. "As it happens, my rural accent didn't go down too well. No one could understand me, and three burly guys took grave offense and chased me around the millpond. But once I'd modified my accent all went smoothly, and I heard a few rumors about Fairfax. I learned he often came to the Hall with one of his company's trucks. This would be full of new iron products; and local men were paid to help carry this equipment inside. Most of it was ordinary domestic stuff—door guards and window hangings, you know—but there were things that must have been bigger, because they filled huge crates. A few days later he'd have it all taken away again. The locals had no doubt what he was doing—he was busy safety-testing new products on the ghosts of Combe Carey Hall. Which in itself," Lockwood said, smoothing back his hair and considering the wall, "isn't wrong—all the corporations must do it. But again it raised the question: if he found the place so useful, why would he suddenly want to snuff it all out? Why call us in?"

"And why not tell us more about the dangers?" I added. "If he's been experimenting here, he must have known stuff about the Red Room at least, if not the hidden staircase."

"Exactly. . . . You know, I think we should do this big block next. If we can get it loose, even George has a chance of squeezing through."

George's brief response was lost in the sound of our crowbars striking stone. For several minutes more we labored at the remaining block; with great exertions we managed to lever it halfway out before it jammed again. We all took another rest.

"Anyway, the long and short of it," Lockwood said, "was that I was deeply suspicious of Fairfax and his motivations. I got further food for thought from George's research, which I read on the train. How Fairfax had started off quite wild as a boy. How his dad had wanted him to go straight into the business, but he'd spent years living it up in London, drinking, gambling, and trying to be an actor. None of which would have meant anything to me at all, if it hadn't been for Lucy's crucial breakthrough." He paused dramatically.

"Which was?" George said. I'm glad he asked; I didn't know either.

"She showed me this." He straightened and, rummaging in various pockets of his coat, produced discarded mint wrappers, candle stubs, and bits of string before, finally, a crumpled piece of folded paper. He passed it across to us.

It was the photocopied sheet, the page from the magazine article George had discovered in the Archives. The one about the young, rich society kids who'd frequented London's top cafés and casinos fifty years before. Annie Ward was there in the midst of the glossy crowd clustered by the fountain. In the individual portrait shot, Hugo Blake's face smarmed smugly up at me.

"Look by the fountain," Lockwood said.

It was hard to make out details in the soft magnesium light, so George switched on his flashlight. At the back of the crowd of merrymakers stood a group of young men, done up to the nines in white ties and tails. They surrounded the ornamental fountain. One had climbed on to the pedestal below the spout; others hung off its sides. They exuded wealth, exuberance, high spirits. The tallest of them stood partly in the shadow of the fountain, a little separate from the others. He was very big man, muscular and barrel-chested, with a resplendent mane of long dark hair. With all the hair and shadows his face was partially obscured, but the essential shapes—the great hooked nose, the heavy brows, the assertive line of the strong squared jaw—were clear enough to see.

George and I stared at the image in silence.

He'd lost a lot of weight in the intervening years, but it was him all right.

"Fairfax. . . ." I said.

George gave a wise, contemplative nod. "I *thought* as much."

I glared at him. "*What?* Don't give me that. You had no idea!"

"Well . . ." He handed the paper back to Lockwood. "I thought he was damned fishy, anyhow."

"So when I showed this page to the ghost of Annie Ward," I began, "and she went mad with terror or distress . . ." I broke off, bit my lip. Beneath my coat, the silver-glass case burned cold against my skin. "But this doesn't prove—"

"You're right," Lockwood said. "It doesn't prove much in itself. Except for one crucial thing: Fairfax is a liar. When he came to see us, he claimed he'd never heard of Annie Ward. He made a big deal about not remembering her name. But quite obviously he *did* know her. He was part of the same set when he was young."

"And not just that!" My heart was pounding now. I felt dizzy; my head spun, like it had back on the spiral staircase, but this time not because of any ghostly tumult. It was my memory that screamed: I'd recalled a detail that had escaped me before. "She was an actor too," I said. "Like Fairfax. Do you remember, in the old newspapers, it said she'd had a promising acting career, but had given it up because of . . . something or other."

"Because of Hugo Blake," Lockwood said. "She fell under his influence, and so—"

"If we're going where I think we are with this," George said suddenly, tapping the protruding block of stone, "don't you think we should keep moving? The night won't last forever."

No one disagreed with him. In silence we mounted a final assault on the block of stone. It took all our strength, and savage attacks on the stubborn mortar with two crowbars and a knife, before the block was loosened. It fell to earth. The sound of the impact faded. We stood staring at the hole.

Lockwood stepped close and squinted through. "Can't see a thing. . . . It's probably the far cellar, where I saw the monk before.

Fine. . . . Once we get upstairs we're out of the front door and away. Give me the flashlight, George. I'll go through first."

Holding the flashlight between his teeth, he hopped up and pushed himself headfirst into the gap. A wriggle, a shuffle, a jerk of legs: he shot forward and was gone.

Silence.

George and I waited.

Dim light shone beyond the wall and with it came Lockwood's voice. "Sorry," he whispered. "I lost the flashlight for a minute. It's okay, it *is* the cellar. Come on—Lucy next."

It didn't take me long. Once my arms and head had reached the other side, Lockwood was there to pull me out.

"Keep guard while I see to George," he whispered. "The night's getting old, so I'd assume the other Visitors are growing quiet now, but . . . you never know."

So I stood by, with flashlight and rapier, while Lockwood wrestled George through the aperture. I could see only a little way. Thick shadows lay across the curved vaults of the cellar; beyond the nearest arch, shrouded lines of wine racks stretched into the murk. All traces of ghost-fog were gone. Perhaps our attack on the well had already affected the entire cluster. It was impossible to say.

But ghosts, right then, weren't my main concern. I was thinking of the blond girl in the photograph, and the man beside the fountain. The implications battered at my mind.

"Everyone ready?" Lockwood whispered, once George was through. "We're going to leave the house and cross the park, fast as we can. I want to reach the ruined gatehouse by the road. If we can get there by dawn, we'll be—"

"Tell me something first," I said. "You think Fairfax planned the burglary too?"

"Of course. When that failed, he fell back on his second plan, which was to get us here."

"So he wanted the locket?"

He nodded. "It's *all* about the locket, and what it proves."

"And what *does* it prove, Mr. Lockwood?" a deep voice said.

Metal clinked. Two figures stepped from beyond the arch. They had the shapes of men, but with monstrous, distorted heads. One held a revolver, the other a lantern that swung directly in our eyes; its strong beam blinded us, gave us searing pain.

"Stop there!" the voice said. Our hands had strayed to our sword hilts. "There'll be no more rapier play tonight. Put your weapons on the floor or we'll shoot you where you stand."

"Do as he says," Lockwood said. He undid his rapier and let it drop. George did the same. I was the last to obey. I stared fixedly into the darkness, in the direction of the voice.

"Quick now, Miss Carlyle!" the voice commanded. "Or do you want a bullet in your heart?"

"Lucy . . ." Lockwood's grip was on my shoulder.

I let the blade fall. Lockwood moved his hand away and with it made an urbane gesture. "Lucy, George," he said, "may I present to you once again our host and patron, Mr. John William Fairfax—Chairman of Fairfax Iron, noted industrialist, onetime actor and, of course, the murderer of Annie Ward."

Chapter 24

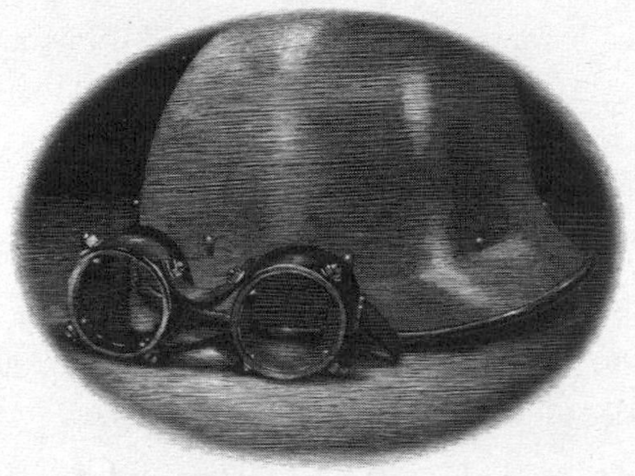

He was still dressed in the same white shirt and gray suit pants he'd worn at the beginning of the night, but everything else about the old man had changed. His slate-gray jacket was gone, replaced by a tunic of shiny steel mesh that hugged his chest and hung loose below his belly in a shimmering cascade. His upper arms were shirtsleeved, but metal gauntlets protected his wrists and hands. As before, he supported himself on his bulldog-handled walking stick—only now the wooden membrane had been removed, revealing a long, slim rapier within. Strangest and most grotesque of all was the helmet that he wore: a smooth steel skullcap with a projecting rim around the back of the neck, and bulging leather goggles strapped below the brow plate. The lenses shone glassily; his eyes could not be seen. All in all, Mr. Fairfax had the look of a demonic frog: both horrible and ridiculous at the same time.

He raised the lantern and stood in its swirling smoke-filled light, considering us. Then he smiled, showing his silver-coated teeth.

"Oh, you're a cool customer, Mr. Lockwood," Fairfax said. "I'll grant you that. I'm more and more impressed with you. It's a shame we didn't meet in other circumstances. You could have had a permanent job with me."

I don't know how Lockwood did it, but despite the revolver pointed at his chest, despite the torn coat, the bloodstains, the spots of plasm, magnesium, salt, and ash on his clothes, despite the trailing cobwebs in his hair and the scratches on his face and hands, he *still* made a decent stab at looking unperturbed.

"You're very kind," he said. "But—aren't you going to introduce us to your friend?" He glanced at the figure with the gun. "I don't think we've had the pleasure."

If not quite as tall as Fairfax, this man was very heavily muscled and broad across the shoulder. His face, what I could see of it, was young and clean-shaven. He too wore a froglike helmet and a set of body armor, and carried a rapier at his belt.

Fairfax chuckled drily. "Percy Grebe, my chauffeur and personal assistant. Used to be an agent with the Hambleton Agency, before it was swallowed up by Fittes. A very capable fellow, and still an excellent swordsman. In fact, you're already acquainted. Percy paid you a little visit the other night."

"Oh yes," Lockwood said. "Our masked intruder. I stabbed you, didn't I? How's your stomach doing?"

"Bearing up," Grebe said.

"Just another little injury to add to the long list you've caused us, Mr. Lockwood," Fairfax said. "Look at this wall!" He gestured at the pile of stones and the ragged hole through which magnesium smoke still gently drifted. "Really, I'm shocked. I *did* request that no incendiaries be brought into my house."

"Sorry about that," Lockwood said. "On the bright side, we've located and destroyed your Source, so we'll be looking forward to our second payment as soon as the banks open later this morning."

Another chuckle. "Insane optimism is another quality I admire, Mr. Lockwood, but I must say it's your ability to survive that most astounds me. I truly thought the Horror of the Red Room would have killed you hours ago. I watched you go inside, I locked the door. . . . Yet now I find you re-emerging like three dusty woodworms from a completely different part of the house! Quite extraordinary. Clearly you found a way out of the Red Room, which is impressive enough, but to discover the ultimate Source . . . Tell me, was it the Red Duke? That was my favorite theory."

"No. It was the Staircase and the monks. We found their well."

"Really? A well? Through there?" The opaque goggles flashed in the lantern light; the voice grew thoughtful. "How interesting. . . . You'll have to show me presently."

At my side, George stirred uneasily. "Yes. . . . Not necessarily a great idea to mention the well there, Lockwood."

Lockwood grinned. "Oh, Mr. Fairfax is a reasonable man. Besides, he wants to talk to us first, don't you, Fairfax?"

Silence from beneath the helmet. At Fairfax's side, the other figure did not stir; the revolver hung suspended in the dark, directed at our stomachs.

"Yes." The voice was suddenly harsh, decisive. "And we can do it in more comfortable surroundings. I'm tired and I need to sit down.

Grebe, take our friends up to the library. If either of the boys tries anything, feel free to shoot the girl."

Lockwood said something, but I didn't hear what. Beneath my shock and terror, anger stirred. This was Fairfax's immediate assumption: that *I* was the least danger, the weak link of the team. That I could be used to bind the others to good behavior and was scarcely a threat myself. I set my face into a neutral mask and stared straight ahead as we filed past the old man and away toward the stairs.

In the library the electric lamps were turned on full. After so many hours in blackness, the effect was viciously bright; we stumbled to the nearest chairs with our arms across our faces. Grebe motioned us to sit; he took up position beside the bookshelves, arms loosely folded, his gun held pillowed on a bulging bicep. We waited.

Finally there came a slow, painful tapping of a stick across the lobby, and Fairfax entered. Light gleamed on the metal skullcap; it shone too on the great hook nose, giving him more than ever the appearance of a stooped and hulking bird of prey. Hesitantly, he advanced to a leather chair below the wall of photographs and, with an extended sigh of relief, sank down into its depths. As he sat, the edges of his metal corset spread out about him with a gentle clinking sound.

"At *last*," he said. "We were hanging around that cursed cellar for hours after we heard the explosion. All right, Grebe; you can take it off. We're safe from ghosts in here."

He bent his neck and removed the helmet, before pulling off the goggles. They'd left a red weal across his brow. The jet-black eyes were screwed up with discomfort; his face was etched with age.

Up on the wall, the photo of his youthful self stared out with all its swash and swagger. Fairfax the actor, smooth and handsome, all codpiece, earrings, and too tight leggings, moodily contemplating a plaster skull. Below the picture, the real thing slumped bent and careworn, wearily coughing in his chair. It was strange to see how completely the years had changed him, how they'd steadily devoured his strength and drained that vitality away.

Grebe took off his helmet too. He turned out to have a remarkably thin head, much too small for his body's muscled bulk. It looked like a bowling pin. He wore his hair in a cropped military cut, and his mouth was thin and cruel.

Fairfax set his goggles and the helmet down on the nearest side table, on top of the books Lockwood had studied several hours before. He glanced around the room with an air of satisfaction. "I like this library," he said. "It's my frontier. At night it forms the borderland between the worlds of the living and the dead. I come here often to test the latest equipment my factories are producing. All the iron keeps me fairly safe, but I have my armor, too, which allows me to walk deep into the house unscathed."

George stirred. "That armor: it looks like you're wearing a dress."

Fairfax's eyes narrowed. "Insults at a time like *this*, Mr. Cubbins? Is that wise?"

"Well, when you're being held at gunpoint by a geriatric madman in a metal skirt, you've kind of hit rock bottom anyway," George said. "It can't really get much worse."

The old man laughed unpleasantly. "That remains to be seen. But you're mistaken to be so dismissive. This 'dress' is made from an advanced type of steel—mostly iron, which gives it its warding power, but with an aluminum alloy that makes it much lighter than usual. Ease of movement and full protection! The helmet is state-of-the-art too. Did you know that the most vulnerable part of every agent is the neck, Mr. Lockwood? This rim removes the danger. . . . Don't you wish you had one?"

Lockwood shrugged. "It's certainly . . . unique."

"Wrong again! It's sophisticated, unusual, but not unique. Fairfax Iron isn't the only company to be working on remarkable innovations. These goggles, now . . ." He collected himself. "But perhaps we're getting off the point."

Fairfax sat back in his chair and regarded Lockwood for a few moments without speaking. He seemed to be weighing his words. "Down in the cellar," he began slowly, "I overheard you discussing a certain *locket*, and a certain *proof* attached to it. In a spirit of casual interest, I'd be keen to know what you mean by 'proof,' if indeed you mean anything. And after that"—he smiled thinly—"perhaps you can tell me where the locket is, and how exactly it may be found."

"We're hardly likely to help you there," George said. "You'll only chuck us down the well." His pale and bloodied face was set in an expression of fierce defiance. Mine (I guessed) was similar, though also laced with deep repulsion. I could hardly bring myself to look at Fairfax at all.

But Lockwood might have been chatting with a neighbor about the weather. "It's all right, George," he said. "I can give the man his proof. It's important we show him just how hopeless his position is." He crossed his legs and sat back with every appearance of contentment. "Well, Fairfax, as you guessed, we found the locket on Annabel Ward's body. We immediately knew that it had been given to her by her killer."

Fairfax held up a hand. "Wait! You knew this? How?"

"Thanks to a psychic insight by Lucy here," Lockwood said. "In touching it, she detected strong emotional traces that linked Annie Ward's unknown admirer with the moment of her death."

The great head turned; the black eyes considered me for some seconds. "Ah yes, the sensitive Miss Carlyle. . . ." Something in the way he said it made my skin recoil. "But, legally speaking," Fairfax said, "that's hogwash. There's no proof in it at all."

"Quite so," Lockwood said. "Which was why I wanted to understand the inscription we found on the locket. On the outside, this was: *Tormentum meum, laetitia mea*: 'My torment, my bliss,' or similar gibberish. That told us little, other than the guy who'd had the necklace made was a pretentious, self-regarding sort of fellow. But then, so many murderers are, aren't they, Fairfax? We needed something more."

Silence in the library. The old man sat motionless, gnarled hands resting on the studded arms of his leather chair. His head jutted forward in an attitude of strict attention.

"Next," Lockwood said, "we came to what we found inside. This, if I recall correctly, was: A ‡ *W; H. II.2.115*. Three letters, A, W, and H, plus the mysterious set of numerals. To begin with, the letters foxed us; in fact, they led us into a serious error. Our instant assumption was that AW stood for Annabel Ward, and that the H might therefore stand for her admirer's name. The newspapers of the time had highlighted her relationship with Hugo Blake, so this seemed a strong possibility. He'd been the last to see her alive, and he had been the only original suspect in the case. The police today also remembered Blake and soon arrested him.

"In fact," Lockwood continued, "Blake was a complete red herring, which I might have realized after a careful study of the inscription. Wasn't it a bit odd that Annie Ward's initials were spelled out in full, while her admirer's were confined to a single letter? And what about the numbers: II.2.115? Was it some kind of code? A date? I'm sorry to say that I was stumped."

He glanced at his watch a moment, then grinned across at me. "Lucy made all the difference, Fairfax. She found a photo showing you in the same group as Annie Ward. At once I knew you'd lied about your purpose in bringing us here. On the train down I read about your early years in the theater and remembered that Annie Ward had acted too. I guessed that might have been your connection. I also noticed that you acted under your middle name: Will Fairfax. At once that gave a new solution to A ‡ W. Not Annie Ward, but Annie and *Will*."

Still the old man hadn't moved. Or perhaps his head *had* dropped a little. His eyes were in deep shadow now and could not be seen.

"I didn't figure out the meaning of the final bit until this evening," Lockwood said. "We were on the Screaming Staircase at the time, and we've been a little busy ever since, so I haven't had a chance to check yet. But I think we'll find that 'H.II.2.115' is a reference to one of the plays you acted in with Annie Ward. I bet it's some soppy quote that somehow binds the two of you together and which, if we investigated, would prove you knew each other *very* well indeed." He glanced up at the painting on the wall. "If I had to guess, I'd say *Hamlet*, since that seems to be your personal favorite, but who can say, except you?" He smiled and folded his hands across his knee. "So, Mr. Fairfax—how about it? Perhaps now's the moment to fill us in."

Fairfax didn't stir. Had he actually fallen asleep? It was almost possible, given how long Lockwood had been talking. Up by the bookcase, the man with the gun shifted; clearly he at least had grown impatient. "Almost four thirty, sir," he said.

A cracked voice from the chair, from the shaded face. "Yes, yes. Just one question, Mr. Lockwood. You had the inscription. Why didn't you instantly show it to the police?"

For a few seconds, Lockwood didn't answer. "Pride, I suppose. I wanted to decode it myself. I wanted Lockwood and Company to have the glory. It was a mistake."

"I understand." Fairfax lifted his head, and if he had looked old before, now he looked positively deathlike, his eyes bright and ghastly, his gray skin clinging to the bones. "Pride does terrible things to a man. In your case, it will be the death of you and your colleagues. In my case, it's led me to a lifetime of regret." He sighed. "Well, your proof is good, and your intuition better. That last reference is indeed to *Hamlet*, in which Annie and I acted long ago. It's how we met. I was Prince Hamlet, and she played Ophelia, his betrothed. The locket refers specifically to Act II, Scene 2, lines 115 to 118, which run:

Doubt thou the stars are fire,
Doubt that the sun doth move,
Doubt truth to be a liar
But never doubt I love."

The old man paused; he stared into the dark. "That's Hamlet to Ophelia," he said at last. "He's saying that his love for her is utterly certain, more certain than anything else in the universe. Of course, in the play she drowns herself, and he's poisoned, but the principle holds true. It's all about the *passion* between them. . . . And passion is what Annie and I shared."

"Didn't stop you from killing her," I said. It was the first time that I'd spoken.

Fairfax glanced toward me, black eyes dull like stones. "You're still a child, Miss Carlyle. You know nothing of such things."

"Wrong." I let my full scorn show. "I know *exactly* what Annie Ward experienced. When I touched the locket, I *felt* it all."

"How nice for you," Fairfax said. "You know, I've always thought that your kind of Talent must be *far* more trouble than it's worth. Feeling another person's death pain? I can't say that's ever appealed to me."

"It's not just her *death* that I understand," I said quietly. "I felt all the emotions that she experienced while she wore the necklace. I know everything she went through with you." And the memories had hardly faded, either. I could still taste the girl's hysteria, her wild jealousies, her grief and anger; and, finally, right at the end—

"What a ridiculous skill you have," Fairfax said. "How terribly pointless and distracting. Still, you'll know then what a dark and difficult person Annie Ward was. She had a volatile personality and a poisonous temper, but she was beautiful all the same. We both acted in a number of amateur productions, and this gave us the excuse to be together, for our relationship had to remain secret. Annie was not of the correct social standing, you see—her father was a tailor, or something of that kind—and my parents would have cut off my inheritance if they'd known about her. Well, finally Annie demanded we go public. I refused, of course—the idea was impossible—so she left me." His lips drew back, teeth glinted. "For a time she went around with Hugo Blake: a fop, a worthless dandy. He was no good, and she knew it. Before long she was back with me."

He shook his head; his voice grew louder. "I'm sorry to say that Annie was wayward. She socialized with people of whom I did not approve, including Blake, though I had forbidden her to see him. We often argued; our arguments grew worse. One night I came to her house in secret and let myself in. She was out. I waited for her there. Imagine my rage when I saw her being dropped outside the door by none other than the vile Hugo Blake himself. As soon as she entered, I confronted her. We had a fearsome row, at the end of which I lost control. I struck her. She fell lifeless to the floor. I had broken her neck at a single blow."

I shuddered. Right at the end: the final pain and terror. Yes, I'd felt that, too.

"Put yourself in my shoes, Mr. Lockwood," Fairfax went on. "Here was I, the heir to one of the largest industrial fortunes in England, kneeling by the body of the girl he'd killed. What could I do? If I called the police, I faced ruin—imprisonment, certainly, and perhaps the rope. Two lives would have been destroyed because of a moment's madness! If, on the other hand, I left her lying there, there was still no guarantee I would escape. Perhaps someone had seen me enter the house? I couldn't be sure. So I resolved upon a third solution. I would hide the body and conceal the crime. It took me almost twenty-four hours, Mr. Lockwood, to create my dear

Annie's impromptu tomb, twenty-four hours that have stayed with me for fifty years. I had to locate a hiding place, knock through the wall, bring materials into the house to conceal that hole—and do all this unseen. Every moment I feared discovery, every moment I had to labor with the body there beside me. . . ." The old man closed his eyes; he took a ragged breath. "Well, I got it done, and I have lived with the memory ever since. But in all my efforts—and this is the bitter irony—I forgot the locket! I didn't think of it; it slipped my mind. It was only weeks later that I recalled its existence, and realized it might one day . . . prove troublesome. And so it has. As soon as I read your newspaper article, I guessed you'd found it and were working on a solution. Subtle inquiries revealed the police knew nothing. That gave me hope; I turned my attention to you. First I tried to steal it. When Grebe failed, I was forced to use more radical measures to ensure your silence." He sighed; air whistled between the silver teeth. "Now the ghosts of Combe Carey have let me down too, and I'm going to have to finish the job myself. However, before I do—one simple question remains. What have you done with my locket?"

No one spoke. When I listened with my inner ears, the house was empty. The Visitors had gone. We were left with only mortal enemies—a killer, his henchman, and a gun.

"I'm waiting," Fairfax said. He was completely calm. The prospect of murdering us didn't appear to distress him in the slightest.

Lockwood, however, seemed just as relaxed, if not more so. "Thanks for the story," he said. "It was most enlightening—and very useful, as it's helped us waste a bit more time. You see, I forgot to mention earlier that we're not going to be alone for long. Shortly before we arrived, I sent word via our driver to Inspector Barnes of DEPRAC. I gave him enough information about you to excite his interest, and I asked him to meet us here by dawn."

George and I stared at him. I remembered the package, the taxi driver, the money changing hands. . . .

"He should arrive quite soon," Lockwood went on blithely. He leaned back in the chair and stretched his arms behind his head. "In other words, it's all over for you, Fairfax. So we might as well relax. Why not get Grebe to make us all a cup of tea?"

The old man's face was ghastly to observe; hatred, fear, and disbelief washed over it in waves, and for a moment he was struck dumb. Then the expression cleared. "You're bluffing," he said. "And even if you're not, who cares? By the time anyone arrives, you'll have sadly met your end while fighting Visitors by the haunted well. One after the other, you all fell in. I'll be terribly distraught. Barnes will be able to prove nothing. So. One final time of asking: *Where is the locket*?"

No one said anything.

"Percy," Fairfax said, "shoot the girl."

"Wait!" Lockwood and George leaped from their chairs.

"Okay!" I cried. "Okay, don't do it! I'll tell you."

All eyes turned as I stood up. Fairfax leaned forward. "Excellent. I *thought* you'd be the one to crack. So . . . where did you hide it, girl? Which room?"

"Lucy—" Lockwood began.

"Oh, it's not at Portland Row at all," I said. "I've got it here."

I was watching the old man's face as I spoke; I saw how his eyes drew tight in pleasure, how his mouth curled sensuously into a secretive half-smile. And something about the expression, fleeting as it was, opened a cracked and dirty window for me onto his truest, deepest nature. It was something he generally kept hidden beneath the bluff, bombastic veneer of the captain of industry; it even underlay the dry regret of his long confession. I'd seen a lot that night at Combe Carey Hall, but that little gleeful smile on those old, wide lips? Yeah, it was the self-love of the murderer, and easily the most repulsive thing of all. I wondered how many others had fallen foul of him over the years, and how he had disposed of them.

"Show me, then," he said.

"Sure." Out of the corner of my eye I could see Lockwood staring at me, trying desperately to catch my attention. I didn't meet his gaze. There was no point. I'd made my choice. I knew what I was going to do.

I reached around the back of my neck and removed the loop of cord. As I pulled the case out, I thought I saw a flash of pale fire from beneath the glass, but the electric lights were bright in the library and I might have been mistaken. I held the case in one hand and shot aside the little bolt.

"Hey, that's silver-glass. . . ." Grebe said suddenly. "What's the locket doing in there?"

I swung the lid open and tipped the necklace out into my palm. As I did so, I heard a little gasp from George. Fairfax spoke too, but I didn't heed him. I was listening to another sound—far off, but swiftly drawing near.

The locket was blisteringly cold; so cold it burned my skin. "Here you are," I said. "All yours."

With that I held my arm outstretched, and turned my head aside.

Up on the wall, the photo of young Fairfax, legs valiantly akimbo, considered thoughtfully the moldering skull. Here in the library, the old, decrepit Fairfax stared in sudden consternation at the necklace in my hand.

Air struck the side of my face. My hair stretched out behind me; chair legs scraped on carpets, tables shifted. I heard a great collective thump as all the books in the room slammed against the back wall of the shelves. Percy Grebe, who had been doing something with his gun, was blown back off his feet; he hit a bookshelf hard and collapsed onto the floor. Lockwood's chair spun into George's. Both were pressed back in their seats by the wave of force erupting from my hand.

All the light bulbs in the library blew.

But it wasn't dark; to me the room grew brighter, because the girl was there. She wore her pretty summer dress with orange flowers. She stood between me and Fairfax, and now the other-light radiated from her like water: it poured in torrents, gushing over chairs and rugs, and spilling around the reading desks in a bright and freezing tide.

"I'm cold," a voice said. *"So very cold."*

Into my head came the little hollow knocking sound I'd heard at Sheen Road the night it all began, like a fingernail on plaster or a nail being hammered into wood. It was rhythmic now, like the beating of a heart. Otherwise it was all dead quiet. For an instant the ghost-girl's eyes met mine, then she turned to face the old man in the chair.

Fairfax sensed but could not see her clearly. He was looking wildly all around. Suddenly his fingers scrabbled on the table. He found the goggles, pressed them to his eyes. He looked, he frowned: at once his face went slack, his body very still.

The ghost-girl drifted toward him, light streaming from her hair.

The goggles drooped in Fairfax's hand, hung at an acute diagonal across his nose. They fell away. His eyes were rapt with wonder and an awful fear. As a gentleman does when a lady enters the room, he got slowly, shakily to his feet. He stood there, waiting.

The girl opened her arms out wide.

Perhaps Fairfax tried to move. Perhaps he tried to defend himself. But ghost-lock had him in its grip. His sword-arm twitched slightly, his hand hung helpless above his belt.

Off to the side, Lockwood fought free of the baleful influence; he tugged at George's arm, pulled him back behind the chairs and safely out of range.

Coils of other-light, like giant fingers, closed in on Fairfax from all sides. And now the girl had reached him. Plasm touched the iron armor; it hissed and bubbled. The girl's form wavered, but held firm. She looked into the old man's eyes. He opened his mouth; he seemed about to speak. . . . She clasped him to her, drew him downward in a cold embrace.

Fairfax gave a single hollow cry.

And the other-light went out.

The room was dark. I tilted my hand; the locket fell and broke into pieces on the floor.

"Quickly! George—get Grebe!" That was Lockwood shouting. The chauffeur's form could just be seen, blundering away across the room, knocking against furniture, making for the lobby. Lockwood grabbed a poker from the fireplace and followed. George leaped in pursuit too, skimming a cushion past Grebe's head. Grebe ducked; his silhouette was outlined hazily against the lobby arch. He turned: a flash, a crack, a bullet whipped between us into the dark.

Lockwood and George reached the arch, paused a moment, and passed through. Then at once there came a shouting and a crashing, and the sounds of voices raised, and despite the pain in my injured hand I too was stumbling to the lobby—where to my astonishment I found the chauffeur sprawling on the ground with Lockwood's poker at his throat, the main entrance doors wide open, and Inspector Barnes and a crowd of grim-faced agents clustering into the Hall.

V

And After

Chapter 25

Whatever it was that Lockwood had scribbled in his note to Inspector Barnes, it had certainly had the desired effect. The taxi driver had delivered the message to Scotland Yard late the previous evening; by midnight Barnes had gathered two vanloads of DEPRAC officers and agency personnel and was on his way to Berkshire. They reached the village of Combe Carey shortly after three, and the estate itself by four. Only their difficulty in opening the park gates (Bert Starkins, thinking they were phantoms risen from his cabbage patch, had shot at them from his window with a blunderbuss load of iron filings) prevented them from arriving at the hall prior to five a.m. Even so, they were two full hours earlier than Lockwood had requested, and just in time to block Percy Grebe's escape.

They didn't turn up a moment too soon for me.

It wasn't ghost-touch or anything, but my close exposure to Annie Ward's final manifestation had left me badly dazed. The chill had cut to my bones, and my right hand—where I'd held the locket—was frost-burned on the palm. Coming on top of everything else we'd experienced in the house through the long hours of the night, it was all I could do to stay upright. Those first chaotic minutes after DEPRAC's arrival, I remember only as a blur.

Things soon started getting better, though. A Fittes medic gave me an adrenaline shot to pep me up. Another bandaged my injured hand. A kindly DEPRAC officer did the best thing of all and made me a decent cup of tea. Even Barnes, passing by my sofa in the midst of barking orders all around, patted me on the shoulder and asked if I was well. I was fine, thanks for asking, but quite content to let someone else take charge.

Of course, events didn't stop just because I was sidelined. There was still plenty going on. The first thing that happened was that the chauffeur, Percy Grebe, was taken into custody. He'd not seen the gruesome details of Fairfax's fate, but he'd *sensed* enough to be left in a state of abject terror. That terror made him talkative. Almost before he was hustled to his feet, he'd begun to spill the beans.

The next thing was that a crowd of agents, armed to the teeth with rapiers, flares, and salt-bombs, and swiveling supersized flashlights zealously all around, advanced slowly out across the Hall. The key word here is *slow*. They were mostly Fittes operatives, with some from Tendy and a few from Grimble's, and all went with extreme caution, taking psychic readings every step of the way. The dark reputation of Combe Carey hung heavy over them, as it did their adult supervisors dawdling at the door. Lockwood and George stood cheerily by as they began to secure the area, painstakingly passing orders back and forth, and jumping at every scrape and shadow.

Their first stop, naturally, was the library, and here, by whirling flashlight beam, Fairfax's body was located. He lay facedown on the rug in the center of the room, with his eyes wide open and his arms outstretched as if in supplication. The medics had the adrenaline needles ready, but they didn't try to use them. It was already much too late. Fairfax had suffered first-degree ghost-touch, and it had left him swollen, blue, and dead. Immediate readings were carried out in the vicinity of the locket and all around the room, but everything came up negative. The spirit of Annie Ward—having been reunited with her killer—was nowhere to be found.

After this, at Barnes's command, the operatives spread out across the hall, routing out Fairfax's servants in the East Wing, and checking the substance of our story in the West. Lockwood and George oversaw their progress to the door of the Red Room, which was discovered to be locked. The key, at Lockwood's suggestion, was found in Fairfax's pocket; the room itself, when a crack team tiptoed in, was empty, quiet, and cold.

Much to George's delight, among the Fittes agents commandeered by Barnes that night was none other than our old friend Quill Kipps, together with his sidekicks, the blond-flick girl and the boy with the tousled thatch. George took great pleasure in standing close as Barnes issued them with orders, occasionally chipping in with suggestions of his own.

"Just through that secret passage you'll find the famous Staircase," he said. "I *think* we cleared it of screaming shadows, but perhaps Kipps should go ahead and check. At the bottom is the well room, where the massacre of the monks took place. Maybe his team should take a peek there, too. No? They seem reluctant. Well, if that's too scary, there's a Gray Haze in the downstairs bathroom they might be able to cope with."

In fact, any remaining danger was soon past. The first dawn rays broke through the windows of the Long Gallery and stretched warm and golden across the floor.

In keeping with tradition, Inspector Barnes managed to remain deeply annoyed with us even while grudgingly congratulating us on a job well done. His mustache hung at an aggrieved angle as he stood in the library half light, lambasting Lockwood for keeping the locket secret for so long.

"By rights I should charge you with withholding information," he growled. "Or stealing evidence from a crime scene. Or recklessly endangering yourself and these two idiots who follow you around. By coming here alone, you knowingly put yourselves at the mercy of a murderer!"

"A suspected murderer," Lockwood said. "I didn't fully understand the locket inscription at the time."

Barnes rolled his eyes. The fringes of his mustache shot out horizontally with the power of his snort. "A *suspected* murderer, then! That's hardly any more sensible! And I notice you didn't see fit to include Cubbins or Miss Carlyle in making that decision!"

This, it had to be said, was a decent point, which was also on my mind.

Lockwood took a deep breath; perhaps he realized he had to explain himself to George and me, as well as to Barnes. "I had no choice," he said. "I *had* to accept Fairfax's invitation. That was the only way I could get the money to pay my debts. And as to the danger we were in, I had full confidence in the ability of my team. Lucy and George are the best operatives in London, as you can see from our results. We've neutralized a major cluster of Visitors *and* overcome a determined and ruthless foe. And all without a single adult supervisor in sight, Mr. Barnes." He switched on his fullest, most radiant smile.

Barnes winced. "Put those teeth away. It's too early in the morning, and I haven't had my breakfast. . . . Hey, Kipps!" Quill Kipps was struggling by, laboring under the weight of three giant see-through plastic crates. Two were filled with Fairfax's theatrical scrapbooks, being removed as evidence; the third contained a chain-mail tunic, neatly folded, and the two strange iron helmets. "Where's the second tunic?" Barnes asked.

"Still on the corpse," Kipps said.

"Well, we need to pry it off him, before he gets too swollen. See to it now, will you?"

"No dawdling," George called. "Chop-chop!"

"That reminds me," Barnes went on, as Kipps departed, scowling. "Those helmets. They were Fairfax's, I assume?"

"Yes, Mr. Barnes," Lockwood said innocently. "We wondered what they were."

"Well, you can go on wondering, because I'm impounding them. They're DEPRAC business now." The inspector hesitated, twisting a corner of his mustache. "Fairfax didn't . . . talk to you about any of this weird get-up, did he?" he said suddenly. "About what he liked *doing* in this place?"

Lockwood shook his head. "I think he was too busy trying to kill us, Mr. Barnes."

"And who can blame him." Barnes appraised us sourly. "By the way, one of the helmets seems to lack its eye-piece. Any idea where it might be?"

"No, sir. Perhaps it didn't have one."

"Perhaps not. . . ." Rewarding us with a final searching glare, Barnes went to organize our departure from the Hall. We stayed where we were, slumped together on the library chairs. We didn't talk. Someone brought us another cup of tea. We watched the daylight spread across the fields.

When cleanup specialists re-entered Combe Carey some weeks later, they found its supernatural activity much diminished in strength. Their first job, acting on our report, was to dredge the well. There, at a considerable depth, they found the ancient bones of seven adult males, previously bound together, but now much mangled and mixed with fragments of silver and iron. The remains were retrieved and destroyed, and after that, as Lockwood had predicted, the rest of the house soon fell in line. A number of secondary Sources were discovered beneath the flagstones of the lobby and in old chests in one of the bedrooms, but with the monks' bones gone, most of the peripheral Type Ones also faded clean away.

Lockwood had lobbied hard for us to be involved in the final cleansing of the Hall, but our bid was turned down flat by the estate's new owners—a nephew and a niece of Fairfax, who had taken control of his company. They disliked the house and sold it soon after it had been made safe. The following year it became a prep school.

Fairfax himself had no direct heirs. It turned out he had never married, and he had no children of his own. So perhaps Annabel Ward *had* been the love of his life, after all.

The remains of the locket were swept up and taken away by Barnes's men in a special silver-glass canister. Whether the ghost-girl's spirit remained tied to it, or whether (as I myself believe) she had permanently departed, I don't know, because I never saw it again.

The body of the missing Fittes agent was recovered from the well room that same night and removed by his modern equivalents. Sometime later, Lockwood received a letter from Penelope Fittes herself, head of the agency and direct descendant of its founder, the legendary Marissa Fittes. She congratulated us on our success, and thanked us for locating the body of her childhood friend and colleague. His name was Sam McCarthy. For the record, he'd been twelve years old.

Chapter 26

HORRORS OF COMBE CAREY

BLOODY TERRORS OF "RED ROOM"

"SCREAMING STAIRCASE" SECRETS REVEALED

EXCLUSIVE INTERVIEW WITH A. J. LOCKWOOD INSIDE

For some days, rumors have been circulating about recent events at Combe Carey Hall and the sudden death of its owner, the noted industrialist Mr. John William Fairfax. Inside today's *Times* of London we are proud to reveal the true extraordinary story of that night, as told by one of its main protagonists, Anthony Lockwood Esq. of Lockwood & Co.

In an exclusive conversation with our reporter, Mr. Lockwood describes the horrific cluster of Type Two Visitors his team uncovered at the Hall, the secret passages they explored, and the terrors of the notorious "death well" hidden at the heart of the house.

He also explains the circumstances surrounding the tragic death of Mr. Fairfax, who suffered a heart attack after being ghost-touched during the final confrontation. "He entered the wing against our advice," Mr. Lockwood says. "He was a brave man, and I believe he wanted to witness the Visitors for himself, but it's always perilous for a non-operative to enter an affected zone."

Mr. Lockwood also speaks openly about new developments in the Annabel Ward murder case. "Fresh evidence has emerged," he says, "which proves the original suspect, Mr. Hugo Blake, had nothing to do with the crime. Although the identity of her killer remains an unsolved mystery, we are delighted to assist in rescuing the reputation of an innocent man. It's all part of the service we like to provide."

Full Lockwood Interview: see pages 4–5

John Fairfax Obituary and Appreciation: see page 56

Today's Most Up-and-Coming Psychic Investigation Agencies: see page 83

A week after our return to London, when we'd slept long and fully recovered from our ordeal, a party was held at 35 Portland Row. It wasn't a very big party—just the three of us, in fact—but that didn't stop Lockwood & Co. from properly going to town. George ordered in a vast variety of doughnuts from the corner store. I bought some crepe paper streamers and hung them up around the kitchen. Lockwood returned from a trip to Knightsbridge with two giant wicker baskets, filled with sausage rolls and jellies, pies and cakes, bottles of Coke and ginger ale, and luxuries of all kinds. Once this stuff was unloaded, our kitchen surfaces (and two shelves in the basement storeroom) had virtually disappeared. We sat amid a wonderland of edible delights.

"Here's to Combe Carey Hall," Lockwood said, raising his glass, "and to the success it's brought us. We got another new client today."

"That's good," George said. "Unless it's the cat lady again."

"It's not. It's Chelsea Ladies College. They report an apparition in the dormitories, a limbless man seen shuffling across the bathroom floor on his bloody stumps."

I took a sausage roll. "Sounds promising."

"Yes, I'm looking forward to it too." Lockwood helped himself to an enormous slice of game pie. "That latest *Times* interview certainly did the job for us. We've gotten the right kind of publicity at last."

George nodded. "That's because we didn't burn Combe Carey down. Though, having said that, we *did* kill our client. I suppose there's always room for improvement."

Lockwood refilled our glasses. We ate in companionable silence.

"I'm just sorry," I said after a while, "that Barnes made you lie about Fairfax. He should have been publicly revealed for what he was."

"I couldn't agree more," Lockwood said, "but we're talking about a very powerful family here, and one of the most important companies in England. If their top man was exposed as a murderer and scoundrel, there'd have been terrible repercussions. And with the Problem worsening daily, that's not something DEPRAC was prepared to consider."

I put down my fork. "Well, *so what* if there were repercussions? This fudge isn't really *justice*, is it? No one's ever going to know the truth now about Fairfax, or about Annie Ward, or how—"

"Thanks to you, Lucy," Lockwood interrupted, "the ghost of Annie Ward got exactly what she wanted. Justice has most definitely been done. In fact it's a great result, whichever way you look at it. Annie Ward gets her murderer, Fairfax is punished, Blake is exonerated, Barnes gets his cover-up. . . . And since Barnes needs us to keep quiet about the true nature of the case, he's had to let me go to the *Times* with all the other juicy details. So that means we've got our free publicity too. Bingo. Everybody's happy."

"Except Fairfax," George said.

"Oh yes. Except him."

"I wonder what *else* DEPRAC's concealing," I said. "Did you see how quickly they moved into that place and started taking away material? It's almost as if they were more interested in Fairfax's suit and helmet than in his crimes. That helmet was so bizarre. . . . I would have loved to take a closer look at it."

Lockwood gave a rueful smile. "Tough luck. It'll be in the vaults at Scotland Yard now, deep underground. You won't see any of *that* stuff again."

"Good thing I grabbed these goggles, then," George said. He pulled down the thick glass eye-pieces, which had been hanging on the back of his chair. "They're very odd," he said. "They don't *do* anything, as far as I can see. They're just a bit blurry; make your eyes feel weird. . . . There's a strange little mark on them, too—just here. What do you think *that* is, Lucy?"

He passed them over. The goggles were heavier than I'd expected, and very cold. When I squinted close, I could just make out a tiny image stamped on the inner edge of the left-hand lens. . . .

"Looks a bit like a funny-looking harp," I said. "One of those little Greek ones with the bendy sides. You can see the strings, look. Three of them . . ."

"Yeah. Well, it's not the Fairfax logo, that's for sure." George tossed the goggles on the table between the jellies. "I suppose all I can do is keep experimenting."

"You do that, George," Lockwood said. We raised our glasses again.

"We're almost out of ginger ale," George said suddenly. "And we need to replenish the doughnuts. This is another serious mission, which you can leave to me." He hopped to his feet, opened the basement door, and disappeared below.

Lockwood and I sat facing each other. We met each other's eyes, smiled, and looked away. It was suddenly just a little awkward, like the old days back again.

"Listen, Lucy," Lockwood said. "There's something I've been meaning to ask you."

"Sure. Fire away."

"When we were back there in the library, and Grebe was going to shoot you . . . You got the necklace out and purposefully freed the ghost, right?"

"Of course."

"Which saved our lives, so obviously it was a great decision. Well done again. But I was just wondering . . ." He studied the sandwiches for a moment. "How did you know it wouldn't attack us, too?"

"I didn't. But since Fairfax was definitely going to kill us, it seemed a risk worth taking."

"Okay. . . . So it was a gamble." He hesitated. "So the ghost-girl didn't talk to you?"

"No."

"She didn't *tell* you to get the locket out of its case?"

"No."

"She hadn't, in fact, told you to take the locket from her body in the first place, back on the night of the fire?"

"No!" I gave him my trademark L. Carlyle quizzical grin. "Lockwood . . . are you accusing me of being controlled by that ghost?"

"Not at all. It's just sometimes I don't quite understand you. In the library, when you held the necklace out, you didn't seem frightened in the slightest."

I sighed; it was something that had been on my mind too, ever since it happened. "Look," I said, "to be honest, it wasn't hard to guess the ghost would focus on Fairfax: I think we all could have predicted that. But you're right. I *was* pretty sure she wouldn't attack us again. She didn't *tell* me, though. I sort of sensed her intentions. It's a thing that comes with my Talent sometimes. I not only read the emotions of the past, but also, faintly, what the spirit's thinking *now*."

Lockwood frowned. "I've noticed once or twice you seem to know subtle stuff about the Visitors we fight," he said. "Like that ghost by the willow the other day. You said he was in mourning for someone dear. . . . But maybe you heard him say that?"

"No, he didn't speak at all. I just felt it. I may have been wrong. It's hard to know when to believe these feelings, and when not to." I picked up a chocolate truffle, toyed with it, and put it back down. I'd made a sudden decision. "The thing is, Lockwood," I said, "I *don't* always get it right. I've made bad mistakes before now. I never told you about my last case before I came to London. I sensed the ghost there was a bad one, but I didn't trust my intuition, and my supervisor didn't listen to me either. Well, it was a Changer, and it fooled us all. But I *almost* saw through it. If I'd followed my deeper instincts, I might've gotten us out in time. . . ." I stared down at the tablecloth. "As it was, I *didn't* act. And people died."

"Sounds very much like it was your supervisor's fault, not yours," Lockwood said. "Listen, Luce, you followed your instincts perfectly at Combe Carey, and because of that we all survived." He smiled at me. "I trust your Talent *and* your judgment, and I'm very proud to have you on my team. Okay? So stop worrying about the past! The past is for ghosts. We've all done things that we regret. It's what's ahead of us that counts—right, George?"

George had kicked open the door. He had a crate of ginger ale in his arms. "Everyone happy?" he said. "Why aren't you both eating? We've a lot of food still to get through. . . . Oh drat, I forgot the doughnuts."

I got up quickly. "No worries," I said. "I'll get them."

It was cool in the basement, which was why we'd stored the food down there. After the warmth of the kitchen, the chill made me shiver a little, and my flushed face stung. I pattered down the iron stairs, listening to the others' voices echoing through the ceiling.

It had been good to chat with Lockwood, but I was happy for an excuse to slip away. I didn't find it easy thinking about the past, or about my close connection to the ghost. Not that I'd lied to him about it. I *hadn't* been getting directions from the girl—at least not *consciously*, at any rate. Unconscious communications? To be honest, that was hard to know. But this particular evening, I wasn't truly bothered either way. Tonight we were relaxing; tonight we were having fun.

The doughnuts were in the high security storeroom, which was the coolest place of all. I'd put the tray on a shelf just inside. It would be easy to reach; I went in without bothering to switch on the lights. As soon as I did so, I tripped over a large box of shrimp cocktail flavored chips that George had helpfully left lying in the middle of the floor. Losing my balance, I fell forward against the shelves, first knocking against something hard, then collapsing on something soft.

Easy to know what I'd sat on, at any rate. The doughnuts. Well, Lockwood could have those.

I got up, brushed sugar off my skirt, and reached in darkness for the tray.

"Lucy . . ."

I froze. The door had swung shut. Four sticks of yellow light were all that showed; otherwise the room was black.

"Lucy . . ."

A low voice, whispering directly in my ear. Far off, yet close at hand. You know the deal.

I didn't have my rapier, I didn't have my belt. I had no defenses at all.

I stretched a hand back blindly, feeling for the handle of the door.

"I've been watching you. . . ."

I found the handle; pulled it a little, not too much. Not yet. The four sticks of light yawned yellow, splintering the dark into an expanding mesh of gray. There in front of me, sitting on the shelf above the doughnuts: a humped shape beneath a polka-dotted handkerchief.

"Yes. . . ." the voice whispered. *"Go on. . . . That's it."*

I reached out, pulled away the cloth. Today the plasm in the ghost-jar glowed pale and green. The horrid face was fully formed, and superimposed so precisely upon the skull beneath I could hardly see the bones at all. The nose was long and the eye sockets cavernous and wide. The mouth grinned evilly; pinpoints of light glinted in the center of the sockets.

"About bleeding time," the ghost said. *"I've been calling you forever."*

I stared at it.

"That's right . . . Little me. Cuddle up close, and let's have a chat."

"Not a chance." I considered the jar. It was silver-glass, which kept the ghost trapped. I'd struck it when I'd fallen, but I hadn't broken it. The glass was whole. So what had changed?

"Oh, don't be like that." The face now wore a wounded look. *"You're different from the others. You know you are."*

I bent closer, inspecting the plastic seal at the top of the jar. Yes: up at the seal, one of the yellow flanges had twisted where I'd knocked against the jar. It had swiveled like a tap, exposing a little grille of iron that I hadn't seen before.

"You're not callous, like that Lockwood, or downright nasty, like

that Cubbins," the ghost went on. "*Ooh, the things he's subjected me to, the cruel indignities! One time, you'd scarcely believe it, he put me in the bath, and . . .*"

I reached out for the yellow tap. At once the mouth in the jar flexed urgently. "*No, wait—! You really don't want to do that. I'll make it worth your while. I can tell you things, you see. Important things. Like this:* Death's coming." The mouth grinned wide. "*There. What do you think of that?*"

"Good-bye," I said. My hand closed on the plastic.

"*It's nothing personal,*" the ghost cried. "*Death's coming to you all. Why? Because everything's upside down. Death's in Life and Life's in Death, and what was fixed is fluid. And it doesn't matter what you try, Lucy, you'll never be able to turn the tide—*"

Maybe not, but I could sure as hell turn the tap.

I did so. The voice cut out. I stared at the face in the jar. Its mouth continued to move; the whole face shook. Bubbles fizzed and spiraled furiously through the plasm.

No. This was our night of celebration. No dumb ghost in a jar was going to spoil it for me.

I pulled the dotted cloth back over the top of the glass, picked up the tray, opened the door, and left the storeroom. I crossed the basement and slowly climbed the spiral stairs.

Halfway up, I heard Lockwood roaring with laughter in the kitchen. George was talking. He was in the middle of some anecdote.

". . . and then I realized he wasn't wearing any! Imagine that! Spending eternity without your pants!"

Lockwood laughed again. *Really* laughed, I mean. He'd thrown his head back, I could tell.

All of a sudden I wanted to be in there, sharing the joke with them. I hastened my steps. Bearing a tray of slightly squashed doughnuts, I climbed quickly out of the darkness toward the warm, bright room.

Glossary

* indicates a **Type One** ghost
** indicates a **Type Two** ghost

Agency, Psychic Investigation—A business specializing in the containment and destruction of **ghosts**. There are more than a dozen agencies in London alone. The largest two (the Fittes Agency and the Rotwell Agency) have hundreds of employees; the smallest (Lockwood & Co.) has three. Most agencies are run by adult supervisors, but all rely heavily on children with strong psychic **Talent**.

Apparition—The shape formed by a **ghost** during a **manifestation**. Apparitions usually mimic the shape of the dead person, but animals and objects are also seen. Some can be quite unusual. The **Specter** in the recent Limehouse Docks case manifested as a greenly glowing king cobra, while the infamous Bell Street Horror took the guise of a patchwork doll. Powerful or weak, most ghosts do not (or cannot) alter their appearance. **Changers** are the exception to this rule.

Aura—The glimmer or radiance surrounding many **apparitions**. Most auras are fairly faint, and are seen best out of the corner of the eye. Strong, bright auras are known as **other-light**. A few ghosts, such as **Dark Specters**, radiate black auras that are darker than the night around them.

Changer **—A rare and dangerous **Type Two** ghost, powerful enough to alter its appearance during a **manifestation**.

Chill—The sharp drop in temperature that occurs when a ghost is near. One of the four usual indicators of an imminent **manifestation**, the others being **malaise**, **miasma,** and **creeping fear**. Chill may extend over a wide area, or be concentrated in specific "cold spots."

Cluster—A group of **ghosts** occupying a small area.

Cold Maiden *—A gray, misty female form, often wearing old-fashioned dress, seen indistinctly at a distance. Cold Maidens radiate powerful feelings of melancholy and **malaise**, but rarely draw close to the living.

Creeping fear—A sense of inexplicable dread often experienced in the build-up to a **manifestation**. Often accompanied by **chill**, **miasma,** and **malaise**.

Curfew—In response to the **Problem**, the British Government enforces nightly curfews in many inhabited areas. During curfew, which begins shortly after dusk and finishes at dawn, ordinary people are encouraged to remain indoors, safe behind their home **defenses**. In many towns, the beginning and end of the night's curfew are marked by the sounding of a **warning bell**.

Dark Specter **—A frightening variety of **Type Two ghost** that manifests as a moving patch of darkness. Sometimes the **apparition** at the center of the darkness is dimly visible; at other times the black cloud is fluid and formless, perhaps shrinking to the size of a pulsing heart, or expanding at speed to engulf a room.

Death-glow—An energy trace left at the exact spot where a death took place. The more violent the death, the brighter the glow. Strong glows may persist for many years.

Defenses against ghosts—The three principal defenses, in order of effectiveness, are **silver**, **iron,** and **salt**. **Lavender** also affords some protection, as does bright light and running **water**.

DEPRAC—The Department of Psychic Research and Control. A government organization devoted to tackling the **Problem**. DEPRAC investigates the nature of **ghosts**, seeks to destroy the most dangerous ones, and monitors the activities of the many competing **agencies**.

Ectoplasm—A strange, variable substance from which **ghosts** are formed. In its concentrated state, ectoplasm is very harmful to the living.

Fittes Manual—A famous book of instruction for ghost-hunters written by Marissa Fittes, the founder of Britain's first psychic investigation **agency**.

Ghost—The spirit of a dead person. Ghosts have existed throughout history, but—for unclear reasons—are now increasingly common. There are many varieties; broadly speaking, however, they can be organized into three main groups (*See* **Type One**, **Type Two**, **Type Three**). Ghosts always linger near a **Source**, which is often the place of their death. They are at their strongest after dark, and most particularly between the hours of midnight and two a.m. Most are unaware or uninterested in the living. A few are actively hostile.

Ghost-fog—A thin, greenish-white mist, occasionally produced during a **manifestation**. Possibly formed of **ectoplasm**, it is cold and unpleasant, but not itself dangerous to the touch.

Ghost-jar—A **silver-glass** receptacle used to constrain an active **Source**.

Ghost-lamp—An electrically powered streetlight that sends out beams of strong white light to discourage **ghosts**. Most ghost-lamps have shutters fixed over their glass lenses; these snap on and off at intervals throughout the night.

Ghost-lock—A dangerous power displayed by **Type Two ghosts**, possibly an extension of **malaise**. Victims are sapped of their willpower, and overcome by a feeling of terrible despair. Their muscles seem as heavy as lead, and they can no longer think or move freely. In most cases they end up transfixed, waiting helplessly as the hungry ghost glides closer and closer. . . .

Ghost-touch—The effect of bodily contact with an **apparition**, and the most deadly power of an aggressive ghost. Beginning with a sensation of sharp, overwhelming cold, ghost-touch swiftly spreads an icy numbness through the body. One after another, vital organs fail; soon the body turns bluish and starts to swell. Without swift medical intervention, ghost-touch is usually fatal.

Gibbering Mist *—A weak, insubstantial **Type One**, notable for its deranged and repetitive chuckling, which always sounds as if it's coming from behind you.

Gray Haze *—An ineffectual, rather tedious **ghost**, a common **Type One** variety. Gray Hazes seem to lack the power to form coherent **apparitions** and manifest as shapeless patches of faintly glinting mist. Probably because their **ectoplasm** is so diffuse, Gray Hazes do not cause **ghost-touch**, even if a person walks through them. Their main effects are to spread **chill**, **miasma**, and unease.

Greek Fire—Another name for **magnesium flares**. Early weapons of this kind were apparently used against ghosts during the days of the Byzantine (or Greek) Empire, a thousand years ago.

Haunting—*See* **Manifestation**

Iron—An ancient and important protection against **ghosts** of all kinds. Ordinary people fortify their homes with iron decorations, and carry it on their persons in the form of **wards**. Agents carry iron **rapiers** and chains, and so rely on it for both attack and defense.

Lavender—The strong sweet smell of this plant is thought to discourage evil spirits. As a result, many people wear dried sprigs of lavender, or burn it to release the pungent smoke. Agents sometimes carry vials of lavender water to use against weak **Type Ones**.

Listening—One of the three main categories of psychic **Talent**. **Sensitives** with this ability are able to hear the voices of the dead, echoes of past events, and other unnatural sounds associated with **hauntings**.

Lurker *—A variety of **Type One ghost** that hangs back in the shadows, rarely moving, never approaching the living, but spreading strong feelings of anxiety and **creeping fear**.

Magnesium flare—A metal canister with a breakable glass seal, containing magnesium, iron, salt, gunpowder, and an igniting device. An important **agency** weapon against aggressive **ghosts**.

Malaise—A feeling of despondent lethargy often experienced when a **ghost** is approaching. In extreme cases this can deepen into dangerous **ghost-lock**.

Manifestation—A ghostly occurrence. May involve all kinds of supernatural phenomena, including sounds, smells, odd sensations, moving objects, drops in temperature, and the glimpse of **apparitions**.

Miasma —An unpleasant atmosphere, often including disagreeable tastes and smells, experienced in the run-up to a **manifestation**. Regularly accompanied by **creeping fear**, **malaise**, and **chill**.

Night watch—Groups of children, usually working for large companies and local government councils, who guard factories, offices, and public areas after dark. Though not allowed to use **rapiers**, night-watch children have long iron-tipped spears to keep **apparitions** at bay.

Other-light—An eerie, unnatural light radiating from some **apparitions**.

Phantasm **—Any **Type Two ghost** that maintains an airy, delicate, and see-through form. A Phantasm may be almost invisible, aside from its faint outline and a few wispy details of its face and features. Despite its insubstantial appearance, it is no less aggressive than the more solid-seeming **Specter**, and all the more dangerous for being harder to see.

Phantom—Another general name for a **ghost**.

Plasm—*See* **Ectoplasm**

Poltergeist **—A powerful and destructive class of **Type Two ghost.** Poltergeists release strong bursts of supernatural energy that can lift even heavy objects into the air. They do not form **apparitions**.

Problem, the—The epidemic of hauntings currently affecting Britain.

Rapier—The official weapon of all psychic investigation agents. The tips of the **iron** blades are sometimes coated with **silver**.

Raw-bones **—A rare and unpleasant kind of **ghost**, which manifests as a bloody, skinless corpse with goggling eyes and grinning teeth. Not popular with agents. Many authorities regard it as a variety of **Wraith**.

Salt—A commonly used **defense** against **Type One ghosts**. Less effective than **iron** and **silver**, salt is cheaper than both, and used in many household deterrents.

Salt-bomb—A small plastic throwing-globe filled with **salt**. Shatters on impact, spreading salt in all directions. Used by agents to drive back weaker **ghosts**. Less effective against stronger entities.

Screaming Spirit **—A feared **Type Two ghost**, which may or may not display any kind of visual **apparition**. Screaming Spirits emit terrifying psychic shrieks, the sound of which is sometimes enough to paralyze the listener with fright, and so bring on **ghost-lock**.

Seal—An object, usually of **silver** or **iron**, designed to enclose or cover a **Source**, and prevent the escape of its **ghost**.

Sensitive, a —Someone who is born with unusually good psychic **Talent**.

Shade *—The standard **Type One ghost**, and possibly the most common kind of **Visitor.** Shades may appear quite solid, in the manner of **Specters**, or be insubstantial and wispy, like **Phantasms**; however, they entirely lack the dangerous intelligence of either. Shades seem unaware of the presence of the living, and are usually bound into a fixed pattern of behavior. They project feelings of grief and loss, but seldom display anger or any stronger emotion. They almost always appear in human form.

Sight—The psychic ability to see **apparitions** and other ghostly phenomena, such as **death-glows**. One of the three main varieties of psychic **Talent**.

Silver—An important and potent defense against **ghosts**. Worn by many people as **wards** in the form of jewelry. Agents use it to coat their **rapiers**, and as a crucial component of their **seals**.

Silver-glass—A special "ghost-proof" glass used to encase **Sources**.

Solitary **—An unusual **Type Two** ghost, often encountered in remote and perilous places, generally outdoors. Visually it often wears the guise of a slender child, seen at a distance across a ravine or lake. It never draws close to the living, but radiates an extreme form of **ghost-lock** that may overwhelm anyone nearby. Victims of Solitaries often hurl themselves over cliffs or into deep water in an effort to end it all.

Source—The object or place through which a **ghost** enters the world.

Specter **—The most commonly encountered **Type Two ghost**. A Specter always forms a clear, detailed **apparition**, which may in some cases seem almost solid. It is usually an accurate visual echo of the deceased as they were when alive or newly dead. Specters are less nebulous than **Phantasms** and less hideous than **Wraiths**, but equally varied in behavior. Many are neutral or benign in their dealings with the living—perhaps returning to reveal a secret, or make right an ancient wrong. Some, however, are actively hostile, and hungry for human contact. These ghosts should be avoided at all costs.

Stalker *—A **Type One ghost** that seems drawn to living people, following them at a distance, but never venturing close. Agents who are skilled at **Listening** often detect the slow shuffling of its bony feet, and its desolate sighs and groans.

Stone Knocker *—A desperately uninteresting **Type One ghost**, which does precious little apart from tap.

Talent—The ability to see, hear, or otherwise detect **ghosts**. Many children, though not all, are born with a degree of psychic Talent. This skill tends to fade towards adulthood, though it still lingers in some grown-ups. Children with better-than-average Talent join the **night watch**. Exceptionally gifted children usually join the **agencies**. The three main categories of Talent are **Sight**, **Listening**, and **Touch**.

Touch—The ability to detect psychic echoes from objects that have been closely associated with a death or **haunting**. Such echoes take the form of visual images, sounds and other sense impressions. One of the three main varieties of **Talent**.

Type One—The weakest, most common, and least dangerous grade of **ghost**. Type Ones are scarcely aware of their surroundings, and often locked into a single, repetitious pattern of behavior. Commonly encountered examples include: **Shades**, **Gray Hazes**, **Lurkers**, and **Stalkers**. *See also* **Cold Maiden**, **Gibbering Mist**, and **Stone Knocker**.

Type Two—The most dangerous commonly occurring grade of **ghost**. Type Twos are stronger than **Type Ones**, and possess some kind of residual intelligence. They are aware of the living, and may attempt to do them harm. The most common Type Twos, in order, are: **Specters**, **Phantasms**, and **Wraiths**. *See also*: **Changer**, **Poltergeist**, **Raw-bones**, **Screaming Spirit**, and **Solitary**.

Type Three—A very rare grade of **ghost**, first reported by Marissa Fittes, and the subject of much controversy ever since. Allegedly able to communicate fully with the living.

Vanishing point—The exact spot where a **ghost** dematerializes at the end of a **manifestation**. Often an excellent clue to the location of the **Source**.

Visitor—A **ghost.**

Ward—An object, usually of **iron** or **silver**, used to keep **ghosts** away. Small wards may be worn as jewelry on the person; larger ones, hung up around the house, are often equally decorative.

Warning bell—Great iron bells used to mark the nightly **curfew**, and rung at times of serious ghostly outbreak. Erected by the government in many smaller towns and villages as a cheap alternative to **ghost-lamps**.

Water, running—It was observed in ancient times that **ghosts** dislike crossing running water. In modern Britain this knowledge is sometimes used against them. In central London a net of artificial channels, or runnels, protects the main shopping district. On a smaller scale, some house-owners build open channels outside their front doors and divert the rainwater along them.

Wraith **—A dangerous **Type Two ghost**. Wraiths are similar to **Specters** in strength and patterns of behavior, but are far more horrible to look at. Their **apparitions** show the deceased in his or her dead state: gaunt and shrunken, horribly thin, sometimes rotten and wormy. Wraiths often appear as skeletons. They radiate a powerful **ghost-lock**. *See also* **Raw-bones**.